VO2 MAX

#HonoluluLaw, #ProTriathletes, and a #SportsAgent

A TRI  ANGLES NOVEL

Katharine M. Nohr

WD
PUBLISHING

Green Bay, WI 54311

V02 Max: #HonoluluLaw, #Protriathletes, and a #SportsAgent by Katharine M. Nohr, © 2018 by Katharine M. Nohr.
Author Photo courtesy of Katharine M. Nohr.

Editor: Brittiany Koren
Copy-editor: Jessie Harrison
Cover Art Designer: Barbra Sprangers
Interior Layout Designer: Amanda Dix

Category: Legal Mystery
Description: *Can attorney Zana West help two new young pro-triathletes stay on the right path?*
Hard Cover ISBN: 978-0-9995872-6-3
Paperback ISBN: 978-0-9995872-7-0
Ebook ISBN: 978-0-9995872-8-7
LOCN: Catalog info applied for.
First Edition published by Written Dreams Publishing in January, 2018.

Green Bay, WI 54311

Praise for Katharine M. Nohr's Tri-Angles Series

Land Sharks

"Katharine Nohr's brilliant debut has it all: smart characters, crisp dialogue, a breathtaking setting, and an ingenious plot that will keep you turning the pages until sunrise."
—Doug Corleone, Author of Robert Ludlum's *The Janson Equation*

"With lots of twists and turns, and interesting characters…in a triathlon, this book really drew me in. An excellent story… Great job, Katharine Nohr!"
—Siri Lindley, USA Triathlon Hall of Famer

Freewheel

"Katharine Nohr's *Freewheel* is a fabulous mash-up of triathlon, law, and punchy characters. A great escape-to-the-beach or lazy summer day read."
—Meredith Atwood ("Swim Bike Mom"), Author, Triathlete and Blogger

"…Zana West and a cast of memorable characters are once again entangled in a non-stop web of page-turning suspense in Katharine M. Nohr's *Freewheel*."
—Jill Marie Landis, Author of the Tiki Goddess Mysteries

VO2 Max

"Zana West is back in this third installment of the Tri-Angles triathlete series, and she goes the distance! It's a fast-paced, entertaining romp through the world of high stakes sports, promotion and profit. Katharine Nohr's humor and witty dialog keeps things moving. It's a great read!"
—Brian Malanaphy, Author of *The Prince of Las Vegas*

"*VO2 Max* continues Katharine M. Nohr's story of pro-triathletes following a young homeless couple in Hawaii who become 'the face' of the sport with sponsorships and big payouts. Nohr surrounds her new characters with her first book's cast, her clean style intertwining their lives flawlessly as they take you through the machinations of triathlete training and temptations of doping."
—Barbara Raffin, Award-winning Author of the St. John Sibling series

The TRI ANGLES Series by Katharine M. Nohr

Land Sharks: #HonoluluLaw, #Triathletes, & a #TVStar

Freewheel: #HonoluluLaw, #FamousTriathlete, & a #Charity

To my brother, Kim Nohr, who has and will forever be one of my best friends, and to his lovely wife, Hannah—my sis-star. She shines so brightly and beautifully, I have to wear shades. I'm blessed to have Kim and Hannah in my life and I thank them for their unconditional love and support.

Chapter One

@Haleyville I wish my #SuperPower was going back in time for 5 minutes. I need a do over!

Haley O'Neill's teeth chattered. She pressed her body even closer against Sean's for warmth. The ground was hard and damp. Their moth-eaten tent, purchased at the thrift store with the last of their money, provided little protection from intermittent heavy rain showers, not uncommon for February in Oahu, Hawaii. She had finally dozed off on her makeshift bed of Hefty bags, a thin army blanket and a pillow made of balled up athletic wear when an announcement from a bullhorn startled her awake.

Haley listened for a few minutes and then nudged Sean, who was bundled up in his University of the Pacific sweatshirt and matching sweats.

"Did you hear that?" she said.

"What?" He groaned.

"We have to move. They're kicking us out of the park," Haley said, sitting upright.

Sean rubbed his eyes. "Now? What time is it?"

"By noon, the guy said." Haley rummaged around the tent and found her Ironman watch. "It's after seven. If you're going to shower at 24 Hour Fitness before your interview, you've got to get moving."

Sean pulled Haley to him, kissed her and slipped his hands under her over-sized T-shirt.

"Your hands are cold." She giggled. "I'm serious, Sean. We're out of money and we only have one energy bar left. You need to get a job."

He closed his eyes and moaned.

"If you don't get up, I'll go. I wish both of us could work, but someone has to watch our stuff." She looked up at their triathlon racing bikes, helmets, suitcases, and gear piled at their feet.

"I'll go." Sean sat up slowly and then fished in his suitcase for his last set of clean clothes he'd been saving for the interview.

Haley clutched her small, ragged stuffed bear she called "Tessie". The little brown bear with its faded blue dress had given her comfort when it traveled with her to every swim meet from the time she was six years old to college, and to every triathlon from age-grouper to pro. She enveloped Tessie in her arms and willed herself not to cry. If Sean landed a barista job at Starbucks, they could save money for plane tickets to leave this expensive island. They couldn't go home to Sacramento, where the tent cities of homeless and unemployment was much worse, but she was sure there were some cities with opportunities for newly minted college graduates with liberal arts degrees.

She watched her boyfriend carefully place his interview clothes into his backpack along with his toiletry pouch and topsider shoes—his only non-athletic pair. He changed into shorts and a T-shirt for the quick bike ride to the gym to use a free 3-day pass to shower and shave.

"I'll be cutting it close," Sean said, reaching into his bag for the last protein bar and handing it to Haley.

"No, you take it." She passed it back to him. "You'll need the energy to answer their questions."

Sean tore open the bar and carefully split it in half, handing Haley her breakfast. They silently chewed their portions. Haley took tiny bites, not knowing when they might be able to scrape up some food again. The night before, when they had shared a Clif Bar for dinner, Sean had commented that people throw perfectly good food away in trashcans. She knew what he was getting at and shook her head. Tonight, they might not have a choice.

"I'll pack everything, but will you promise to return by eleven o'clock?" she said, then took the last bite.

"I should be back well before then." He leaned down to kiss her. "We'll be okay."

She nodded, and gave him her most reassuring smile.

He grinned back at her, unzipped the tent and wheeled his bike out.

After Sean rode off, Haley folded up the Hefty bags along with their only blanket, and squeezed them into her big suitcase stuffed with almost everything she owned, save for a few boxes she'd left with her mom and siblings, who were crammed into a two bedroom apartment in Sacramento. She also had the large black case to pack that had been used to fly their bikes to Honolulu for the Freewheel Movement Triathlon last week.

She grimaced as she thought of their failed plan. They had used the last of their frequent flyer mileage earned from years of traveling to triathlons and swim and track meets with the hope of one of them winning the trip to Paris offered to the winner of each age group. As professional triathletes, Sean had been sure they had it in the bag. How could they lose? They hadn't counted on stiff international competition, a few flat tires (him) and a stomachache (her).

Ever since the Freewheel Movement founder Ryan Peterson had announced the prize, she and Sean had envisioned their trip of biking south of Paris to explore the French countryside for a few weeks. Thoughts of *foie gras*, baguettes and wine picnics had motivated Haley to finish up the five credits needed at the University of the Pacific, where she attended on a swimming scholarship. Haley thought Sean's idea of winning the all-expenses paid Paris trip was the perfect way to celebrate their college graduation, and instead of flying back to Sacramento, they could fly to Houston, Atlanta, Miami or whatever city Monster.com led them to for their first *real* jobs. Unfortunately, not winning never entered their minds.

Haley sipped the last of the water from her Hydro Flask and felt the urge to pee. She zipped the tent and carefully placed a U-Lock she used for her bike through some thin nylon rope Sean had strung through the tent's zippers. This would only delay thieves from getting to her expensive triathlon bike, their gear and suitcases, but she had no choice. Wearing running shorts, an oversized T-shirt and flip-flops, she walked across the street. It was another two hundred yards to the public park bathroom with working drinking fountains and stall doors. She'd put on her Oakley sunglasses to protect her eyes from the bright sun and put her long, wavy auburn hair into a high ponytail, which she had threaded through a white Nike hat.

When she reached the restrooms, she drank to quench her thirst and then filled the two water bottles she'd brought with her.

While she waited in line, Haley heard some shouting and sounds of trucks in the distance, but thought nothing of it. The park had its share of crazy people who awakened her at night with their screaming and loud chatter. After finally taking her turn in the grubby bathroom stall, she again drank from the fountain before heading back.

As Haley walked across the street, she didn't see their tent where she'd left it. That was odd.

Shaking her head in disbelief, she sprinted toward the palm trees where Sean had tied a line across to hang wet clothes. The tent was gone. All their belongings gone. The only thing left was her pink T-shirt blowing in the breeze on the line.

Haley grabbed the shirt. "Oh, My God!"

She scanned the park, searching all corners of it. The other tents, filled to the brim shopping carts, and tattered rolling suitcases that had littered the park only twenty minutes before were also gone. She then heard the rumbling of a large truck in the distance near the Honolulu Zoo.

"They got your stuff, too?" a man with a toothless smile said.

Haley could only nod. She felt sick—like her insides were going to burst.

"Every few months they haul our stuff to the dump like it's rubbish." He swatted at a few flies with his hand. "It took me weeks to collect all my newspapers and bags. Now, I've got to do it all over again."

"Where did they take everything?" Haley swallowed hard.

"The dump on the other side of the island. Even if you can get there, they won't let you in," the man said, shaking his head.

Haley slumped to the ground and put her face in her hands, letting the tears flow down her cheeks.

"Is this yours?"

She looked up and saw the man bend down to pick up something. It was Tessie. She reached out and enveloped her little stuffed bear in her arms, and cried harder.

Chapter Two

@ZLaw The third wheel (#Me) is sent rolling away. Does anyone have a couch I can crash on? Homeless in #Honolulu

Zana West, still wearing her bright blue and yellow cycling jersey and padded black lycra shorts from her morning ride, sipped a latte at the Kahala Mall Starbucks. She had swapped her bike shoes for rubber slippers and did her best to freshen up with anti-bacterial wipes. She looked at her watch, and then scanned the entranceway for her roommates.

"Hey, you're here," Andrew said, approaching her table with two steaming cups.

"I guess we didn't notice you when we came in," Kelly said, taking one of the coffees from her fiancé and sitting down.

Zana watched her friends stir sugar in their drinks, and when they looked up, she smiled. "I miss you two."

"It's hard to believe we work in the same firm and live in the same house and go so long without seeing each other," Andrew said, crumpling his napkin and tossing it aside. His leg bounced under the table. Zana noticed that Kelly's hands were shaking, too, as she took her hair out of its elastic band and then redid it again, putting it back into a ponytail.

Sensing the tension, Zana asked, "Do you want me to move out?" She knew this moment was coming for months—ever since Andrew had proposed marriage to Kelly when they had gone to New York over the holidays. She laughed, attempting to ease her roommates' apparent anxiety. "I can, if you want me to."

"We don't *want* you to move out. You've been an amazing addition to our little household. It's just that with the wedding coming up…" Andrew glanced at Kelly.

"We need your room for Andrew's parents." Kelly finished his sentence.

"Okay," Zana felt a knot growing in her stomach at the thought of being kicked out of the only place that felt like home since her mother died. She had known it was only a matter of time before her roommates would want to live alone, but she had hoped it wouldn't be so soon.

"You're not okay with this," Kelly said.

"You'll find an even better place to live, Zana." Andrew ran his hand through his thinning hair.

"I know," Zana looked down, willing herself not to cry. She had become emancipated from her drug addict father as a teenager, and with Andrew and Kelly, she felt like she was part of a family.

"Hey, do you want help finding a place?" Andrew asked. "I know a rental agent."

"Maybe," Zana said, looking up to see concern in his eyes. "When do I need to move out?"

"We're not trying to rush you." Kelly paused, then took a sip of coffee. "My mom wants to help me with the wedding plans and it seems like every mainlander relative has asked if they can bunk with us."

"Wouldn't it be less stressful if they stayed in hotels or an Airbnb?" Zana asked.

Andrew laughed. "When I told my parents there wouldn't be an available bedroom, they insisted on staying the entire month of May, even if they had to sleep on the floor."

"Sorry, Zana." Kelly sighed. "We have no choice. I wish we had enough space for everyone."

"We're thinking about turning the garage into a family room and parking in the driveway, so we can sleep more people." Andrew grinned, lightening the mood.

Zana raised her eyebrows. *Was he serious?* "I'm not sure your posh Kahala neighbors will appreciate an open garage family room, but I'll help decorate."

"My country club parents will be impressed." He laughed.

"He's joking. You know Andrew would never park his pristine car outside." Kelly paused and fingered her necklace. "Are you okay with this?"

Zana nodded and sipped the rest of her latte. "It's okay. I'll be fine. Just focus on your wedding."

"I'm so happy you're one of my bridesmaids." Kelly beamed. "You'll get to meet our families and be a part of everything."

"Uh huh," Zana said. *Just not in their home.*

They sat in silence while Andrew and Kelly drank their coffees and

Zana calculated in her head how much she could afford to pay for rent. With paying off her student loans, there was little left after her salary each month to cover Hawaii's high housing costs. And, she'd have to come up with a deposit, *and* first and last months' rent.

"I'll find something and be out of your hair within the next month or two." Zana managed a smile.

Andrew stood up. "Kelly is letting me watch the game while we work on our wedding invitations later. Zana, if you can demonstrate envelope stuffing skills, you can help."

"Sorry, I'm only an attorney," Zana said. "Besides, Shelby and I are hiking up Diamond Head."

"Didn't you already go biking?" Andrew raised his eyebrows. "Isn't hiking up hundreds of steps a little overkill?"

"Not to me. You never can be too fit or too rich," Zana said, standing up and following her friends to the parking lot.

"Ain't that the truth," Andrew said, putting his arm around his fiancé. "I can safely say I don't happen to fall into either of those categories."

"You're rich in love," Zana said.

"Damn straight," Kelly said, and all three burst out laughing.

* * *

On her way to meet Shelby, Zana stared out her car's windshield as if she was driving on autopilot, still thinking about her dilemma. The sound of a sharp car horn startled her out of her thoughts. Had she just driven through a stop sign? She gripped the steering wheel firmly and forced herself to pay attention, to stop visualizing herself pushing a shopping cart full of ragged business suits and triathlon gear. She had a good job, and if she couldn't find a place, her friends would surely not turn her out into the streets. Would they?

Shelby was leaning against her car in the Kapiolani Community College parking lot when Zana pulled her SUV into an adjacent stall. *Maybe the hike would get her mind off her troubles?*

After changing into running gear and slathering on sunscreen, they jogged across the street to begin their hike.

"Where's Jerry today?" Shelby asked as they sped briskly up the hill towards the Diamond Head tunnel.

"He had to fly to LA early this morning for some studio filming," Zana said. "Now that 'Fighting in Paradise' has been picked up by a network, he's spending a lot of time in California."

"That sucks. Do you ever get to see him?"

"Not as much as I'd like." Zana moved closer to the side of the windy steep hill as cars passed by. They walked in silence as they entered the tunnel, falling into single file on the side of the narrow road.

"When are you two going to take your romantic trip to Paris?" Shelby asked as they exited the tunnel into the bright sunlight. She slid her sunglasses back on, then paused to take a drink of water. "It's been a few months since you won that trip. If it were me, I would've hopped on a plane immediately."

Zana shrugged. "Frank gave me all those days off for the race. I'll have to wait until I've accumulated more vacation time."

"Is he still firing associates as often as he changes his boxers?"

Zana laughed, increasing her pace as they walked through the parking lot to the entrance kiosk. "He's slowed down a bit now that he's not trying to scare me into billing more hours."

"There's no way he fires attorneys just to harass you." Shelby shook her head.

"Frank will fire employees if they wear the wrong colored shirt. It's sort of like skeet shooting to him."

"I don't see why you don't quit that place." Shelby said, handing her money to the guy manning the entrance kiosk.

Zana fished out a dollar from the tiny pocket in her running shorts and handed it to the man. "He has some new female associates to pick on and so I'm no longer his favorite target."

"Good to hear."

They walked to the restroom building adjacent to the trailhead and leaned against the outside wall to stretch their calves before entering the path clogged with tourists.

After nudging their way through a pack of teenagers on a school outing, Zana said, "Let's run." She kicked up a cloud of dust and ran past a family of Japanese tourists taking selfies. Shelby followed her and they raced up the winding rocky path. A man wearing a San Diego Zoo T-shirt and fanny pack stepped out in front of Zana and bumped her. "So sorry," she said breathlessly, slowing to a walking pace.

"Any interest in going to Kona next weekend?" Shelby asked, walking a step behind. "We could bring our bikes and ride the Queen K Highway."

"I can't. I have to start looking for a place to live."

"You finally got kicked out, eh?"

"Yup. I knew it was only a matter of time." Zana wiped sweat from her brow with the back of her hand.

"Where are you going to live?"

They squeezed past a large couple wearing rubber slippers.

"I guess I'll look for another room in a house to rent. I can't afford my own apartment yet."

"Maybe, you can move in with Jerry." Shelby raised her eyebrows.

"I don't think his parents would appreciate us living together in their cottage only yards away from their house."

"He's a big boy. Is he ever going to move into his own place?"

"Well, he's forty-three years old and it hasn't happened yet."

Shelby stopped in the middle of the path. "Are you saying that he's never lived away from home?"

Zana stepped up a few stairs to a look-out point. "I don't think so. He's lived in that two-bedroom cottage since he was eighteen years old and attending UH. At least he's traveled all over the world, so he's not completely a mama's boy."

They zipped past a group of middle-aged women and ran halfway up the steep, narrow steps until a slow-moving family stalled their progress.

"We always talk about my dramatic life. So who's your flavor of the week?" Zana said after they reached a long, cave-like, dimly lit tunnel at the top of the stairs.

"You know, I'm sick of hearing that question," Shelby said. "I wish I could find a nice guy and get married. How do people do that?"

"I have no idea. You should ask someone who might have a clue."

"You never know. Jerry might have already bought a ring."

Zana laughed again. "It took him ages to tell me that he loves me. I'm not exactly holding my breath waiting for him to propose. But, it would be nice."

They made their way up the steep spiral stairs and around teenagers blocking the path with a selfie stick.

When they emerged into a cement room at the top, a local man selling "I Survived the Climb up Diamond Head" T-shirts gave them a shaka sign with his hand, meaning "hang loose", before they ascended the few stairs leading to the next level.

"Just a second." Zana stopped suddenly on the path. It had an expansive view of the Pacific Ocean. She grabbed her vibrating phone out of a neoprene pocket clipped to her running shorts. "Hello."

"Hey sweetie," Jerry said.

"Jer-bear!" Zana beamed. "What's going on?"

"I miss you," Jerry said. "We're taking a short…"

"This isn't a great connection. I'm on Diamond Head with Shelby. Let me walk up higher and maybe I can hear you better." Zana pushed her way through a group of teenagers clogging the narrow dirt path until she found an open space with a stunning ocean and Koko Head view.

"Can you hear me now?" Jerry asked.

"Okay, that's a little better," Zana said. She signaled to Shelby to run ahead.

"Take your time," Shelby said, before heading up the last flight of stairs to the lookout area on the top of the mountain.

"Anything new, honey?" Jerry asked.

Zana sighed. "I have to move out."

"You knew that was coming."

She sighed. "Yeah, but it's still rough."

"I know. I wish I was there to make you feel better."

"Me, too. I've got to start looking for a place, but I don't know where to start." Zana stretched her right calf as she talked, seeing a cruise ship in the distance.

"I have an idea."

"The connection is getting crackly again." She moved a few feet to the left.

"My tenants moved…my condo."

"I'm sorry, Jerry. You sound like you're under water. Did you say you have a condo?" She moved a few more feet to the left.

"Yeah. I'm…renting…out." Jerry's voice cut in and out.

"I think I got that right. Did you say you're renting it out?"

"Yes. It's a one bed…in…Waikiki. You want to move in?"

Zana paused, not sure she had heard him right.

"Are you there?" he asked.

"Jerry, this connection is really bad, but I think you asked me if I want to move into your condo."

"Yeah, that's what I said."

"I'd love to," she said, wanting to jump up and down with excitement. She dared not move though.

"Zana, I'm so sorry. I've got to go. They're calling me back on the set. We'll talk later. I love you," Jerry said clearly.

"I love you, too." Zana grinned, putting her phone back into its pouch. She then ran as fast as she could up the remaining stairs to the top. Shelby was drinking from her water bottle and leaning against the rail at the lookout point. Zana had been up to the top of Diamond Head so many times that she barely noticed the spectacular view of the south shore of Oahu from where they were standing.

"He must have proposed marriage, you look so happy," Shelby said.

"Just as good. It turns out that Jerry has a condo in Waikiki. He's asked me to move in with him." Zana squealed. She looked out at the expansive ocean view and couldn't help but daydream about cooking his meals and re-decorating.

Chapter Three

@Haleyville And they call this #paradise? There's so much rain, I'm looking around for wood to build an ark.

"You might want to start getting ready," Sandy said to her husband, Bud, through the open door of his man cave.

"Rory McIlroy is putting." Bud was stretched out on his brown leather sofa. "Just give me a few more minutes."

"Okay, it's your function." Sandy smoothed her hair. "It doesn't matter to me if we're late."

"He missed the putt. It looks like Henley is going to win," Bud said, slowly rising. "I'll be ready in ten minutes."

Bud wasn't looking forward to the premier showing of "Fighting in Paradise" on a big screen on Magic Island in front of one hundred or so invited VIP guests. He had argued unsuccessfully with the network execs that the show should be a highly publicized red carpet event and open to the public. Instead, he was wearing an Aloha shirt and slacks to an informal late afternoon picnic and early evening showing, which would exclude their Hawaii fan base.

"I'm amazed you got ready so quickly," Sandy said, following him to the three-car garage, which only had room for one of their vehicles.

"It's not like this event is anything special. The network knows where I stand. They have my money for sponsorship, but I don't agree with how the show is being launched," Bud said as they made their way past his work bench and through piles of boxes and a half dozen bicycles.

"Shit!" Sandy yelped and then leaned against their Cadillac XTS.

"Are you okay?" he asked. Bud couldn't remember the last time he had heard his wife swear.

"Yeah. I tripped on a helmet." She bent down to pick it up. She examined her ankle and gently walked a few steps in her one-inch heels. "I'm fine."

She turned her head away, but he had seen the pained look in her eyes. He wordlessly took the helmet and placed it on top of a tower of plastic bins.

After he helped his wife into the front passenger seat and had buckled his own seatbelt, Bud asked, "Is Emma here with the kids?"

"She's taking them to see a movie." Sandy checked her lipstick in the visor mirror as soon as the garage door opened behind them.

"I think I'd enjoy that better."

"Do we have an umbrella?" Sandy asked after the car emerged into the daylight. "It looks like it's going to rain."

Bud nodded. "There's a golf umbrella in the trunk."

"I'll bet you're excited that 'Fighting in Paradise' is finally going to be on a network station after being on cable for so long."

"Yeah, it's quite an accomplishment. Jerry Hirano will now be seen by millions of viewers," Bud said, pulling the car out of the driveway and onto the street.

They rode in silence from their home in Portlock through Hawaii Kai, and then onto the H-1 Freeway in Kahala. Bud clicked on the stereo to play some soft jazz, hoping it would replace the tension in the air. Since their son Terry had died, they had done their best to get back to normal for the sake of their grandchildren, but there always seemed to be an issue to debate or a thorny problem to resolve for which he simply had no energy.

"I'm so relieved you dismissed the lawsuit," Sandy said.

"Yeah," Bud nodded, slowing down to a crawl in the ever-present H-1 traffic. He hoped she'd drop the subject. He wasn't in the mood to rehash the legal action he'd brought against triathlete Olympic gold medalist Ryan Peterson.

"I know this isn't the best time to bring this up, but one of these days we're going to have to clean out the garage, Bud."

He grunted, gripped the steering wheel tighter and kept his eyes on the road. Had she not tripped on the helmet, he wondered if she would have brought the subject of Terry's bikes, clothes and race equipment up. She wasn't a fan of pulling her Prius into the garage making parking space not an issue. He had lost the argument about preserving their son's room as it was the morning of his accident and, mercifully, their granddaughter, Chloe, had moved in when he was away on a business trip. She now had her own bathroom and space for her doll collection.

"You're not even listening to me," Bud heard his wife say.

"Huh?" He glanced over at her. Now she was turned to him with her lips pursed.

"I said that it's time to go through Terry's things," her voice cracked. "And give most of them to charity."

He felt his stomach clench. "I would prefer not to just throw my only son's possessions into a donation bin," Bud said, keeping his eyes on the road.

"I agree." Sandy placed her hand gently on his arm. "We can probably have someone put the bikes on e-Bay for us before they're destroyed by rust. We spent at least fifty thousand dollars on his triathlon gear."

He let her words sink in as he watched rain drops collect on the windshield for a few minutes before activating the wipers. "It's good we brought an umbrella," he said. "The rain is really coming down. I'll bet the organizers will wish they had listened to me and held this event in a hotel ballroom."

Sandy shrugged. "I get it. You're not ready to talk about this."

After he took the freeway exit, she asked, "Are Kenny and Preston going to be there tonight?"

"Of course—all of the producers, cast, crew and their significant others," Bud said, pleased that Sandy had changed the subject. He turned the windshield wipers to a higher speed. The rain was now coming down hard against the windshield.

"I wish I hadn't worn sandals," Sandy said. "Is that thunder?"

"Probably." Bud pulled the Cadillac into the Magic Island parking lot. Beach-goers holding towels over their heads to protect themselves from the heavy rain were running to their cars. "Let's wait for a few minutes until the rain dies down a bit."

"There's Jerry and Zana," Sandy said.

Jerry's red Ferrari pulled up next to Bud's car. Jerry opened his car door and immediately popped open a large black umbrella. He walked to Bud's side of the car, signaling for Bud to roll down his window.

"Can I escort each of you under my umbrella?" Jerry asked.

"I have one in my trunk," Bud said, opening the door and joining Jerry. After retrieving a black and white Titleist golf umbrella from the trunk, Bud helped Sandy from the passenger side of the car. They followed Jerry and Zana to a large tent erected in the grassy Magic Island section of Ala Moana Park.

Producer Kenny Paxton greeted the couples at the entrance of the shelter where they added their wet umbrellas to a growing stack in a large plastic bin.

"Lovely weather," Jerry said.

"I'm sure it'll clear up—at least in time for the show," Kenny said. "There's no assigned seating so make yourself comfortable wherever you'd like. Waiters will come round and get your drink order. We have delicious Hawaiian, Korean and Japanese food—whatever you're in the mood for today."

Bud led Sandy to an open table at the edge of the tent so they had a view of Diamond Head and the boat marina adjacent to Magic Island. He didn't feel like making small talk now that Sandy had darkened his mood.

A waiter delivered a glass of pinot noir to Sandy and a bottle of Stella Artois to Bud. Pupus of sushi and sashimi were served, but what Bud wanted was a big, juicy steak like he used to eat in Texas. He wondered if he could talk Sandy into saving her appetite and heading over to Morton's Steakhouse at Ala Moana after the event, even though she had already filled her plate with thin slices of ahi sashimi and a California roll.

"Mr. Schubert, would you like some kalbi ribs?" A waiter held out a plate to him.

"You must've read my mind," Bud said. He looked up and caught Kenny's eye from a nearby table and smiled. The producer knew him well.

As he ate the ribs, Bud stared out at Diamond Head, which looked greener than usual because of the recent rain. A few outrigger canoes were swiftly moving towards the boat harbor to escape rough seas. He then noticed a young couple huddled under a thin, grimy beach towel. They were wearing shorts and soaking wet T-shirts and sitting directly on the ground. The young woman, who had long auburn hair, was sobbing.

"Excuse me," Bud said to his wife. "I'll be right back." He went to the umbrella bin and grabbed his Titleist umbrella and a second one, which he opened to protect himself from the rain as he walked over to the couple.

"Hi, I thought you could use this," Bud said as he handed his umbrella to the young man.

"Thank you so much," the young woman said.

"I noticed your bike," Bud said. "My son had the same model. He passed away last year."

"I'm so sorry to hear that," the young man said. "Was he a triathlete?"

"Yeah, a pro."

"We're professional triathletes, too," the young woman said. "I'm Haley and this is my boyfriend, Sean."

"Nice to meet you," Bud said. "I'm Bud. I don't want to be rude, but why are you sitting on the ground soaking wet? Don't you have a home to go to?"

"It's a long story. You're obviously busy," Sean said, motioning to the large party tent about 20 yards away.

"Excuse me a minute. I'll be right back," Bud went to the tent and spoke briefly to one of the waiters. He then returned to the young couple and crouched next to them under the umbrella. "Please tell me your story."

"Okay," Sean said. "Well, in January, Haley and I graduated from the university in Sacramento with liberal arts degrees and no hopes of getting jobs. We heard that the Freewheel Movement Triathlon in Honolulu was offering all-expense paid trips for two to Paris to the top age group finishers. Since we're both pros, we figured that for sure one of us would win in our age group, so we used all of our frequent flyer mileage to get one way tickets to Honolulu for the race."

Two waiters emerged, setting up folding chairs for Sean, Haley, and Bud and another waiter brought the young couple plates of hot Hawaiian food and bottles of cold water.

"Wow, thank you so much," Haley said, her eyes wide.

Bud watched as Sean stopped talking and rapidly ate the chicken long rice, kalua pork, lomi lomi salmon, poi, and haupia pie without looking up. He then swigged half a bottle of water.

"After you tell me your story, I'll have the waiters bring you some more," Bud said. Haley wiped her mouth on her oversized, wet T-shirt.

"Hmm, that was delicious." Sean smiled, put his fork down and rested his empty plate on his thigh.

Bud remembered the last time he and Terry went to their favorite Korean restaurant. His son had grinned broadly after polishing off a plate of barbeque chicken—just like Sean. Both of them had boy-next-door good looks, with a hint of mischief in their eyes. Or, was that confidence? Bud looked at Sean more closely.

"So, you were telling me..." Bud said.

Sean's smile faded. He glanced at Haley as if to ask her approval to continue. She nodded slightly. He gulped. "Neither of us won our age groups. The competition was just too stiff, so here we are stuck in Honolulu."

"We bought a tent with the last of our money and camped out at Kapiolani Park. Our plan was to have Sean work while I stayed with our stuff," Haley said, wringing out water from the large Freewheel Movement Triathlon T-shirt.

"We used to have suitcases, with all our belongings and triathlon gear." Sean turned his head. Bud could see his eyes were welling with tears.

Bud placed a hand on Sean's shoulder. "Was it stolen?"

"Worse, city workers were clearing out the homeless camps and hauled everything away," Sean said, wiping his eyes with the back of his hand.

Haley leaned over and put her face in her hands.

"I was at a job interview. Haley had to use the restroom and get water." Sean placed his hand gently on Haley's upper back. "The trucks came while she was away for only a few minutes."

"I went back to our camp site and everything was gone." Haley sobbed. "Everything."

"I got the job at Starbucks, but I couldn't take it. How could I work with no change of clothes? Besides, I couldn't leave Haley alone," Sean said.

Bud could see tears streaming down their faces.

"We've had to beg people for money for food and we've been sleeping on the ground," Haley said. "This was never part of the plan."

Bud looked down at his hands and felt a lump in his throat. He reached into his wallet and handed Sean a $100 bill. He then excused himself and went to his car, returning with the scratchy wool blanket he kept in the trunk for emergencies, 2 golf towels, a few granola bars from his golf bag, a golf shirt and a T-shirt with the Sony Open logo.

"At least you can change into something dry," Bud said as he handed the shirts to the young couple.

"Thank you so much," Haley said. She carefully folded them and placed them in her lap.

"You remind me of my son." Bud sat back down on the third folding chair. "He passed away last year at a triathlon."

"I'm sorry," Sean said. "What was his name?"

"Terry Schubert," Bud turned to look at the ocean. "Have you heard of him?"

"Yeah, we all raced against each other. I remember Terry. He always joked around," Sean said. "The last race I saw him at was Wildflower. His goggles broke and so I lent him my extra pair so he could race. He kicked my ass."

"Yeah, he was fast," Bud agreed. "He was so excited to be a professional triathlete, but his mother and I wondered how he was going to make a living. It's too bad there are so few triathlons with decent prize money."

"Yeah, tell me about it," Sean said, shaking his head. "If we could make money as pros, we wouldn't be in such a hopeless situation."

"It's so frustrating that almost any other pro athlete has the opportunity to make millions, and here we are—endurance athletes. We need day jobs," Haley added. "I just don't get it."

Bud nodded in understanding. "My son and I used to talk about that all the time while watching golf and tennis matches. One day, pro-triathletes should make as much money as Tiger Woods, he'd say. I read once that Woods made seventy-one million dollars in a year, mostly with partnerships with big brands."

"Or Serena Williams," Haley said. She put her hand in Sean's, and they exchanged looks.

A waiter came up and brought a few more plates of food for Sean and Haley, who took them gratefully. "Sir, Mr. Paxton asked that you return to the tent. The evening event is going to be starting soon."

"Do you have a cell phone, Sean?" Bud asked.

"I do, but it's been turned off."

Bud frowned. "Will you be staying here in this park?"

"Most likely. We might get a bed in a shelter now and then, but we have to sleep apart and that scares Haley."

"I'll be in touch. Take care of yourselves." Bud shook hands with Sean, nodded to Haley and then walked to the tent.

He returned to his seat next to Sandy, who was talking with Kenny's partner, Preston. He feigned attention to their conversation, keeping an eye on Haley and Sean. They had changed into his shirts and were using the scratchy wool blanket to keep warm. Bud noticed that a waiter had retrieved the plastic chair he had been sitting on, but had let the young couple keep the other two folding chairs. Sean had moved his bike off the ground so that it was leaning against the back of the chairs and was partly shielded from the rain by Bud's large Titleist umbrella.

The rain had stopped by the time the first "Fighting in Paradise" epidsode of the season was shown on the large screen to an enthusiastic group of VIPs. Bud was pleased to see a few of his commercials play before and after the main feature. After the showing, Kenny introduced Bud and thanked him for his generous sponsorship money. Now that Bud was semi-retired from running his empire of real estate developments and other business concerns, he was focusing his time and money on special projects. "Fighting in Paradise" was one of the shows he and his son had watched together. Sponsoring it so it wouldn't be cancelled had been one of his priorities.

After the show and some polite chitchat with other VIPs, Bud suggested to Sandy that they head home. He felt a wave of exhaustion and was a bit unsteady on his feet as they walked to the parking lot, now partially illuminated by streetlights.

"We forgot your umbrella," Sandy said as Bud opened the car's passenger side door for her.

"No, I gave it to those homeless kids," he said.

"That's nice, dear."

"They knew Terry."

"Really?" She turned to him. "How is that possible?"

"They're professional triathletes."

"Why are they homeless?"

"Because the sport of triathlon is completely messed up," Bud said as he pulled their Cadillac out of the parking space and joined the line of cars waiting to exit.

"You and Terry talked about that for years."

"It's time things change." Bud clenched his hands tightly on the steering wheel, his brow furrowed.

As he pulled out of the parking lot, he looked in the rearview mirror and saw Sean and Haley making a bed on the sodden ground with his blanket.

"I'm ready to clear out the garage, Sandy."

Chapter Four

@FreewheelMV My #parents advise arriving at the airport 4 hours before your flight for full enjoyment of TSA cavity search.

Ryan Peterson leaned back in his black leather chair, put his bare feet on the matching ottoman and checked his Twitter feed. There were a few snide comments alluding to his past pro cycling doping scandal, the Olympic trials accident and Bud Schubert's more recent wrongful death lawsuit that was thankfully dismissed, but otherwise the online chatter wasn't so bad today. His tweet about the success of The Freewheel Movement triathlon in Honolulu was re-tweeted 929 times.

"Ryan dear, could you please give me a hand?" his mother called from his master bedroom upstairs, where she and his father had been staying for the past month.

"Sure, just a second." Ryan set his phone on the coffee table and raced up the stairs.

She had her 30" Samsonite suitcase filled with clothes, and it lay open on his king size bed.

"There's not enough room." She shook her head, causing her graying ponytail to swing. She motioned to a half dozen shopping bags of souvenirs on the floor.

"What do you have there?" Ryan asked, raising his eyebrows. He shouldn't have been surprised considering all the shopping she had done.

"The usual—chocolate covered macadamia nuts, Kona coffee, T-shirts, puka shells…all sorts of delightful goodies for my book group, the ladies at work and our neighbors," she said, beaming. "I should've bought an extra suitcase like your dad suggested."

"No worries. I'm sure I have something you can use." Ryan stepped into his walk-in closet and emerged with a large Team USA duffle bag. "Will this work?"

"Perfectly," she nodded and immediately began stuffing the bag with her purchases.

"I'm going to miss you," Ryan said, putting his hand on his mother's shoulder.

"You mean you're going to miss my cooking." She winked and gave him a hug.

Ryan heard his father's footsteps before he entered the room. "Are you packed yet?" he asked. "My bags are in the car. Let's get moving."

"Dad, your flight doesn't leave for almost four hours."

"I like to get there early. You never know how long the TSA cavity search is going to take." Dad chuckled.

"He's right. And, what if we hit traffic? There could be an accident." Mom slathered some tuberose scented lotion on her hands before placing the bottle in her suitcase and zipping it closed.

"I've never had a problem leaving two hours early," Ryan said, wasting his words. Once his parents agreed on anything, there was no persuading them to another point of view, whether it was as inconsequential as what to have for dinner or as significant as who to vote for as president. He lifted his mother's suitcases off the bed and carried them downstairs, with his parents following.

Ryan opened the rear passenger door of his SUV for his mother and then loaded her luggage into the back. His father sat next to him in the front, studying a fold out map of Oahu.

"You can take H-3, the Pali Highway or Likelike Highway to the airport," Dad said.

"Don't worry, Dad. I know how to get to the airport."

"It looks like the Pali is faster," Dad said, squinting at the map through his wire frame glasses.

"I'm going to take H-3," Ryan said.

Before he pulled out of the driveway, the song "I'm Yours" by Jason Mraz began playing from his phone. "It's Alexia," he said and clicked onto the call.

"Hey, you."

"Did I call you at a bad time?" Alexia asked.

"Sort of, my parents are late for their flight so I'm going to race them to the airport," he said, winking at his mother who was leaning forward in her seat, probably hoping to hear the other half of the conversation.

"I called to wish them a good flight," Alexia said.

"I'll put you on speaker, so you can tell them yourself," Ryan said, pressing the speakerphone button and placing the phone closer to his parents. "Go ahead."

"Oh, hi Mr. and Mrs. Peterson. I just wanted to tell you that I enjoyed meeting you." Alexia's voice carried loudly through the phone.

"We enjoyed meeting you as well, dear. Thank you for the beautiful leis," Mom said.

"Your Canasta game is coming along," Dad said. "I hope you'll visit us in Long Beach. Our invitation is always open."

"Mahalo, I'd love to. I know you have to catch your flight," Alexia said. "Travel safely! Aloha!"

"Aloha!" Ryan's parents said in unison before he hit the End button on the phone.

"Such a nice girl," Mom said as Ryan backed out of the driveway. "You seem quite serious."

Ryan glanced at her and grinned. "I am."

"Will you be meeting her parents soon?" Dad asked, folding the map up and tucking it into his fanny pack.

"I hope so," Ryan said, focusing on the road.

"Make sure you meet them. It's important to know where someone comes from," Mom advised. "Otherwise, you'll only see what they want you to see."

"What do you mean by that?" Ryan made eye contact with her in the rear view mirror.

"Alexia is so beautiful and perfect—like a Barbie doll. I'm curious about her mother. What traits do her parents have? What will she be like when she ages?" Mom rummaged in her purse for her lipstick and then applied it, using a small mirror. "You'll learn more about her after you meet her family."

"I see." Ryan nodded as he drove through the 5,000 foot long Tetsuo Hirano Tunnel, cutting through the Ko'olau Mountain Range. "Alexia never talks about them."

"Maybe, you haven't asked," Dad said.

"I have." Ryan frowned. "Come to think of it, she's changed the subject every time I've asked about her family or her past."

"I'm sure she'll open up more as you get to know her," Mom said, patting him on the shoulder. "You seem happier than you've been in years."

Ryan beamed at her. "Yeah, things are finally coming together. The Freewheel Movement has taken off and I won lots of races last season."

"You don't have as many talk show appearances as you used to," Dad commented.

"That's fine with me. It's nice to stay on Oahu and train, and spend time with my girlfriend. The first race of the season is in a few weeks."

"What's the prize money?" Dad asked.

"Not much," Ryan said and then noticed his father's frown. "Don't worry, I'm making plenty of money from the Freewheel Movement. We're signing up hundreds of new members each week."

"That's good, dear," Mom said.

Ryan switched lanes to pass a car as they sped down the mountain. "I forgot to tell you. We just landed another national sponsor for the Freewheel Movement triathlons. And, I just got a call from Bud Schubert." Ryan laughed. "He said he felt so bad about the litigation that he's considering sponsoring our Honolulu triathlon. He wanted to know more about the Freewheel Movement. He asked me to email him information about placing an ad on our website."

"Good for you, son. I just hope you can avoid litigation for a change." Dad winked. "Does Freewheel have a good attorney?"

Ryan looked at his dad for a brief moment. "That's an interesting question. I hired a law firm for start up. But now that we've grown, it makes sense to hire an attorney for day to day issues."

His father put a hand on Ryan's arm. "It might help you stay out of trouble—"

"For once." Ryan finished his father's sentence. "Don't worry. I'm not doping anymore and I'm doing my best to avoid cycling accidents."

"You must know plenty of attorneys with all of the legal trouble you've had in the past five years," Mom said.

"Don't remind me. I've got the perfect attorney in mind." Ryan grinned.

"Oh?" Mom leaned forward in her seat.

Ryan nodded. "Zana West."

"She helped you with the Schubert case, didn't she?" Dad said.

"Yeah, she's perfect," Ryan said. "My plan is to hire Zana to be Freewheel's attorney and my agent."

"Don't you already have an agent?" Mom asked.

"I gave him the boot a few months ago. He was more interested in his commission than in helping me develop my career."

"Why do you think Zana will be any different?" Mom asked in her worried tone of voice.

"She has something to prove," Ryan said and then smiled. "She has the nastiest boss—Frank Gravelle. It will piss Frank off if I hire her."

"How does that help you, Ryan?" Dad asked.

"Because I know Zana will work night and day for her clients. She wants more than anything to move to the sports agency side of her firm."

"It sounds like a win-win situation then," Dad said, pulling out his plane ticket and studying it.

They were silent as Ryan drove the remaining few miles to the airport.

He was pleased his parents were supportive of his Freewheel Movement plans, hatched during long training bike rides. If they had voiced concerns or objections, he would've listened and reconsidered. His mother patted him on the shoulder again when he turned the steering wheel to take them to the airport. He grimaced at the thought of saying goodbye to them for what he knew would be months before he saw them again.

Rather than drop them off at the curb, Ryan parked and helped them with their luggage through the agricultural inspection station and then through the airline's special line for first class passengers. He had traded his accumulated miles for their seats.

When they reached security, Mom whispered in his ear, "We're going to miss you."

His father silently hugged him and looked at him with sad eyes before joining the long line.

Ryan waited while his parents wound their way through the queue and intermittently waved and smiled until they mouthed good-byes and "I love you's."

Ryan took his time heading to his car, stopping for a tall black coffee at Starbucks and checking his Twitter feed. Instead of driving back to Kailua as he had planned, he headed toward downtown, hoping he could have an impromptu meeting with Zana. When she had served as his attorney for the Schubert lawsuit, his insurance carrier and Alexia's employer, Friendly Isle Mutual, had paid her fees. He would now propose that Freewheel Movement pay her attorney's fees and an agency fee of 10% of his earnings as a professional triathlete, model and television personality. His prize money from triathlons wasn't significant, but he had recently picked up a few new sponsors for print and television ads. Now that his reputation was finally on the upswing, he expected to attract more sponsors. Plus, there was talk that he might be a frontrunner in the men's triathlon at the next Olympic games.

Ryan arrived at the Gravelle, Parsons & Dell law firm in record time, since it was mid-morning and there was very little traffic. The firm's receptionist had just hung up the phone when he stepped toward her desk.

"Hi Jasmin, is Zana in?" he asked.

"Good morning, Mr. Peterson. I'm sorry, but Ms. West is in a deposition this morning," Jasmin said. "Would you like to speak with her secretary?"

He put his index finger to his mouth and thought for a moment. "Is Frank in?"

She nodded. "Libby, Ryan Peterson is here to see Frank," the receptionist spoke in hushed tones into the phone. "Have a seat. Mr. Gravelle's secretary will be right with you."

Ryan wasn't sure that he was making the right move by talking with

Frank first, but in the past, he had found the man easily manipulated as long as he appealed to his pocket book. Libby didn't keep him waiting and led him down the corridor lined with legal secretary cubicles to Frank's corner office. Ryan ignored the stunning ocean and Diamond Head view and looked the man directly in the eyes as he firmly shook Frank's hand.

"How may I help you, Mr. Peterson," Frank said after Ryan had taken a seat across from his desk.

"I'm in need of an attorney to represent my charity business, the Freewheel Movement," Ryan said.

"Yes, I saw it on the news. It's nice to see the private sector taking care of underprivileged people rather than the government," Frank said, rubbing his chin.

Ryan nodded. "It's a new way of giving back and making peoples' lives better."

"We can help you with your legal needs." Frank smiled.

"I understand that you have a sports agency group in your firm," Ryan said, taking a sip from the G, P & D coffee cup Libby had placed on a coaster on the edge of Frank's desk for Ryan.

"You've come to the right place. My partner, Donald Reno is heading up that group," Frank said, leaning back in his chair. "And, I'd be happy to represent Freewheel."

"That's not what I'm asking." Ryan was amused at Frank's assumption that he was seeking *his* help. "I want to hire Zana West to be the Freewheel Movement's attorney and my agent."

Frank leaned forward with furrowed brow and pursed lips. After a moment he said, "Ms. West is hardly qualified—"

"That's for me to decide," Ryan interrupted. "If you have any problem with my hiring Zana, then I'll simply offer her a job at my company and your firm will not see any of the fees."

"I see no problem in having Ms. West represent your firm and serve as your agent," Frank backpedaled. "I'll let her know to call and set up an appointment with you."

"Mahalo," Ryan said. He'd noticed Frank's face turn crimson.

Ryan relaxed his shoulders and sat back in his seat to watch the meanest son-of-a-bitch attorney he knew squirm. He couldn't wait to tell Zana how she would soon escape the old codger's supervision.

By the time Ryan left the firm, it was lunchtime. He decided to walk over to the FIM building and surprise Alexia. He found her sitting at an outdoor table shaded by a large umbrella, eating a salad and engrossed in a magazine. Her long blonde hair cascaded down her back. As he approached her, he noticed her snug, teal, cleavage-revealing blouse, which meant she had so far escaped male attention that day. He'd learned that as soon as a man ogled her, she'd drape a scarf over her breasts to ward off further advances. *She does look like a Barbie doll.*

He tiptoed behind her, putting his hand softly on her shoulder.

Alexia made a high-pitched scream and jumped out of her chair, causing people at the surrounding tables to look up from their meals and away from their conversations.

"Oh, my God!" Alexia shrieked.

"It's just me, sweetie." He enveloped her in a tight hug. "I didn't mean to scare you."

"Please don't sneak up on me," Alexia sobbed, tears streaming down her face.

"Alexia, I'm so sorry. Most people don't react as dramatically to someone touching their shoulder from behind them. I wanted to surprise you."

She shrugged and wiped her tears away with a napkin. "I know."

"Are you going to tell me why you startle so easily and why you seem to be afraid of everything?" Ryan asked as he sat down next to her. He pulled her to him and kissed her gently on the lips.

She broke eye contact with him and looked away. After a few minutes of silence, she asked, "What are you doing here?"

"I had a meeting." He cupped her face in his hands and looked into her bright blue eyes framed by long false eyelashes. "Alexia, every time I ask you about yourself, you change the subject. If we're going to have a relationship, you're going to have to start trusting me and opening up."

"I know," she said softly. "I do trust you."

"Well, let's start with a simple question. How come when I say your name, you sometimes don't respond?"

"I do," she insisted. "I respond."

"No, I've noticed this quite a few times. At first, I wondered whether you might have a hearing problem, but then I realized that Alexia is probably not your real name."

"Alexia is my name," she said, averting her eyes.

"If you tell me the truth, I promise I won't love you any less."

"Ryan, we're in a public place. Do you mind if we have this conversation sometime in private?" Alexia whispered.

He swallowed hard. "I want you to promise me that we'll talk about this."

"We'll talk." She looked around and then whispered, "Just not here, okay?"

He sighed. "How much more time do you have left?"

She looked at her phone. "Fifteen minutes." She took a few bites of her salad, swallowed, and then said, "Did you hear the news about Zana?"

"What news?"

"Jerry asked her to move in with him."

"Into his parent's cottage?" He raised an eyebrow.

"No." She giggled. "It turns out that he owns a luxury condo in Diamond View Tower and he asked her to move in."

"Wow, that's amazing," Ryan said. The high rise at the Ewa end of Waikiki made front page news when the opulent units with spectacular views went up for sale, drawing investors from Japan, China, Europe and the US Mainland. "When is she moving?"

"Next weekend. Jerry is stuck in LA filming and Andrew and Kelly are busy with wedding plans," Alexia said. "She wondered if we could help her move."

"Sure," Ryan said. He put an index finger to his mouth, wondering how Zana and Jerry went so quickly from being broken up to living together. "Does she have furniture?"

"No—mostly boxes of clothes and books. She needs a second SUV to move everything in one load."

"Not a problem. Is the condo furnished?"

"Yeah. Jerry told her that it's a one bedroom, fully furnished apartment on the eighteenth floor with an ocean view."

"Lucky her. That's such an elegant building. A triathlete buddy of mine was staying there last year and invited me to work out in the gym and swim in the infinite lap pool. There's a spa and a restaurant and bar," he said. "I wonder how Jerry was able to buy a condo there. When they were up for sale, there was a lot of competition, and if I recall, they were selling for at least a few million bucks apiece."

"I guess there are some things we don't know about Jerry," she said, finishing the last bite of her salad.

"Or, you, my dear," Ryan said.

She averted her eyes.

He took her hand and squeezed it. "Things are turning around for Zana after their break up."

"I think it was more of a *mix up* than a break up, but they do seem happy together now." She smiled and leaned forward to kiss him lightly on the lips. "Would you ever consider living together?"

"Possibly." His eyes widened.

Alexia bit her lip and said, "You may not want to after our talk."

He saw what looked like fear in her blue eyes before he noticed for the first time that it looked like she had a ring of brown around them. *Was she wearing blue contacts?*

Chapter Five

@Hayleyville Living the #goodlife: PB&J sanwiches for every meal, sleeping on a beach towel and used underwear. #spoiled

"These are disgusting." Haley made a face as she rummaged through the underwear bin at the thrift store.

"No, they're not. What's disgusting is not having any clean underwear to change into," Sean grimaced.

"I know. At least we'll have enough clothes so we can wash the ones we're not wearing." She held up some pink panties. "Hey, look Shay—Victoria's Secret. They still have the tags."

"Score!" Sean gave a thumbs up. "Don't get carried away. We need to save *some* money for food."

Haley moved on to the sportswear section and began looking through a rack of shorts. She examined a brand-new pair of Nike running shorts, but dismissed them when she saw the price. She felt her stomach growl, reminding her that a plate of food was far more valuable to her than clothes. Before they found themselves homeless and broke, she would've alerted Sean to her hunger and suggested they leave to get a bite to eat. Nothing fancy. Even when they were students, they ate fast food or from reasonably priced grocery stores. Instead, she bit her lip, then took a sip from her water bottle and tried to shift her focus from her grumbling stomach to the clothes.

Haley was well familiar with the hunt for gently worn clothing, but her mother had always bought her and her siblings' new underwear from Target or Sears. Growing up, if she wanted something besides her school uniform to wear, she and her younger sisters would frequent thrift stores and consignment shops. If she'd saved up enough babysitting money, they would take a bus to an outlet mall. They had a roof over their heads, a closet and dresser to organize their purchases, and even though her large family lived in a small apartment, there was always something good for dinner, cereal for breakfast and clean clothes to wear.

Sean interrupted her thoughts. "Hayleyville, you might want to check out the socks, too, so you don't complain about your feet being cold at night."

"I will," Haley said. She watched Sean add up the cost of his items. She could only imagine what he was feeling. She suspected that his childhood had been far worse than hers, but he seldom talked about it. Whenever she asked questions, his canned response was, "we now have each other," which was either followed by a kiss or sex, depending on their location and schedule.

"Do you have everything you need?" Sean asked as Haley examined the clothes she'd selected, checking for stains, holes or major flaws.

"Yup. These will work." Haley held up the small pile of clothes for Sean to see.

"I found a pup tent and flashlight that still has working batteries." Sean pointed to the pile in the cart. Haley's eyes widened when she saw a blanket and two towels.

"Are you sure we have enough money for all this?"

"Yeah, thanks to Bud Schubert," he said.

They wheeled the shopping cart filled with their purchases up front and asked the young man at the register to cut off the tags before placing the merchandise in the orange and pink duffle bag Sean found for a dollar.

After they left the store and had begun their several-mile walk back to Ala Moana Beach Park, Haley said, "If we hadn't met Bud, I don't know what we'd have done."

Sean shifted the weight of his backpack and the duffle bag on his shoulders. Haley pushed his bicycle as they walked on Ward Avenue past Jack-in-the-Box. In order to get her mind off the strong aroma of French fries, she commented, "It's amazing that you knew his son, Terry."

"Yeah, what a coincidence. I think he believed me when I told him that I lent Terry some goggles at Wildflower."

"You lied to him?" She stopped in her tracks and stared at her boyfriend.

"Yeah, I was hoping he'd give us some more money." He laughed.

Haley could feel the bile rising up in her throat. "Shay, just because we're destitute doesn't mean you should lie."

"I know what it takes to survive," Sean said, gesturing her to keep moving. "I'm not going to apologize for doing whatever it takes to provide for us."

"I totally disagree. The only thing we have left is our honor. I would rather skip meals and be miserable than lie."

"You're a better person than I am," he said as they walked towards the park in silence.

"Were you lying when you told Bud that his son was always joking around?" Haley asked.

"Yeah, Terry hardly ever cracked a smile at races. He wasn't very friendly to me."

"Then, why didn't you tell him the truth—at least about that?"

"You can't say negative stuff about dead people. It's just not nice."

Haley could feel tears welling in her eyes. "How do I know if you're telling the truth to me?"

"I wouldn't lie to you, Hay. Come on, you know me better than that."

Haley stopped to look at Sean, wanting to see reassurance in his eyes, but she couldn't see anything but her reflection in his sunglasses. "I hope so," she said quietly.

The heat and hunger were making Haley feel so light-headed, she no longer cared about her boyfriend's dishonesty. All she could think about was food and the smells of barbeque emanating from picnics scattered throughout the park. "What should we have for dinner?" she asked even though she knew the answer. They had a loaf of bread purchased at Love's discount bakery for a dollar and half empty jars of peanut butter and jam.

"We don't have many choices tonight," Sean said. "Delicious PB & J."

"Well, you could lie to me and tell me that we're having barbeque ribs, corn on the cob, biscuits and chocolate cake for dessert."

"Okay then, that's what we're having," he said, leaning over to kiss her.

It was getting close to sunset by the time they found the ideal spot in the expansive beach park to pitch their tent. No camping was allowed, but the police hadn't been enforcing the law in the wake of the homeless sweeps of Kapiolani Park. There were dozens of tattered tents scattered amongst the temporary umbrellas and canopies erected by tourists and locals, who were busy packing up to head back to their hotels and homes for the night.

Together, Haley and Sean quickly set up the pup tent and made a bed of blankets and towels, using their clothes as pillows. After they took cold showers on the beach, they changed into sweats and socks and ate their peanut butter and jam sandwiches while they watched the last moments of the sunset. Haley was relieved to finally sleep in a dry, warm bed and appreciated the privacy of the small pup tent. They didn't want to burn out the batteries on their newly purchased flashlight, so it was turned off as soon as they got settled into bed at 8 p.m. Despite the hard ground, Haley slept through the entire night for the first time in weeks.

Breakfast was more peanut butter and jam sandwiches, but Haley didn't complain. It was better than rummaging through trash cans for partly eaten food, or begging strangers for money. A few times, Haley or Sean had gone up to families who were picnicking on the beach and asked if they could spare a plate of food. This usually worked and yielded some delicious meals, but was even more embarrassing than asking for money.

Haley watched Sean wolf down his sandwich, knowing that he would still be hungry after he ate it. Even when she heard his stomach growl he didn't utter a word of complaint. She sensed that this wasn't the first time in his life he'd experienced hunger.

"Here," Haley said, handing Sean part of her uneaten sandwich. She wasn't satisfied, but it didn't seem fair that they divided the food equally when she was 50 pounds lighter than he. Sean took a small bite and then handed it back to her.

"Hayleyville, you are the sweetest woman I've ever met." He stood up. "Do you mind watching the tent while I take a quick run around the park?"

"Sure. I promise I won't leave and go to the bathroom."

"I can wait for you to go, if you need to."

"No, I'm okay. Go for it." Haley watched Sean run across the grass and then onto the sidewalk adjacent to the beach. She kept her eyes on him until he turned a corner and was out of sight. It would probably be about a half hour before he reappeared, so she tried to get comfortable on the beach towel. She wished she could go for a run, but her running shoes were among their possessions they'd lost with the camp sweep.

She didn't have anything to help her pass the time—they didn't have any reading material or electronics of any kind. She listened to the birds chattering and watched the waves in the distance.

They had tried to set up camp in an area as far from other people as possible, but families had begun spreading large blankets with rolling coolers filled with soft drinks. The adults were sunbathing, with their kids playing nearby. She could hear bits of peoples' conversations as they passed her. They were talking about normal things—relationship problems, issues at work, and about movies they hoped to see. Haley sighed, wishing that those were the topics of her and Sean's conversations instead of where their next meal was going to come from.

Haley lay down on the beach towel and was almost dozing off when she heard the sounds of loud rap music. She opened her eyes to four teenage boys sitting on the grass about 20 feet from her. Aside from their loud music, they caught her attention, because three were wearing hoodies and the skinny one was wearing a stocking cap. If they were on the mainland they would look fashionable, but their clothes were far too heavy for Hawaii's heat and humidity.

Haley smelled the smoke from the joint they were passing around, making no effort to conceal it. She couldn't help but stare at the largest guy's leg, which had a tattoo of breasts.

"Hey, you fuckin' haole. Whatcha lookin' at?" The guy with the breast tattoo asked her harshly.

She immediately looked away, toward a family who was setting up their blanket about 50 yards to the right. She wondered if they had heard the guy's profanity or had smelled the pot.

"She must be deaf," the tall, skinny teenager said. He was wearing a knit cap over his long, greasy black hair.

Haley didn't move. She continued to stare at the family, willing the father to look towards her.

"Are you fucking deaf?" another boy asked loudly, and the others responded with laughter.

"The haole chick is a homeless whore," a boy whose face was almost hidden within his hood said loudly, catching the attention of the father who Haley was staring at.

She felt the urge to run, but she didn't want to leave Sean's bike unattended for fear the boys would steal it. She was also terrified that they would lose everything they owned again if she left her post.

She saw the shadows of the boys approaching. When she looked up, two of them were standing over her. She could smell the woody alcohol scent of Jack Daniels as one of the boys took a swig from a bottle and splashed the liquid on the front of his hoody, spraying a few drops on her arm. She ignored them and kept her gaze on the father who had apparently told his wife that they should move away, because they were busy packing up their belongings.

"Let's get some of that," the larger boy said. His pants were low on his waist so that most of his briefs were showing. He threw a lit cigarette stub at Haley, which bounced off her breast and onto the grass.

She felt a sting from the cigarette, but kept her eyes on it as it smoldered in the moist grass. She sat frozen, trying not to look away from the hooligans. She felt a hand reach down to touch her hair. She glanced to see that the overweight boy's pants had fallen down even lower and his erect penis was visible through his gray briefs. She was about to scream when she saw Sean run up from behind them.

"Move along guys," he said in a loud, firm voice.

"You fucking haole," the large guy said, taking a swing at Sean and hitting him squarely on the cheek. The other guys laughed as Sean momentarily lost his balance.

"We don't want any trouble." Sean put his hand to his cheek and backed up a few steps.

The guy with the long, greasy hair slammed his fist into Sean's face, knocking him down. Then the heavily tattooed teen kicked Sean in the ribs.

Haley stood up and stepped toward Sean, a scream muffled in her throat as the large guy grabbed her from behind. He pressed his body against hers so she could feel the hardness of his erection through her shorts. She tried to wrestle out of his grip, but he just laughed and pressed himself tighter against her.

Sean started to pull himself up, but the long haired teen kicked him in the head, knocking him to the ground.

"Hey, I want some of that," the long haired boy said and grabbed Haley's arm.

She involuntarily let out a shrill scream, which startled the large boy who knocked her to the ground. In the distance, she heard a police siren.

"Let's bolt," the teen said. He tossed the almost empty liquor bottle onto the grass and took off running in the direction of the beach with the others following close behind.

Haley rushed to Sean's side where he lay on the ground unconscious.

Chapter Six

@ZLaw One can never have enough packing boxes or moving helpers. Can I borrow your boxes @ UltimateAndrew? I pay in pizza.

"What do you think he wants now?" Zana placed her "Fighting in Paradise" mug in the box alongside the other coffee cups and wine glasses she was packing.

"How were your billable hours last month?" Andrew asked in response, pausing to sip a glass of wine while he washed dishes at the kitchen sink.

"Not bad. Over two hundred." She carefully wrapped the glasses and mugs, one at a time, in newspaper.

Kelly peered into her box. "Do you want some help?"

"No thanks. I'm almost done," Zana said. "I just need to find my wine opener and vegetable steamer."

"Maybe he's going to give you a raise." Andrew laughed and nearly choked on his wine.

"Ha ha—very funny," Zana said. She wrapped the last wine glass, placed a lid on the box and set it on top of a small pile of boxes. She poured a glass of wine for herself and took a seat at the kitchen table.

"What are you two talking about?" Kelly asked, rummaging through a drawer and producing a wine opener and handing it to Zana.

Andrew wiped his hands on a dishtowel and turned to his girlfriend. "Zana got an e-mail from Libby telling her that Frank wants to meet with her in the conference room tomorrow morning."

"That doesn't sound good." Kelly grabbed the dishtowel her fiancé had tossed on the counter and folded it neatly.

"Do you want my cardboard moving boxes? I can help you pack your office before the meeting." Andrew reached into a cupboard and pulled out Zana's vegetable steamer, then placed it in one of her boxes.

Zana grimaced. "I'll let you know." They had been through this routine before and Frank hadn't fired her. She sipped the wine, feeling her body relax. "I'm not going to let Frank's weirdness interfere with my good mood. I'm so excited about moving in with Jerry."

"He's sure spending a lot of time in California," Kelly said. She poured herself a glass of wine and sat at the kitchen table next to Zana. "Is he ever coming home?"

"This month he's working in LA during the week, but he'll be back on weekends." Zana pulled a napkin from the holder on the table and used it as a coaster for her wine glass.

Andrew sprayed Clorox on the countertop and cleaned it with paper towels. "Did he give up his law practice yet?"

"Not completely. He still has some cases, but he did hire another attorney to help him while he's gone." Zana couldn't stop grinning. Ever since Jerry had suggested they move into his Waikiki condo, she had felt giddy. Even if Frank fired her, she felt confident that her life was moving in the right direction. *Finally.*

"You're so lucky to be moving to Diamond Head Tower. You'll be living the good life with the beautiful people. I'll make us a snack," Kelly said as she rose out of her seat and rummaged through the fridge for hummus, which she placed on the table with a plate of carrot and celery sticks and crackers.

"Is Jerry making you pay rent?" Andrew dipped a carrot stick into the hummus.

"He didn't say anything, but I plan to give him money every month for my share," Zana said, reaching for a handful of crackers. "It's such an elegant building, the mortgage must be super high."

Andrew reached for another carrot stick. "It's going to be weird for him to move out of his parents' cottage after all these years."

"Yeah," Zana said with her mouth full. "When we get settled, I hope we can have a dinner party."

"That would be so cool." Kelly smiled. "Sorry we can't help you move this weekend. We're having a tasting with the caterers, and we have dress and tux fittings scheduled."

"No problem. Alexia and Ryan are helping me."

"I know you don't have time this weekend, but let me know when you can try on your bridesmaid's dress," Kelly said.

"Is it hideous?" Andrew asked before crunching on a celery stick.

"Andrew!" Zana gasped.

"He's just kidding." Kelly laughed. "He helped me pick out the bridesmaid dresses—they're really cute."

"I'm sure they are." Zana frowned.

"They're bright orange with feathers all over them. You'll look like an orange chicken." Andrew raised his eyebrows, clearly egging Zana on.

"That sounds absolutely lovely." Zana rolled her eyes. "I hope it has a matching hat with a beak." She got up from the table, and with a huge smile on her face, carried the boxes out to her SUV.

***

Zana arrived at her office extra early that morning and by the time she was to report to the conference room, she was caught up with most of her work. She hoped Frank had a new assignment for her—maybe, another triathlon case. Since Frank seemed to measure associates' value to the firm by billable hours, she felt reasonably confident that she wasn't going to be fired. Her billable hours had been in the top 10% of the firm's associates for the past 6 months. She decided that she wasn't going to panic before meeting him for a change. If she *was* fired, at least she was moving in with Jerry and not likely to become a homeless bag lady, even if it took some time to find a new job.

She headed to the conference room a few minutes early, but when she approached the door, Jasmin, the receptionist, intercepted her. "They aren't ready for you yet, Zana. You can wait in the reception area."

Zana could feel sweat bead on her forehead while she thumbed through the latest issue of *Hawaii Business Magazine*. Once she finished that, she paged through the latest issue of *Pacific Business News* without reading a single article. The door to the conference room was still shut. Jasmin was concentrating on her computer screen. It was now 10:15.

"Are they ready for me yet?" Zana asked.

"Let me check." Jasmin typed on her keyboard, presumably e-mailing someone in the conference room. "They'll be with you shortly."

Frank doesn't do e-mail, so Zana concluded that associates were in there with him. She picked up a *Hawaii People Magazine* and studied pictures of her and Jerry at the Hospice Fundraising dinner at the Hyatt Regency last month. *We look good.* She smiled. There was an entire page devoted to "Fighting in Paradise" with a picture of Jerry posing with Kenny and the other producers. Bud and Sandy Schubert were in another picture. Zana put the magazine down when she noticed the picture of Jerry and Annabelle Wong, the sexy and flirtatious martial arts choreographer. She couldn't stop her eyeroll.

"They're ready for you," Jasmin said.

Zana smoothed her gray pencil skirt and adjusted her black suit jacket as she stood up. She was surprised there were six men sitting around the conference table when she walked in.

Frank rose and introduced her to Donald Reno, the head of the firm's sports agency department, whom she had met only once before. Donald had an unbelievably fake-looking dark tan. He had been a professional golfer before going to law school later in life. When he joined the firm five years ago, he brought a number of pro golfer clients with him, starting the sports agency section.

"Hi Zana," Donald said, standing up to greet her and shake her hand firmly. He was wearing plaid golf pants and a matching green golf shirt. "I'd like to introduce you to Mika Savea. He's my right hand man."

"Nice to meet you, Mika," Zana said, shaking his hand. Mika was at least 250 pounds of muscle. She had read a number of articles about him and had seen him on the news. He was one of a string of successful Samoan football players who graduated from the University of Hawaii and played in the NFL for a year before having a short career on an Arena football team. Afterwards, he went to law school.

"Mika represents our male football, basketball and baseball players," Donald said.

Zana nodded.

"I'd like you to meet Christopher Presley. He's our CPA. Joshua Chan is our sponsorship and marketing expert. And Glenn Inouye is our go-to guy for travel, hospitality and operations," Donald explained as each of the young men stood up and shook Zana's hand. "We also have two secretaries, Nina and Rainy, and a few interns. I'm sure you'll enjoy working with our team."

She looked at Frank and raised her eyebrows before she sat down next to Mika at the conference table.

"Zana, we're transferring you out of litigation to the sports agency department. You'll be moving to the 28th floor this afternoon," Frank said, rubbing his chin. "Kim McCall and Lucas will be taking over your cases."

"That's terrific," Zana beamed. She had been hoping for this day since law school graduation. It was hard to believe that her dream had finally come true—and so early in her career.

"Ryan Peterson has hired you to be his agent and to be the attorney for the Freewheel Movement. Our agents don't usually represent companies, but you are only starting out with one professional athlete client so you should have plenty of time," Frank said.

"I think you'll like being a member of our team," Donald said. "No billable hours, but we're on call 24/7 for our athlete clients. We've been hoping to add some women golfers, tennis, and basketball players and having a female agent should mean new clients for the firm." Donald rose to his impressive 6'3" height and poured coffee from a carafe on the credenza. "You can go ahead and clean out your office. Nina and Rainy can help you move."

"You'll need to contact Ryan Peterson soon to discuss your representation," Frank said, making a note on his legal pad.

"He and his girlfriend, Alexia, are helping me move this weekend. I'll talk to him then." Zana smiled.

"That's unacceptable. We can't have an athlete helping his agent move," Frank rubbed his chin. "If you need help, I'm sure that Christopher, Joshua, and Glenn can use their firm cars to assist you."

Zana noticed that the three young men didn't look up from their smart phones when Frank offered their services. "I'm sure I can find other arrangements."

After the meeting was adjourned, Zana made a beeline to Andrew's office.

"Can I borrow your packing boxes?" she asked, trying to frown.

"Oh, my gosh—Zana, I'm so sorry," Andrew said. "You've been a billing machine. I'm sure I'll be next."

"Do you mind helping me pack?" Zana asked. She couldn't hold back her happiness any longer. She started laughing hysterically.

"You shithead!" Andrew socked her in the arm. "I believed you."

She rubbed her arm. "Actually, I do need to borrow your boxes. I'm moving up to the 28th floor."

"To the real estate transaction section?"

"No." Zana grinned. "I'm now a sports agent."

"Congratulations! That's amazing." Andrew pulled some boxes out from behind his desk and handed them to her. "You're going to get to play golf and go to games every day like Donald and Mika. Good for you."

"Yeah, I'm representing Ryan."

"Very cool," Andrew said. "I do have some advice."

"What's that?"

"Wear sunscreen. You can't be in our wedding if you look like Donald."

"Won't a tan clash with my orange dress with feathers?"

"Yeah, and it will especially clash with the matching orange beak hat."

Zana laughed at Andrew's joke, not because it was especially funny, but because she felt elated to finally be moving away from Frank and up one floor to her dream job.

"Do you need help?" Andrew asked.

"No, thank you. Donald is sending his secretaries to help me."

"Classy. Don't forget to visit us down here in the trenches."

"Maybe." Zana had no intention of setting foot on the 27th floor ever again, if she could help it.

She had been upstairs once, when she accidentally pressed the wrong elevator button. The reception area on the 28th floor, with its tasteful Japanese décor, was designed to cater to wealthy Asian clients who sought counsel for multi-million dollar real estate transactions in Hawaii and the Pacific Rim. She had heard that the 23 attorneys in the section were all bi-lingual, frequently traveled to Japan and China for work, and had posh offices. The real estate transaction attorneys were all Asian-American men wearing crisp Reyn Spooner shirts, dark slacks, and freshly shined shoes. They wisely never ventured to the 27th floor, but Zana had seen them on the elevator, usually with their clients, speaking in what she assumed was Japanese.

The sports agency section occupied only a small portion of the 28th floor, with its eight large offices facing either Diamond Head or the ocean. The firm's partners reasoned that the clientele for the real estate and sports sections would base their impressions of the firm partly on the grandeur of its décor, so they spared no expense.

In contrast, the 27th floor had less aesthetically pleasing furnishings thought to appeal to hard working insurance adjusters and small business owners, who wouldn't take kindly to their fees being spent on frivolity. Soon after Zana started at the firm, she heard Brian Ching suggest that a sofa in the waiting area be replaced because of a small coffee stain. Frank pointed out that if insurance carriers observed their attorneys working in extravagant surroundings, they would likely have to cut their already low fees. The reception area was finally refurnished after client criticism reached Frank's ears, but the changes were modest in comparison with the elegance of one floor above.

When Zana returned to her office, Nina and Rainy were already packing her framed certificates in their own boxes and loading them onto a cart labeled "GP&D Sports". Zana placed her personal items into a box while she instructed Lucas and Kim briefly about the status of her cases. After the secretaries left with the cart, the three of them sat in her now almost-barren office with its view of Dole Cannery, the warehouses and the airport in the distance.

"I'm so jealous," Lucas said. "You were wrong about nepotism. You don't see me moving up a floor."

"True. But, you do have that swanky office with the ocean view, thanks to your dad," Zana said. Her irritation about Frank giving his son a far better office than associates who had been at the firm for many years before him was now extinguished by her own good fortune.

"You'll both be working in luxury while I slave away in my tiny shit hole in the low rent district." Kim frowned. He was one of Zana's favorite associates on the litigation team and so she sympathized with him. He had been at the firm for close to 2 years and was still in one of the associate offices in the row facing industrial Honolulu.

"I'm sure it won't be long before you move near Lucas," Zana said, giving him a sympathetic look.

"Right," he said. There was no basis for her optimism. He would likely spend his remaining years at the firm in his current office.

"I'm sorry, but I've got to get to a status conference." Kim reached out to shake her hand and then pulled her in for a hug. "Congratulations, Zana. You deserve it. Don't forget us little people."

"It's not like I'm moving away. Just upstairs." She'd never seen any of the 28th floor attorneys or employees socialize with those on the 27th floor and didn't expect she'd behave much differently. The hug she'd given her secretary, Sylvia, felt more like a good-bye than a see you later.

After Kim left, Zana explained in more detail the status of each of her cases to Lucas while he typed notes on his iPad. After they were finished, Zana leaned back in her chair and looked out the window. These were her last moments in what she had considered hell for over a year.

"What's wrong?" Lucas asked.

"Nothing." She didn't think he'd sense the butterflies in her stomach or the ache in her chest.

"You look worried."

"I'm super excited about my new job." She forced a smile. "But, I have only one client."

"You'll get more."

"I'm going to be an agent with one client who hardly makes any prize money. It's ridiculous."

"Apparently, Donald, Mika, Frank and everyone else believes in you," Lucas said, rubbing his chin—an action she'd seen his dad do one too many times. "I wouldn't worry about it."

"I've never been an agent," Zana said with furrowed brow. "I don't even know what to do. I went to law school, but I didn't take any classes to be a sports agent."

"I guess you'll learn on the job, then."

"Everything is happening so fast. I'm moving into Jerry's condo in a few days and today I'm changing jobs and moving upstairs," her voice cracked. "It's a little too much change."

"You can handle it."

Zana leaned forward and looked Lucas in the eyes. "You told me once that you had a shitty childhood. Well mine was horrific. My mom died while competing in a marathon and then my dad fell apart and became a drug addict. Did you know that I'm only twenty-eight years old and I've been taking care of myself for 15 years already?"

Lucas's eyes widened. "I had no idea."

Zana swallowed hard. "I'm sick of moving and change. I want security. I need stability."

"You're just having a temporary meltdown. You'll see. Everything will work out fine."

Zana was afraid that if she responded, she'd break out in tears. She closed her eyes briefly and finally said, "I know."

"Would you like me to go upstairs with you to check out your new office?"

"I'd love that. I think I'll feel more comfortable if you come with me." Zana was surprised to hear the words come out of her mouth. "Could you please do me a favor?"

"What's that?"

"Don't tell Frank that I'm anxious about this move."

"I promise. I have no reason to tell him about how you feel," Lucas said. "When has Frank ever cared about feelings anyway?"

"Good point." Zana followed him out the door but paused to turn the light off in her office for the last time.

Chapter Seven

@Haleyville I'm not sure if I'm dreaming or if Santa Clause is giving me everything on my wish list. #getmeoutofhere #nomorePBJ

"Are you okay?" Haley bent over Sean, who was still lying on the grass, groaning. Blood trickled out of his nose and onto his lips.

He opened his eyes and wiped his mouth with the back of his hand. "I'm sorry," he said and managed to sit up. "I should've been here to protect you." He winced when she pressed on the spot on his cheek where the punch had landed. She sat down next to him and dabbed at his face with a paper napkin. "You were. You got here just in time." She noticed his cheek was swelling and there was a small cut—probably made from the guy's ring. Haley reached for a small bottle of hand sanitizer from inside Sean's backpack and poured some on a clean part of the napkin. "This is going to sting."

"Ouch," he winced. "I'm not much of a fighter, I guess."

"That's fine with me." Haley studied the small cut. It wasn't big enough for stitches, and after cleaning it the best she could, she tossed the bloody napkin in a nearby trashcan. "I hope it doesn't leave a scar."

He ignored her concern. "Are *you* okay?"

"Yeah—just a little shaken up." She was a lot more than a little shaken up, but she didn't want Sean to know. She forced a smile.

He nodded. "I hear you. We better move camp."

Haley wished they could go back to Kapiolani Park where they had no problems. But, it wasn't an option. "Is there a safer place?"

"When I was running, I noticed a few tents of homeless people camped out under a tree. If we stay near them, maybe no one will bother us."

"Okay." She didn't want to tell him that she was equally afraid of the homeless people she'd seen at Ala Moana Beach Park. Some of them talked to themselves or yelled profanities. She assumed that some of them must be violent. *What would they do to her when Sean left the tent to use the bathroom or for any other reason?* She would prefer not to find out, but there was no way she would stay where they were, so she reluctantly helped Sean pack their gear.

They trudged across the grassy park, carrying their backpacks with heavy steps in stark contrast to the light and joyous steps of the tourist family who carried an ice chest, picnic basket and beach ball less than 30 feet away. When they reached their destination, a woman with a few remaining crooked teeth gave them a big smile.

"Lookin' for a place to stay?" she asked with a lisp.

Sean answered, "Yeah, do you mind?"

"You look like you was beat up," a dark skinned bald man said, who was sitting on the ground.

"Yeah—a group of teenagers." Sean put his pack down on the ground next to a large tree.

"Thugs. They don't come near us since Bobby pulled a knife on one of them," another man said. "I'm Pete. Go ahead and set up under that there tree."

Haley tensed when she heard about the knife, but helped Sean set up their tent. Listening to Pete, Jenny, Bobby, Truck and Fred talk about the weather, they were normal people airing their opinions about local politicians and fishing. The group was friendly. They seemed to be happy to have more ears to bend about opinions and stories Haley suspected were repeated endlessly in order to pass the time. Truck and Fred shared butts of cigarettes they found abandoned by tourists in the park. Jenny had a dog-eared partial deck of cards she used to play solitaire on the grass. Pete mostly dozed, and Bobby used a knife to whittle sticks as he leaned against a tree.

As soon as it grew dark, Haley and Sean retreated into their tent to eat their sandwiches in private. They didn't have enough to share, and after watching Jenny and Truck rummage through garbage cans, they dared not accept the scraps of food they offered. Despite the terror she felt that morning, Haley felt safe snuggling next to her boyfriend in their tiny tent while listening to their new acquaintances drone on about the same tired subjects late into the night.

The next morning when Sean and Haley emerged from their tent, the others were still asleep, either on blankets on the ground or in their own tattered tents. After Haley took her turn walking to the park restrooms, she made their peanut butter and jelly sandwiches while Sean filled their water bottles at a nearby water fountain. They moved their beach towels to an open grassy area about 50 feet from their tent so they could eat and talk in private.

"How's your face?" she asked, stretching out on her beach towel and soaking in the warmth of the morning sun.

"Sore," he said, stretching out next to her. "I hate fighting."

"Yeah, me too." Haley adjusted her sunglasses. "Have you ever been punched in the face before?"

"Never." He shook his head and winced. "Ouch, I guess I shouldn't do that. I've been in situations where people have been fighting, but I've always been able to walk away."

"That's one of the reasons I love you so much," she said, leaning over to kiss her boyfriend. She handed him a sandwich and took a bite of her own.

"Who's that?" he asked, gesturing towards a woman who looked to be in her forties. She wore a white peasant blouse and a flower-patterned skirt with clipboard in hand, and she was walking directly towards them.

"Do you think we should leave?" Haley asked.

"She looks harmless," he said, puffing out his chest. "I think I can take her."

Haley laughed. "I'm sure you can."

"Good morning. I'm wondering if you might know a young couple by the names of Sean and Haley," the woman asked.

"Maybe, what do you want with them?" Sean peered at her over his sunglasses.

"My name is Debbie Jacobsen. I'm an outreach worker with the Freewheel Movement."

"What's that?" Haley asked.

"Have you heard of the Olympian Ryan Peterson?"

"Yeah," Sean said.

"The Freewheel Movement is his charitable organization. It's designed to match people who want to help with people who could use their help," Debbie explained. "We have someone who has joined Freewheel in order to help a couple by the names of Sean and Haley."

Sean set down his sandwich on his towel and stood up. "I'm Sean Bennett and this is my girlfriend, Haley O'Neill."

"Do you have an ID?" Debbie asked.

"I have my driver's license," Sean said. He reached into his shorts pocket for his wallet.

"My ID was stolen," Haley said softly. She hoped she wouldn't have to go into detail about the homeless sweep.

Sean handed over his California driver's license, and Debbie made some notes on her clipboard before handing it back to him.

"What's this all about?" Sean asked.

"A gentleman by the name of Bud Schubert would like to give you some items. I've got the list right here." Debbie handed a piece of paper to Sean.

Haley peered over his shoulder and read from the list:

> *1 triathlon bike of Terry's that will fit Haley*
> *1 bicycle pump*
> *1 bicycle tire repair kit*
> *1 pair of bicycle shoes that will be purchased for Haley that will fit the clipless pedals on the bicycle of her choice*
> *1 bicycle helmet for Haley*
> *1 bicycle shorts that will be purchased for Haley*
> *1 bicycle jersey for Haley*
> *Sean's and Haley's selection of any workout gear they would like from a box (Terry Schubert's gear)*
> *A swimsuit to be purchased for Haley*
> *Running shoes to be purchased for Haley*
> *Running clothes to be purchased for Haley*
> *Haley's selection of clothes, shoes, and accessories from a box (Sandy Schubert's clothes)*
> *Sean's selection of clothes, shoes, and accessories from a box (Terry's clothes)*
> *Miscellaneous camping gear, including a large tent*
> *2 small gym bags*
> *iPad*
> *2 mobile phones*
> *Misc. charging cords*
> *2 phone plans paid for 3 months.*
> *Private backyard to camp in for 3 months, with use of pool house with bathroom and shower*
> *$500 Safeway gift card*
> *Use of outdoor BBQ equipment, camp stove, refrigerator, and sink in pool house for 3 months*
> *Two bus passes for 3 months*
> *Two entries for the Terry Schubert Classic Pro Triathlon scheduled for July 5th*

After reading through the list, Haley felt tears well in her eyes. *Could this be true?*

"Is this some kind of a joke?" Sean frowned.

"This is unbelievable," Haley stammered.

"No, this is not a joke. When someone joins the Freewheel Movement,

50

they can design their gifts or contributions however they want. In this case, Mr. Schubert wants to donate his late son's triathlon gear, clothes and possessions, his wife's old clothes, and use of the back yard of one of their houses, as well as other items to help you two get back on your feet," Debbie explained.

"Have a seat." Sean motioned for Debbie to sit on their beach towels. She joined them without hesitation.

"How will this all work?" Haley looked at Debbie. The woman knew theirs and Mr. Schubert's name. She seemed to be telling the truth.

"First, I'll need you to review the Freewheel Movement recipient contract and sign it." Debbie handed the contract to Sean.

"Where do we sign?" he asked.

"In order to receive the gifts, the recipient has to adhere to any rules imposed by the gift giver. In your case, Mr. Schubert wants you both to get back on your feet. He's asking that you get part-time jobs and return to triathlon training so you can compete in the Terry Schubert Pro Classic Triathlon race on July 5th." Debbie consulted the paper on her clipboard. "You must agree to compete in the race or he'll withdraw his gift."

"That's a no-brainer. Of course, we'll do the race." Sean grinned.

Debbie handed him a pen.

Sean and Haley quickly reviewed the two-page Freewheel Movement Recipient Agreement and took turns signing it.

"Mr. Schubert doesn't want you to camp out at Ala Moana Park any longer than necessary," Debbie explained as she rose up from the beach towel. "I'll come by here tomorrow morning at ten to pick you up. Can you be ready by then?"

"Yes. Where are we going?" Haley said in a shaky voice. With all they had been through, she wondered if they should trust this woman.

"I'll take you to one of Mr. Schubert's houses in Hawaii Kai where you'll be selecting the items that have been offered to you and setting up camp in the fenced backyard."

Haley reached for Sean's hand and met his eyes.

"Are the Schuberts living in the house?" he asked, rising from the beach towel and helping Haley up.

"No. They live at another location," Debbie said. "A caretaker is staying at the house while it's being remodeled. All of the work is being done during the day. It shouldn't interfere with your sleep."

"Where does Mr. Schubert expect us to find part-time jobs?" Haley wiped sweat off her forehead. The late morning sun was beating down and the water she sipped from her bottle was warm already.

"There are some shopping centers nearby where you can both apply for jobs," Debbie said. "Mr. Schubert is willing to serve as a reference for you.

If you have any trouble getting employment, let me know and I can make some phone calls."

Haley rolled up their beach towels while Sean gathered the jars of peanut butter and jam, and placed them in his backpack.

"Is there a reason why he wants us to work part-time," Sean said. Their things put away, he and Haley walked with Debbie toward her car parked at the Magic Island parking lot.

"Only that Mr. Schubert wants you to devote most of your time to triathlon training." Debbie held out her key fob and clicked it to unlock her Honda.

"Will we be seeing him again?" Haley furrowed her brow. She wondered if there was a catch to this man's generosity.

"The Freewheel Movement allows for whatever relationships that the giving party wants to form—with the recipient's consent, of course. In this case, Mr. Schubert would prefer to have some intermittent contact," Debbie explained. "Once you get settled, he'll be contacting you. Until then, if you have any questions, you can call or e-mail me." She handed a business card to Sean.

When they reached Debbie's car, Haley hugged her. "We appreciate your help so much."

"I'll see you tomorrow morning at ten. I'm going to pull up at that curb." Debbie pointed to a spot near the restroom at the east end of the park. "I'll wait no longer than a half hour so make sure you're here."

"We'll be here," Sean said, reaching out to shake her hand.

"You'd be surprised at how many people are offered help from the Freewheel Movement who don't accept it. We don't force this on you, so if you decide you're not interested, you don't have to show up. I'll tear up the contract." Debbie opened her car door. "This is an opportunity to change your life. I hope you take full advantage of this chance for a fresh start."

"We're very grateful." Haley wiped a tear from her eye. "We'll be packed and ready."

She waved at Debbie as she drove away.

"Keep in mind that the offer for a place to stay is only for three months, Shay. We'll have to save every cent we earn to afford a deposit and first month's rent for an apartment," she said as she walked hand-in-hand with him back to the camp.

"Maybe we need to get full-time jobs." Sean paused to kiss her lightly on the lips.

"The contract said that we have to get part-time jobs and train. I think we better follow the rules."

"We'll see," he said. "I don't want to be back in the same position we're in now after the race."

After they returned to their tent, Haley pulled their remaining food out of Sean's backpack.

"I'm sick of peanut butter and jam sandwiches. Can we use some of our money to buy something else?" she asked.

"I don't want to blow our money yet. What if something goes wrong?"

She nodded.

"Let's not say a word of this to anyone," he whispered.

"Why?"

"I'm not sure." He rubbed his neck. "Let's be careful. We don't want anyone to sabotage our chances of getting out of here."

"I agree."

They ate the rest of the bread and peanut butter and jam for lunch and dinner, offering some to the others who shared some fresh mangoes they'd picked from a nearby tree. After sunset, Sean and Haley whispered with excitement as they lay on the blankets inside their tiny tent, flashlight on, no longer concerned about using up the batteries.

The next morning, Haley woke with a start. She had a sick feeling that she'd slept past 10 and missed the pick-up time. She rolled over, expecting to feel Sean's warm body, but the blanket next to her was empty. *Maybe he made a trip to the bathroom or he's sitting outside.*

Haley crawled out of the pup tent, slipped her sunglasses on and scanned the park, but saw no sign of her boyfriend. Even though the other homeless people were fast asleep nearby, she didn't dare leave their belongings unattended. She had no choice but to pee in a plastic cup while crouching inside the small tent, trying not to splash the blankets.

It was 9:15. Haley began packing up their gear, hoping Sean would reappear so they could leave this awful place together. She was sick of sleeping on the hard ground, listening to nonstop chatter from their camp mates late into the night and smelling unwashed bodies, not to mention the rotting garbage from the dumpster nearby. Her hands trembled as she dismantled the tent. She wondered whether her feelings of anxiety were more from fear of Sean being gone or from what would happen after Debbie picked them up.

After she had packed up their camp, Haley sat on a beach towel, staring across the park in the locations of the bathrooms, hoping to see her boyfriend emerge. She glanced at her watch every few minutes. It was now 9:40. *Would she have to leave and meet Debbie alone?* There was no way she was going to stay in this place for one more night.

She let out a sharp cry when she felt a hand on her shoulder from behind.

"It's me," Sean said.

"You scared me." Haley placed a hand over her heart.

"Sorry. I've got breakfast." He raised the McDonald's bag and a tray of coffees he was carrying.

Her eyes widened. "Thank you, thank you!" Haley squealed. "It feels like Christmas."

He sat down next to her and pulled out two Egg McMuffins. "It will feel even more like Christmas later today when we move into our new digs," he whispered.

She smiled broadly before she savored every bite of her sandwich.

Chapter Eight

@ZLaw #Wine, steak and #chocolate decadence. Is there any other way to a man's heart?

The only thing missing is Jerry. Zana absent-mindedly sipped from a glass of 2010 Luna Pinot Grigio left behind by the previous tenants in the wine fridge of his Diamond Head Tower condo. She stared out of the floor-to-ceiling window as the setting sun turned the sky orange and yellow. Jerry was supposed to make it back last night and she had even experimented with cooking beef stroganoff for the first time. The black lacquer dining table was still set for two with a centerpiece of unlit votive candles in geometric glass holders. He'd called from the airplane the moment he touched down to break the news that he was needed immediately on the studio set. Then, more bad news. He would be heading home to his parent's cottage when he was finished—likely in the wee hours of the morning. The beef in the stroganoff was tough now, the sauce was runny and so after eating a few bites, she dumped the rest in the garbage disposal. *At least Jerry hadn't tasted her cooking yet.*

She spent the day unpacking boxes of clothes and books, neatly arranging them and making sure to only use half of the walk-in closet and dresser drawer space, leaving the other half for Jerry. She was careful to allow him sufficient bathroom drawers and medicine cabinet shelves, placing feminine hygiene products discreetly in the back of the cabinet. As far as she knew, he had never lived with a woman before. She didn't want to scare him off with tampons.

Alexia and Ryan had helped her move—even after she'd called Ryan and told him that Frank had forbidden her to allow a client to aid in menial labor.

Ryan had laughed hysterically at Frank's directive and told her that his ambivalence about helping her had turned into unbridled enthusiasm. Just as Zana promised, hauling her boxes took them only one load using both of their SUVs, and afterwards, she treated her friends to lunch at the Ocean View Lounge on the top floor of her new building.

"Do they have steak and lobster? I'm sure Frank wouldn't approve of a client ordering a BLT." Ryan studied the menu.

Zana laughed. "I would have no problem if you ordered toast, but order whatever you want—my treat." The three decided on a round of beers and shared the edamame hummus, a few orders of spicy tuna roll, the seafood dynamite, the cheese plate, and then several lemongrass shrimp salads. Who knew moving worked up such an appetite.

"You're stylin' with your new condo and office." Ryan raised his beer in a toast. "I'll pop over on Tuesday so we can discuss your representation of me and the Freewheel Movement. We've got a lot to talk about."

"Sounds great." Zana beamed and clinked her glass with his and Alexia's.

"Congrats, Zana," Alexia said.

But now, she again had the condo to herself. She had texted Jerry, but his response was simply, "filming—xo". Even though tomorrow would be a workday for both of them, she hoped he would at least load up his dad's truck with some boxes.

She pulled her Rachel Ray cookbook off the shelf and thumbed through it, searching for recipes for a romantic first night living together dinner. *Maybe, there was something easier than beef stroganoff.*

***

When Jerry awoke, he thought he was still in Los Angeles…until he felt the trade wind breeze coming through his louvre windows. He breathed in the faint scent of ginger, which his mother had picked from the yard to welcome him home. It felt good to be sleeping in his own bed for a change, and it was comforting to know that his parents were in the main house nearby.

He couldn't wait to tell Zana all that had transpired in the last few weeks. His agent had negotiated his contract with the network, which had ordered 13 episodes of "Fighting in Paradise" and he was now raking in close to $100,000 per episode. If the show continued to show promise, the network would order nine more episodes. He smiled when he thought of Zana visiting him at the condo he'd just bought in Marina Del Rey so he'd no longer have to stay in a hotel room while filming.

Visiting, no living.

Jerry stretched out on his bed, wishing he could linger, but his schedule was packed as usual. Although he wasn't an endurance athlete like his girlfriend, he felt like each day must be as tough as an Ironman competition. If they were filming, he was at the set or on location from early morning until late at night. In his trailer, he memorized and practiced his lines, read script changes, and intermittently responded to law practice-related e-mails. His least favorite part of the day was in make-up, hair, and wardrobe. There were the martial arts training and work outs, which he was now obligated to do under his contract. Those were usually done at either 4 a.m. or late at night, unless a rare chunk of time during the day opened up.

Now that he was back in Honolulu for a week, Jerry had a few trial setting conferences on his calendar which required attendance by the lead attorney. After the network had acquired "Fighting in Paradise" and he became aware that the show had suddenly become more than a part-time Oahu based job, Jerry hired an experienced insurance defense attorney to handle the day-to-day operations of his law practice.

Kate Scrimshaw's timing had been impeccable. She came by Jerry's office with a résumé in late February on a day when he was sitting at his desk, polishing up a memorandum in opposition to a motion. In the wake of the problems he had with flirtatious Annabelle Wong, he welcomed Kate, a mousey, middle-aged, overweight woman. Jerry was impressed with her 25 years of insurance defense litigation experience as an in-house counsel for MEI-CO in a handful of states and at an insurance defense law firm on the mainland.

Kate's soon-to-be ex-husband was a US Naval officer who had been stationed in California, Florida, Virginia and Texas, where she had passed the bars and practiced law over the years. When they were stationed in Italy, she took some time off, learned to speak Italian and took cooking lessons. Years ago, she had lived on Oahu shortly after graduating from law school and passed the bar, but they had an unexpected change of duty station, and so she had never practiced law in Hawaii. When her husband had replaced her with a younger woman he met on Match.com, Kate quit her job at MEI-CO and moved back to Honolulu.

She seemed intelligent, knew how to handle insurance defense cases and work with claims adjusters, and she had a warm, friendly personality that didn't quite match her no-nonsense appearance.

After checking her references, Jerry had hired Kate and installed her in the empty office adjacent to his. She seemed delighted to work for him, and so far, had efficiently managed his caseload while he was busy with the show. He'd initially planned to hire a man, because he didn't want to make Zana feel uncomfortable after the Annabelle debacle. However, Kate was so non-threatening and competent that he knew his girlfriend would be pleased with his choice.

While sipping his morning coffee, Jerry checked his iPad calendar. He had time to meet with Kate to go over the status of his cases before walking to court. This was his first time back to Honolulu after his contract had been negotiated to include the retention of a bodyguard at the network's expense. He thought the notion of having a bodyguard when he was a black belt in multiple martial arts disciplines was ridiculous—until there had been a mob of fans surrounding him at a grocery store in Honolulu.

Kaiko, a large Hawaiian man who wore an earpiece like a secret service agent, was assigned to accompany Jerry in Honolulu whenever and wherever he went out in public, which meant that he had to text or e-mail his schedule and any changes to Kaiko throughout each day. This new requirement felt oppressive and was a price of fame Jerry didn't appreciate. In LA, when his bodyguard, Neil, followed him, Jerry kept looking back until Neil finally told him to relax and ignore him. Jerry constantly felt like he was being stalked, but understood that it was necessary to keep the paparazzi and fans at arm's length so he didn't end up on the front page of a tabloid because of a round-house kick to an over-eager selfie seeker.

After his meeting with Kate, Jerry walked to court with Kaiko in his shadow. As he passed the First Hawaiian Bank building, a woman rushed up to him. Jerry's body tensed until he recognized that the woman was Moana, one of Zana's best friends.

"Hey Moana," Jerry said, turning to nod at his bodyguard. Kaiko stepped back and whispered something into his earpiece.

"I didn't think you'd be back yet," she said as Jerry kissed her cheek.

"I'm only here for the week. Then I have to return to LA."

"I'm rushing off to a meeting, but I wanted to tell you congratulations. I'm so happy for you and Zana." She smiled broadly and rushed to cross the street.

"Mahalo," Jerry called after her, wondering what she meant. He didn't think there was anything to congratulate them for. Maybe she was referring to their being back together after several months of separation.

He continued to the courthouse, feeling the presence of Kaiko behind him, even though his bodyguard was well practiced at keeping his steps light and his breath silent. As they approached the First Circuit Court Building, a number of attorneys wearing dark, tropical weight suits passed Jerry. They exchanged greetings, but Jerry hoped they didn't guess that Kaiko was ready to pounce on them if they made a threatening move. Once they got through security at the courthouse, his bodyguard was content to stay downstairs and wait while Jerry met with judges and opposing attorneys on the fourth floor. He had to set trial dates and discuss other trial-related matters.

Just as Jerry walked out of the courtroom and was heading towards the elevator, his phone began playing Katie Perry's "Roar"—Zana's ringtone.

"Hey you," he said softly into the phone.

"Are you coming home tonight?" Zana asked. "I've made a special dinner for you."

"Sure." He slowed so he could talk to her without getting cut off if he stepped on the elevator. It had been a long time since he had had a day off or even an evening free. "What time shall I be there?"

"As early as you can," she said. "I really miss you."

"Would six be okay?" Even if Kenny called insisting that he report to the studio, it was time to say no. Kate could more than handle the office. Jerry planned to work out in the late afternoon and then spend time with his girlfriend for a change.

"Perfect. I have a new work situation so I can leave here anytime I want," she said. "I'll have dinner on the table for you and then we can have dessert."

"Can we have dessert first?"

"We'll see. Maybe, if you're a good boy." She giggled.

Jerry felt butterflies in his stomach at the thought of spending an evening with Zana. After he delegated more tasks to Kate, drank a protein shake for lunch, lifted weights, hit a punching bag and ran on the treadmill, Jerry stopped by his favorite florist to pick up two dozen red long-stemmed roses for his girlfriend. Kaiko followed him to a wine store where he picked up a bottle of Columbia Gorge Chardonnay. Then, he headed home to pack his overnight bag.

Jerry noticed Kaiko following him in a black SUV from his house in Manoa to Diamond Head Tower in Waikiki. He had to give the guy credit, even though they had encountered quite a few red lights, Kaiko managed to stay less than two cars behind Jerry's red Ferrari. He was tempted to speed away, but knowing Kaiko, he wouldn't lose him. Once he reached the condo's parking garage, Kaiko followed him to the well-staffed lobby and then disappeared for the night.

Jerry knocked, even though he was the owner of the tastefully appointed one-bedroom condo with its stunning ocean view. As soon as Zana opened the door, accepted his gift of roses and wine, he carried her to the bedroom for a long overdue evening of lovemaking.

It took him a few seconds to remove her tank top, shorts and the matching bra and thong she wore underneath. She almost ripped his shirt in an effort to press her bare skin against his well-muscled torso. Their bodies came together on top of the duvet cover. He was overwhelmed with how good she felt underneath him, causing him to finish much too quickly.

"I'm sorry—you're too sexy," Jerry said, kissing her neck.

"That was only round one." Zana winked.

"Is that right?"

"I've got dinner in the oven, so if you want to eat something that isn't burnt, we'll have to take this up again later."

"Sounds delicious." He smiled. "Dinner and later."

"Perfect. Would you mind grabbing my robe in the closet, Jer-bear?"

"Sure." He opened the walk-in closet while Zana went into the kitchen naked. He noticed that she'd put her clothes and shoes in one half, leaving the other half empty. He grabbed her black satin robe off a hanger and then went to the bathroom to wash his hands.

The soap dispenser was empty. He opened the cupboard below and saw that her cosmetics and toiletries took only half of the space and the rest remained empty. He opened the medicine cabinet. It was half empty as well.

"Wow!" He helped her into her robe. "Something smells delicious."

"Sit down and relax." She motioned to a kitchen chair. She'd put the roses in a large vase on the black marble coffee table in the living room. "Let me pour you some wine."

"This looks amazing, Zana," he said, stunned at the filet mignon, baked potato, and steamed asparagus on the plate before him. She rarely cooked and he'd never seen her near red meat.

"I hope you like it." She sipped her wine.

Jerry tasted a bite of steak and without completely swallowing, said, "This is delicious, but I didn't think you ate meat."

"I do, sometimes." She winked.

"You're a fabulous cook. I'm a lucky guy." He patted his stomach.

"It's wonderful to have you home."

"I agree." He put down his fork and looked into her sparkling green eyes. "You look beautiful, sweetheart."

"You do, too." She reached out to caress his freshly shaved face.

"It must be my outfit." He was wearing only black briefs—his torso was bare.

"Very attractive." She caressed his abs.

He moved his chair closer to hers. "Are you enjoying the condo?"

"I'd be enjoying it more if you were here."

"I know. It's been rough on me, too." He leaned closer to kiss her gently on the lips. "This is my first night off in ages."

She sat back in her chair. "It's amazing how much our lives have changed in the past month."

"I'm so proud of you. What's it like being a sports agent?"

"I'm not sure yet. I haven't even done anything for my only client." She swallowed. "We're meeting tomorrow morning so at least I'll have something to do."

He noticed the edge in her voice. "You're not just sitting in your office looking out the window, are you?"

"Far from it. I'm researching sponsorship opportunities for Ryan. I've also done an exhaustive research of triathlons with prize money worldwide so I can advise him tomorrow on racing possibilities."

"Sounds interesting." Jerry took his last bite of steak. He then put his fork and knife on his plate and leaned back in his chair. "Yum."

"I've got chocolate decadence for dessert."

He frowned. "My new contract has a no chocolate decadence clause."

"You can have some bites from my piece." Zana cleared their dishes and placed a plate with small slivers of chocolate decadence cake with raspberries on the table.

"I'm so full, but this is incredible." He took a bite of chocolate and held it on his tongue for a moment to savor its rich flavor.

"Get used to it," she said, raising her wine glass.

"Zana, you know I love you," Jerry reached across the table for her hand.

"I love you, too."

"This has been a really nice evening, but I think you've misunderstood something," he said gently.

"What do you mean?" She stared at him.

"I'm sorry, sweetheart, but I'm not moving in here with you."

She put her wine glass down and looked at the king-size bed through the open bedroom door and swallowed hard.

Chapter Nine

@Haleyville From #baglady to tent queen. What's more luxurious than a refrigerator, hot water, and groceries? #HappyHaley

"Did you know that almost half of all American women fear becoming bag ladies, even if they're making a six-figure income?" Haley asked as she helped Sean unfold a large tent in the corner of the Schubert property backyard.

That task finished, Sean pulled the tent poles out of the large box and placed them next to the unfolded tent. "I find that hard to believe."

"I read it in a sociology class." Haley leaned against the pool house. "I was thinking about how I became a bag lady at twenty-two years old, before I even got the chance to make any income."

"You're not a bag lady." Sean reached for the directions inside the box.

"Shay, we're homeless," she said, hands on hips. "How am *I* not a bag lady?"

He paused and looked up at his girlfriend. "We've got this amazing tent and backyard to camp in. Haleyville, if you were a bag lady, you aren't any more."

"I know," she said softly. She slumped to the grass and put her face in her hands. "I'm the first person in my family who's earned a college degree, and what have I got to show for it?"

"Yeah. This really sucks." He put the tent poles down, sat down next to her and put his arm around her.

"My mom always had a job and kept a roof over our heads. She only had a tenth-grade education." Haley sobbed. "Look at me."

Sean kissed the tears on her cheeks and held her in silence for a long moment. "All during college, I dreamt about graduating and having a full-time job—wearing a suit and going to an office."

Haley saw the hurt in his eyes and said, "I'm sorry for being such a downer. I do appreciate all of this."

The neighborhood was beautiful, with large homes and well-kept tropical landscaped yards. Schubert's home had a large backyard—complete with a rectangle swimming pool surrounded by chaise lounges and a covered barbeque area in an equipped outdoor kitchen. The pool house was separated into men's and women's shower and changing sections and each area had a clothes rack with shelves they could use as closets.

"Look at the bright side." Sean stood and offered a hand to assist Hailey up. "We can take hot showers and we have cold water to drink."

She nodded. "It's nice to have our own clean bathrooms with mirrors."

"And a refrigerator. We can buy milk for our cereal."

"I wish he would've let us live inside the house." She gestured to the large house on the property with all its blinds closed.

"He didn't have to do anything to help us. Let's appreciate what we've got."

"I love my new triathlon gear." She smiled. "I can't believe Terry's old bike fit me. I miss my Cervelo, but the Specialized isn't too bad."

"And we can both leave at the same time without fear of someone taking our stuff."

She rolled her eyes. The jibe still stung. They were given a key to the pool house where they could lock their valuables. She wished it were big enough to sleep in. Sean stood up and returned to the task of erecting the tent.

"Do you know how to put that thing together?" She pulled herself up.

He shrugged and handed her the instructions written in four languages.

"You have more patience than me." She handed them back to him. "And, you're always so calm."

"That's a very sweet thing to say," Sean said, leaning over to kiss her. "One thing at a time—that's all we can do."

She watched him as he inserted tent poles through the frame. "Once we get this put together, let's go to Safeway and shop for food."

"We can fire up the barbeque and have chicken or hamburgers for dinner."

"Oh yum! Let's get corn on the cob and salad." Haley brightened. "I'm so sick of peanut butter and jam and stale bread."

"After dinner, we can take a swim in the pool using our new goggles. How cool is that?"

"Or we can go for a run." She handed him the last tent pole. "It's amazing how we used to take our ability to do simple things for granted."

They raised the tent together.

"Now, we have the freedom to work, exercise, sleep, eat, and shower." He admired their handiwork.

She nodded. "We can't let Schubert's generosity go to waste."

He bent down to hammer the tent pegs as Haley stood over him and watched. When he finished, he looked up at her. "I had it rough as a kid, but at least we were never homeless. It's not an easy life."

She reached for his hand and squeezed it. "Shay, let's promise to work our asses off."

"I promise, Haleyville." His eyes were moist. He averted them and focused on setting up the rain fly. Then they ducked inside.

"It's huge." She stood up to her full height inside the tent.

"We're not done yet." He stepped out. Sean carried in a queen size airbed that she helped him inflate. They made it up, using clean sheets, blankets, and pillows donated by the Schuberts. When the bed was made, he pulled Haley onto it for a long kiss. She sighed as she felt the thick softness of the bed underneath her.

"This feels nice."

"I know," Sean breathed, pressing his body against hers and reaching to unbutton her shorts.

She could feel her stomach growl beneath his touch and pulled away. "Shay, we need to go grocery shopping." There was no way she was going to let anything get in the way of buying food and eating a real meal—not even sex.

He frowned.

"Later, okay?" She kissed him, stood up and buttoned her shorts.

They walked to Safeway and pushed a cart through the aisles, filling it with fresh fruit, vegetables, cereal, hamburger, chicken, yogurt, milk, cheese, coffee, rice, and potatoes—all the food they had been daydreaming about. Haley added a few chocolate cupcakes as a treat.

The moment they left the store, Haley ripped into the Wheat Thins box. She felt the urge to gobble the crackers by the handful, but instead savored one salty cracker at a time.

As soon as they reached the back yard, Sean fired up the barbeque. They prepared their meal of hamburger patties, corn on the cob and roasted potatoes, which they ate on the patio table next to the swimming pool. Sean inhaled his food and then piled more on his plate. Haley ate slowly. Aside from their breakfast sandwiches that morning, it had been weeks since she had eaten anything hot and substantial. She bit into the hamburger and closed her eyes as she chewed. Sean had suggested buns, but she reminded him that they had had nothing but sandwiches for the past two weeks. So they agreed not to purchase bread of any kind. They washed down their meal with glasses of cold, filtered ice water instead of the rust-flavored warm water from park fountains.

After dinner, Sean cut a cupcake in half for his girlfriend, but she took a whole one, smiling with each bite. He laughed at the chocolate frosting smeared on her cheek, wiped it off with his finger and let her lick it off.

After washing dishes in the pool house sink, Haley changed into her bathing suit and lowered herself into the pool's cool water.

"Come in," she called to Sean, who was cleaning the grill with a wire brush.

"I'll be right in," he said.

It felt good to swim lap after lap of freestyle as she stretched out her body and lengthened her strokes. This was Haley's first swim since the city took away her goggles. Her body felt more relaxed with each stroke as she moved quickly through the water. Her stomach was finally full, and she let her mind wander rather than worry about where their next meal would come from. Sean soon joined her and they swam side-by-side, picking up their pace until sunset.

After their swim, they took a hot shower together, taking turns soaping each other. Later, they dried each other off using fluffy blue towels. Haley giggled when Sean wrapped her up in a towel, carried her to the tent, and then almost dropped her while he fumbled with the flap.

"You should put me down."

"I've got it." He held her in his arms and squatted as he tried to unzip the tent.

After a few minutes of her uncontrollable laughter, he set her on the grass and used both hands to gain entrance into the dark tent.

She dropped her towel and fell onto the bed with Sean. She breathed in his clean scent and writhed in pleasure as they kissed deeply. She felt him explore her legs with his fingers and didn't stop him this time. His hardness pressed against her and her fear from weeks of homelessness seemed to melt away as they fumbled in the dark. Safety was an aphrodisiac.

Haley pulled him on top of her, and their bodies moved together as they moaned with pleasure. His breathing became quicker and she tensed her body, hoping to prolong the intense sensation. Then she let out a gasp just as he moaned loudly. She felt the dampness of his chest against hers as he relaxed. She pulled him even closer and closed her eyes, feeling the softness of the pillow and the warmth of his body. Exhausted, she fell asleep.

Haley woke with a start.

"Hay, are you okay?"

She reached for him and he pulled her close.

"Did you have a nightmare?" he asked, stroking her hair.

"I'm not sure, but when I woke up I thought we were still in the park."

He reached down and clicked on a flashlight. "We'll have to get some lanterns."

The light was dim, but the tent was so large she could envision furnishing it with a love seat and chairs if they could manage to earn extra money.

"All we need are pictures on the walls and this would be nicer than my college dorm room." She snuggled closer to Sean.

"What do you think the neighbors will think when they see this big ass tent?"

"It's not much different from their kid's forts and princess houses," Haley observed. "They can probably put up with it for a few months."

"Bud Schubert must be some sort of big shot so he can probably do whatever he wants on his own property." Sean stroked her hair.

"What time is it?"

He fumbled for his backpack next to the bed and pulled out his phone. "Eight-thirty."

"I wish we had a TV." Haley sat up in bed, wide-awake now.

"That's what the iPad is for." Sean pulled it out of his backpack. "Do you want to watch a movie before we fall asleep?"

"Only if we can have popcorn."

"There's a microwave, but we forgot to buy popcorn."

"Next time." Haley curled up under Sean's arm to watch *Hangover 3* until she fell asleep.

***

In the morning, Haley stepped out of the pool house wearing one of the two-piece jacket and skirt suits she'd selected from the boxes of Mrs. Schubert's old clothes.

"You look beautiful, Haleyville." Sean's eyes widened.

"It's hard to believe anyone would give this away." Haley put her hand on the lightweight silky black fabric. "It's Armani."

"It looks brand-new." Sean took a few steps closer to examine it.

"Debbie said that Mrs. Schubert has put on some weight and has given up on ever being a size four again." Haley sat on a lounge chair and slipped on some shiny black pumps. "Her clothes are a little big on me, but I'm not complaining."

Sean pulled on a navy polo shirt to match his khaki slacks. "Are you sure you want to wear an Armani suit job hunting at Petco and Ross's Dress for Less?"

"Good point." Haley grimaced, and stepped back into the pool house. She had automatically picked the nicest outfit without giving it much thought. After examining Mrs. Schubert's cast-off garments, she changed into a simple, blue, Ann Taylor dress with a white collar. At least wearing this outfit, she'd fit in at the strip mall shops where they planned to submit résumés.

"You look nice." Sean smiled. "I'd hire you in a nanosecond."

Haley bit her lip. "I'm not sure it's realistic for us to land even part-time jobs."

"Yeah, we've just blown into town from the mainland and both of us don't have much work experience," he said as he combed his hair.

"Shay, we've got to think positive." Haley frowned. They hadn't bothered with résumés. Their work experience would barely fill the lines of the form job applications they anticipated filling out. She doubted the stores cared much about college degrees.

"I fucked up my opportunity to work at Starbucks." Sean tucked in his shirt. "All I've ever done is work at coffee shops."

"It's my fault. If our stuff wasn't hauled away, you would have shown up for work." She didn't want to see the disappointment in his eyes again, and so she busied herself with putting a few things into one of Mrs. Schubert's discarded black shoulder bags.

"It's okay," Sean said softly. "Hopefully, my coffee shop experience will get me an interview somewhere."

"Well, you do know a lot about history."

"Yeah, I seriously picked the wrong major," Sean said. "At least you have retail experience."

"It wasn't in Hawaii, though. Why would anyone give us jobs over local people?"

Sean shrugged. "We've got to make an effort so Bud doesn't kick us out."

"At least one of us needs to get a job. If we have to, we can sell the Schuberts' stuff on eBay."

"Just in case, I suggest you don't use those designer handbags. We might have to sell them to buy groceries." Sean eyed her purse.

"I'm way ahead of you." Haley gestured to the bag on her shoulder. "This one has stained and torn lining."

Sean slung his backpack on his back. "You'll get blisters walking all the way to the stores in those heels."

"Let's ride our bikes. I can put my shoes in my back pack."

"Aren't you worried about helmet hair and grease stains on your dress?"

"I'll be careful. After washing my hair in a cold shower on the beach with soap for a few weeks, helmet hair doesn't seem like such a big deal anymore." She smiled, meeting his eyes. "You look nice all cleaned up, Shay."

His eyes sparkled when he grinned, reminding her of graduation day last month. Both of them had felt so hopeful about their future. They'd talked incessantly about their planned trip to Paris, never imagining that the field would be so competitive that neither of them would win the trip. Haley carefully slipped her bicycle helmet on and clicked into the pedals with her new bike shoes. She couldn't remember ever riding a bike wearing a dress before. It was late morning and the traffic was so light they rode side-by-side on the wide neighborhood road. She was careful to ride slowly.

"The applications are going to ask how long we've lived in Hawaii," Haley said as she pedaled.

"Hmmm, you're right. We'll have to lie." Sean matched her cadence. "We're never going to get jobs if we say we've been on the island for only three weeks."

Haley shook her head. There was no way she'd lie about anything. That's not how she was brought up. As they rode in silence, Sean passed her, and she followed behind, her dress blowing in the warm island breeze.

The first shopping center was only three blocks away. She hoped that she could avoid sweat stains on her dress from the late morning heat. They rode through the empty parking lot to a bike rack, where they locked up their bikes and stowed their helmets in their backpacks.

"Where are you going to apply?" Haley smoothed out her dress with her hands.

Sean ran his fingers through his hair. "Everywhere—until someone hires me."

"Should we go into the stores together or separately?" Haley's voice quavered, and she felt knots tighten in her stomach. She hadn't applied for a job since sophomore year when she had made the rounds at the mall close to campus. The Gap was short staffed and hired her immediately. The J. Crew manager had lured her away with an offer of higher pay until she had to quit, because of the demands of school, swimming and triathlons.

"We can start at opposite ends of the strip mall and meet up here when we're finished." Sean pulled the rubber bands from the bottom of his pant legs he'd put on so his pants wouldn't get caught in the bicycle chain.

"Good luck!" They said to each other in unison, followed by a kiss before they walked their separate ways.

Haley systematically went from store to store, asking to speak to the managers. She filled out application forms that were routinely offered to be "kept on file" once completed. Besides The Gap and J. Crew, she added the grocery store where she'd worked during a few summers in high school to her job experience list. When asked how long she had been at her current address, she wrote "1 day", not feeling comfortable lying as Sean suggested.

She filled in her new cell phone number and Bud Schubert's address—

they wouldn't guess that she was living in a tent in the back yard. For a local reference, she gave their benefactor's name and phone number, hoping one was sufficient. She didn't know anyone else in Hawaii besides Debbie and the homeless people.

A manager or employee had accepted her application at each store, but none offered an interview or any encouragement. There were no signs advertising job openings. She'd seen a few other people filling out applications at the same time. The only encouragement was a brief conversation she had with a friendly male manager at Chun's Dry Cleaners, but she couldn't be sure he wasn't hitting on her. Just when she was about to enter Petco, she heard the ringtone of her new cell phone for the first time.

She rummaged through her purse and after the fourth ring, croaked "Hello."

"May I speak with Haley O'Neill?" A male voice said.

"I'm Haley."

"This is Adam Kessler. I'm the manager at Costco."

"Oh, yes." He'd looked over her application in front of her and told her that they didn't have any openings, but he'd call her if anything changed.

"Haley, I called Bud Schubert. He's a friend of my fathers," Mr. Kessler said.

Haley nodded, without saying anything.

"He was quite insistent that I hire you."

"Oh, okay."

"As I told you this morning, we're fully staffed, but I can give you a part-time job. Are you okay with that arrangement?"

"Absolutely." She grinned.

"Bud suggested that I hire you to work from ten a.m. to three p.m., Mondays through Fridays so you can train for a triathlon."

"Are you serious? I mean, thank you so much," Haley squealed. "When do you want me to start?"

"How 'bout tomorrow?"

"Sure. I'll be there. What time?"

"Can you be here at ten to fill out the paperwork? Then you'll start our training program."

Haley was so excited to land a job that she didn't think to ask Adam what she'd be doing before hanging up. If she weren't wearing a dress and heels, she'd have jumped for joy. Instead, she walked as fast as she could to the bike racks. Her bike was where she'd left it, but Sean's was missing. Had she really taken that much longer than he had filling out forms?

Maybe he'd ridden to another area to submit more applications. If it was stolen, she might be able to catch the person. She almost forgot she was wearing a dress that was dry clean only. After changing her shoes, she hiked her dress up and sprinted around the parking lot, looking for Sean or his bike. After about twenty minutes, she raced the three blocks home.

Sean was already changed out of his interview pants and sitting by the pool when Haley leaned her bike against the pool house.

"You're back already?" Haley asked, pulling her helmet off.

"Yeah, sorry. I guess I should've texted you. Did you give up?"

"No, I got a job at Costco. I guess Bud pulled some strings."

"Congratulations!" He stood up and hugged her.

"Did you give up?"

"Bud's name must be gold around here." Sean grinned.

"What do you mean?" Haley searched his face for an answer. "Did you get a job, too?"

"After I said good-bye to you, I rode my bike over to Starbucks to apologize for not following up with their offer at the Waikiki store. The manager acted like he was expecting me and told me to start tomorrow."

"Do you think Bud called them?"

"He must have." Sean sat back down on the lounge chair. "I told him and Debbie about the missed opportunity."

"What are your hours?" Haley asked.

"Monday through Friday, ten to three."

"Okay. This was a total set-up." Haley sank into the chair next to Sean's. "We have the same hours."

"Yeah, and those aren't normal shifts. It's perfect for triathlon training, but this is a ridiculous coincidence." Sean furrowed his brow.

"I guess Bud Schubert really wants us to win that race in July." Haley smiled before she leaned over to kiss her boyfriend.

Chapter Ten

@ZLaw My own private #barista, a luxurious office, and now my very own autographed picture of Olympian #RyanPeterson. Can life get any better?

"It's fantastic," Zana said the moment Ryan tore the brown paper off the large framed, autographed poster of himself accepting his gold medal at the London Olympic Games. "It'll look perfect over my desk."

Her eyes moved to the large framed photograph on the wall of Donald mid-swing on the fourteenth hole during a pro-am golf tournament. There were half a dozen similar photographs in every office, inspiring her new boss to tell the story behind each whenever there was a lull in the conversation. She hoped never to hear another.

Ryan crumbled up the brown paper and tossed it into a small waste can. "I can't have my agent surrounded by golf pictures when she doesn't even golf." He sat down on the olive and light-yellow leather guest chair. "Aside from the art work, this office is exquisite."

"You think so?" Zana took a seat behind her desk and caressed its koa wood surface. Donald had offered to let her redecorate, but she liked the light wood and exquisite modern furniture. It made her feel as if she no longer worked for a revolving door law firm with disposable associates.

"I feel like I'm in a Tokyo office—everyone is so polite up here." Ryan squinted at her. "And the bags under your eyes aren't as prominent as they were when you worked downstairs."

Zana leaned back in her olive-green leather chair. "It's a different world. It's not only beautiful, but no one bats an eye if someone doesn't stroll in until the afternoon."

"Why's that?"

"The real estate transaction lawyers are always flying to Asia for client meetings, and when they're on Oahu, they often work from home. Donald spends most of his time on golf courses or at meetings at the 19th hole. Mika goes to every ball game and practice he can. He only pops into his office to meet clients every few days."

"So, what are you doing here?" Ryan raised his eyebrows. "Shouldn't you be out meeting clients?"

"You're here." She laughed. "My one and only."

"I'm sure you'll have a bunch more clients soon."

"It's not like pro triathletes need agents." She frowned. "They hardly make any money."

"That's going to change, Zana." He smiled.

"How so?"

"That's one of the reasons I'm here." He scooted his chair closer to her desk. "After Bud Schubert apologized about the lawsuit, he contacted me to discuss ways to honor his son. I'm helping him produce a race series, but we also discussed a topic of interest to Terry when he was alive—how to make triathlon more like golf, tennis, and ball sports so pros can earn more money."

"How do you propose doing that?" She fingered a turtle-shaped paperweight on her desk. "Fans want to watch their home teams or root for their favorite golfer. Sponsors aren't interested in a sport hardly anyone watches or cares about."

"True, but what if the public became infatuated with some pro triathletes?" he said, his face becoming animated. "Wouldn't that increase television viewership?"

She shrugged. "I suppose so. Do you have some triathletes in mind?"

"Bud does. He met some homeless triathletes on Magic Island. Have you ever heard of Sean Bennett or Haley O'Neill?"

She shook her head. "No, I can't say I have. I wonder if he was with them in the pouring rain during the premier of 'Fighting in Paradise' at Magic Island." She put down the paperweight with a thud. She remembered seeing Bud give some homeless people an umbrella, but she had been paying more attention to Annabelle Wong who was sitting at their table, thankfully flirting with another attractive male cast member rather than Jerry.

"I'm not sure. Maybe. According to Bud, they're attractive young athletes and have a compelling story."

"How does that translate into big bucks?" She pursed her lips.

"Bud signed up with the Freewheel Movement so he can sponsor Sean and Haley by giving them clothes, triathlon equipment and a tent to sleep in on one of his properties. In return, they have to compete in the Terry

Schubert Pro Triathlon Classic to be held in July."

She pulled out a notebook and wrote down their names. "The race you were talking about."

"Exactly."

"Do you want some coffee?" Zana asked, hoping he'd say yes. She could feel her eyelids drooping. Even though she no longer had bags under her eyes, she felt less energetic with no pressing work.

"Sure."

"Listen to this." She pressed a button on her phone.

"May I help you?" Nina's voice asked through the speakerphone.

"Could you please bring me a latte and, what would you like, Ryan?"

"Coffee." He leaned forward to speak into the phone.

"You can have anything—espresso, cappuccino—whatever." Zana hoped he'd order something more fun than a plain coffee.

"Okay, cappuccino."

"Anything else?" Nina asked.

"That's fine." Zana grinned. "Thanks." After she pressed a button on the phone, she turned back to her client. "And, you were saying?"

"Bud asked me to find race directors for his national triathlon series. He's enlisted Kenny Paxton to be the producer."

She tilted her head to the side. "Okay, now you've lost me. What does he need a producer for?"

"He's going to make the races huge TV events," Ryan said, his eyes sparkling.

"So how will the triathletes make any money?"

"You do know that Bud is wealthy?"

"Of course."

"He's planning to fund a series of Terry Schubert Pro Triathlon Classics across the country and put up prize money of two million dollars for each race."

"Are you kidding me?" She could have leapt out of her seat to hug Ryan, but the door opened and Nina entered with a tray. The woman placed small, olive-green place mats on Zana's desk and then carefully set down cups and saucers with their drinks, a small glass bowl of a variety of sweetener packets, and a plate full of grapes, apple slices, almonds, vegan super seed crackers and organic oatmeal cookies. She then handed them each a pale yellow cloth napkin.

"Anything else?" Nina asked.

Zana looked at Ryan who shook his head. She reached for her latte. "Mahalo, Nina."

"This *is* quite a change from the Styrofoam coffee cups downstairs." Ryan sipped his cappuccino.

Zana nodded and popped a grape into her mouth. "So, there's finally going to be a big money race series for pro triathletes. That's great!"

"Bud is starting with races in Honolulu, San Diego, Colorado Springs, Chicago, Salt Lake City and Miami. His initial contribution will be about twelve million dollars, but we're also looking for other sponsors."

Her eyes widened. "Are you going to compete? Will you be allowed to?"

"Are you kidding? Of course." He laughed.

She turned the page on the legal pad and took up her pen. "What's the break-down of prize money?"

"Each male and female winner earns five hundred thousand dollars. Second place finishers each get two hundred grand. Third place finishers get one hundred grand. The prizes diminish from there for the top ten males and females."

She wrote notes about the winnings and then looked up. "How does that couple fit into the plan?"

"Bud doesn't know how they're going to place so he wants to give prize money to the top ten. He figures that if one of them gets at least fifth place, it will allow them a fresh start. They'll be able to have enough money to move out of his tent and into a place of their own."

She scrunched her forehead and put her pen to her lips. "I'm still not getting it. How does this turn triathlon into a big money sport?"

"Kenny is going to create a televised special to showcase these homeless triathletes who are competing for prize money. The plan is for them to go from rags to riches in a matter of hours. Hopefully, the public will eat this up."

"So—what if they do?"

"We hope Sean and Haley will be able to get individual sponsors and more media opportunities." Ryan paused and sipped his cappuccino. "The public likes these athletic human-interest sob stories. The winning triathletes who we spotlight will attract a huge number of eyeballs. The sponsors will come flooding in."

"Interesting plan." She chewed the end of her pen and stared at the golf picture behind Ryan's head. If this couple came into money, maybe they'd need an agent.

As if he could read her mind, Ryan looked her straight in the eyes and said, "I think Bud is planning to refer Sean and Haley to an agent he golfs with."

"Who?" She picked up her coffee cup.

"Mansfield." He bit his lip. "Rip Mansfield."

She felt her hand begin to shake and put down her cup. She looked out the window and stared at a distant cruise ship for a few moments before saying quietly, "He's been disbarred."

"According to Bud, he's now a sports agent, dividing his time between LA and Honolulu."

Zana stared at Ryan, bile rising in her throat. She would never forget the image of Rip Mansfield calling her a whore as long as she lived. She was also sure he wouldn't forget the hand Jerry and she played in his disbarment. Even if she managed to sign Sean and Haley on as clients, Mansfield would do everything in his power to steal them away.

"That snake is going to represent pro triathletes?" Zana moved the small trashcan under her desk towards her in case she got sick.

"I'm sure you'd be better," Ryan said. "There's plenty of time for you to meet Sean and Haley, and try to win them over."

Her chest tightened, and dampness spread under her arms.

"You've got one advantage over Mansfield."

"One?" Her eyes widened.

"You're a triathlete—you can swim, bike, and run with prospective clients. Mansfield can golf, but I can't imagine he'll don a Speedo." Ryan chuckled.

Zana smiled thinly. She didn't stand a chance against Mansfield. He'd pay off anyone to get what he wanted. "How can I possibly train with Sean and Haley?"

"I talked Bud into paying for their triathlon coaching with Dieter Weiss."

Zana had heard that Weiss was a former Olympian and one of the best coaches in the sport. He'd never agree to coach her, and she surely couldn't afford his rates. She again turned her gaze to the window, hoping Ryan wouldn't notice her discouragement.

"You should join his training group."

She swallowed hard.

"I'll put in a good word and you can expense your training to the firm." Ryan rose and leaned against the floor to ceiling window, looking in the direction of the cruise ship that was now pulling into port at Aloha Tower.

"Maybe I can improve enough to race in the Schuster Pro Classic." If she managed to come in 10th place in her age group, the money could go to pay down her student loans.

Ryan shook his head and turned toward her. "That would be a conflict of interest with your triathlete pro clients."

"You mean my imaginary clients?" She laughed.

"The clients who you'll land after you start training with Dieter." Ryan stepped back to her desk and reached for a few apple slices, which he munched while standing. "He coaches most of Hawaii's elite athletes as well as thousands of triathletes remotely."

"What can I train for?"

"For an Ironman. The Schuster Pro Classics are all going to be intermediate distance, so if you train for long distance events you'll have fewer conflicts—even if you become an elite athlete."

She rubbed the back of her neck. "We'll see." She'd always raced short and intermediate distance triathlons. The thought of swimming 2.4 miles, biking 112 miles and then running a marathon was overwhelming.

"With the proper training, you can do it." Ryan winked, then resumed his place by the window. "Now, onto another subject. I need you to work on the liability waivers for the Freewheel Movement races. We've been using something we got off the Internet, but now we need a release that will work for each state where the race is held. I'll email you the details tomorrow."

"Sure, I can do that for you." Zana sat up straighter in her chair. It would be nice to have work to do. She'd been so bored, she'd considered secretly helping Andrew. "Anything else?"

"A few things. I'll e-mail you some documents and contracts for your review."

"Sounds good. What can I do for you as your agent? I've been researching possible races for you for the rest of the year." She turned to her computer. "I've got a list—just let me pull it up."

"Don't bother. I plan to race in all the Schuster Classics in order to maximize my income. I've already signed up for the Lifetime and the ITU series. That should be enough."

"I can make a calendar for you and then we can discuss strategy," she said, clicking the keyboard. "I'm also working on finding sponsorship opportunities for you."

"Let me know what you find." He walked towards the door. "I need to get going. I'm meeting Alexia for lunch."

"Tell her I said hi. I'm going to miss working with her now that I'm no longer in litigation." Zana followed him.

"She wanted me to thank you for lunch on Sunday." He paused, turning toward her in her office doorway. "When's Jerry moving in?"

"He's not." The knots in her stomach returned in full force.

He raised his eyebrows. "I thought that was the plan."

She swallowed hard, feeling tears well in her eyes. "So did I."

Ryan put his hand on her shoulder.

"He wants to continue living in his parents' cottage and said that I can live at his condo rent free."

"That's generous."

She shrugged and motioned him forward. She didn't want her only client to see the hurt in her eyes. "I don't want to feel like a kept woman and insisted on paying rent."

"Makes sense." He followed her down the hallway, through the exquisite reception area and to the elevators. "Isn't Jerry going to be in LA most of the time anyway?"

"Yeah. He bought a condo there. He doesn't want to keep putting money into hotel rooms." She pressed the elevator button.

"With the money he's probably making now, I would think he would've bought a house."

Zana managed a smile. "I asked him the same thing. He's worried that the show could be cancelled anytime and doesn't want to get stuck with a house in California. The condo he bought sounds nice—he said it has an ocean view."

They stood in silence until the elevator doors opened. Ryan stepped in, pressed the hold button and said, "Be patient. He might surprise you."

After Ryan left, she ducked into the Ladies room to blow her nose. Until the news about Mansfield and the mention of Jerry, her meeting with Ryan had been a welcome distraction from her disappointment about her living situation. She almost missed the days with Frank breathing down her neck and piles of work on her desk. At least she had had something other than her boyfriend to fill her thoughts.

She was tempted to go downstairs and talk to Andrew, but didn't want to feed the secretary and associate rumor mills. Instead, she plopped down behind her empty desk and soaked in her ocean view. She dozed off for a while in her comfy chair and when she awoke, the door to her office was still closed, the phone was silent and if she had wanted to lay down on her olive-green leather couch to nap for the rest of the day, no one would care.

Zana rubbed the sleep out of her eyes, clicked on her computer and typed "Haley O'Neill" into the search engine.

Haley was twenty-two years old and had been racing as a pro for two years. She had won a few small pro races, but hadn't earned more than $5,000 in prize money in her entire career. She was a strong swimmer and runner and so had great potential in the sport. Images of Haley showed a tall, shapely young woman with long, curly auburn-brown hair, large brown eyes and a few freckles on her cheeks. She was beautiful, even in pictures showing her after crossing a finish line not wearing make-up.

Zana's research of Sean Bennett took a little more effort, because his name was more common. There was a senator, NFL player, and geography professor, among others who shared his name. After sifting through pages and pages of unrelated content, she discovered that the highest Sean had placed as a pro triathlete was second or third. He wasn't a strong swimmer, but was a very fast runner. When she searched "Sean Bennett track and field", she discovered that he had competed in the USA Olympic Trials in 2012, but didn't make the team. Sean was even more photogenic than

Haley. He had an inviting smile, lively brown eyes, a full head of brown wavy hair and a ripped torso. One picture of Sean posing in his Speedo made him look like an underwear model.

With little else to do, Zana spent the next few hours clicking on every link she could find on Sean and Haley. She then opened files on them and stored all relevant information she might need if she ultimately served as their agent. Just when she was ready to close down her computer, another link about Sean Bennett caught her eye.

She clicked on it and her eyes widened. *If the press got wind of this, his pro career could be over before it had barely begun.* She copied and pasted it in a separate file. *Should she call Ryan to warn him?* She shifted in her chair and frowned. A text from Shelby interrupted her thoughts. Sean's secret was safe for now.

Chapter Eleven

@Haleyville Coach Dieter says we're not washy-wishy. Is that a good thing?

Haley raced from the checkout counter to the cereal aisle. She grabbed two boxes of Ancient Grains cereal and then hustled over to the medications aisle, located a large bottle of Aleve, and made her way through the long lines of shoppers.

"Here you go, sir," Haley said with a smile, placing the items she had retrieved on the conveyor belt so they could be scanned along with the man's mountain of other family-sized products.

"That was fast. Mahalo." The man's eyebrows shot up. "I wish *my* employees were as efficient as you."

"I'm happy to help." She moved on to the next customer who had grabbed the wrong sized shirt the woman was buying for her son. Haley raced back to the clothing tables and found the correct size and color.

After she returned to the check-out area, Kara, the cashier Haley was assisting said, "I'm going on break. Adam wants you to take over."

"No problem." Haley stepped behind the register and took the next customer's Costco card. "How are you today?"

"Not bad." The man was wearing a "Weiss Scientific Tri Training" T-shirt. "You look familiar."

Haley studied the man's thin, tanned face, wondering if she'd met him before.

"I've seen you biking in the mornings," the man said. "Are you a triathlete?"

"Yeah. I just moved here." She turned her attention to scanning a huge can of protein powder, an 8-pack of dental floss, a jumbo oatmeal cannister, several large containers of vitamins, and a 40-pound bag of dog food. Male customers often flirted with her, so she wasn't sure whether this man was doing the same.

"I'm Jeff Paris." He extended his hand.

"Nice to meet you." She smiled at him, now recognizing the well-known professional triathlete. "I'm Haley."

He helped her put his purchases into the shopping cart.

"My boyfriend and I just moved here." She didn't want him to get the wrong idea. She pointed to his shirt. "What's that?"

"My coach is Dieter Weiss—a former Olympian from Germany. He moved here last year to coach triathletes."

Her thoughts flashed to her beloved collegiate coaches. She wouldn't be the athlete she was today without them. "We could use a coach."

"Dieter's phenomenal," Jeff said as he took control of the large shopping cart. "Check out his website—Weisstri.com."

"Will do. Mahalo."

"Hope to see you." He grinned at her, then pushed his cart towards the exit.

Haley worked the check-out stand until Kara returned from her break. She was then tasked with folding and straightening clothes piled high on tables.

"How does this look?" Women would ask as they held up garments, trying to assess fit without the luxury of a mirror or dressing room. Haley did her best to help and always told each customer if she thought the purchase would be a mistake. Even though the clothes were inexpensive, she didn't want them to waste their money. She folded clothes until 3 o'clock, punched out, and headed home on her bike.

Sean was nowhere in sight when she returned to the tent. She sat on an umbrella-shaded chair next to the pool house with their new iPad and searched the Internet.

After a few minutes, he appeared, leaned his bike against the pool house, and bent down to kiss her.

"What are you looking at?" he asked.

"Some triathlon scientific training program." She looked up at him. "How was work?"

"Good. Decent tips." He took off his bike helmet and ran his hands through his hair. "How can I complain about a five-hour workday?"

She nodded. "Everyone else is working long shifts. I feel guilty when I leave."

"I don't." He pulled up a chair next to her and examined the website. "That name sounds familiar."

"I wish we could afford coaching." She clicked off the site when she saw how much Weiss charged.

Sean pulled his wallet from his pants pocket and thumbed through it until he found a business card. After examining it, he smiled at her.

"What's that?" Haley asked, putting the iPad down on the table.

"Dieter Weiss's business card," Sean said, handing it over.

She sat up straighter. "How did you get this?"

"Debbie stopped by the café to see how things are going. We talked during my break. She said Ryan Peterson suggested to Bud that he pay for coaching for us."

"Why are you just telling me this now?" She punched him in the arm.

"I totally forgot." He waved his hand to shoo away a fly.

"Will Bud pay?"

Sean's wide grin told her that Bud would.

Haley furrowed her brow and stuck out her tongue at him. She had begged him to communicate with her and had even threatened to break up with him when they were in college when he'd pulled the same stuff. Now, she wasn't in any position to make such a threat. But it still irked her that he kept things from her.

He leaned forward and kissed her, placing his hand gently on her chin. "Sorry, I forgot to tell you."

She refused to look him in the eye and stared at the swimming pool. After a few minutes, she said, "Dieter Weiss coaches Jeff Paris."

"How do you know that?"

"He came into Costco today."

"And why am I just hearing about that now?" Sean pulled her close to him.

***

"It's good to have you join us," Dieter Weiss said to Haley and Sean when they walked through his warehouse training facility in Kakaako a few days later.

Haley's eyes widened when she saw a portion of the large space was filled with 20 high-end spinning bikes with computer screens attached to each. There was another section with weight machines, free weights, and a handful of treadmills. She noticed some VO2 Max testing equipment and more computer monitors on stand-up desks. There was another area with resistance bands attached to poles, which Haley presumed were used for swim stroke training.

They walked past an informal classroom with comfortable leather chairs facing a podium, a Power Point screen, and a large flat screen television. There was a refrigerator with a glass door containing a variety of energy and electrolyte replacement drinks, and adjacent to it, were shelves holding an assortment of protein and electrolyte powders and bars.

"This place is amazing," Sean commented.

"Before I give you a tour, let's talk in my office." Dieter led them to a back room. There, he sat behind his large stainless-steel desk topped with a computer and six flat screen monitors. "Have a seat." He motioned for the couple to sit in leather chairs facing him.

"I've never seen so many monitors." Haley gasped.

"I use them to analyze and compare race splits and videos," Dieter said in his heavy German accent, looking intently into her eyes. "I only train serious athletes who are coachable. I'm not interested in anyone who's out to have a good time."

"Makes sense." Haley shifted in her seat. She hoped they met his criteria.

"Bud Schubert has offered me a lot of money to train you." Dieter pressed a few keys and looked at a computer screen. "I told him I'd let him know after our interview."

"We understand," Sean said, his right leg shaking so much that it shook his chair.

Dieter turned his attention to Sean and motioned for him to still his leg. "What are your goals as an athlete?"

"We have a race coming up in July—the Terry Schubert Pro Triathlon Classic. I want to win." Sean straightened his posture.

"So do I," Haley added, hoping she sounded serious.

"It's good you're not washy-wishy," Dieter said.

Haley opened her mouth to correct him, but then decided against it when Sean shot her a look. She habitually corrected anyone who used improper English, which was one of her boyfriend's pet peeves.

"Have either of you won a pro race?"

"Haley has," Sean said and then added, "I've been close."

"I was not only a top triathlete in Germany, but one of my PhDs is in sports science. I train each of my athletes using scientific methods, which includes testing your VO2 Max regularly. Have you been tested before?"

Sean nodded enthusiastically. "At our university."

"I've watched people being tested, but I never got to do it. Can you remind me what VO2 Max is?" Haley hoped he wouldn't hold her ignorance against her.

Sean's stare bore into her. He had a tendency to feign knowledge of everything to avoid being thought of as a dumb jock.

"Excellent question." Dieter smiled broadly at Haley. "VO2 Max is the maximum capacity of an individual's body to transport and use oxygen during incremental exercise, which reflects the physical fitness of the individual. Simply put—it's an athlete's aerobic capacity."

"Interesting," she said.

"I work with endurance athletes to improve their VO2 Max which often translates into better results in races. I'm also a trained sports psychologist—my second PhD—and so I also work with athletes to address psychological issues related to performance."

"Do your athletes use EPO, human growth hormones, testosterone, or any blood doping techniques to improve their performance?" Sean studied a hangnail rather than looking at Dieter for his answer.

"Sean, that's not nice," Haley interjected.

Dieter formed his hands into a pyramid shape and leaned back in his chair. "Absolutely not. My research has been focused solely on naturally improving performance without using any banned substances. I prohibit my athletes from doping or using any performance enhancing drugs not approved by WADA."

Sean nodded.

Dieter glared at Sean. "Athletes who violate this rule are kicked out of my program immediately."

"Good to know." Sean raised his eyebrows.

"Have either of you ever used banned substances in a race or during training?"

Sean placed his hand on his face. "Not to my knowledge."

"No way," Haley said.

"Good." Dieter handed them clipboards with at least an inch of documents attached. "Fill out these questionnaires. The first one is basic information. You don't have to address the financial arrangement portion. Just so you know, Mr. Schubert is paying my charges of two thousand dollars per month per athlete for coaching." He paused and looked at them intently. "You are very fortunate."

"Thank you for this opportunity." Haley set her clipboard on the edge of Dieter's desk and wiped her palms on her shorts.

"I have my reasons for telling you how much Mr. Schubert is paying for your coaching." Dieter frowned. "People don't appreciate what they don't pay for. I expressed my concerns to Mr. Schubert about this, and so we agreed that I would disclose the cost to you with the hope that you'll understand the value of my training."

Sean nodded and caught Haley's eye.

"Another rule I have is that athletes who I work with have to be committed to my process. You have to follow all of my directives."

"What if we have questions?" Haley asked.

"I'm happy to explain my methods. However, I will not tolerate defiance or lack of trust." Dieter glared at Sean. "Let's get back to the forms. The next form relates to medical history. You'll need to disclose each and every medication—including all vitamins, herbs, and supplements of any kind that you use. If you ever add anything that I don't know about, I must be informed immediately."

"What if we eat poppy seeds?" Sean grinned.

"My training methods are serious. I will not suffer foolishness."

"I'm sorry." Sean shrugged. "I was joking."

Dieter ignored him and continued. "The third set of forms is your race and athletic history. This goes back to when you were a child. I need to know details of all of your sports training and your times in competitions. I don't expect you to remember it all, but I do require that each of you do some research and e-mail me all of your race results for the past five years. The last set of forms are psychological assessment tests, which you'll need to complete in order for me to understand the best way to motivate you and to address issues that might prevent you from reaching your potential."

Sean sighed. "Is the psych testing really necessary?"

"Yes, Sean. It is essential, if you wish to reach your peak performance. If you elect not to do it, there are other coaches who will be much easier on you. I promise you that if you want to be a top professional triathlete, I will get you there."

"May I ask what other pros train with you?" Haley asked softly.

"I'm training the pros in Honolulu who are committed to be the best— Ryan Peterson, Jeff Paris, Sam Donahue, Trini Waimea, Eric Low, Penny Feldman, Tessa Banks, Gary Ching, and Dave Sumida. I'm also training a handful of age group athletes—Bev Chong, Daria Pendleton, and Rick Kessler. I've also just accepted a new age group triathlete." Dieter rummaged among some papers. "Her name is Zana West."

"So, what do we do now?" Sean asked.

"I'll give you some time to complete your paper work and then I'll do baseline measurements of VO2 Max, resting heart rate, blood pressure, EKG, blood and urine tests, flexibility, and strength tests. The other athletes will be spinning and then going for an eight-mile run at five p.m. While I work with them, my assistant, Shannon, will complete your testing."

"Any chance we can have a work out this afternoon and finish the testing tomorrow?" Sean asked.

"Absolutely not. Testing, evaluation, and assessment come first. You'll then have to go through a process of reaching a resting base before training with the group. You will not be working out with the others for at least a week."

"That will put us behind in our training." Haley furrowed her brow.

"No, it will allow you to rest. Sleep and rest is fundamental to the training process. My athletes don't over-train. In order for you to achieve maximum results from my coaching, you will have to come into the training well rested and open to change. You're required to get ten hours of sleep each night for the first week."

"That's fine with me." Sean yawned.

"For the first five days, you will be attending yoga, meditation, biofeedback, and psychotherapy sessions. I'll need you to complete a two-day fast and then adhere to a vegetarian diet for four days to cleanse your systems. It's all in my manual, which you'll take home and read." Dieter reached into a drawer and pulled out two loose leaf binders with the Weiss Tri Scientific Training logo on the front.

"Wow, this is complicated." Haley's eyes widened as she thumbed through the binder. "Are there athletes who drop out?"

"Unfortunately yes, a fair number don't have the motivation to adhere to my rigorous demands. The athletes call it boot camp," Dieter said. "It's the price you'll pay for becoming one of the top pro triathletes in the world."

"Okay—sign me up." Sean puffed out his chest.

Chapter Twelve

@ZLaw My Type-A personality gives me the competitive edge in sleeping, #yoga and #meditation. Too bad those aren't the three sports in #triathlon.

Zana popped out of bed before her alarm dinged. Ordinarily, she groped her way to the coffee maker, but this morning she didn't bother to turn it on. Instead, she opened the fridge and reached for a bottle of Dieter Weiss's fresh green juice and eagerly consumed the bitter liquid. Within minutes, her body responded to its nutrients and she felt a sensation similar to the natural high of running.

Still wearing her sleep T-shirt and panties, Zana lowered herself to the yoga mat in front of the TV and began the warm-up poses she'd learned on day one of Coach Dieter's program, which prescribed ten hours of sleep each night for a week, plus yoga and meditation.

Jerry had laughed when she told him of the regime, and he wagered that Weiss could not possibly tame her type A tendencies.

In an effort to prove him wrong, she harnessed her ambition and drive and, like every other item on her to do list, excelled at sleeping. She went to bed at 9 p.m. on the dot and stayed there until 7 a.m.—keeping her eyes tightly shut if she woke up a few hours early since her internal clock was still set to leaving for the office before 6 a.m. The peace and strength she now felt reminded her of the morning of the Freewheel Movement Triathlon after Ryan had arranged for her to spend the days leading up to the race resting at the Ala Moana Hotel.

Several weeks ago, when Zana had met with Dieter at his warehouse, he had cautioned that his scientific method wasn't compatible with her squeeze-every-moment-out-of-every day philosophy. He had expressed reluctance to let her even try to accomplish the rest phase when, after its explanation, she asked, "Can't I sleep when I'm dead?"

Now, she relished long hours of REM sleep and was relieved that Donald would make no objections if she continued this practice and rolled into the office late in the mornings.

Zana's downward dog was interrupted by a call from Jerry.

"Good morning," she chirped.

"It's almost afternoon in LA," Jerry said. She could detect the smile in his words. "Before they call me back to the set, I wanted to hear your voice."

"You're so sweet." Zana leaned against the black leather living room sofa. "I finished phase one."

"It's okay. You can say, 'I told you so'," Jerry laughed. "How do you feel?"

"Amazing, but I can't wait to get out there and move. I feel like I've been in a submerged submarine for a week." Zana looked out the window and could see joggers on the sidewalk below.

"Don't overdo it," he cautioned. "They're calling me back to the set."

After exchanging "I love you's", Zana clicked off her phone and headed to the shower. She faced another excruciating slow day at the office before she would put in her first training day with pro triathletes instead of the hodge-podge of age groupers she ordinarily swam, biked, and ran with before races. She looked forward to talking with the other athletes rather than simply executing yoga poses next to them.

She had spent the previous week silently meditating on a thin yoga mat and sweating through the crane and firefly poses and other pretzel twisting positions next to Haley O'Neill and Sean Bennett. They were not permitted to talk to each other during their first "cleansing" week, but they exchanged curious and sometimes bored glances at one another.

Zana noticed that Haley would always let her long, wavy auburn hair out of its elastic ponytail holder and sigh at the end of every two-hour session. Her large brown eyes framed with long eyelashes, and her porcelain face were almost doll-like.

Sean, on the other hand, looked like he belonged on the cover of *People Magazine*'s "Sexiest Man Alive" issue. He apparently disliked wearing a shirt. When they were supposed to be closing their eyes, silently focusing on their mantras, Zana would sometimes stare at his six-pack abs and the tattoo of three Chinese characters on his upper right pectoral muscle. She wondered what they meant.

She also endured biofeedback and psychotherapy sessions with Dieter. After some prodding, Zana described her unfortunate childhood to her new coach. He seemed sympathetic when she calmly explained that her mother had died of a heart attack during a marathon and that her father had escaped his pain from losing his wife by using marijuana, cocaine and heroin. He ultimately abandoned her in favor of drugs.

This revelation led to additional intensive therapy sessions and a trial of hypnosis. Dieter explained that her past traumatic experiences undermined her self-confidence. He worried aloud that she might not be able to push herself, knowing that she could suffer the same fate as her mother. He questioned her ability to feel safe in a relationship with a partner because of her father's abandonment. These insights were new to Zana. Instead of feeling restoration from these sessions, she felt more anxious than usual.

When Dieter suggested an additional week of cleansing, she feigned composure, and in her most measured voice, explained she was ready to begin the next phase. Perhaps he believed her, or maybe the complexity of her psyche exceeded his therapeutic training.

Whichever it was, he agreed to let her move to the next step. Dieter then cautioned her that unless she completely adhered to his plan, she wouldn't likely achieve improved athletic performance. Zana saw what she thought was a twinkle in her coach's eye when he emphasized compliance and she wondered whether he knew that while she was supposed to be meditating she was formulating to do lists in her head.

Energized by her green drink, Zana greeted each of the support staff on her way to her office. Just as she'd made herself comfortable in her Italian leather chair, Donald entered without knocking.

"Good morning, Zana!" He grinned at her with his bleached teeth. He was wearing a peach golf shirt and matching pants, which accentuated his dark tan.

She returned his smile and positioned herself to listen to what he called his daily "coaching".

"Years ago, there was this brilliant high school golfer—he was just as good as many of the pros. I found out his practice schedule and made sure I had the tee time immediately before him. I'd let him catch up, and after a few months, he was my client."

Zana nodded. The story was always the same, but with a different athlete. Her boss made it loud and clear that she was to get close to Sean and Haley, win their trust, and then sign them. It wouldn't seem as daunting if Rip Mansfield wasn't her competition.

"And then there was Leah Cunningham. She was..." Donald went on and on for another ten minutes while Zana smiled and nodded without hearing a word he was saying. It wasn't that she didn't like her new boss. She adored him. He was just—a bit too much.

She folded her hands before her on the desk and when Donald had exhausted his daily parables, he headed off to the golf course. She closed her door behind him and sighed. *How could she complain?* Working without Frank's constant threats hanging over her was heaven.

A knock on the door disrupted her thoughts. Rainy walked in without waiting for an invitation and set a box on her desk.

"Your business cards," Rainy explained.

"Mahalo." Zana waited for the secretary to leave her office before she lifted the lid of the large box and discovered a dozen smaller boxes. She opened them one by one. Her name and firm were the same on all the cards, but each box contained cards with a different specialty. She could present herself as a sports agent, specializing in the representation of multi-sport and endurance athletes. Or, by passing out a different card, she was an agent for pro women athletes. Another set branded her as a pro golf and tennis player agent.

Her head was spinning with all of these *alleged* specialties. She couldn't fathom whom she could pass out thousands of cards to, and stuck most of them in her bottom desk drawer.

Zana spent the morning finishing up some work for the Freewheel Movement before she analyzed Hawaii pro triathlete's race times. Her heart beat faster when she visualized training with the pros. *Would she be able to keep up with them?* At least there were a few other age group triathletes in the program. She felt confident about her swimming ability— she was as fast as many of the pro men and women. Her biking and running skills were not on par with the professionals, but as Dieter said, the only way to improve her skill was to work out with people faster than she. He had counseled her to have courage and patience when she found herself at the back of the pack on training days.

It was almost lunchtime. Zana scanned the list of approved foods in the Weiss Scientific Triathlon Training Manual. There were items on the list that she had always thought were healthy, but for some inexplicable reason, they were on Dieter's Do Not Eat or Drink list.

She wasn't allowed to drink certain vitamin waters, fruit juices, specified energy drinks, protein powders and drinks, or eat protein or granola bars. She wasn't surprised with Dieter's recommended food list, including: blueberries, walnuts, sweet potatoes, red peppers, chia seeds, strawberries, egg whites, wild salmon and dark leafy greens. There were other lists of acceptable foods and obvious foods to stay away from. She didn't need to be told not to go near fast food restaurants. Dieter's manual was so complete that he included daily meal plans and calorie and nutrition information. She decided to have a salmon salad for lunch at Hula Salads, requesting that they throw in some walnuts and red peppers.

After her afternoon snack of cold cut up sweet potatoes purchased at the sundry store in an adjacent building, Zana felt fueled for her first day of training. She met up with the group at Ala Moana Beach Park where they would swim 2,000 meters and do a series of two-mile runs at varying paces.

"Hey, Ryan," Zana said when she saw her client.

"Welcome to our humble training group." Ryan winked. "Do you know Jeff Paris and Sam Donahue?"

Zana nodded and smiled at the men, who wore swim trunks and caps.

"Are you a pro now?" Sam asked.

"Not quite." Zana joined the guys in some stretching moves on the grass adjacent to the beach as they waited for Dieter and the other athletes.

"She won her age group in the Freewheel Movement Triathlon," Ryan offered as he bent his body into a yoga pose.

"How was France?" Sam asked, copying Ryan's pose.

"I haven't gone yet." She put her towel down on the grass and stretched gently.

"Now that you're in this group, Dieter will never let you go." Jeff held his pose.

"Even if you do go, you can't eat any of the croissants, cordon bleu, or crepes." Sam paused to breathe in and then exhale. "Are you sure that you want to work out with us?"

"The sacrifices are worth every minute I get to spend with you guys," Zana quipped.

"What are you training for?" Jeff asked.

"An Ironman, I guess."

"You guess? Haven't you decided which one you're doing?"

"Probably Lake Placid or Colorado at the end of July," she said. "Or, I could go to Louisville or Wisconsin in August. I'm not sure yet."

Jeff and Sam exchanged looks.

"What?" Zana wondered if they doubted her ability to finish an Ironman.

"It's probably too late to sign up." Sam shifted into another pose. "Most of the Ironman races fill up in a matter of hours after they open for registration."

Zana felt the heat of her face flush. She didn't want her prospective clients to think she didn't know anything about the sport. "Maybe there's still a slot available." She was relieved to see Dieter approach, followed closely by Eric Low, Bev Chong, Trini Waimea, Sean and Haley.

"Listen up," Dieter barked. "I want you to swim down to the far white pole and back without stopping. Stretch out your strokes and focus on swimming in as straight of a line as possible. I want each of you to wear a different color swim cap so I can track you. I have extra caps here. I need to know what color of cap you're wearing before we start."

Zana had a florescent pink cap, and since no one else had that color, she wore her own.

"Where's the white pole?" Haley asked.

Zana jumped slightly at hearing Haley's voice after their week of silent yoga and meditation sessions.

"See the radio tower in the distance?" Zana pointed to the far end of the protected swimming area. "You should sight off it. When you get to the end, there's a white pole—kind of like a buoy in the water."

"We'll find it." Sean stepped towards them. "Hey, you can speak."

"Yeah." Zana laughed. She glanced to see if Dieter was looking their way. He was busy passing out swim caps. In a low voice she said, "I'm not really a big fan of meditation."

"It's a lot harder than it looks." Haley rolled her eyes. "How long have you been a pro?"

"I'm not," Zana said. "I'm training for my first Ironman."

"Zana's my agent," Ryan interjected. "Hi, I'm Ryan Peterson."

"Yeah—the Olympian. We know who you are," Haley gushed. "I'm Haley O'Neill and this is Sean Bennett."

"Let's get going," Dieter interrupted. He waved the athletes to follow him to the water.

"I've never done a swim like this—with the coach spotting athletes wearing different colored caps," Haley whispered as she walked alongside Sean, Zana, and Ryan to the beach.

"Dieter has unconventional methods, but he knows what he's doing." Ryan pulled his orange cap over his ears.

"How long has he been your coach?" Sean asked.

"Only a few months. I had to get to a place financially to be able to afford his steep rates," Ryan said, dropping his towel and rubber slippers off at the lifeguard stand.

"How did you find out about him?" Haley placed a small backpack next to Ryan's towel.

"Dieter coached the German athletes who came in second and third in the Olympics." Ryan put his goggles on his head as they walked on the sand in bare feet.

"But you won the gold medal. Your coaches were clearly better," Sean said.

"I wasn't expected to win and so I didn't really have anyone other than the US Olympic coaches leading up to the Games." Ryan reached the water, took off his goggles and spit on the inside lenses. He then stepped into the ocean. When he was waist deep, he rinsed them before placing them back on his head. "After my problems with the Tour de France, no one was willing to coach me until after I won the gold medal. Even then, I had to wait until WADA cleared me."

"With your doping history, I'm surprised Dieter agreed to train you." Sean stood next to Ryan and adjusted his goggles.

"It wasn't easy to convince him." Ryan secured his goggles on his face. "I have to submit to random drug tests."

"Let's go!" Dieter shouted from the shore.

Zana had been listening to Ryan and Sean's conversation, but at the same time was anticipating her first swim with the pros. If she kept up with them, they would have more respect for her and she wouldn't feel so out of place.

At first, she drafted off of Haley, who was swimming at a fast pace. After a few minutes, Zana saw that Haley was headed for the coral instead of the radio tower in the distance. The shoreline was bent and anyone unfamiliar with the course was bound to make the same mistake at least once.

She adjusted her course away from Haley. Zana and her friends had been swimming back and forth at Ala Moana at least a few times each week for the past year and they had almost perfected their skill of swimming from end to end in a straight line. When she lifted her head to sight, she saw a handful of the pro men swimming ten meters in front of her.

She managed to catch up and draft on their feet for the remainder of the workout. When they approached the beach near the Magic Island lifeguard stand, Zana kicked into high gear and passed several of the men, running out of the water with Jeff Paris and Eric Lowe.

"Great job, Zana," Dieter said as she ran out of the water. He was holding a clipboard and jotting notes.

She made a beeline for her towel and water bottle under the lifeguard stand. After she'd taken a few gulps, she turned around and saw Haley, Sean, Ryan, Bev, and Trini run up the beach. They grabbed their gear and gathered on the sand to wait for the few remaining athletes to finish.

"It looks straight, but I swam right into coral." Haley peeled off her swim cap.

Zana nodded. "It takes practice."

After they were all finished and Dieter had joined them, he consulted his clipboard. "Do you want to know who swam the most efficient course?"

"Yeah," a few of the pros said in unison.

"Gather round." Dieter held up his diagram of the courses swam by each athlete. "See—Zana swam the most direct course down and back. Eric and Jeff swam together and did very well. Sam was right behind them. Ryan, you veered off a bit. Sean, Haley, and Trini—you were all over the place."

"I messed up big time." Trini leaned over to examine the diagram.

"So did I," Ryan said. "I should've concentrated on the course more. I was focusing on my stroke."

After the athletes all had a chance to look at the chart, Dieter clapped his hands. "Shower quickly and change into your running gear."

Zana, with her mesh bag of her shampoo and conditioner in hand, went with the others to the outdoor shower. The water was cold, but she managed to wash the salt water off of her body quickly. There were four shower nozzles attached to the shower pole, and Haley and Sean were showering next to her.

"Any chance you could show Sean and I how to navigate Ala Moana?" Haley asked as the three walked away from the shower to the bench where they had placed their towels and backpacks. "We're training for the Terry Schubert Pro Classic and can't afford to mess up this course."

"Sure." Zana smiled and finished drying her hair with a towel. She wondered what Rip Mansfield would think if he knew another agent was spending so much time with his prospective clients.

"Can you swim with us a few mornings each week?" Sean asked.

"I'd love to." Zana beamed. Donald would be over the moon that she was spending time with pro athletes in the mornings. "Any time is fine with me."

"Terrific!" Haley exchanged looks with her boyfriend. "We need to warn you about something."

"What's that?" Zana raised her eyebrows.

"A TV producer contacted us about filming most of our workouts for a special feature. If you work out with us, you'll probably end up on the show," Sean explained as he pulled his running gear out of his backpack.

"Who's the producer?" Zana asked.

Haley paused to think for a moment. "Kenny Paxton."

Zana grinned.

"Do you know him?"

"Yeah." Zana slipped on her socks and running shoes. The plan to make Sean and Haley celebrities was moving forward faster than Zana expected. She might play a role after all.

Chapter Thirteen

@Haleyville Up close and personal is up close and annoying! Life of a #Realitystar, I guess.

Bud gently placed his hand on Sandy's back and guided her to their usual table at the Queen's Club. The waiter followed, carrying a Dewar's & soda and margarita on a small tray. Bud waved away the offered menus and ordered their usual—the special fish for her and a medium rare filet mignon for him with mashed potatoes instead of rice. The club was slow for a Thursday night, but they were early. The tables around them would soon fill with leaders of business and industry, doctors, lawyers, legislators, judges, and members of Hawaii's old boys' network. Bud used the club during the day to negotiate business deals, but when he came here with his wife several evenings a week, it was for relaxation only.

"There's Trudy and Robert." Sandy gestured toward an elegant couple being escorted to a nearby table.

Bud nodded. Trudy and Robert lived next door to their Hawaii Kai house where the triathletes were camping. Robert was a psychiatrist who spent more time providing expert witness testimony in court than he did seeing his own patients. Trudy was a stay-at-home busy body who called them often with updates about the neighborhood now that they were living in Kahala.

"Sandy!" Trudy shrieked when she saw her. The couple abandoned their menus and walked over to Bud and his wife's table. "I was going to call you today and here you are."

"Yes, here we are," Bud said and instantly felt Sandy's nudge to his foot under the table. His wife didn't care for sarcasm. He reached out to shake Robert's hand and Sandy kissed each of them on the cheek.

"Your campers are a real nuisance," Trudy complained. "That tent is an eyesore. Tell me they're moving along in a few days."

Robert grimaced and nodded his head vigorously in agreement with his wife.

"I'm sorry you feel that way, but they'll be camping in the back yard until the end of July," Bud said. He had been anticipating the onslaught of complaints from the neighbors, but was determined to move forward with his plan.

Trudy's face scrunched up so he could see a long protruding chin hair. "Are you fucking serious?"

"Now, now." Robert placed his hand gently on his wife's arm.

"I'm going to take this up with the association," Trudy spat.

"Feel free." Bud took a long sip of his drink. "I've already gotten their approval." He didn't add that it cost him a hefty donation to the common grounds improvement fund.

"Approval, my ass." Trudy stood facing them with her hands on her hips. "We'll be talking to our attorneys." She turned to her husband for his agreement and he bobbed his head up and down, steering his wife back to their table.

Sandy's eyes widened, and she turned to Bud. "What are you going to—"

The waiter interrupted her by placing their dinners before them. Bud picked up his knife and fork and cut into the thick, juicy filet mignon. He closed his eyes and savored the first bite.

Sandy finished asking her question, "What are you going to do?"

"Nothing," Bud said with his mouth full.

"I don't see why they can't move into the house." Sandy shook her head. Glaring at him, she took a bite of mahi mahi.

Bud sighed. "It would be too disruptive to the remodeling."

"They could stay in one of the condos in Kapolei. Isn't the house in Pacific Heights empty?"

"We have plenty of places for them to stay, Sandy, but you're missing the point." Bud picked up his drink.

"What point is that?" She put her fork down so it clacked loudly on her plate.

"In order for Sean and Haley to become self-sufficient, they need a strong incentive to work and train hard." He paused to take a drink. "I can't just give everything to them on a silver platter."

She furrowed her brow. "What if they don't win the triathlon? What then?"

"The reason the prize money goes so deep is to ensure that one of them wins enough money so they can rent their own apartment." He and Ryan had spent several hours analyzing how to make his plan fail-proof. He reached out for Sandy's hand, hoping to reassure her.

"Ever since you met this couple—you've been obsessed." She held his hand and looked him in the eyes. Her shoulders seemed to relax after a few moments.

"They're so young—Terry's age." He looked down at his partly eaten steak. "If our son were in their shoes—"

"I know," Sandy interrupted softly. She squeezed his hand and then smiled brightly. "Since you've been helping them, you've been happier."

He assured her that he was, and they both resumed eating. After the waiter cleared their plates and brought Bud a brandy and Sandy a coffee, he said, "I have to give Ryan credit. If he hadn't started the Freewheel Movement, I wouldn't have felt comfortable helping."

Bud swirled the brandy in his glass and looked over at Trudy and Robert. She caught his eye and raised her wine glass and mouthed something.

Bud shrugged his shoulders and read what he thought was, "I'll sue." He mouthed, "Go ahead" and returned his attention to his brandy. Sandy had been stirring cream and sugar into her coffee and didn't seem to notice the exchange.

She sipped her coffee and smiled. "Did you hear that the President is giving Ryan a humanitarian award for his work?"

"Where did you hear that?" Bud's eyes widened.

"On the news this morning."

"Well, he deserves it," Bud said. He sipped the brandy, the warmth spreading through his chest. "He's inspired me."

"How so?"

He sat back in his chair. "I've been thinking about how I can use our money to make a difference in people's lives instead of just accumulating real estate and businesses."

"What's your plan, honey?" Since they had acquired wealth, she cared more about animal charities than money. He filled her in on the race series in Terry's honor.

Her eyes lit up.

"I want these pro triathletes to have a real chance to excel."

"The chance that Terry didn't have?" she said softly.

"Yeah. Even if Terry had won an Olympic gold medal like Ryan, he'd probably still be living at home." Bud clenched his fist under the table.

"Ryan's done well for himself."

"Only because of the Freewheel Movement. Face it. The public isn't interested in triathlon." Bud spoke from experience. If Terry hadn't taken up the sport, he wouldn't know a thing about it. Even now, he preferred watching golf, tennis, football, or any other sport on television.

Sandy took a sip of coffee, then said, "There's nothing you can do to change the public's perception."

"You'll see." Bud sat up straighter in his chair. "Triathlon will be more interesting once people become emotionally involved with the athletes."

"You think the public will connect with Haley and Sean that way?"

"Absolutely." The word sounded stronger than his conviction. He hoped they would connect, but Kenny had warned him it was a long shot. It was hard to predict public opinion and almost impossible to *intentionally* make media go viral.

"I can see it with team sports—everyone roots for their favorite. Face it, honey." She put her empty coffee cup back on its saucer. "Triathlons are not spectator sports. It's boring to watch and the pro triathletes all look alike. There's really nothing interesting about them."

"You like those housewife shows and *The Amazing Race*, don't you?"

"You know I do, but you can't make triathlon like that. It's a sport."

"Watch me. Kenny said that he can turn any sport into a reality show."

***

"Good morning, Sean." Haley emerged from the tent, smiling stiffly.

"Good morning, Haley," Sean said after he stepped out of the tent behind his girlfriend. "It's such a beautiful day."

"Cut!" Dominic barked. "This is a *reality* show. You're not acting real at all."

"Sorry." Haley looked at the ground, not wanting him to see the frustration in her eyes. This was the third take and it was already too late for them to go for a run before work.

Dominic took a few steps towards the couple and lowered his voice. "Listen. I want you to act completely natural. Just ignore the cameras."

"How can we do that? You guys are in our face." Sean slumped down in a lounge chair next to the pool.

"We'll back up and be more discreet. Just do what you'd normally do, okay?" Dominic said. "None of this cheesy *good morning* stuff."

"What we would normally be doing is working out. It's already eight forty-five and we have to get to work." Haley tried not to raise her voice, but she couldn't help it. She wondered if it was a mistake for them to have agreed to this. They were only getting paid $500 per month for opening up their lives to the public.

"I have an idea." Dominic flashed his bleached smile. "We'll install a few discreet cameras here and we'll limit the number of cameramen who follow you."

"That's better." Sean nodded. "I'm not sure how long my boss is going to put up with cameras filming me at work."

Dominic paused for a few minutes and drummed his fingers on the umbrella-shaded table. "The new format I have in mind won't require much more filming at your workplaces. I'll have to clear it with Kenny, but I think you'll find us a lot less intrusive."

"Can I take my microphone off?" Haley scratched her neck. The microphone was a small clip on, but she felt more allergic to the attention than to its metal.

"Not yet," the director said. "Before you go, we're going to do some up close and personal interviews with you in private. Can we start with you, Haley?"

"Sure, but I need to get ready for work soon," she said as she followed Dominic and a cameraman to an area on the side of the house farthest away from the tent. She had been encouraged to disclose her private thoughts about what was going on in her life in these twice-daily interviews and it was starting to feel more comfortable.

Haley wasn't wearing any makeup and her auburn hair fell in loose, uncombed waves down her back. She was still in the soft black T-shirt and pink sweat pants that she had worn to bed. Her feet were ice cold inside her rubber slippers.

"Haley, how does it feel to be working at Costco as a clerk after graduating from college?" Dominic asked while the cameraman moved in closer.

"My degree is in sociology, so it's not like I'm trained to do anything special. I'm thankful to have a job," she answered.

Dominic motioned with his hand for her to continue talking.

"I really like working at Costco. The people are so nice there. It's a fun challenge to help customers find products."

"What don't you like?" Dominic pressed.

"Not much." She smiled. "It's a great job."

"Oh, come on. I'm sure there are things you don't care for." Dominic raised his voice.

She paused, hoping he'd move onto another topic.

"What don't you like?" His eyes bore into hers.

"Men constantly hit on me." She squirmed.

"And?"

"One creep—a customer followed me around the store. When I reached for some paper cups on a shelf, he actually touched my breast."

Dominic's eyes pierced into her, but he smiled and asked, "How did you handle that?"

Haley paused and stared into the camera.

"How did you handle that?" He repeated.

"Well, I knocked his hand away." Haley motioned with her hand. She hoped she wouldn't have to tell the rest of the story, because she didn't want to get into trouble at work.

"Then, what did you do?"

She turned her head and looked away from the camera. "I'd rather not say."

"It's okay, go ahead." Dominic signaled the cameraman to zoom in closer.

Haley paused, scrunched up her face and said, "I was so angry. He was shorter than me, and I guess I caught him by surprise. I pushed him against the paper towel shelf and told him to leave me alone."

"Did he leave you alone?"

She nodded and shifted in her chair.

"How are you and Sean adjusting to living in a tent?"

"I'm thankful we have a roof over our heads." She smiled warmly.

"What happens if you don't win any prize money in the Terry Schubert Pro Classic Triathlon?"

Haley paused and swallowed hard. "I guess we'll be back on the street."

"How would that happen? You both have jobs."

"True, but we work part-time at low wages," she said. It seemed so obvious, but the director signaled with his hand for her to continue. "Hawaii is expensive. In order to come up with a deposit and first and last month's rent, we'd need at least three thousand dollars, probably more if we don't want to live in a bed bug and cockroach-infested studio."

"If you don't win the prize money, will you fly back to the mainland?" Dominic asked in his measured voice.

"That's possible. It would be less expensive to live there, but maybe not so easy to find jobs." Haley swatted a fly away. She could feel sweat pouring down her back as the morning sun beat down on her. She hadn't remembered to put her sunglasses on and so she squinted at her watch now. It was 9:25 already. She was running out of time to get ready for work. She and Sean had signed a contract agreeing to fully participate in all interviews, but this was cutting it *too* close.

"Can't you go back and stay with your families?"

"My mom has her hands full working two jobs and taking care of my brothers and sisters. There's no room in their tiny apartment for me." Haley felt tears streaming down her cheeks, not from her mother's or her own dire situation, but from frustration. "I'm so sorry, but I'm already going to be late for work. Can we finish this later?" She wiped her face with the back of her hand.

"Of course," Dominic said, and the cameraman lowered his equipment. Haley nearly flew into the pool house, took a 3-minute shower, not bothering to wash her hair. She quickly applied lip gloss, dressed, and grabbed her backpack. Sean was waiting with their bikes. Haley buckled the chinstrap of her helmet and sighed.

They pedaled out of the driveway and rode side-by-side on the empty street.

"I have a breakfast bar and a sandwich for you in my backpack," Sean said.

"Thanks, baby." Haley picked up the pace, which Sean easily matched.

"How was the interview?"

"Horrible. It seemed like Dominic purposely made me late for work so I'd become emotional on camera," Haley said, pedaling harder.

"Did it work?"

"Yeah. I guess he knows what he's doing."

***

After work, Sean waited for his girlfriend outside Costco. She was a few minutes late, so he munched an energy bar as he waited. There wouldn't be much time for an afternoon snack before they left to meet up with Dieter's training group.

"Sorry," she said, when she finally joined him. Ordinarily, she kissed and hugged him when she saw him. Instead, she climbed on her bike and sped home at a pace she ordinarily reserved for racing.

They leaned their bikes on the side of the house and he followed her past the row of hibiscus bushes to the locked gate.

As they reached the gate, Haley screamed and pedaled into Sean, throwing him off balance. He grabbed her and righted himself before he fell down. He could feel her body shake.

"What?" Then he saw it. Three dead rats were hanging by their tails on the gate, dripping blood onto the stone walkway. **Leave!** was written in blood on the side of the house.

Chapter Fourteen

@ZLaw Played the #JerryHirano's girlfriend card today. It worked, #Bitches!

Zana kept her freestyle strokes long and steady, and skillfully swam in a straight line, never veering into the paddle boarders' lane or the coral reef. She hoped her florescent pink cap was visible enough to Sean and Haley, but she couldn't feel any splashing against her feet. No one was swimming next to her on her way back towards the lifeguard stand.

Before this first session with the couple, Zana had researched their swim splits from triathlon results on the Internet. Haley was a strong swimmer and was often the fastest of her competitors. Sean consistently finished the swim in number 5 or 6 position among the pro men and then made up time on the bike and run.

Zana suspected that most of their race experience had been in lakes, but that they had trained primarily in pools. Ocean swimming is far more difficult than mind-numbing lap swimming in a pool, which means staring at lane lines, doing flip turns and never having to consider the current or navigating in a straight line to stay on course.

She took a quick look back between strokes and was relieved to see both Haley and Sean a few feet behind her. They hadn't drifted off course. As they drew closer to shore and there were no more concerns about navigation, the couple suddenly sprinted ahead. Zana kicked into gear, but couldn't keep up with the pro triathletes, who switched to butterfly stroke as soon as they reached water shallow enough to stand.

Zana swam freestyle until she felt her hand touch the sandy bottom and then pulled herself up and ran to the beach where Haley and Sean were already standing.

"How was it?" Zana asked when she reached them.

"Fantastic!" Haley's eyes were shining. "Thank you so much."

"We'll just need to replicate that in the race." Sean stretched his shoulder by pulling his arm across his chest.

"It takes practice." Zana pulled her cap and goggles off. "You might want to swim this course a few times a week before the race to make sure you have it mastered."

"As it gets closer, we should practice swimming on our own. It's not like the three of us will be swimming together on race day." Sean switched arms.

"I agree," Haley said. "It's a different feeling when you're swimming against competitors. They always want to punch me with their down strokes. I have to break away early."

"You should see the men. Open water swimming is like a boxing match. I usually have bruises afterwards." Sean grimaced. "If I were fast enough, I'd swim out of the mayhem, but I end up in the main pack and can't escape the battering."

"Age group swimming is a nightmare, too," Zana said. "My problem is that when we line up there are people who think they're good swimmers and I run right over them." Zana gathered her belongings from under the lifeguard stand and led them to the outdoor shower. "Now I ask people what their expected time is before we start and if they're likely to be snails, I insist on getting in front of them. It prevents black eyes."

After they showered and dressed, Haley looked at her watch. "We've got to get to work."

"What time is the next bus?" Sean directed his question to his girlfriend.

"If you'd like, I can give you a ride," Zana offered.

"Are you serious?" Haley's eyes widened. "We're all the way in Hawaii Kai."

"No problem at all," Zana said, pleased at the prospect of being away from the office longer, and she could report to Donald that she spent the morning with pro athletes.

Before they piled in her SUV, she ducked into the park restroom to change into the T-shirt and shorts she'd pulled out of her gym bag.

Sean gave Zana directions to the private residence in Hawaii Kai with its perfectly manicured lawn similar to the other houses in the upper middle class neighborhood, save for the large beige tent in the back yard. Zana watched the couple walk to the gate on the side of the house, rather than to the front door. *How did these homeless triathletes stand a chance to win against athletes who had roofs over their heads and spouses or parents supporting them?*

She was well aware of the challenges of being homeless and trying to compete in triathlons. It simply didn't work. During the times when she lived in her car, there was no way she could train or compete. All of her energy and resources were devoted to her survival. Pro triathletes were flying to Hawaii from all over the world for the Terry Schubert Pro Classic Triathlon hoping to win the biggest triathlon purse offered in the history of the sport. She wouldn't dare tell Ryan her true thoughts, but this couple didn't stand a chance against their competition.

Zana stopped at Starbucks for a latte. There was no rush to get to work. She relaxed at a table and sipped her drink while scrolling through her Instagram feed. A picture Kelly posted of a pile of bridal magazines reminded her of her friend's many texts, imploring her to try on her bridesmaid dress. She sighed and finished her latte. If she didn't swing by the bridal shop at Kahala Mall on the way to the office, Kelly would surely fire her from her bridesmaid role in their wedding this coming Saturday. And, if the dress didn't fit, she doubted there would be time for alteration.

The mall had just opened and the bridal shop was nearly empty. Two middle-aged sales clerks responded in slow motion to Zana's request to try on her dress. The moment she had walked into the luxurious shop with its white marble floor and pillars, and its lavender and white furnishings, she regretted not changing into her work clothes first. Her hair was still damp from her post swim shower. Her old race T-shirt and shorts were wrinkled, and her two-dollar rubber slippers had seen better days.

The sales lady with a gray pageboy haircut stared at Zana over the top of her tortoise shell glasses and gestured to her hair. "Is that sweat?"

"No. Sorry—I just went swimming and my hair is still wet from a shower." Zana felt her face flush. It was probably rude to try on dresses in a fancy bridal shop wearing beach clothes.

"Whose wedding are you in?" the tall salesclerk with the blonde chignon asked.

"Andrew Bergen and Kelly Campbell," she croaked. Zana reached into her backpack for her water bottle and took a long swig.

"You must be Jana West."

"I'm Zana. Like Dana, but with a Z."

"You're the last bridesmaid to pick up her dress," the sales woman said sternly, looking her up and down. "Please have a seat." The woman gestured to a tasteful lavender loveseat positioned behind a white ornate coffee table with carefully stacked bridal, fashion, and tabloid magazines. As Zana waited, she thumbed through a back issue of *People*.

The tall blonde woman disappeared. She emerged a few minutes later with a garment covered in plastic, which she carefully took off, revealing a light peach silk chiffon dress with a plunging neckline.

She signaled Zana to follow her into a large luxurious white and lavender dressing room with floor to ceiling mirrors. As she placed the dress carefully on a gold hook inside the dressing room, the sales woman said, "It's a size four. Most girls who order such a small size can't fit into it by the wedding day."

"That's my size." Zana crossed her arms over her chest while she waited for the woman to leave her alone. She wasn't wearing a bra and hoped she didn't need one for the fitting.

"We'll see. You're very tall." The woman scrutinized her and then left her to try on the dress.

Zana wrapped her damp hair in her T-shirt for about 30 seconds to make sure it didn't drip onto the stunning garment. She easily slipped into the dress, which was a little roomy. It would've been knee length on most women, but because of Zana's height it reached mid-thigh. The light peach color flattered her skin tone, and as she studied her reflection in the mirror, she admired how it made her look sexy with its open back and plunging neckline. She rarely wore such a revealing dress and so she looked forward to seeing Jerry's reaction. She stepped out of the dressing room to be scrutinized by the sales ladies who were hovering by the door.

"It certainly fits," the gray-haired woman glared over her glasses. "Turn around."

"I'm not sure about the length," the tall blonde woman said.

"I like the length." Zana smiled. "I think it's perfect."

"It won't be uniform with the other bridesmaids who are shorter than you," the gray-haired woman said.

"That's fine." Zana studied her reflection in the mirror. "I'll take it."

The blonde woman scrunched up her face. "I think we should call the bride and discuss it with her."

"Kelly will be fine with it. I've got to get to work. I'll take it as is." Zana noticed the saleswomen exchange glances.

"You don't seem to understand fashion," the gray-haired woman said. "I'm sure you seldom wear evening clothes."

Zana retreated back into the dressing room, fuming at the saleswomen's condescending comments as she changed back into her damp T-shirt and shorts. She made a beeline for the coffee table piled with magazines and grabbed a select few. She calmly walked to the counter to purchase her dress.

"Do you recognize anyone in this photo?" Zana showed the saleswomen the cover of *People Magazine,* which pictured her and Jerry at a red carpet event. She was wearing Alexander McQueen and he was wearing Prada.

The women stared bug-eyed at the photo clearly recognizing who it was. Zana then presented the cover of *Star* with a photo of Jerry wearing Armani and her wearing Christian Siriano.

"I'm *so* sorry." The woman looked mortified.

"We didn't realize." The blonde woman stared at Zana for a moment before processing her credit card.

The gray-haired woman's hands shook as she placed the dress in a lavender garment bag, which bore a tasteful imprint of the shop's logo.

"Please, come again." The woman handed the bag to Zana.

"And, bring Mr. Hirano."

Zana raised her eyebrows. "You might want to be careful next time you judge someone by their appearance." She then walked out head high, swinging the garment bag.

***

"It's gorgeous," Zana said to Kelly through her iPhone as she drove home to Diamond Head Tower. She didn't dare tell her friend about her encounter with the women at the store. Kelly had too much on her plate already with the wedding only four days away.

"You're going to look stunning," Kelly said. "I'm so excited. It's a mad house here."

"You're not staying with Andrew the night before your wedding, are you?"

"No, the Royal Hawaiian is giving me a special deal on a room for wedding eve," Kelly said. "You're lucky. Your condo is within walking distance."

"That will come in handy if you need anything on the big day. Just let me know." Zana waited in traffic at a red light.

"I'll keep that in mind." Kelly paused. "Remember, the rehearsal dinner is at Hard Rock Café on Friday night."

"Why the Hard Rock?"

"Andrew insisted we keep it casual. Since his parents are paying for it, he wanted to keep the cost down."

"It'll be fun. What's most surprising is that Andrew agreed to an Oahu wedding. I thought he wanted it to be off island so he didn't have to invite the partners of the firm." She'd been so busy adjusting to her new job and Dieter's triathlon training, there hadn't been time to catch up with her friends about their constantly changing wedding plans.

"The Royal Hawaiian had a cancelation and offered us the Coconut Grove—you know, the grassy courtyard area in the center of the hotel. It's perfect for an intimate wedding," Kelly explained. "We've only invited family and close friends to the ceremony, but the reception in the Monarch Room will be much bigger. We've seated the firm partners and their wives at a few tables. No worries—you and Jerry will be at a reserved table with the bridal party."

"No head table?" Zana asked as she drove up the parking ramp.

"No, we thought it would be too difficult to chat with our friends. We want to have fun, not preside over the wedding."

"You can play a trick and put Frank Gravelle's name card next to Andrew's. He'll have a heart attack." Zana laughed. She and Andrew had traded practical jokes against each other almost since they met, and she was always trying to come up with something new.

"Great idea. Do you know any good divorce attorneys?" Kelly asked. "Promise me you won't do that? I want the wedding to have as little drama as possible."

"Okay, I'll try to behave myself for a change." Zana pulled into an empty parking space. "Are you sure you don't want a bachelorette party? You still have a few days."

"If I wasn't working so many hours so I can take a week off for our honeymoon I'd probably take you up on your offer. I just don't have the time or energy to go out for a night of putting dollar bills into dancing men's G-strings," Kelly said. "What's gotten into you, Zana? You seem so relaxed. It's not like you to even suggest wasting precious time going out."

"Until I sign some more pro athlete clients, I don't have much to do at work. It'll probably be noon by the time I roll in today." Zana slid out of her car.

"You've got it made. Now, it's time for me to get going. Unlike you, I work for a living."

Zana smiled and retrieved her dress from the back seat. She was tempted to blow off work, but she couldn't wait to tell Nina and Rainy about the scene at the bridal shop.

Chapter Fifteen

@ZLaw I discovered #JerryHirano's super power today. #Yawn. Yes, it's a #Yawn.

The rabbi and the pastor were talking, but Zana couldn't focus on their words. She stood a head above the other four bridesmaids and looked out at the sea of phones pointed at them by the guests. It was easy to spot Jerry, because many of the phones were aimed in his direction.

She turned her attention back to the rabbi and pastor who took turns imparting sacred words to the bride and groom. Kelly wore an eggshell strapless, organza gown and Andrew wore a black tux. Their foreheads were glistening from the humid air, but their eyes shone.

Zana recognized the look of concentration on Andrew's face. He'd confided his fear of zoning out during the key parts and Zana had nearly doubled over with laughter when he'd acted out various scenarios of blowing the most important moment of his life. She pinky swore not to tell Kelly. Now, as she watched him scrunch his face in concentration, she had to ball up her fist and pinch her lips together to keep from laughing.

Zana hadn't been privy to her former roommates' wedding plans, which had taken shape after she moved out of their house. The only contribution she'd made was the use of co-officiants. Both Andrew and Kelly had texted her about the impasse they'd reached. Both wanted to please their parents and wondered if their marriage stood a chance if the other wouldn't compromise. Zana did what she always did when faced with a problem. She turned to her friend, Google.

After tapping away on her computer, she learned that Chelsea Clinton's wedding was co-officiated by a rabbi and a Methodist minister. A few emails later, the thorny problem was solved, and her former roommates were finally tying the knot—with their parents beaming in the front row.

As Andrew and Kelly tearfully shared their wedding vows, Zana's attention was drawn to a wedding guest nudging another out of the way with her Galaxy phone. The hired videographer and photographer were mouthing what looked like angry words to each other until the wedding planner intervened and spoke softly in their ears.

Zana waited for someone to gently ask the guests to put their phones away, but the couple was pronounced man and wife before rules were imposed. They kissed passionately for the phone cameras and paused for guests to post the happy news on social media.

Jerry escorted Zana to the receiving line where the beaming bridesmaids were hugging guests—friends and strangers—in their usual Aloha spirit. Before taking her place next to them, Zana made a beeline to the bride and groom.

"Congratulations Mr. and Mrs. Bergen!" Zana squealed.

Kelly beamed and kissed her husband. "It was such a beautiful ceremony."

Zana nodded. "There were *a lot* of phones."

"Yeah—wasn't it great?" Andrew put his arm around his wife.

"All of our friends and family on the mainland who couldn't make it got a play by play of the wedding ceremony." Kelly smiled.

"Were the rabbi and pastor okay with that?" Zana asked wide-eyed, surprised the paparazzi-style wedding was tolerated. "What about your parents?"

"No one seemed to mind—except you. And Jerry's body guard." Andrew laughed.

Zana smirked. "Maybe I'm old-fashioned."

"Or, maybe you're a bit jumpy about paparazzi," Kelly offered.

"That's probably true." Zana felt Jerry's hand press against the bare skin of her open back dress.

"Congratulations!" Jerry kissed Kelly on her cheek and then shook Andrew's hand. "Beautiful wedding."

"Your girlfriend didn't seem to think so," Andrew said.

"It *was* beautiful." Zana frowned, now regretting her comment about the phones.

"Maybe you'll be next," Kelly offered.

Zana felt her face flush as she gave a sideways glance to Jerry. It was embarrassing enough that he didn't want to live with her after she had made the announcement to all of her friends that they would be.

"You never know." Jerry winked at Zana.

He escorted her to the Monarch Room for the reception. It wouldn't start for twenty minutes, but they found their seats early and sipped wine while they waited. The chairs and tables were decorated in light peach and ivory, and each table had a centerpiece of peach orchids that matched the flowers on Kelly's bridal bouquet.

Within a few minutes, guests began filing in and the other bridesmaids and groomsmen joined Zana and Jerry. Kelly's childhood friend with a southern accent sat next to Zana and recounted the story of baking their first pie, because her grandmother insisted they learn to bake to keep their future husbands happy.

"It finally occurred to me why everything is peach colored." Zana turned to Jerry who was seated on her other side.

"Oh, you mean that Kelly wanted to incorporate her Georgia roots into the décor?" Jerry asked.

"Yeah. How did you know that?"

"I was talking to Kelly's mother in the receiving line earlier and she mentioned how much she loved the Georgia peach theme," Jerry said.

Zana grimaced and looked at the floor. "I'm a bad bridesmaid."

Jerry reached over, put his hand on her chin and gently moved it so her eyes met his. "I love you anyway," he whispered and kissed her on the lips.

She felt her body relax and rested her head on his shoulder. Guests streamed in and found their seats at the large round tables. When Frank and his wife, Arlene, walked through the ballroom threshold, she sat up straight and smoothed her dress with her hands. Frank wore a black tux and Arlene a beaded rose-colored gown. Behind them, Zana saw a handful of other partners and firm associates accompanied by their significant others.

Jerry squeezed her hand under the table and kept his gaze on her while Zana focused on her colleagues.

"Next to his wife, he looks like someone's grandfather," she commented.

"You mean Frank?" Jerry turned his head to look.

"Yeah, Amanda Priestly." She rolled her eyes. It was Andrew who had coined the nickname, referencing the film, *The Devil Wears Prada.*

Jerry chuckled and pulled his girlfriend closer. "Let's enjoy tonight." She followed his lead and turned her attention to the others at their table.

After some pre-meal speeches and toasts, waiters placed elegant salads in front of guests, that, according to the program menu, were Hirabara Farm baby romaine Caesar salads. The main course of roasted lemon grass chicken, choi sum, Hamakua Shitake mushrooms, caramelized onions, and Ho-Farm colored tomato and rosemary garlic potatoes followed.

Zana saved room for the Waialua Estate chocolate tart with chocolate sorbet and lilikoi fruit pearls, which she preferred over a slice of the five-tier wedding cake elaborately decorated with peach orchids.

When Andrew announced they were ready to cut the cake, Zana led Jerry by the hand to watch the couple politely smash small bits into each other's mouths while the guests snapped pictures. After the newlyweds had wiped the messes off their faces, Jerry grabbed Zana's hand and led her back towards their table.

"We're not done yet." Kelly grabbed Zana by the arm. "It's time for the bouquet toss."

There was no way Zana was going to let her work colleagues see her scramble to catch a bunch of flowers in her desperation to "be next." So as soon as Kelly let her go, Zana headed for the bathroom.

"Oh no, you don't!" Andrew grabbed her by the arm and led her to the giggling young women surrounding the bride. They were holding their hands up in front of them like catcher's mitts.

Zana let her arms dangle to her sides. She towered over the other girls and felt all eyes on her.

Andrew cheered on his wife with the other guests, and just as Zana took a step in the direction of the restroom, she felt the bouquet hit her forehead. Her reflexes kicked in and she caught it before it fell to the ground.

Claps and cheers of excitement followed. Women of all ages, shapes, sizes and marital status echoed, "You're next."

Her face flushed as she escaped to a bathroom stall, hoping the guests, particularly Jerry, would quickly forget about her "lucky" catch. Her boyfriend appeared by her side the instant she exited the Ladies room.

"I hear there's a scout for the Red Sox here. He's considering signing you to play right field," he said, putting his arm around her.

"It wasn't like I was trying," she said, hoping to diffuse any concerns he might have that she had cooked up a scheme with Kelly to catch the bouquet. She didn't want him to think she'd pressure him into tying the knot before he was ready.

"Never mind the Red Sox—bouquet tossing is more like basketball. The taller players have an edge over the competition."

"Yeah, I guess I'm the Michael Jordan of bouquet catching," she said, relieved that he could joke about something as serious as her being destined to be next. As they headed back towards the Monarch Room, they ran into Andrew, who was pacing back and forth in the hallway by himself.

"Is something wrong?" Zana asked.

"I'm fucking pissed off," Andrew said, brushing his hand through his thinning hair. "I told you that I didn't want *him* here."

"Has Frank done anything horrible?" she asked.

"No. It's just stressful to have him—" Andrew's voice caught "—watching me."

She nodded. "Can you ignore him?"

"I've tried," Andrew hissed. "Wherever I look, there he is."

"I'll take care of him," Jerry said.

"What are you going to do?" Zana's eyes widened. "None of your Jerry Ho Kung Fu moves, please."

"Don't worry, martial arts aren't necessary. Zana, do you want to come with me?" Jerry placed his hand on her back. "I promise you, Andrew, Frank and his wife will hurry home after I get done with them."

"Thanks," Andrew said weakly.

Zana followed her boyfriend across the ballroom to Frank and Arlene's table.

"Hey, Frank!" Jerry grinned. "You look lovely, Arlene."

"Hello, Jerry," Frank said stiffly.

"This is—" Jerry let out a big yawn. "Excuse me." He then yawned again, covering his mouth. "It's a nice wedding, don't you think?"

"It is," Frank said. He then imitated Jerry's yawn. Arlene yawned in turn.

"It's been a long day." Jerry yawned again—even more loudly. "Excuse me."

"It sure has." Frank yawned. "Arlene, shall we call it a night?"

"Yes!" Arlene yawned. "I'm beat."

"It was great seeing you," Jerry called after them.

Zana repressed a giggle as she followed Jerry. "That was brilliant," she said.

Jerry beamed. "It works every time."

"You've done that before?"

"Whenever I want people to leave who are overstaying their welcome," he said, leading her to their table. "Now Andrew can have fun at his wedding."

By now, the lights had dimmed and the DJ had announced the first dance. Andrew and Kelly began swaying to Norah Jones' "Come Away with Me." Jerry pulled his chair close to Zana's and kissed her on the lips.

"Thanks for coming home for the wedding, Jer-bear," Zana whispered. "It means a lot to me."

"I'm so happy to be here with you. It gets lonely in LA," he said softly.

"Everyone give a big hand to Mr. and Mrs. Andrew Bergen," the DJ said as the couple finished their first dance. The crowd had thinned out a bit, but the applause was loud. "Join the happy couple on the dance floor."

"Let's go," Jerry said as he led Zana to the dance floor as soon as the first bars of the song, "What Does the Fox Say?" came on. More than a dozen couples imitated the animal-like dance moves from the music video.

Zana had never danced with Jerry before, so she was surprised at his rhythm and sexy moves. Halfway through the song, Andrew and Kelly moved to their side of the dance floor.

"I saw Frank and Arlene leave," Andrew shouted over the music to

Zana. "How did that happen?"

"You know how yawns are contagious?" Zana shouted back to her friend who was now dancing next to her.

"Yeah."

"Well, Frank and Arlene caught a case of the yawns from Jerry. You would've thought that he literally booted them out the door, they left so fast."

"You rock, Jerry," Andrew grinned, giving Jerry an enthusiastic fist bump before returning to his bride.

The dancing went on for several hours before Zana discovered something about Jerry she hadn't known. He was an energetic dancer, never sitting out a song. They shimmied, twisted, grinded, hip hopped, Electric Slided, slow danced, YMCA'd, and even moon walked until only a handful of wedding guests were left.

Andrew and Kelly had already retreated to their bridal suite by the time Jerry was ready to walk Zana the few blocks back to Diamond Head Tower.

As they were collecting their wedding favors, Jerry handed Zana the bouquet, which was still on the table where she'd abandoned it. "Don't forget this."

She took the delicate peach and white roses and orchids from him, and looked at Jerry curiously.

"You could be next," he whispered in her ear.

Chapter Sixteen

@TheGreatShayB Grrrrr! Don't tell me I screwed up your drink. I don't care if you wanted no foam and extra hot. You will survive. #firstworldproblems

"Training for a triathlon is like planning a wedding," Haley said as she ran at a slow pace next to Sean.

"How so?" Sean bristled at the wedding reference. *Why are women so enthralled with putting on a white dress and making a spectacle of themselves?* The few weddings he'd attended seemed sort of depressing. The couples got drunk and gave maudlin speeches in front of hundreds of usually ignored distant cousins and friends of their parents.

"There's so much planning and scheming." Haley adjusted her sunglasses. "Zana said she was a bridesmaid a few weeks ago. With all of our focus on training menus and race strategy leading up to the Schubert Pro Classic, it's sort of like we're prepping for a wedding or something."

"I guess so." Sean frowned.

He pulled his cap down lower so the brim partially covered his eyes. A part-time job at Starbucks didn't bring in enough money for rent, let alone pay for a diamond engagement ring. Before his parents died in a car accident, his father had worked as a pharmacist and his mother had stayed home and taken care of Sean, their only child. He could still hear his father's words, "It's the man's job to bring home the bacon." Sean assumed that after college graduation, things would be different.

"I want to get married in a church and wear a white dress with a veil," Haley squealed.

Sean purposefully let his mind drift while Haley continued on about her dream wedding. When they went for long runs they often talked about their plans for the future and this morning's boredom-inspired conversation wasn't much different from the others.

But his legs felt wobbly and his heart was racing faster than it should've been at such a slow pace. It wasn't the wedding talk that was bothering Sean. He heard his labored breathing. *I have to win this race. It's my only chance to make money.* There was no hope of landing a decent paying job with his history degree. Going to law school or graduate school was out of the question. He sighed.

Why hadn't I thought to take some business classes so I'd have some work skills? It had just seemed easier with his track and field training and his budding pro triathlon career to relax in the familiarity and comfort of taking one history class after another. He read history books for fun and getting A's and B's was easy, even when he was on the road a lot for track meets and had to miss classes.

"You're so quiet." Haley glanced at him while keeping the same running pace. "I've been chattering away and you haven't said a word. Are you okay?"

"I'm fine. Just tired, I guess." He didn't want to let her in on his troubled thoughts. She had no idea how much he stewed about their precarious situation. He'd never told her about his sleepless nights. He needed her to continue to be their cheerleader and he usually managed to feign enthusiasm and optimism. Occasionally, when she sank into the depths of despair, he had to take over her role and reassure her that their lives would get better.

When they finished their run, Sean quickly showered and dressed in his black pants and polo shirt. He folded his freshly washed barista apron and placed it in his backpack, along with a turkey sandwich and apple.

Haley, wearing her Costco uniform, was putting rubber bands on her pant legs to ready herself for the bike ride to work. Without glancing up, she asked, "Did you get a chance to look at our training schedule for this afternoon?"

"Yeah, we've got a bike ride from Triangle Park starting at four-thirty. We'll have to hustle in order to ride there and meet the group," Sean said, slipping his backpack on.

"Dieter wants us to take The Bus so we conserve energy for the workout."

"That's ridiculous." He narrowed his eyes. "Let's just ride easy. If we have to, we can take The Bus home."

He watched as his girlfriend placed her hands on hips in her usual righteous posture. She was so concerned about adhering to every rule. She had no capacity for telling even a little white lie.

"I'm following what Dieter said. He's going to ask us how we got there."

"Okay, sweetheart." Sean sighed. It would be easier to do what she asked. He had no energy to argue. He mounted his bike and rode to work with Haley riding in his slipstream behind him.

When they returned home that afternoon, Dominic and his cameraman were waiting. Sean unbuckled his bicycle helmet and let out a loud sigh as he approached the director.

"What, you're not happy to see us?" Dominic asked.

"It's not a great time. We need to get ready for our workout." Sean ran his hand through his helmet hair.

"I need a few minutes of your time, Sean. When we were editing, we had plenty of Haley's footage, but not much from you."

"Okay, but can you make it quick?" Sean followed the director and the cameraman to the far side of the house and plopped down in the plastic chair that hadn't been moved from its position after several interviews. He sighed again as the cameraman got in position and Dominic adjusted a lapel microphone on Sean's black polo shirt, damp from work and riding his bike in the hot sun.

After the camera was rolling, Dominic asked, "What do you find the most challenging about training for a pro race?"

"Waiting. I'm not the most patient person." Sean clenched his fists in his lap.

"Really?" Dominic's eyebrows shot up. "When Haley described you in an interview, she said that was one of your best attributes—patience."

"My best attribute is *pretending* to be patient," Sean blurted out, not giving much thought to Haley seeing the interview if it didn't land on the cutting room floor.

"How will you feel if you don't win any prize money at the Terry Schubert Pro Classic?"

"That's not an option. I plan on winning." Sean clenched his fists tighter.

"How will you feel if Haley does better than you?"

"I hope she does. She's worked hard." Sean could feel the sweat trickle down his face.

"Do you think that your competition is tougher than Haley's?"

"Yeah. The pro men's field is always deeper than the pro women's field, from what I've seen."

"What's your strategy?"

"Go out hard. I've got to get ahead of Ryan Peterson on the swim. If I can get a decent lead and stay up with the main contenders on the bike, I should be able to beat all of them on the run."

"Why do you say that?"

Sean paused and swallowed hard. He could see Haley pacing in his peripheral vision. "If you look at their times, I'm probably the fastest pro triathlete runner competing right now."

Dominic leaned in. "How does it feel living in a tent?"

"Not great. We've got a good set up right now, though."

"How do you feel about not being able to give Haley a home?"

"It's rough." Sean rubbed the back of his neck. "I want her to have a house to live in. She deserves it."

"What's the worst thing that's happened to you since you've been in Hawaii?"

Sean paused and looked down. "I would say when the city took all of our stuff. Things weren't too bad when we first got here and if I worked for about a month, we would probably have been able to fly back to California."

"Are you angry at the city for throwing away your possessions?"

"Yeah." Sean's voice cracked.

"Was there anything they threw away that was irreplaceable?"

"Yeah, there was. I had some pictures of my mother and father—my only photos of them—in my suitcase. Now they're gone. Just like my parents." Sean sniffed. "Are we done yet?"

"Yeah. We got it." Dominic reached out and patted Sean on the back. "We're done for the day."

***

After Dominic and the cameraman left, the couple changed into their workout gear and took The Bus with their bikes to Kahala Avenue. From there, they rode a few blocks to Triangle Park. Dieter was there already, leaning against his SUV.

"Good. You're here early," Dieter said after Sean and Haley dismounted their bikes next to his car. "I need to talk with both of you."

"Okay," Sean said. "What about?"

"You've been following the protocol well. Analyzing the data, it looks like both of you are contenders for the top ten. Haley's data is stronger than yours, Sean, but not by much."

"Is there any way we can improve?" Haley asked.

"You've got less than two weeks before the race. So right now, you can only get worse," Dieter said in his thick German accent.

"What do you mean by that?" Sean couldn't keep the irritation out of his voice. The day had deteriorated further after Haley's early morning wedding talk. He had to remake a half dozen drinks at work, and then he'd revealed to Dominic the loss of his parents' pictures. Even Haley didn't know about that. Now, Dieter was planting negative thoughts in his head, which he didn't want any part of. He couldn't walk away without risking everything. Bud Schubert demanded compliance with his coach's training methods and Sean didn't want to test Bud.

"My analysis of your previous training schedules and results tells me that both of you have a tendency to over-train." Dieter wrinkled his brow and squinted at the clipboard in hand.

"How is that possible?" Sean raised his voice. "We haven't been training hard enough. Too much time spent on meditation and yoga. Not enough time putting in the miles."

"A lot of my new clients think that." Dieter nodded. "I'm concerned about your morning pulse rates, which are a little high. I realize that when you take them yourselves, they might not be done properly so I'm going to ask my assistant, Angela, to swing by and take your pulses first thing in the morning for a few days."

"How will she know when we wake up?" Haley asked.

"If you're following my schedule, she'll be there when your alarm goes off," Dieter said. "If you decide to wake up earlier or later, you'll need to text her. This data should give us important information."

"Okay," Sean said.

"There are other symptoms of over-training. How's your sex drive?" Dieter glared at them over his sunglasses.

"Good," the couple said in unison. Sean looked at the ground.

"Are you feeling more irritable than usual, Haley?" Dieter asked.

"Not at all," Haley said, smiling.

"How 'bout you, Sean? Are you experiencing irritability?"

"No," Sean lied. He had reason to be irritable. No man likes to hear his girlfriend talk on and on about expensive weddings. The few instances at work that pissed him off today would have made anyone angry. The cashier must have typed in the wrong drink orders. Dominic had goaded him into telling personal information that would have made anyone upset. Haley had pushed his buttons by making him take The Bus when it would've been easier to ride their bikes. And now, Dieter was going on and on about over-training. Sean just wanted to work out. If he weren't trying to hide his irritability, he would have used some choice curse words.

"What workout did you do this morning?" Dieter asked.

"We ran an easy ten miles at talking pace," Haley said.

"I want you to go home," Dieter commanded. "Sleep in until 8:30 and no workout tomorrow morning. Angela will be there to take your pulses shortly after you wake up. Stay in bed until she arrives."

"What? We rode The Bus all the way here." Sean's nostril's flared.

"See—you *are* irritable. You need to get your resting heart rates down. The problem with having too much time on your hands to train is that you work out too much and don't give your bodies enough time to rest." Dieter looked down at his clipboard.

"Can we work out with the group tomorrow afternoon?" Haley asked.

"Yes. You can join us for our swim and run at Ala Moana." Dieter made a note. "Sean, if you continue to be irritable, I need to know about it. If this goes on much longer, it could make a significant impact on your performance."

"Okay," Sean said, lowering his head. He needed to win the race. *If this crazy bastard coach thought that he needed to rest more, so be it.*

"I'm going to e-mail a revised schedule to you. It will have new sleep hours and diminished training up until race day," Dieter said in his clipped accent. "I advise you to follow the schedule flawlessly."

The couple mounted their bikes and rode away. When Sean pedaled past The Bus stop, Haley shouted after him. "We have to follow coach's orders!"

His instinct was to ignore her and ride home, but after about a block, he turned back and waited with her at The Bus stop for a few minutes before it arrived. They loaded their bikes on the bike racks on the front and then boarded the crowded bus. There were no seats available, so they stood the entire way to Hawaii Kai. It felt good to get off and ride a few miles to their makeshift home.

After their dinner of microwaved chicken, brown rice, and salad, Haley asked, "What do you think about Dieter's theory that we've over-trained?"

Sean put his fingers on his chin and thought for a moment. "It *might* have some merit."

"Then, why did you act like he was crazy when he mentioned it?"

"I want to train. I hate sitting around and waiting for the race."

"Me, too. There's not much to do without a TV." Haley frowned. "It's too early to go to bed."

"We could watch a movie on the iPad."

"Or you could make love to me." Haley raised her eyebrows.

"Sweetie, I would love to, but I'm feeling really tired all of a sudden."

He didn't want to admit that he'd lost his sex drive—another one of Dieter's over-training symptoms.

Haley stuck out her lip in a pout and changed into her nightgown. After they slipped into bed at 7:30, Sean closed his eyes to feign sleep. *Coach was right.* He normally couldn't keep his hands off of Haley.

Chapter Seventeen

@FreewheelMV Coach is happy with my blood test. Those who don't know the #RealMe might be surprised. #RacingClean

I'm on my way! Ryan had texted. Alexia responded immediately with a smiley face emoticon, which made him smile. His steps were light as he went up the path overgrown with red ginger and a jungle of tropical plants. A faded garden gnome stood guard and seemed to glare at him as he knocked on her door.

"Who is it?" Alexia's voice sounded anxious.

Hadn't he just texted that he was on his way? He heard her unlock at least three deadbolts and open the door slowly, pulling him into her small house by the hand and shut the door quickly behind him.

"This is Honolulu, not Compton," he said. She shrugged in response. She was probably the strangest woman he'd ever met, but her face, hair, and body were so exquisite he hardly noticed her shaking hands and quivering bottom lip. He pulled her into his arms and kissed her. Finally, he felt her body relax.

They fell onto the loveseat, and after a few moments, she pulled away. "How was your bike ride?"

He groaned and shifted in his seat. "Good," he said breathlessly. He'd hoped they were headed for the bedroom, but her erect posture told him otherwise. Plus, she had straightened her blouse. It wouldn't be coming off quite yet.

He followed her lead and sat up straight on the small sofa, which worked well in the tiny living room. "Only Jeff, Sam, and Trini were there."

"Why so few?" She gathered her long blonde hair into a ponytail as she looked at him quizzically.

"Dieter sent everyone else home to rest. He's got this hang-up about over-training, especially since the race is a few weeks away."

"So, he doesn't think that you've over-trained?"

"I guess not. He's happy with all of my blood tests and heart rate."

"I'll bet you like that." She winked at him.

He sighed. "It's been years since Tour de France. Those days are long over."

He reached for her small, perfectly manicured hand and placed it gently in his. "Speaking of the past, when are you going to tell me about yours?"

"Soon," she stood up, "I've got dinner ready."

He didn't let go of her hand but pulled her back onto the loveseat. "Dinner can wait. I really need to know about *you*."

She yanked her hand away, stood up and stared at him.

"When you're ready," he said softly.

She continued to stare at him for a few more moments before she said, "That's better" and retreated into the kitchen.

Ryan followed Alexia and then watched her as she pulled a pan of baked, skinless chicken breasts out of the oven. From where he stood, he could almost see the entire 1,200 square feet of the tiny, old house—except the bedroom. There was not one personal photograph displayed. All of the pictures on the walls were of Hawaii landscapes—generic looking. He scanned the rooms for something personal to Alexia and didn't find anything other than her sweater draped over a chair. The house looked like a vacation rental.

"You don't own this place, do you?"

"No. I rent it. Why?"

"Just wondering."

Ryan managed to make small talk over dinner, but if she didn't open up soon, he'd lose interest. Her physical beauty was not enough to make up for her lack of personal history and growth. Just as he had overcome so many obstacles, he knew that any woman he shared his life with would have had to triumph over challenges herself. Alexia seemed too perfect. He yearned to know more of what lie underneath her Barbie doll exterior.

After dinner, Ryan held Alexia's hand while they finished watching the DVD of a romantic comedy she'd selected. Bedtime was 9 o'clock so they could both wake up at 4 a.m. for morning workouts. He delighted in making love to Alexia every chance he got, and they had never before fallen asleep in the same bed without first enjoying each other's naked body.

This time, he kept his T-shirt and boxer shorts on. He wasn't in the mood. *How could he be intimate with someone who wouldn't share her life with him?* He kissed her, said he was tired, and rolled over onto his side facing the wall.

It was 3:50 a.m. according to the dial on Ryan's illuminated Ironman watch when he woke with a start. Alexia's side of the bed was empty and the only noise he heard was the hum of the refrigerator.

He stepped out of bed quietly and walked a dozen steps to the living room where Alexia sat with her hands gripping a baseball bat, staring at the locked front door.

"Are you going to tell me what this is all about?" Ryan asked.

"Huh, oh—you startled me." Alexia was wearing a camisole and panties with her long blond hair hanging loose. Her eyes were open wide and her body was tense.

He took the bat out of her hands and laid it on the floor. "I'm listening," he said, and sat in the chair across from her.

Alexia stared down at her empty hands for what seemed like five minutes and then she looked up at him with tears welling in her eyes. "My real name is Elaine Finnegan. I was married to a police officer—a detective. We went to high school together, but we didn't start dating until after we graduated, and he'd already graduated from the police academy. I thought he was a good guy." Her voice caught, and the tears started to fall.

"After we got married something changed—or, maybe the change came after one of his buddies was killed. I don't know." She stared down at her hands again.

"Uh huh." Ryan moved next to her on the loveseat and reached for her hand.

"Stan started to hit me. He was always the jealous type and had never approved of me spending time with my family or friends. After a few years, he wouldn't allow me to go anywhere except to work—I was a bank teller." With the back of her hand she wiped at the tears now streaming down her face.

Ryan stood to retrieve a box of tissues from the bathroom and quickly returned. He gently wiped her face. "That must've been so hard for you."

"It was horrible. The violence escalated. He'd threaten to kill me and remind me often that because he was a police officer he'd get away with it. One time while he was choking me, he said that he knew how to hide a body. I was so scared." She paused and put her face in her hands.

Ryan closed the distance next to her on the loveseat and stroked her hair.

"He told me he would make it look like one of the scumbag criminals was responsible so he could get rid of me and put someone away at the same time."

Alexia's voice was barely audible and Ryan strained to hear her as she continued. "He wouldn't let me see my parents or any family members. I'm sure they thought I'd abandoned them. A friend from high school came into work one day and asked me to join her for lunch. She told me about our mutual friends and some things about my family members I didn't know. I pretended that I knew some of the things she told me so she wouldn't get suspicious. I don't know how he found out about that friend, but when I got home, he raped me and broke my arm with his night stick." She began sobbing.

Ryan pulled her to him and held her tightly. "I'm here now," he whispered.

"I was rescued and came here to hide," Alexia said softly, her crying subsided.

After a few minutes of silence, she pulled away from his embrace. "I'm a different person now."

"Honey, I don't know what to say." Ryan felt tears welling in his own eyes and his chest ached for her. "That's so awful. I'm amazed that you escaped."

"Now you can understand why I've been so reluctant to date and why I'm so scared all the time," Alexia said, her voice shaking. "I'm so afraid Stan will find me someday."

"Why are you out here with the bat? Did you hear something that scared you?"

Her body stiffened. "Yeah, I keep hearing tapping outside that sounds like Stan's night stick."

"Do you think he's found you?" Ryan stammered.

"No." She reached out and put her hand on his bicep. "I look completely different than I did when I was in Seattle. I've got a new name, a new social security number, and work in a different profession. I haven't been in contact with my family or any friends from back home since I've been in Honolulu."

He hesitated in asking the question, but he had to know the answer. "Are you still legally married to him?"

Alexia shrugged. "My rescuers told me not to talk or think about him. They were adamant that I become Alexia Moore and leave Elaine Finnegan in the past. Stan was married to Elaine, not Alexia."

Ryan nodded. He couldn't imagine not having his parents in his life or abandoning the friends he grew up with. Alexia was forced to give up everything, simply because she married the wrong guy.

"There's something else you should know, Ryan."

"What's that?"

"I Googled his name a few years ago." She took a deep breath. "I found out that since I've been missing so long—they believe I'm dead."

"Oh, Lex." Ryan drew her to him and held her tightly.

"My parents think I'm *dead*." She sobbed.

"Sweetie, that's horrible." Ryan loosened his embrace and looked into her deep blue eyes. "Would you feel better if I took you over to my place for a while?"

She shook her head. "No, I can't. I need to work out and get to the office on time."

"You can skip a workout, and if you don't feel up to it, you can call in sick."

"No, I never skip a workout."

"Of course, you can. There are some days you have to rest."

Alexia pulled out of his embrace and stood up. "You don't understand. My disguise is my fit body. If I don't keep it in amazing shape, someone could recognize me."

"Or, you could recognize yourself," Ryan said, looking closely at her face to see if she reacted to this proposition. He noticed her eyes widen with his suggestion.

Alexia paced the floor for a few minutes. He watched her as if for the first time. She paused directly in front of him, put her hands on his waist and said, "Now that you know the truth, you must swear to me that you will never tell a soul about my real identity." She moved her hands to his face and looked intently into his eyes. "Please... My life depends on it."

"I swear. I won't say a word." Ryan returned her gaze. She seemed to believe him and slumped down next to him on the couch, putting her head on his shoulder.

After a few minutes, he asked, "Do you think you'll ever be able to relax and be yourself?"

"Hmmm. I don't know who I really am anymore." She paused and looked up, not meeting his eyes. "I'm who I've become, I guess. I'm Alexia."

"If you're no longer Elaine Finnegan, then maybe there's no reason for you to be afraid anymore," Ryan said. He waited as she pondered his words.

"I'm afraid. But, I'm courageous."

"Yeah—you have managed to do many things, despite the fact that they've been frightening. That's the definition of courage."

"It's time for me to go to the gym."

"Do you want me to work out with you? I can."

"No. I'll be okay," Alexia said weakly.

"If you change your mind about staying at my place, that's fine. You can show up or call me and I'll come over to get you."

After Ryan left her apartment, he decided to head home instead of to the early morning masters swimming workout as Dieter had directed. He needed to process what she had just told him, and he couldn't do that amongst a pool full of swimmers.

As he drove towards Kailua, he remembered the time when he had been threatened with a gun at his deposition and Zana told him to get out of the state for his own protection. On his way to the airport, Alexia had called him. When he told her of his fear and his feeling about having to flee for his life, she had told him that she knew how he felt. At the time, he thought she could relate because of her experience with irate claimants. Now that he knew her story, so many of her comments and behaviors made sense.

In some ways, Ryan wished that he wasn't burdened with such a huge secret. He wanted so much to discuss it with his parents. Alexia's clandestine life reminded him of his pro cycling days when secrecy was his way of life. From the time he was hired by a pro team, the weight of his family and friend's aspirations lay squarely on his shoulders. Their pride in his accomplishments put him under so much pressure he'd felt that the only way to meet their expectations was to take performance-enhancing drugs. After he was exposed for lying and cheating, he had promised himself and his family that those days were long behind him. But it was a tough road.

Despite Ryan's efforts to live an honorable life after pro cycling, trouble seemed to find him. Now that he was finally free of litigation, he was excited about the opportunity to make decent money for the first time in a pro triathlon. But he felt frustrated that he was again facing challenges.

After he got home, he changed into his biking shorts and a sleeveless biking jersey. His best thinking was always done while working out, so he hopped onto his spinning bike in his exercise room and pedaled hard while focusing on Alexia's circumstances.

Ryan had worked up a sweat by the time he realized what was troubling him so much. Of course, he was worried about Alexia's safety. She had gone through so much. He realized that he had no control over those things and was helpless to do anything about them, aside from offering her a safe place to stay, which so far, she'd declined. What he *could* control were his own actions.

As he pedaled his bike, he realized that he was likely dating a married woman. Even though her husband was the lowliest of scumbags, Ryan knew that he couldn't continue a romantic relationship with Alexia if she were still married.

Still dripping with sweat, Ryan turned on his computer and Googled Stan Finnegan, Washington State police officer. He felt sick to his stomach as he read about Stan's commendations and involvement in charity work with kids. Stan's name even came up as having completed some 5K fun runs.

Ryan was surprised that Stan had placed in the top three in his age group for some of the races. He then did a search of Stanley Finnegan, which revealed even more information. There had been a Finnegan family reunion, which Stan had attended. Almost all of the pictures were of Stan posing formally in his police uniform, looking dark and serious.

Ryan studied a picture of Stan that had been taken only a few months ago that someone had included in an online Finnegan Family Reunion Newsletter. The picture showed Alexia's estranged husband posing with a little boy who looked to be about two or three years old. It was the only picture showing Stan with a smile on his face. His dark eyes were covered by sunglasses and he wore a blue ball cap. There was no information as to the identity of the little boy, who also had dark hair and brown eyes. Ryan realized that he'd forgotten to ask if Alexia had any children. There was also the possibility that the boy was a nephew.

Ryan asked Siri to call Charles Keaton, an attorney in New York who had represented him in his doping cases.

"Chuck, I have a favor to ask."

"What can I do for you, Ryan?"

"Can you have your investigator dig up whatever you can find on Stanley Finnegan? He's a police officer in Seattle."

"What kind of information are you looking for?"

"I want to know if he was ever divorced from Elaine Finnegan."

"That shouldn't be hard to find out. You could probably do a Google search."

"I tried. Nothing came up. Also, could you find out if he and Elaine had any children, or whether he had any children with someone else?"

"Sure. What's your timeframe on this?"

"I need it as soon as humanly possible. It's urgent."

Chapter Eighteen

@Haleyville The race organizers rank me number 12. Planning to prove them wrong. Not over confident; just well-trained. #Winner

Haley woke to the smell of fresh coffee brewing and the morning chatter of birds, one of which had made its way into the tent.

"Get out of here, little birdie!" Haley was in no mood to clean up bird crap. She shooed the tiny bird out through the flap of the tent as two more birds flew in. "Out—now!" She shouted, trying to scare the birds so they'd leave on their own.

"You're up." Sean poked his head into the tent and handed her a steaming cup of coffee.

"Can you get these birds out of here?" Haley pleaded.

It'd always been Sean's job to scare off birds or kill cockroaches, spiders, centipedes, flies and mosquitoes. She didn't mind geckoes, because they ate the bugs. Sean stomped his feet and rushed towards the birds making their only avenue of escape to fly out of the tent.

"Got 'em!" He quickly closed the tent flap.

Haley headed for the pool house to brush her teeth. She noticed that Sean was wearing running shorts and shoes, and his bare chest was glistening with sweat. "You look like you went for a run."

"Yeah, it felt good," he said. He sat down in one of the camp chairs.

"Dieter specifically told you not to work out this morning. You were supposed to sleep in like I did." She could feel her face grow hotter with the confrontation. *Was she the only one that was serious about winning?*

He shrugged. "I know. I woke up early and couldn't sleep." He rose and fetched the coffee pot to top off her partially empty cup. "I'm sure I'll be fine."

She sighed. There was no use talking to Sean sometimes. "How far did you run?"

"Twelve miles."

"No way!" Haley raised her voice. "That's ridiculous. The race is only a few days away."

"I'm going to win because I'm training hard." He puffed out his chest and flexed a bicep.

"Sean, I'm so pissed off right now—" She got up and walked past the pool, then spun around. "I don't know what to say." She glared at him.

"I'm sorry, Haleyville. I promise you, I'll be fine." He put his coffee cup down stepped across the pool deck to reach for her arm.

She moved to avoid his touch.

"I'm not over-trained."

"You do realize that if we don't win prize money, we'll be on the streets again," she spat.

"We'll win." He flashed his biggest smile. "Don't worry so much."

Haley gave him an icy stare, grabbed her coffee cup and headed to the pool house for a long, hot shower.

She let the hot water rush over her. She tried to relax her muscles and calm her mind. Sean wasn't taking his training seriously and so it was up to her. If she won fifth place, she'd get $7,500.00—enough for them to move into a small apartment. Placing higher would mean winning money to pay their travel expenses for the next Terry Schubert Pro Classic to be held in San Diego in six weeks.

Haley took her time drying off with a beach towel, and then put on a clean Costco uniform. Before leaving the pool house, she made both of them turkey sandwiches and filled plastic baggies with baby carrots.

As she handed Sean his lunch sack, she said, "We lost Freewheel Movement Triathlon."

"What do you mean by that?"

"We were over-confident and neither of us won our age groups," she said, looking him squarely in his eyes. "The Terry Schubert Classic is a pro race with top triathletes from all over the world coming here for a chance to win decent prize money. Now is not the time to ignore our coach. If you continue to be so arrogant and we end up on the street, I don't know if I can forgive you." Haley pursed her lips tightly when Sean stared back at her. "Do you understand what I'm saying?"

"Yeah, I get it," he said. He grabbed his bike and got on without making eye contact with her. They rode in silence, and he gave her the slightest peck on the cheek before heading to work.

She racked and locked up her bike and went across the parking lot to Costco. She turned back in time to see Sean kick a piece of trash on his way to Starbucks.

***

Haley and Sean were seated in the back of The Bus and on their way to Weiss's Training Center for a briefing session the Thursday evening before the Saturday race. Dieter had left them in the dark about the agenda, but had told the competitors to wear street clothes rather than workout gear.

"How are you feeling?" Sean put his arm tenderly around his girlfriend.

"Really good. I'm rested, and there isn't much I can do to improve between now and Saturday," Haley said, resting her head on her boyfriend's shoulder. "How are you?"

"Fantastic!" Sean grinned. "I'm going to win."

Haley suppressed a laugh. She had heard Sean say those words as long as she knew him. When he was on scholarship for track and field in college, he'd boldly declare—Muhammad Ali style—that he was the greatest. Sure enough, he was right. He won so many blue ribbons, gold medals, and trophies competing in running events that they filled a half dozen boxes now stuck in her mother's storage unit. When Sean became a pro triathlete, he'd make brash statements, but didn't quite live up to them—placing second, fourth, tenth or sometimes even being disqualified for breaking a rule.

From Haley's perspective, Sean's arrogant attitude didn't serve him well in triathlons. His overconfidence led to carelessness. He'd take too long at transitions; he'd get flat tires that were preventable if he hadn't run over glass, or he'd forget to buckle his chinstrap. Sometimes, she wondered whether Sean had a fear of success. Or maybe he made careless mistakes he could use as excuses for not winning. Whatever his problem was, Haley hoped that Dieter's counseling would help him.

Haley was startled awake. She felt the dampness on Sean's shoulder, and embarrassed, quickly wiped the drool off her mouth.

"Come on, sleepyhead." He grabbed her hand and pulled her through the maze of standing bus riders.

Haley almost tripped over a woman's shopping bag in the aisle as she followed Sean out the door. They squeezed past a half dozen people trying to board before finally exiting the crowded bus.

"We can buy an SUV with our prize money," Sean said as they made it past the throng of people waiting at The Bus stop.

"I hope so. Let's focus on one thing at a time," Haley said, holding Sean's hand as they crossed the street to the training facility.

"After this season, we'll have enough money to buy a house."

"I'd be happy to have enough money for a decent haircut and a pedicure."

"It sounds like you're plotting how to spend your prize money," Zana said, ducking in the door that Sean was holding open for her and Haley.

"Yeah, we'll need a good accountant," Sean said, winking at Zana.

"Are you ready for your big day?" Zana asked.

"More than ready. You're looking at the winner," Sean said, flexing both biceps.

Haley rolled her eyes and then grabbed Sean's hand, leading him to the classroom where Sam, Trini, Eric, and Dave were already seated. The others were milling around, and from what Haley heard, were talking anxiously about various aches and pains, concerns about the competition, and what they were going to eat the night before the race.

"Everyone gather 'round," Dieter announced in a loud voice. He was standing in front of the room between a screen for his Power Point presentation and a large, flat screen TV. Dieter pressed his clicker and a slide with the Weiss Scientific Training logo appeared on the large white screen.

After everyone had taken their seats, Dieter clicked to slides of the Terry Schubert Pro Classic that Haley recognized from the website. "This is the transition area. You'll have to check your bikes in at four-thirty and get body marked. I've been given your race numbers. They're based on how the race director ranked each athlete," Dieter explained.

"Can you tell us our numbers now?" Ryan asked. A few other athletes also voiced their eagerness to know where they stood.

"Yes. Ryan, you're number one. I don't want any of you to place too much meaning on these numbers. Ryan, just because you have race number one doesn't mean that you're going to win or that there isn't a target on your back. You have to run your own race," Dieter said.

"Understood," Ryan nodded.

"What's my number?" Jeff asked.

"Jeff, you're number two," Dieter said. "I'll read down the list. Sam is number eight; Eric is number twelve; Sean is eighteen; Gary is twenty-seven; and Dave is thirty-three. In Women's, Haley is twelve; Trini is seventeen; Penny is twenty-two; and Tessa is twenty-three."

Haley let out a gasp when she heard her race number and covered her mouth with her hand. She thought that she'd be at least number 6, but wondered if the competition was going to be stiffer than she'd imagined.

She saw Sean's face tighten in response to his number 18. She wondered if it might take some of the pressure off of him if he wasn't expected to win. *On the other hand, if both of them were ranked so low, how did they stand a chance at winning prize money so they could move into a place of their own?* According to Bud, the tent would no longer be available to them after the race. This was their only shot at staying off the streets. They hadn't saved enough money from their part-time jobs to pay first and last month's rent yet on even a modest apartment.

"How many pros are competing?" Eric asked.

"There are thirty-five men and twenty-seven women from the US, Canada, Australia, Germany, Japan, Great Britain, Switzerland, New Zealand, Sweden, Czech Republic, Portugal and Spain." Dieter consulted his notes.

"I'm number twenty-three. It doesn't look like I have a shot in hell at winning any prize money," Trini complained.

"You are all prepared to do well in this race," Dieter said. "You've followed my program, and I assure you that you will be delighted by the results of my scientific and holistic approach." Dieter paced the room and gestured with his hands as he spoke. "We've been training on the course for months and so you should know it well. That's where you have the home court advantage. There are only a handful of other Hawaiian athletes competing."

"Who are they?" Sam asked.

Dieter looked at his list. "Megan Alexander, Drake Littlefield, Kevin Chong, Arielle Kennedy, and Perry Fujita. The only athlete in that group who is ranked high is Megan. She's number four."

"She's fierce," Trini said, and others voiced their agreement.

"As you know, this race is draft legal. You'll have to draft off of the bike in front of you to gain any advantage." Dieter clicked to a slide showing cyclists drafting close behind each other allowing for the following cyclist protection from the wind, which increased their speed. Next, he clicked to a photo of a group of swimmers in the ocean. "As we've practiced, you'll need to draft off other swimmers in order to gain advantage in the water. I expect you to use run tactics on race day."

Dieter moved through a dozen more slides and then glanced at his watch. "Any questions?" Without looking at the athletes to address any raised hands, he turned off the projector and picked up the remote for the TV.

"I have a surprise for you tonight. We're watching a TV show that airs at seven. We have about twelve minutes before it starts."

Haley noticed Kenny Paxton enter the room. Bud Schubert and Dominic, the director, followed close behind.

"Athletes, I'd like to introduce you to Kenny Paxton, the producer of 'Fighting in Paradise'. He'd like to say a few words before the show begins." Dieter smiled at the men—now standing on his left.

Haley wondered if Kenny was there to talk about their reality show, but she hadn't heard anything recently, so she assumed they would be treated to a "Fighting in Paradise" episode to help them relax before the race. Since they didn't have a television in the tent, this was a rare treat for her.

"Good evening, everyone. It's great to be here before the first Terry

Schubert Pro Classic Triathlon. I'd like to introduce you to Bud Schubert, the founder of the race, who is also the sponsor of the show you'll see in a few minutes," Kenny said, gesturing to Bud.

"Thanks, Kenny. I want to wish you all good luck in our first Terry Schubert Pro Classic." Bud beamed. "I'm sure my son, Terry, would have been thrilled to see the sport he loved offer big prize money. That's the reason for this race in his name. Terry thought triathlon should be like other professional sports."

The athletes clapped enthusiastically.

"In a few minutes, you're going to see a thirty-minute prime time, nationally televised network show about two triathletes who are here in this room," Kenny said.

Haley felt her heart race and she suddenly felt lightheaded. She closed her eyes for a moment, feeling her face flush. Her first reaction was to run out the door to avoid the embarrassment that she was sure to endure while her life was exposed to millions of television viewers and, more importantly, her friends and competitors in this room. Sean's hand gripped hers and she glanced at him. He gave her a big smile.

"This is great," he whispered in her ear.

"If you think so," she whispered back.

"Our hope is that by bringing the lives of these two special triathletes into the living rooms of the American public, they will understand your passion for the sport and become fervent fans," Kenny said. "It is my great pleasure to introduce the premier of 'Racing in Paradise'."

Haley leaned into Sean and he held her close during several commercials before the show began. She noticed that everyone in the room was mesmerized with the screen as the camera zoomed in on her and Sean running on the beach at sunset. He wasn't wearing a shirt and his abs looked particularly chiseled. In response to Dominic's direction, Haley's hair was flowing loose while she ran so she looked more like a cover model than a triathlete.

The show told the story of their challenging lives—how they struggled through college in Sacramento on athletic scholarships, graduated, and because of the down economy couldn't find jobs, and had no place to go. As a last resort, they gambled the last of their frequent flyer mileage to race in the Freewheel Movement Triathlon, hoping one of them would win the trip to Paris prize.

Haley couldn't stop the flow of tears during the reenactment of the city taking away all of their possessions at Kapiolani Park. The story glossed over Bud Schubert's role, but credited the Freewheel Movement for providing them a tent and part-time jobs so they could train. Towards the end of the show, there was footage of them swimming, biking, and running. And then, to Haley's embarrassment, there was at least three minutes of her and Sean's up close and personal confessions to the camera.

The last shot was a close up of Haley sans makeup, tears streaming down her face, saying, "If we don't win any prize money, I don't know what we're going to do. We'll be back on the street."

After the show was over, an advertisement for the Terry Schubert Pro Classic Triathlon was shown, encouraging viewers to tune into the race coverage on Saturday at 9 a.m. to see how Haley O'Neill and Sean Bennett fared in the race.

Enthusiastic clapping erupted as soon as Dieter clicked off the TV.

Haley managed to smile, even though her chest tightened and it was hard to breathe. It wasn't a secret that they were homeless and in need of the prize money, but during their training, they had not brought attention to their plight.

Kenny came up first to them, with Bud, Dominic, and their fellow triathletes following in hugging them and wishing them good luck. Haley felt the weight of all of their hopes and expectations on her shoulders.

Chapter Nineteen

@ZLaw Schmucks lose every time. #bestdayever

"Still only the one client, Zana?" Donald asked in a rare passing of the two in the firm hallway.

Zana nodded. "Yeah. I've done as you suggested. I'm spending lots of time with pro triathletes."

"LOL," Donald chuckled. "It's not as if triathletes make money. Do you have a plan to get real clients?"

"You'll see." She smiled. Her boss wore black pants and a green polo shirt instead of his usual plaid ensemble. "You're not golfing today?"

"Late tee time with a few UH golfers. I'm blending in by wearing their school colors."

"Smart."

She stopped by Nina's desk for Ryan's file and then headed to her office to her perfect, clean desk. She sometimes missed being so busy at work that popping an Ambien was the only way she could manage to sleep at night. She didn't miss the wrath of Frank, though. Donald had proven to be a most congenial boss—rarely saddling her with thorny projects, and his jokes were harmless. He gave his underlings the freedom to do their jobs, preferring not to micro-manage the way Frank did.

Zana actually *enjoyed* running into Donald. He would rib her good-naturedly, using what he thought were hip words and phrases he'd picked up using a slang dictionary app on his Android phone. From what she'd seen, his young pro golfer clients appreciated his efforts in about the same way a Parisian waiter appreciates an American tourist ordering dinner with the help of a French phrasebook. But his heart was in the right place.

Her calf muscles were sore after her solo 14-mile run that morning.

Coach Dieter had ordered the rest of her training group to sleep late before their race, but since she was training for the Arizona Ironman in mid-November, she didn't get the same luxury. She had risen at 4 a.m. for her run. However, it *was* nice not having to worry about the race tomorrow. She didn't envy the pressure the pros were under the day before the biggest prize money race of their lives.

When she'd checked in with Ryan that morning, he seemed fairly relaxed about the race, but anxious about what he called his "personal life". He said the race was a welcome diversion. She guessed his personal life meant Alexia. Zana hadn't wanted to pry, so she'd quickly changed the subject back to work.

After her talk with Ryan, Jerry had called just to say he loved her.

Even though her boyfriend was living mostly in Los Angeles, they talked every day and he flew back home anytime she needed him. Now that Bud was no longer intent on breaking them up and temptress Annabelle Wong had her hooks into one of the other actors on the show, their relationship was stronger than ever.

Zana turned her attention to a contract she was reviewing for Freewheel. Ryan's charity was expanding internationally, and so a steady stream of documents needed her attention. After concentrating on her computer screen for roughly an hour, she heard a light tap on the door. Rainy didn't wait for her to respond but walked in with the day's Star Advertiser Zana had asked for.

"Mahalo," Zana said, focusing on the photograph and headline on the front page of the newspaper. She studied the picture of Sean Bennett and Haley O'Neill under the banner, **Homeless Triathletes Racing in Paradise**.

She'd first noticed the photo of the couple when she ran past a newsstand in Waikiki earlier that morning. Sean's tattoo of Chinese characters on his chest and Haley's swinging auburn ponytail had immediately caught her attention.

She'd been surprised by the showing of the couple's reality show at the training facility last night. Dieter wanted his amateur athletes to work out on the spinning bikes, but she decided to take a break when Kenny, Bud, and Dominic came in to speak to the pros. It was clever that they named the 30-minute primetime show, "Racing in Paradise" in order to build on the "Fighting in Paradise" brand. The camera seemed to love Sean and Haley. They looked like models even when they were sweaty from exercise.

Ryan had told her about the plan to monetize the sport of triathlon in a big way, and last night's show was clearly the inauguration of his scheme. The public would go wild over this—with Haley and Sean being a homeless couple that stood to win enough money in one race to put a roof over their heads and food on their table. Even if the sport were Tiddlywinks, television viewers would eat it up.

She leaned back in her chair and closed her eyes. Last night would have been perfect if Rip Mansfield hadn't showed up. The moment she saw the Pierce Brosnan look-alike enter the room, she'd retreated to the bathroom to pace back and forth. When Trini had walked in, she retreated back into the main room just in time to see Mansfield sharing a laugh with Sean. All of the time she'd spent with the couple had been wasted. Bud Schubert had gotten his wish. Mansfield would be their agent. She could feel bile rise in her throat.

Her ringing phone interrupted her thoughts.

"This is Zana," she said, picking up her usually silent landline.

"Mr. Sean Bennett on line 1," Nina said.

"Thanks, Nina." She clicked over to line 1. "Hello, Sean."

"Hi Zana, did you see the show?"

"Yeah, I was there last night. Remember?" She picked up her pen and started to doodle on a yellow legal pad.

"Oh, yeah—that's right. What did you think?"

"It was *amazing*. You and Haley looked fantastic on camera."

"I guess you're not the only one who thinks so," Sean said. "We slept in this morning just like coach told us. When we got up, we had dozens of phone messages and emails."

"People wanted to congratulate you, I bet." She smiled into the phone.

"A few did. Mostly, they were PR and marketing people asking to speak to our agent."

"Oh?"

"Yeah. One of the callers was from a national talk show inviting us to appear on Monday morning."

She wrote a note—*Monday morning*. "That's exciting. Are you going to do it?"

"Absolutely, we'd like to. The problem is, Haley and I can't handle all of this by ourselves. We need an agent," he said.

"You mean, Rip Mansfield?"

"He's a schmuck," Sean said, and then paused. "We need you, Zana."

She jumped up from her chair and threw up her hands, dropping the pen and phone in her excitement.

"Are you there? Hello?"

"Yes, I'm here. Sorry. I dropped the phone." Her grin was ear to ear, but she calmed herself enough to speak in a serious, business-like tone, "Let's set up an appointment for you to come in next week." Even though she knew her calendar was clear, she pulled it up on her computer screen.

"That's too late. We need you today," Sean said, clear desperation in his voice. "We need you to return all of these calls. Can you represent us starting *now*? I can give you all the information over the phone."

Zana paused. "Hmm, I suppose I can. I'm not sure you should be coming into my office to sign the agent representation contracts today though, with the race tomorrow."

"We'll sign them electronically. Just e-mail them and we can sign it on our iPad."

"Don't you want to go over the contracts with me in person? I don't mind coming to your tent—I mean, your home," she said, hoping she hadn't offended her new client.

"We took the day off from work, but if we could sign the contracts electronically, you can start returning the calls immediately. We want to get as many appearances, sponsorships, and modeling jobs as possible—but only if we make money."

"Sure, I understand. I'll e-mail you the contracts later today. Please e-mail me the phone messages and I'll take care of those," Zana said, clicking onto the athlete contract forms on her desktop. "You should also provide me with your work schedules so I can try to work around them."

"No need. If we have any conflicts with work, we'll quit. »

"You'll want to see how the race goes first, don't you think? The media frenzy might be short-lived. I'd recommend that you not quit your jobs just yet," she advised. "The public has a very short attention span. If you don't do well tomorrow, it's possible any sponsors will cancel before you've had a chance to make any money."

"Don't worry. We're going to do *very* well tomorrow," Sean said. "Can you fly to New York with us for the TV appearance?"

"I'll check my schedule to confirm, but I don't see why not." She smiled. "First things first—I'll get the contracts to you and then I'll make the calls."

"Thanks so much, Zana."

"No problem. After you sign the contracts and e-mail me the messages, please do me a favor."

"What's that?"

"Focus only on the race. Put all of this other stuff out of your mind," she said.

He laughed. "Will do."

"I think you should both have a session with Dieter today. He can put you back on track mentally."

"If you say so."

"I'm serious, Sean. Would you like me to call him?" She chewed the end of her pen.

"No need. I'll take care of it," he said.

After they hung up, another call came in immediately.

She answered the phone with the pen in her mouth. "This is Zana."

"You don't sound like my girlfriend," Jerry said.

She laughed.

"There she is. Hey gorgeous."

"What are you up to, Jer-bear?"

"Great news! I'm calling from LAX. I'm on my way home."

"Fantastic. When will you arrive?"

"Not until seven tonight, but I have another surprise."

"Really. What's that?"

"Well, actually I've got a few surprises. Kenny wants me to attend the race tomorrow. He thinks having me there will attract even more media attention to the event."

"That's terrific! If you stay overnight at Diamond Head Tower, we can go together. What's the other surprise?" She giggled.

"Kenny gave me the week off. We can finally go to Paris."

Zana frowned, and started to chew on the pen again. "Oh Jer, that would be perfect, except that Sean Bennett and Haley O'Neil just hired me to represent them. I'm probably flying to New York on Sunday with them for a national TV appearance on Monday."

"I can go to New York, too, and then we can fly to Paris from there."

She sighed and shook her head. "I wish I could. It looks like I'm going to be super busy the next few weeks with them."

"Bummer. At least we can spend some time together after you get back from New York."

"Yeah, that'll be a treat. Aren't you going to congratulate me on getting two new clients?"

"Congratulations, baby," he said. "I'm so proud of you."

"Thanks, Jer-bear."

"I know you're busy, but can you do a big favor for me?"

"Sure, how can I help?"

"I need to sign a document that my associate, Kate, is finishing up. If you can pick it up from my office and bring it home with you tonight, I can review, sign, and mail it tomorrow."

"Will do. I was going to head out for a bite soon, so I'll stop by your office after lunch."

After Zana hung up, she finished preparing the standard form contracts for her new clients. She had to plug in names and dates and tailor them to the sport of triathlon before she could e-mail them to Sean with instructions. After lunch, she'd return phone calls for them and take care of any necessary travel arrangements.

As she headed to Jerry's office, she wondered what his associate was like.

They had never met, but Jerry mentioned Kate often. After the kerfuffle with Annabelle, Zana wasn't in the mood to meet another woman Jerry worked with, assuming she would be beautiful, sexy, and flirtatious—and a threat to their relationship.

Zana had gotten into the habit of dressing casually for work on days when she wasn't meeting with clients—almost every day. As she passed a mirrored building, she glanced at her reflection. Her sleeveless white top was flattering, but her black skinny jeans made her legs look stilt-like, even with flats. She wished she were dressed more professionally for this first meeting.

When she walked into Jerry's reception area, his secretary was nowhere in sight so she rang the bell on the counter. Within seconds, she was towering over a frumpy, middle-aged woman.

"Hello," the woman said.

"I'm here to see Kate Scrimshaw."

"You must be Zana." The woman held out a pudgy hand. "I'm Kate."

Zana could feel her entire body relax. It was as if she'd held her breath since Jerry had asked her to do this favor. She extended her hand to Kate and said, "It's nice to meet you."

"Jerry has told me so many wonderful things about you," Kate said warmly, handing over a large envelope.

"Mahalo," Zana said, staring at Kate, who looked the exact opposite of Jerry's usual Victoria Secret model-type hires. Kate was certainly not ugly. She was about 25 pounds over-weight and her brown skirt, with its hemline below her knees, did nothing for her figure. Zana was startled at Kate's appearance, but even more surprised that Jerry had told Kate "wonderful things" about her.

"You're gorgeous—no wonder Jerry is so smitten with you," Kate said, giving her a big smile that made her whole face crinkle.

Zana grinned back and slipped the envelope in her tote. She was used to women gushing about Jerry, but not complimenting her. She liked Kate instantly. "Jerry is fortunate to have you working with him. Since you've been here, he's been able to live his dream and focus on the show."

"I aim to please." Kate picked up a stack of mail from the receptionist's desk. "Practicing law in Hawaii is a dream come true. I definitely made the right decision moving here. Now, if you'll excuse me, I have to get ready for a settlement conference."

Zana spent the rest of the afternoon returning calls for Sean and Haley. She confirmed their appearance for Monday, providing the information needed so the producer could arrange for their flights and accommodations. Surprisingly, the companies that expressed interest in sponsoring her clients sold cars, cell phones, shampoo, sunscreen, and hotel rooms, rather than bicycle components, energy bars, and running gear. It was rare for any triathlete to attract the attention of a non-sports industry sponsor and, after the airing of only one prime time half hour show, Sean and Haley were being offered sponsorship opportunities Olympians would drool over. It was impossible to negotiate the contracts before the next morning's race and so Zana hoped her clients would do well enough to keep the sponsors interested until Monday.

On her way out at the end of the work day, Zana saw Donald in his office through its open door as she walked by.

"Good news," she said from his doorway.

"What's that?" Donald asked, flashing his bleached smile.

She beamed back at him. "The triathletes I've been training with—Sean and Haley—hired me to be their agent."

"Good for you." He rose from his leather chair and gave her an awkward fist bump, followed by his version of a hand explosion—complete with sound effects.

Zana bit her lip so as not to laugh and concentrated on not rolling her eyes.

"You can probably land a Speedo or Power Bar sponsor."

"Good idea. It looks like we've already got Honda, Samsung, Hawaiian Tropic, Pantene, and Marriott—all in one afternoon."

Donald raised his perfectly manicured eyebrows. "Are you serious? I'm lucky if I can get Titleist or Ping after a month of playing phone tag."

"The sponsors are hoping to cash in on their compelling human-interest story," Zana said. "And, it doesn't hurt that they both look like models."

Donald gave her a fatherly pat on the shoulder and resumed his seat. "See, hard work pays off."

"My new clients have a big race tomorrow morning. If they don't do well, I'm not sure what opportunities will be left by Monday."

"I've been in your shoes. Years ago, I represented a young pro golfer who was only fourteen years old. Sponsors were mad about him and he got more media attention than some pop stars get during their entire careers. His game was impressive until he got his driver's license and a few DUIs." Donald frowned, picked up a handgrip strengthener from his desk and began using it. "He lost one sponsor after another."

"What happened?"

"He dropped out of pro golf. After losing his license and completing the court-ordered community service, he came to his senses. I held him back from tournaments until he turned eighteen and then we re-branded him as an adult instead of a teen phenom. With the pressure off, he played well and attracted the typical golf sponsors—Nike, Taylormade, and Calloway."

"It seems like the sponsors are more interested in Haley and Sean's appeal as beautiful, athletic young adults who are struggling with homelessness than in their prowess as triathletes."

"There's nothing wrong with that," Donald said as he switched his grip strength exercises to the other hand. "Keep in mind that the sponsors are hoping they're first in line in case Sean and Haley win tomorrow but if they lose, you may never hear from them again."

"That's what I'm afraid of."

Donald looked at her over his grip strengthener. "You better tell them to keep their day jobs."

"I have. I'll keep you posted."

Chapter Twenty

@TheGreatShayB Winning in Paradise. #Terry-SchubertProTriathlonClassic

Even though it was still dark outside, Sean slipped his sunglasses on to shield his eyes from the portable lights erected by the 'Racing in Paradise' crew. A race volunteer stenciled his new number 5 on his arms and calves while another volunteer stenciled number 3 on Haley. Apparently, their reality show had moved them up in the standings.

Sean tried to focus on the race, but instead, he adjusted his expression for the camera. He stared into the distance and locked his jaw to create a steely determination-to-win look. The butterflies in his stomach were more about the TV appearance on Monday than the race in less than an hour. As the camera moved in closer, Sean flexed his bicep and said, "I'm the greatest" in his best Muhammad Ali imitation.

After their bodies were marked, Sean watched Haley offer best wishes to fellow competitors who she didn't know. She agreed to trade transition spots with another athlete who mentioned that she preferred the prime location of Haley's bike and gear. Per Dominic's direction, she let her auburn hair flow during the pre-race filming and would only tuck it into her swim cap at the water's edge.

Dominic and his two cameramen, Tim and Pete, with cameras poised on their shoulders, followed them and their newly appointed agent, Zana West, to the swim start, a short walk down the beach. The couple embraced and whispered into each other's ears.

"I love you, Shay. No matter how we do, we'll get through this."

"We're going to win, Hayleyville!" Shawn kissed her, and then pulled away and pumped his fist for the camera.

***

Zana watched the pro men line up two layers deep. Sean had pulled and zipped up his one-piece triathlon suit so his chest was no longer exposed. The body positions of the men were a cross between swimmers poised to dive and track stars on their marks. She could identify them easily, because their last names were stenciled on the rear-ends of their suits.

A loud bang sent the men sprinting from the shoreline into the ocean. They launched their bodies to open water so they could get away from their thrashing competitors and freely move in the direction of the first large orange buoy marking the turn-around point. She watched the white water dotted with florescent yellow swim caps of the men swimming swiftly away from shore. She tried to keep her eyes on the cap she believed was Sean's, but questioned her choice as that swimmer lagged behind the breakaway group of about five athletes. A few men veered into the coral, but she was sure Sean had followed her instructions and was among those swimming in a straight line.

When five minutes had elapsed and a large gap had opened up behind the pro men, the race director announced that it was time for the women to line up. Third from the end, Haley lined up next to Megan Alexander. Jackson was on one side of her and Okuda and Pang on the other.

Zana noticed that Dominic made sure that cameraman Pete was in place to capture close ups of Haley before she took the plunge to begin the race. The instant the starting pistol sounded, Haley rocketed into the water. From what Zana could see from the shore, Haley was tied with three other swimmers for an early lead.

When the swimmers were in the distance, Zana glanced at Jerry, who was standing with Kenny Paxton and Bud Schubert in a roped off VIP area. His bodyguard was standing off to the side.

Zana watched Coach Dieter as he stood on the grassy area that separated the beach and the transition area so he could see competitors. The men finished their swim and then ran out of the water and up the sand to collect their bikes positioned on numbered racks. Whenever he saw one of his triathletes he would cheer for him or her, and run to the transition area to shout out encouraging words.

No surprise—his first athletes out of the water were Jeff, Sam, and Eric. Within about 30 seconds, Sean emerged, followed by Ryan. Ryan executed a lightning speed transition from swim to bike. Sean didn't have Ryan's transition speed and had never been a top cyclist in the pro field, so it seemed odd that a cameraman poised on the back of a motorcycle was filming Sean as he rode his bike out of the transition area. Ordinarily, the media focused their attention on the leaders.

Even though she expected other swimmers to come out of the water within minutes, her gaze lingered on Sean as he positioned himself on his aero bars and rode out of the park.

***

Haley's hand hit the sand and she swiftly pulled her body up and ran up the shore to the transition area. She instantly located her bike and wasted no movements transitioning to the next leg of the triathlon. She felt calm thanks to the last minute psychological counseling Zana insisted on. Haley had felt overwhelmed with the possibilities presented by potential sponsors and afraid that her performance in today's race might not live up to their expectations. She had become tearful when she admitted her fear of being cast to the street with no money, job, or home. As she pedaled at top speed on Kalanianiole Highway, her mind drifted to her conversation with Dieter.

"Do you enjoy competing in triathlons, Haley?" Dieter asked.

"Yeah, I love it."

"What do you love about racing?"

"I feel alive," she said thoughtfully. "It's painful—but in a good way—and I always have a big sense of accomplishment when I finish."

"How do you feel if you don't win or if you finish in a position lower than expected?"

"Of course I'm disappointed, but that doesn't take away from my enjoyment and satisfaction."

"Will you take pleasure from the race tomorrow, no matter what the outcome?"

"I suppose I could."

"It's still the same sport that you've enjoyed competing in for years, right?"

Haley paused and then smiled at her coach. "Yeah, I'll have fun."

Dieter had confessed to her that he was not only impressed with her progress in training, but also in counseling. She had been open about her childhood, explaining that her father had left her mother for a French woman. He had met the woman at a company party her mother couldn't attend, because she was pregnant and on bed rest. Although Haley didn't have contact with her father anymore, she knew that he lived in Paris. That was years ago, and she hadn't had any contact with him since.

"Are you sure what I say to you is in confidence?" Haley had asked.

After he responded "yes," she confided in Dieter the real reason Sean had been able to talk her into flying to Honolulu in the first place. She was counting on winning the trip for two to Paris. When both of them had lost, she felt the heavy weight of their dire situation as well as deep disappointment that she couldn't look for her father all on her shoulders.

Haley turned her attention back to the race. She smiled, increased her cadence and moved to pass the two women she was trailing.

***

Zana strained to identify the lead male cyclists in the distance as they approached the transition area. She was able to make out the leader because of his red helmet. It was Ryan. She cheered enthusiastically for her client, not even caring about the $100,000 prize money that was at stake and that, as his agent, she was entitled to a share. Ryan expertly slipped his feet out of his bike shoes that remained clipped to the pedals, dismounted, and racked his bike. He pulled his helmet off, slipped his bare feet into his running shoes and grabbed his running hat, which he popped onto his head while in motion towards the transition area exit.

Jeff and his other competitors were still on the bike course, so Ryan took the time to adjust his sunglasses and take a long swig of water from a paper cup handed to him by a volunteer. She watched him toss the empty cup to the ground as he ran out of sight at an impressive pace.

When she turned her attention back to the transition area, she saw Jeff, Sam, and some of the Japanese athletes dismount their bikes. As they were starting the run segment of the race, she noticed Eric, then the German athletes, and behind them was Sean. She estimated that Sean was in 9th or 10th place at that point. He fumbled a bit with his running shoes as at least five other men rode into the transition area. When Sean finally ran out, he was grouped with those men, and unless he kicked it into high gear, he'd place out of contention for any prize money. Zana's stomach was in knots.

She moved into position to watch the top women ride into the transition area. As she was waiting, she felt someone put their hands on her waist from behind.

"How's the sports agent?" she heard Jerry ask.

"I'm okay, but it's not looking so good for Sean. Ryan's in first, though."

"What about Haley?"

"She'll be in any second," Zana said. "Oh, I see a pink helmet. That could be one of the Japanese women."

"What color is Haley's helmet?"

"Yellow."

"Sweetheart, I see a yellow helmet."

"Yeah? Oh, my gosh, Jer-bear! She's in second." Zana jumped up and down, clapping her hands. "Megan Alexander is on her tail."

"Go Haley! Keep it up!" Zana yelled as she watched her client quickly change from bike to running gear. Zana and Jerry shouted encouraging words until Haley and the two other front-runners ran out of sight.

"Let's go to the finish line and wait for the men to come in." Zana grabbed Jerry's hand and led him quickly in the direction of a finishing arch that read "Terry Schubert Pro Classic Triathlon" at the top and on both sides.

As they made their way over there, Zana noticed spectators taking pictures of *them* with their phones. Even one of Dominic's cameramen was filming them. She smiled at the camera and saw Jerry doing the same. He was used to the attention. Before they reached the finish line, an announcement was made over the loud speaker that the men were on their way in.

"Let's run," Zana said.

They made it to the finishing arch just in time to see Ryan dash victoriously through the finish line tape held on one side by Bud Schubert and on the other by the race director. Jeff Paris finished a close second behind Ryan.

"Ryan Peterson is the winner of the Terry Schubert Pro Classic and the winner of $100,000 in prize money," the race announcer said. "Congratulations, Ryan!"

Zana gave Ryan a quick congratulatory hug before he was draped in leis, given a small Gatorade logo towel and a bottle of water. A local news reporter rushed up, almost knocking Zana down in order to capture Ryan's first words after his victory.

"How does it feel to win one hundred thousand dollars in prize money?" The reporter asked.

"Fantastic. It was a tough race. Lots of wind today." Ryan smiled at the camera.

"It looks like Sean might be coming in," Jerry said in Zana's ear.

"Excuse me." Zana walked away from the impromptu interview and back into the crowd gathered by the finish line, with Jerry on her heels. She saw a stream of athletes running her way. Sean was in the mix, but she couldn't quite make out what position he was in. Since he was a very strong runner, it wasn't surprising that he was picking off one athlete at a time and improving his position.

"And, seventh place goes to Sean Bennett!" the announcer said.

"Great job!" Zana said, giving Sean's sweaty body a partial hug. He was gasping for air. He bent over and put his hands on his knees, puking onto the ground.

Zana grabbed a towel and bottle of water from a race volunteer for her client.

"Let's get you some medical attention," Zana said, leading Sean away from the crowd with Jerry's help. The medical tent was about 100 yards away. Tim, one of Dominic's cameramen, was trailing them. She wanted to tell him to knock it off, since her client was sort of green and certainly not his usual attractive self, but decided it was more important to focus on getting Sean help.

The cots in the tent were empty, save for one female athlete with fresh road rash. The doctor, nurse, and EMT swooped in. They connected Sean to an IV in no time while Tim filmed every moment of the drama. Once Sean was situated, Jerry excused himself to take a phone call.

"Do you know how Haley is doing?" Sean asked Zana as he lay on the cot, the color returning to his face.

"She'll probably be coming in soon," she said.

"Go watch her," Sean directed. When Zana hesitated, he said, "I'm fine. Go. Please."

"I'll be right back." Zana dashed out of the tent, running at full speed to the crowd that was now chanting the names of the front-runners, including Haley's.

Just as Zana reached the finish line, she saw Haley finish in third place—and winning $25,000. Relieved, Zana realized there was still a chance for sponsorships.

Chapter Twenty-one

@Haleyville Moving up in the world. Samsonite instead of Hefty Bags. #Class

Unaccustomed to being on a talk show television set, Haley sat stiffly next to Sean on the sofa, not knowing what they were expected to do next. Neither of them had watched television for years. Even before they were homeless and had access to such luxuries, they didn't have the time to waste in front of a TV screen with their busy school, study, training, and competition schedules.

Haley suppressed a yawn. It was 1 a.m. Hawaii time, and even though she'd slept almost the entire plane ride, she was still tired from their long day on Saturday. After the race, every local TV station and some cable news stations wanted interviews. Rather than offer a press conference, they'd met with each reporter separately until she'd become so desperate for a shower and meal, she'd begged to take a break.

Zana was with them every step of the way. After the interviews, they met at her office to go over their itinerary for their New York trip and discuss possible sponsorship opportunities. Zana had driven them home after buying them a late dinner, and then reminded them to pack their suitcases. A car was picking them up at 10 o'clock the next morning to take them to the airport. *What suitcases?* The city had scooped up their 27-inch Samsonite rollers, the large cases used for transporting their bikes, and their carry-on duffle bags with the university logo, along with all of their other possessions.

"We're not going to get on a plane with Hefty bags," Haley announced. Then she called for an Uber to take her and Sean to the nearest 24-Hour Walmart. By midnight, their brand-new 20-inch roller board suitcases and Oakley backpacks were neatly packed.

Now, on the set, Haley noticed that Sean was nervously shaking his leg.

She reached out and put a reassuring hand on his knee. She felt his sweaty hand squeeze hers just before the director signaled that they were on the air.

"Haley, how does it feel to have won twenty-five thousand dollars in prize money?" Matt, the host, asked.

"Great," Haley said through a forced smile. If she were truthful, she would've said she felt tired and a little dazed at how fast everything was moving. Just last week she was running around Costco fetching family-sized boxes of Cheerios and jumbo bundles of toilet paper for customers. Now, she was wearing a heavy layer of pore clogging make-up and trying to smile, answer inane questions, and keep her core temperature from plummeting in the ice cold television studio.

"I know the race was only a few days ago, but have you decided what you're going to do with the money?" he asked.

"I really haven't had much time to think about it. Of course, we're going to move out of the tent where we've been staying and find an apartment." Haley suddenly felt a wave of relief wash over her. The crushing worry of the last few months was gone, making her feel light and giddy. "My mom is working two jobs to support my ten brothers and sisters, so I'm going to send her five thousand dollars to help her out. Maybe, she can take a few days off and pay some bills."

"I'm sure your mother will appreciate your help. It sounds like you had it rough growing up with such a big family and being raised by a single parent," Matt said.

"Yeah, it wasn't easy." Relief flooded Haley when she realized she wouldn't have to share the details with millions of television viewers.

"Sean, how are you feeling about your seventh place finish?" Matt asked—his tone had changed from compassion to something more biting.

Haley felt her shoulders relax when the questioning was shifted to her boyfriend, but she noticed Sean shift in his seat at the quick change of subject.

Sean paused and stared at one of the cameras for a tense moment. He seemed to recover and answered, "The competition was tough. It was a windy day, which made for a challenging bike ride."

"Are you disappointed you only won a thousand dollars with so much prize money available?"

"Sure, I'm disappointed. I've been an athlete all my life. You win some and you lose some." Sean shrugged. "That's the way it goes."

"I'll bet you're proud of Haley and relieved that you two can finally afford a home?"

"Yeah. Haley did well," Sean said. "I'm proud of her."

Haley felt his body stiffen next to her, even as he patted her knee.

"How will your lives change, aside from being able to move into an apartment?" Matt asked, directing this question flavored with kindness towards Haley.

"We've been given a lot of sponsorship opportunities, with those and upcoming Terry Schubert Pro Classic races in other venues, we're going to be busy," Haley said, relieved that Sean was temporarily off the hook. Since the race, he hadn't said much about his disappointing finish. Instead, he had launched into his typical list of post-race excuses to anyone who was willing to listen.

"Haley, it's my understanding that you've been working part-time at Costco and Sean, you've been working part-time at Starbucks."

They both nodded in unison.

"Are you planning to continue working at those jobs?"

"I don't think we're going to have time," Sean said.

"I'm hoping to keep my job," she interjected—worried that her boss was watching. "We took this week off from work, but I plan to go back next week."

"I know you've been through a lot with being homeless. Has anyone helped you during this difficult time?"

"Yes. We owe everything to Bud Schubert and the Freewheel Movement." Sean brightened. "Without them, we wouldn't have had a tent to sleep in, food, jobs—so many necessities. Bud came to our rescue. If it weren't for his race series, we wouldn't have had the opportunity to make much money in the sport we love."

"We're so thankful to Bud Schubert. He's been more than generous," Haley gushed. "I'd also like to thank Ryan Peterson's Freewheel Movement, who made it possible for Mr. Schubert to reach out to us."

"It's been a delight to meet with you, Sean and Haley. I'm sure we'll be seeing much more of you in the future." Matt smiled at the camera.

Haley noticed that his smile seemed to be frozen on his face until the director signaled to cut to commercial. Before Matt completed his hasty good-byes to them, a makeup artist blotted shine off his head and an intern handed him papers.

Haley followed Sean off the set and into the green room where Zana was waiting.

"Great job, you guys," Zana said.

Haley accepted her warm hug. "What's next?"

"Coffee." Zana headed toward the door.

"What's wrong with this?" Sean said, motioning to the coffee pot on a burner next to a tray of bear claws.

"It's crap." Zana winced. "There's a Starbucks down the street. Let's go there."

***

"What did you think of the interview?" Haley asked after they had waited in a long line to order their drinks and managed to find an open table in the busy cafe.

"The questions weren't at all surprising. I think you both handled them well." Zana stirred some Equal into her coffee. She was impressed with how elegantly her clients had responded on live television and how comfortable they appeared on camera. They had come across as the boy and girl next door, which was the image they'd need to keep the attention of the many sponsors hoping to cash in on this newly popular couple.

Sean leaned towards her. "How much money are we going to make in sponsorship?"

"One thing at a time, Sean." Zana suppressed a laugh. She could understand the question. She had wondered the same thing and had already begun daydreaming about putting a down payment on a house with her earnings. "I have messages from a few more companies. Not sure if you're interested. Let's see—Smooth Condoms, Mason's Mayo, and Bandy Soap."

"Can we *have* lots of sponsors?" Haley's eyes widened.

"Yes. You can have multiple sponsors, but we're going to have to be strategic. I suggest that you consider the sponsors who have products or services that you can stand behind," Zana said.

"I can stand behind Smooth Condoms. Do they want me to demonstrate the product?" Sean asked.

Zana rolled her eyes. "Not necessary. You might want to pass."

"Why? I don't mind being the face of Smooth," Sean said.

"I don't know if they're just looking for a face," Zana said, and all three of them laughed.

"I hate mayonnaise. There's no way I'm doing an ad for Mason's Mayo." Haley grimaced.

"I don't mind. I want to make money," Sean said.

"Sean, do you trust me?" Zana placed her hand on his forearm.

"Yeah."

"You've got to stop this talk about only wanting to make money."

"I'm just being honest."

"The public is falling in love with you for your vulnerability. They want to see you and Haley succeed, and if you only talk about money, this isn't going to last very long,"

"I'm telling this to you and Haley. It's not like I'm tweeting it."

"People could overhear, and if you have an attitude that you only want to make money, you'll turn a lot of people off." Zana withdrew her hand when she saw understanding in his eyes.

"I hear you," Sean said, looking at his coffee. "I'll tone it down."

"Let's get going. Maurice is expecting us in forty-five minutes. You'll have to change into bathing suits for the pool shots." Zana stood up and tossed her paper cup and napkin in the trash. The hotel was only a block away, and if they hurried, there would be enough time for Haley and Sean to prepare for their photo shoot with the sports model photographer Donald had recommended. She had arranged with the hotel to close their pool and gym for an hour for their photo session and the makeup artist and hairstylist that had done their magic on her clients this morning had agreed to stop by for touch ups.

While Haley and Sean were changing, Zana took the elevator down to the swimming pool to meet Maurice. She was surprised at how fragile he looked—not at all like a former Olympian as Donald had emphasized. Zana looked him up and down. Maurice wore gray snakeskin pointy boots, which matched his pencil thin gray pants. He wore an expensive form-fitting white T-shirt with a pop of red in a scarf wrapped artfully around his neck. Zana noticed that Maurice's face was somewhat frozen—probably from Botox; his straight blond hair looked highly processed and his cornflower blue eyes had the wisdom of someone much older.

"What's our plan for the day?" Zana asked after introducing herself.

"I'll get some pictures of them in front of a screen first," he said. "I want them to hold off getting in the pool in case their hair and makeup is destroyed."

"Have you got the lights set up in each room?" Zana asked, not really knowing what was expected of her, but she wanted to make sure she properly handled her clients and so she resorted to a bit of cross examination.

"We're all set." Maurice fiddled with his camera for a moment longer before he met her gaze. "I'm sure you're wondering how I could have been an Olympian."

"Not at all," Zana lied. She hoped to hear him explain why he didn't look even a tiny bit athletic.

"I was a figure skater. I made the Canadian team for the 1976 Innsbruck Olympics. I had a few falls and didn't make it into the finals due to injury," he said. "That was the end of my skating career. I'd always adored photography and have been taking pictures of athletes ever since."

"My boss, Donald Reno, speaks very highly of you," she said. Now that she knew that he'd been a figure skater, she noticed how gracefully he moved. "Did you have sponsors during your skating career?"

"I had quite a few over the years—mostly Canadian."

Zana paused, hoping she wasn't being too pushy. "Do you have any tips about seeking sponsorships?"

"Appreciate the offers. They might be short-lived." Maurice pressed his finger to his cheek. "Also, your clients will need to dress and behave professionally at all times. Bad behavior reflects on the sponsors' brands. I suggest you tell your clients to *toe the line* or they'll be old news."

"We'll *toe the line*—whatever that means," Sean said as he walked into the swimming pool room wearing only a red Speedo swimsuit. Zana noticed that his legs were shaved smooth and his abs were so ripped they didn't look real. Haley followed him, also wearing a red one-piece swimsuit, carrying her backpack.

"Like what you see?" Sean flexed a bicep.

"You're both gorgeous." Maurice extended his hand to Sean then Haley, before fixing his gaze on Sean's torso. "Let's get your head shots and full body shots in front of the screen first. I'll film you in the weight room. Lastly, you can get in the pool."

"Do they need to change into other clothes?" Zana asked.

"Workout gear for Haley. Sean doesn't have to wear anything if he doesn't want to," Maurice winked at him.

Sean seemed so focused on the lights and camera set-up that he probably didn't notice Maurice flirting with him. After they posed in front of the screen for 15 minutes, Haley ducked into the women's restroom to change.

"Sean, could you quickly change into your running clothes?" Zana put her hand on his shoulder.

Sean nodded and headed for the men's room with his backpack.

"Do I have any chance with that heavenly man?" Maurice asked Zana as he watched Sean walk away in his red Speedo.

"Absolutely not," Zana said.

"Are you sure?"

"He's skating for a different team," Zana said, hoping Maurice would abandon his infatuation with her client and focus.

"If you say so." He sighed, adjusted his red scarf, and then led Zana to the exercise room, set up with bright lights and a large backdrop screen with a stool for portrait and full body shots.

Once the couple had changed into the colorful running outfits Zana had helped them select, she watched with fascination how Maurice efficiently directed their poses and interacted with both of them in a flirty way as he shot hundreds of photos. The couple changed back into their swimsuits after the dry land shots and then slipped carefully into the swimming pool so they wouldn't get their faces and hair wet for the initial shots.

Then, Maurice encouraged them to play and swim in the water disregarding the camera while he clicked away.

"You can have a rest, or put on your caps and goggles and swim laps," Maurice said. "I'll be right back."

Zana wished she had her swimsuit on. She longed to join them in the pool despite its small size. When Maurice emerged, he was wearing a tiny black Speedo and holding a mask, snorkel, and underwater camera.

"Now for some fun." Maurice entered the water and Zana giggled as she watched his snorkel moving back and forth across the pool, chasing after Sean.

Chapter Twenty-two

@FreewheelMV Never be fooled by what you see from the outside. Everyone has #secrets. Not all can be learned from drug testing. Not all women can be tamed with flowers—or a jade plant.

"Congratulations, Ryan! I saw in the paper that you won a triathlon," Charles Keaton said.

"Thanks, Chuck. Have you heard anything?" Ryan tapped the speaker feature of his phone so he could keep his hands on the steering wheel while driving over the Pali on his way to Alexia's house. They were planning to spend a quiet evening at her home, something he'd been looking forward to after a busy week of meetings with prospective sponsors.

"I just got the report." Charles paused. Ryan heard papers rustling. "Stan Finnegan is married to Renee Hunt Finnegan and they have a three-year-old son, Stanley Finnegan, Jr."

Ryan pulled over to the side of the highway so he could focus on his attorney's words. "Are you sure about that?"

"I checked the court records myself."

"What about Elaine Finnegan? Is Stan divorced from her?"

"There's a court document finding that Elaine Finnegan was legally presumed dead because she was missing for seven years. The kid was born before the seven years were up."

"Did Stan marry before that?"

"No. They got married a few weeks after Elaine was presumed dead," Charles said.

"Interesting."

"Is there anything you want to tell me?" Charles asked.

"No." Ryan wasn't interested in breaking Alexia's confidence. He only planned to tell Charles what he needed to know in order to do his research.

"Do you have any information about Elaine Finnegan?"

"No. I was just wondering."

"Just so you know, there are exceptions when a person disappears following a threat made on his or her life. If a person would have a valid reason for voluntarily leaving and concealing his or her identity, the court may examine that situation in a different light," Charles said. "Is there something that you know about Elaine Finnegan that you're not telling me?"

"Charles, I don't know Elaine Finnegan," Ryan said. From what Alexia had told him, he really didn't know Elaine. He wished he did, but knew that she was someone he'd never meet.

After he hung up, Ryan sat in his car for a few minutes before pulling back onto the highway. The tension that he'd held in his shoulders for weeks seemed to relax. Instead of driving directly to her home, he stopped by a florist to buy her flowers, then he remembered her aversion and bought a jade plant instead.

Alexia met Ryan at the door with her usual caution, pulling him in furtively before she locked the deadbolts and fastened the chain.

"What's this?" she asked when he handed her the plant.

"You don't like flowers," he said, pulling her towards him. She placed the small plant on the coffee table and kissed him so passionately that Ryan's instinct was to push her towards the bedroom.

"Let's eat first," she said, pulling away.

"Dinner can wait." Ryan hungrily kissed her neck.

"No it can't. I baked some butterfish, using a recipe."

"I'm sure it will be as delicious as you." He followed her a few steps to the kitchen. "Mmm, smells good."

"I've got brown rice, zucchini, and salad," she said as she opened the oven to check on the fish.

"Can I help?" He put his hands around her tiny waist.

She laughed and twisted away. "Sit down and relax."

Ryan sat at the table and watched her dish up the food onto plates. His stomach growled at the thought of eating something besides rabbit food at her place. He had never seen a person eat as little as Alexia did. She never seemed to be tempted by comfort food or sweets, so if he wanted something more substantial besides salad, he usually ate before they saw each other. He found her perfectly formed body beautiful. It would be more fun if she enjoyed eating, and he wouldn't mind it if she gained some weight.

"I got some news today," Ryan said after Alexia sat down and took a bite of fish.

"Oh, what's that?"

"Your husband has remarried," he said tentatively.

"What?"

"He married and they have a three-year-old boy."

"How do you know that?" She put her fork down.

"I did a little research."

"You didn't get that from the Internet." She stared at him. "I've looked and haven't found anything."

"I asked my attorney to have an investigator look into it."

"You *fucking* did what?" She raised her voice.

"I'm sorry if you don't like it, but I needed to know."

"Why did you need to know about something that's none of your fucking business?"

"I'm sorry, Alexia," he said softly and reached out to touch her hand. "I was concerned about dating a married woman."

She turned away from him and put her face in her hands. They sat in silence for a few minutes. Then she looked up and asked, "I'm legally dead, right?"

"Elaine Finnegan is." Ryan swallowed hard. "Alexia Moore is alive and is the most beautiful woman I've ever set my eyes upon."

Ryan couldn't read what Alexia was thinking. She had put her hands in her lap and was staring at him.

"Are you okay?" he finally asked.

"You need to leave," she said in a low tone.

"Let's talk about this."

"There's nothing to talk about, Ryan." Alexia picked up both of their uneaten dinners and emptied the food into the trash. She walked to the door and opened it.

"Can't we be adults and talk this through?" Ryan implored.

"What I told you was in confidence. You had no right to call your lawyer."

"Alexia, he doesn't know anything. I promise."

"Leave," she shouted. "Now!"

He walked out the door—stunned by her anger at what he thought would be closure for her. Instead of driving home, he went to Kapiolani Park and changed into his running shorts and shoes in a public bathroom. A six-mile run at a fast pace would clear his head.

***

Haley admired the shiny key in her hand before using it to open the door of their very own two-bedroom/ two-bathroom condo in Hawaii Kai. Their new furniture wouldn't be delivered until Thursday and so the living room was empty, save for some boxes and their packed suitcases. The hardwood floor gleamed as the morning sun shone through the sliding glass door.

Sean opened it and they stepped onto their large dock-like lanai built over the ocean-fed waterway that snaked along the edge of the condominium complex. A young man with a cocker spaniel waved as he paddled by in a kayak.

Haley sighed. "This is so beautiful."

"It's hard to believe it's ours." Sean pulled her close to him. "Too bad we don't have a bed yet."

"Everything has moved so fast. It was just two weeks ago when we were in New York and now we have a condo, furniture on its way, and a new car," Haley said, referring to the Kia Soul the company had given them as part of their sponsorship agreement.

She felt the weight of the key still in her hand. They'd already earned so much in sponsorship money that it made more sense to put a down payment on their own place, rather than rent.

"How did Caroline take it when you gave her your notice?" Haley asked while she stared out at the water.

"What notice? I handed her my apron and said I was done, and left. Did you give them two-weeks' notice or something?" He laughed and shook his head.

"No." Haley felt her chest tighten at Sean's question. He never seemed to care if he left someone in the lurch. "I asked Adam if he needed me to stay on longer until he could train my replacement." Adam had appreciated her concern but was happy for her success.

She breathed in the freshness of the ocean air. She thought she could smell a hint of the plumeria flowers from the tree in their tiny yard.

"What did he say?"

"He said my position was created as a favor for Bud Schubert and there was no need to find a replacement."

Sean's eyes widened.

"Do you think your job at Starbucks was the same?"

Sean shook his head slightly, but Haley could see from the look in his eyes that his answer was yes. It had been too easy to ask for days off, and neither of them had suffered any consequences the day they'd both forgot to call in and tell their employers that they were staying another day in New York.

"What are we going to do with all of our free time?" Sean said, interrupting her thoughts.

"Have you seen the schedule that Zana e-mailed yesterday? I don't think we'll have much downtime." Haley sat down on a shady spot of the wooden lanai and pulled her knees to her chest.

He sat down at the edge of the dock and let his bare feet dangle into the water. "I haven't looked yet. What does she have us doing?"

"We've got photo shoots, filming for commercials, talk show interviews, publicity appearances, and some travel to the mainland. Plus, filming for our show."

"I'm exhausted just hearing about it. I wish we could hang out in our new place for a while and kick back."

Haley stood up and walked over to the plumeria tree, reached up, and grabbed a flower for her hair. She sat next to Sean and felt the cool ocean water wash over her feet. "We're not going to have much time to train for our next race in San Diego."

He shrugged. "We don't have to do all of them."

"Yes, we do," she said. "Zana has us signed up for the entire series. The sponsors insist that we don't skip any. They want us to publicize their brands at the races and on 'Racing in Paradise'."

"I don't see how racing in Colorado Springs, Chicago, and Salt Lake City are paradise." Sean adjusted his sunglasses.

"Well, it's not like there are many pro races in Hawaii," Haley said, "We'll be lucky if we spend much time here at all."

They sat in silence. Two young women paddled by in kayaks.

Sean broke the silence. "Since we'll be traveling so much, I wonder if we made the right decision by buying a condo in Hawaii—it's so expensive."

"Yeah, for what we pay for our mortgage for this small condo, we could've bought a large house in a lot of places on the mainland."

"But, we wouldn't be living in paradise on the water with this amazing view, and you wouldn't have a tropical flower in your hair."

"True. Sean, I know it seems like we've got it made with the prize money and the sponsorships, but we better watch our expenses. We're shelling out two thousand dollars each for training each month, plus our mortgage and the rest of our bills."

"We've been broke for so long, we've got to live a little," he said.

"Zana set up an appointment for us to meet with the accounting guy at her firm—Christopher Presley. Hopefully, he can give us some good advice so we can keep up with our expenses."

"Let's buy a huge flat screen TV for the living room. It's about time we had one."

"Sean, did you hear what I said. Do you know that sixty percent of NBA players go bankrupt? That's what Zana's been telling me," Haley said. "You always hear about players who signed big contracts and get injured, and then get cut from the team. Meanwhile, they racked up huge bills for fancy lifestyles and end up destitute."

"We'll be okay." Sean draped his arm over her shoulder. "Can we change the subject? This is supposed to be one of the most exciting days of our lives. We've got to celebrate our new home a little."

"Maybe. There are some bottles of water in the fridge. Are you thirsty?" Haley took Sean's hand and led him to the kitchen where they paused for a passionate kiss. There were two champagne flutes on the counter with an envelope addressed to them.

She picked it up and read the note out loud. "Congratulations, Sean and Haley! Wishing you much happiness in your new home. Toast to your success (champagne chilling in the fridge—I'm sure Dieter won't mind just this once). Aloha, Zana."

The refrigerator was bare, except for the champagne and a carton of strawberries. Sean uncorked the bottle carefully and filled their glasses.

"Shall we toast?" Haley lifted up her glass.

"To the best day of my life so far. I'm with the woman of my dreams, living in our first home in paradise. What else could a man ask for?" He clinked her glass.

They leaned against the counter in the kitchen and drank their champagne in between kisses.

"I wish we had a bed," Sean said, pulling her close.

"I wish we had a bed, furniture, food—anything." She broke away from his embrace. "We desperately need to go shopping. We'll be sleeping on the floor tonight if we don't pick up a blow-up air mattress and some sheets from Costco."

"We should've borrowed the air mattress from Bud."

"The caretaker and his people packed up everything and took it away," she said. "Let's go to the store and get what we need before it gets too late."

She grabbed her purse and tossed the car keys to Sean. As they walked out the door, Haley gasped. More than a dozen paparazzi and news reporters were gathered in their carport and on the walkway.

"How does it feel to have your own home?" a well-spoken Japanese-American female reporter asked, thrusting a microphone near Sean's mouth.

"It's wonderful. We're very happy." He beamed.

"Are you feeling the pressure of your next race?" another reporter asked.

"Not yet. We've got to focus on getting settled first," Sean said.

"Any talk about getting married at this point?" a young female reporter asked with a wink to Sean.

"We'll let you know if we do." He laughed.

"Is that your new car?" another reporter asked.

"Yes, we're very happy to be sponsored by Kia," Haley said, posing next to the car as if she was doing so for a commercial. "We can't wait to drive our new Kia Soul."

Sean and Haley then posed hand in hand in front of the car. Haley knew that this kind of media attention would soon get old, but for now it was so novel and unexpected that she happily answered the reporters' questions.

"Haley, why are you staying in Hawaii rather than moving back to Sacramento?"

"This is a beautiful place and we can train here in this perfect weather all year long," she responded, noticing that a male reporter with greasy, long dishwater blonde hair tied together in an unkept ponytail was whispering something to Sean. Sean's expression went from joyful to distress during the course of their brief conversation.

"What was that all about?" Haley asked when Sean returned to her side.

"I'm not sure what you're talking about," he said, opening the car door. "Let's get out of here."

She climbed into the passenger seat, smiling at the paparazzi who continued to take pictures. She wished she'd made more of an effort with her hair and makeup that day, but she was not yet accustomed to the constant media attention.

After Sean pulled the car out of the driveway, Haley noticed his face looked unusually stern.

"Will you tell me what that guy with the ponytail said to you?" Haley pressed.

"Who?"

"That guy who was talking to you before we got in the car."

Sean's face turned ashen and his lip trembled.

"He said that if I don't pay him five thousand dollars, he's going to leak something to the tabloids about me."

Chapter Twenty-three

@ZLaw My clients have been abducted by aliens. That's what the #tabloids say. Is it true?

"When you weren't in your office, I was sure you'd been canned," Zana said, admiring the view of Andrew's new office, which was a few doors down from Lucas's swanky ocean front digs. "Did you have to kill a partner to move in here?"

"Almost. I'm not sure if you heard—Peter Dang had a heart attack and decided to retire early." Andrew leaned back in his Italian leather chair and propped his feet on his koa wood desk.

"No, I hadn't heard. There are so many more attorneys that are senior to you. Don't tell me that you had to resort to sexual favors." Zana winked at her former roommate and sat on the black leather loveseat facing him.

Andrew laughed. "Not quite. I think inviting Frank and the other partners to my wedding helped, because Frank has been civil to me ever since."

"Amazing. How are your billables?"

"Super high." He grinned. "Ever since my parents came for the wedding and forgot to go home, I've escaped the craziness by coming into the office every chance I get."

"Now I'll bet you wish that you'd followed my advice and kept me as your housemate to block imposing relatives?"

"Yeah, maybe. Do you want to move back in?"

"No way. I love the ocean view, gym, and infinite pool. Jerry even pays for a massage for me every week."

"You've got it made." He shook his head. "You hardly work, have no stress, and you get to work out as part of your job."

"It's not quite as cushy now that I have a few more clients." Zana yawned. "I'm losing sleep."

"Tell me about it," Andrew said, taking his feet off his desk and leaning forward in his chair.

"Ryan and Alexia had some sort of falling out and he's been cancelling appointments with big sponsors." Zana was pleased she could confide in another attorney in the office about their firm client. Because of confidentiality concerns, she hadn't been able to discuss her challenges with Jerry or any of her friends.

"That's probably just temporary. I wouldn't worry about it too much. He's such a great athlete the sponsors will still be interested in a few weeks."

"The problem is, I've only been an agent for a short time and I don't have many connections. If I need to find a new sponsor, I have no idea who to call."

"I'm sure you'll make those connections with time," Andrew said.

Zana sighed. "Hopefully. Sean Bennett is an even bigger challenge."

"Yeah, he's really been taking hits in the tabloids lately."

"Sounds like you're all caught up with your reading."

"When I'm waiting in line at the grocery store and I see our firm's client on the cover of almost every tabloid, I can't help but pick them up." Andrew frowned. "Seriously, Zana. What's up?"

"It's a mess."

"Is any of it true?"

She cocked her head to the side. "What do you think of the situation as someone who doesn't know Sean? Do you believe any of it?"

Andrew shrugged. "I don't know what to believe."

Zana paused and looked out the window at the expansive view of Diamond Head, the ocean and Iolani Palace in the foreground. "Sean confirmed with me that he was disqualified at a few college track meets for using steroids. When his urine tested clean, he competed with no more problems."

"That doesn't seem like a huge deal."

"It sort of is, considering all of the negative press that Ryan Peterson and so many other athletes have gotten. Sean's lost a few sponsors."

"When you took him on as a client, did he tell you any of this?"

"No, but after some Internet searching I had seen reference to the incidents. The story isn't exactly breaking news."

"What about his illegitimate child? Is that true?"

"I don't think so. Sean denies knowing the woman who claims to be his baby-mamma. He's even willing to submit to a paternity test, if necessary."

"Haley must be freaking out."

"Yeah." Zana gazed out the window. "I can only imagine."

162

"Isn't there another allegation against Sean?"

"Oh, the one that he was abducted by aliens?"

"No." Andrew laughed. "Something about him cutting the course in the last race in order to improve in the standings. Is that true?"

"There's no proof. He came in seventh, so it's not likely," Zana said. "The problem is, a lot of people believe these allegations and it hurts his image."

"Is it affecting Haley's sponsorship opportunities?"

"A few. But she still has some good sponsors."

Andrew leaned forward in his chair. "What does Donald have to say about all this?"

"He's gone through it before with some of his golfers. He just shrugs his shoulders and says it's part of the business."

"Don't they say that any publicity is good publicity?"

"Yeah, but I'm not sure who 'they' is. That's what I've heard."

"I guess your job isn't as glamorous as I thought. Do you miss being a billing machine on the twenty-seventh floor?" He grinned at her.

She rolled her eyes. "No. I'll take the twenty-eighth floor any day. I just wish I could get some sleep. It seems like there's a new crisis every day lately."

"Remember, if there weren't problems, there would be no need for lawyers or agents."

"True enough."

"So, counselor, I'd advise you to become very comfortable with problems, otherwise you'll make yourself crazy," Andrew advised.

She nodded. "This swanky office has made you a wise man."

"I'd like to think so," he said, putting his feet back on his desk.

Zana laughed all the way to the elevator.

***

Jerry was nudged awake by the flight attendant. His first thought was that he had just landed in Hawaii, and then he remembered it was a workday. He was back in LA. Most of the first-class passengers were disembarking while Jerry gathered up his iPad and phone, stashing them safely into his briefcase.

"Good morning, Jerry," a familiar voice said from behind him.

"Oh, hey Rip," Jerry said as he turned to see Rip Mansfield, the attorney who was disbarred last year because of his actions on a case.

"It's been awhile," Rip said, following Jerry off the plane.

"Yeah. What are you up to now?"

"I'm a sports agent."

"Are you serious?" Jerry realized his voice sounded shrill.

"Yeah, I'm commuting to and from LA," Rip said as they walked down the jetway.

"I can relate to that. What athletes are you representing?"

"A few golfers, a surfer, and a few football players." Rip glanced at his Rolex. "Keeps me out of trouble."

Jerry wanted to make a snide comment, but refrained.

"How long are you in LA for?" Rip asked as they entered the airport.

"Not long. We've got three days of filming."

"I've got a week of meetings with sponsors," Rip volunteered.

"Well, it was nice seeing you." Jerry ducked into a restroom.

He usually waited until he got to his condo to brush his teeth, but needed any possible excuse to escape that vile man. Now that Zana's nemesis was also an agent, he hoped they wouldn't cross paths. The good news was that Rip's clients weren't triathletes and so Zana would probably avoid any interaction with the jerk. Just talking with him for a few minutes had given Jerry the creeps.

After freshening up, he stopped for a coffee, stalling so he wouldn't run into Rip at baggage claim. Jerry kept clothes in LA and normally didn't check a bag, but this time he'd brought back a suitcase filled with chocolate covered macadamia nuts for the show's cast and crew.

He spotted his bodyguard, Neil, waiting by the baggage claim carousel.

"You didn't have to park." Jerry scanned the area, but Rip was nowhere in sight. "You could've met me at the curb."

"I can't leave you unattended with fans."

"I got it. I'm now imprisoned in this famous body and you've been hired to protect me from evil fans." Jerry laughed.

"Something like that," Neil said in his gruff voice. "What luggage do you have?"

"It's that black bag right there—the one with the 'Fighting in Paradise' sticker."

"Not too subtle."

Jerry remembered to switch his phone out of airplane mode after he climbed into Neil's black SUV. He had only one text from Zana sent to him late last night.

So much stress with S&H. Feels like the terror before bungee jumping. Do you ever feel like that, J? xox -Z

Jerry stared at the word *terror* and felt his stomach churn. Neil was taking him to the Hollywood set where his best acting was pretending he belonged. He'd grown up in Kalihi with plenty of martial arts training and no theatre experience. He'd only taken one acting class as an adult on Kenny's strong recommendation. Now that they were filming in LA with a new format, a big-time director and real actors making guest appearances, he was completely out of his element.

He responded to her text: **Every Day. xoxox**

Jerry longed to hear Zana's voice, but it was only 5:30 a.m. and with the time difference, she'd be sleeping. He was dying to tell her about Mansfield, but worried that it would add to her stress. He decided to keep the incident to himself.

On the set, he ducked into his trailer for a brief nap, a short session of pushups and crunches, and a hot shower. Kenny popped in to tell him they were running late with another scene and so Jerry relaxed on the sofa, sipped a protein shake, and read the morning news on his iPad. Through the window, he could see Neil standing guard. Jerry rejected his urge to invite him in for coffee.

Growing up, he had seen his father offer ice teas to gardeners and on the few occasions they could afford a housekeeper, his mother shared homemade cake and conversation with the housekeeper at the kitchen table after her duties. Jerry turned his attention back to his tablet. Neil had made it perfectly clear that it was against company policy to fraternize with his clients. He wouldn't even accept a cup of coffee.

The first person to greet Jerry on the set was Annabelle. She wore tight black jeans and a black T-shirt. Even though Annabelle's shirt showed some cleavage, it was probably the most conservative piece of clothing he had ever seen her wear.

"Good morning, Jerry," Annabelle said in a tone more appropriate for the bedroom.

"Hey, Annabelle." He avoided eye contact. "What's the plan for today?"

"Kenny wants me to work with you on a fighting sequence before shooting." She led him to an area with thick mats on the floor. He imitated her graceful mixed martial arts moves, combining stances, punches, kicks and blocks from kung fu, karate, judo, and boxing. Jerry picked up the sequence quickly before he read over his lines that Kenny had e-mailed to him over the weekend.

After an unusually light day with only a half dozen takes for several scenes, Jerry was released before sunset. Kenny drove him home to pick up his white Mercedes Benz CLA-250.

"Make sure you call Neil," Kenny urged. The bodyguard had left as soon as they began filming and wasn't back on duty until midnight.

"Sure thing," Jerry said before thanking the producer for the ride. He had no intention of calling his bodyguard. Instead, he climbed in his Mercedes and headed straight for the gym for an extra long weight training session and an hour on the treadmill, listening to a playlist of Zana's favorite workout tunes.

After eating an egg white and broccoli omelet at the gym café, he slipped into his car and drove back to Marina del Ray. He tried to call Zana, but she didn't pick up. *She's probably swimming, biking, or running.*

Jerry didn't feel like going home. He stopped by the Starbucks a few blocks away from his condo where he could enjoy a decaf coffee while reading his e-mails in the presence of others. He never felt lonely when he spent evenings alone in his cottage in Manoa, because he knew his parents were in the next house, and Zana and his friends were only a phone call away. Without any real friends in LA, he was pleased that work and the gym took most of his time so he could avoid the aching loneliness of his sparsely furnished condo.

He settled in with his steaming decaf at a table surrounded by what looked to be mostly students staring at their laptop screens. A few older people, some reading newspapers, others holding Kindles, nibbled at pastries and sipped coffee.

"May I join you?" a male voice asked.

Jerry turned around to see Rip Mansfield holding a Starbucks cup and a plate with a slice of banana bread.

"Sure," Jerry said tentatively, gesturing to the empty chair.

"Are you staying in the area?" Rip asked.

"Yeah, I have a condo here."

"I bought a house down the road."

"We're neighbors," Jerry said, trying not to roll his eyes.

"I don't know about you, but I've had a long day."

"We finished shooting early. We usually go as long as fifteen hours."

"I've been meeting with prospective sponsors. It just so happens that Thin Mix Cereal and B-Box are in the market for young, attractive professional athletes and I was able to score some lucrative contracts with them," Rip said smugly.

"That's great." Jerry raised his eyebrows. Rip had landed some of the most profitable brands in the world. "I'm not too familiar with what you do as a sports agent. It must be hard to find the right people to talk with at those big companies."

"It took months to make the connections, and then I found this gal, Teri Casey at Thin Mix—she's a hot piece of ass. She directed me to Eddie Phillips at B-Box stores." Rip placed his hands in a steeple position. "Everything has come together. My clients will make big bucks and I'll collect my six-figure commission."

Jerry sat stiffly, listening to Mansfield for a half hour. When the man finally took a breath, Jerry excused himself and drove the two blocks home where he saw Neil sitting in his car waiting. He didn't look happy, but then, Neil never did.

As soon as he walked in the door, he texted Zana. Big sponsorship opportunities for Ryan and S&H. Contact Teri Casey at Thin Mix Cereal; Eddie Phillips at B-Box. Big $$$$!! You can thank me when I get home. —J xoxox

Chapter Twenty-four

@Haleyville Landed cash cow sponsorships even though the tabloids seem to think I'm a former cow. What's up with that? #Haleythecow

Haley opened the front door, bent over, and picked up the tabloid magazine laying on the welcome mat with a large yellow sticky note on it. She flung it on the table and headed for the kitchen to make coffee. There was no way she could handle another scandalous story about Sean without caffeine. Her anger and frustration had reached their boiling point yesterday and so she'd packed up his clothes and left them in suitcases on the doorstep with a note. She felt steam coming out of her ears when she had read his text that he was staying at the expensive Kahala Resort and Spa.

The coffee brewed slowly while Haley sat in a chair at the kitchen table staring into space with the tabloid magazine lying in front of her on the table. *Was there another woman claiming Sean was the father of her baby? Was he accused of cheating in another triathlon?*

When Haley first saw a picture of Sean on the cover of a tabloid she was in line at the grocery store to buy laundry soap. She'd felt dizzy and she'd put the soap on the floor, retreated to her car and called Zana. "Remember, I warned you this would happen," Zana said. "It's the price of fame."

When a beeping sound alerted her that the coffee was ready, Haley took her time washing her favorite mug. She added a dash of milk and stirred honey into the steaming liquid. She sighed as she returned to her seat. The sticky note was in Sean's handwriting and read, "I don't believe this."

Haley peeled it off and saw a picture of an obese woman who'd been photo shopped with Haley's head on her body. Underneath the photo, the caption read "Before". An "After" photo showed a recent picture of Haley with her thin, toned body wearing a bikini. The headline of the story was **Haley O'Neill: From Fat to Fabulous!**

"Oh, my God," Haley shrieked aloud. She slammed the magazine on the table and began pacing. The pacing wasn't enough, so she changed into her running gear and dashed out the front door and down the street. She wound her way around the neighborhood, running as fast as she could. If a thought entered her mind, she sped up the pace. After over an hour of sprint intervals, she collapsed on her doorstep. *If the tabloids could blatantly lie about her, they'd likely made up the stories about Sean as well.*

She texted Sean. Come home

While waiting, she showered and then cut off the tags of a new skort and top she'd bought a few days ago, poured a cup of coffee and slumped into a kitchen chair.

"Hey, babe," he called as he walked in the door.

Haley didn't get up from her seat. "I'm not sure how much more of this I can take."

Sean sat in a chair next to her and reached for her hand. "It might be better if we don't read them."

"Maybe." She noticed bags under his eyes. "We'll need to hire someone to do our grocery shopping."

He leaned forward and kissed her lightly. "If that's what it takes to protect you from lies about us, then yes, we should."

The tenderness in his eyes and touch made her forget her anger. She reached for him and he pulled her into his arms, kissing her tenderly. She breathed in the fresh scent of his skin, feeling his muscular chest pressed against hers. His fingers slipped under her top, caressing her back.

"Shall we try out our new bed," she said huskily. The king-size bed had been delivered the day before *after* she'd kicked him out. They made their way to the bedroom, undressing each other along the way. Haley caressed his six-pack and then pulled his body onto hers as they rolled in their new Egyptian cotton sheets.

Haley was awakened by the beep of a text coming from her phone she'd left in the living room.

"It can wait," Sean said groggily.

"What time is it?"

"I have no idea."

"We should go swimming or for a bike ride," Haley said, now feeling guilty that they'd been dozing when they should have been training.

"Didn't we just have a workout?" He pulled her close to him.

"I'll let Dieter know that we completed the sex portion of the triathlon." She giggled.

"He'll probably want to know the details about cadence and heart rate."

"They were through the roof." She began to tickle him and sent him into hysterical laughter. She loved it when Sean was playful and loving. They lay in each other's arms and gazed at the ceiling. Ever since she won the money in the race, he had cooled towards her. If they could somehow survive the tabloid scandal, maybe her dream of getting married and having babies with him might ultimately be fulfilled.

"What are you daydreaming about, Haleyville?" Sean asked, using the pet name she loved.

"I'm happy."

He grinned broadly and kissed her.

"Stay right here." Haley jumped out of bed and ran naked into the living room to grab her phone. She then sprinted at full speed back into the bedroom and jumped on the bed—phone in hand. They looked at the text message from Zana together: Amazing news: Thin Mix and B-Box are super interested in both of you. Big bucks!

***

"Was that my thank you?" Jerry asked Zana as their bodies lay intertwined on the bed.

"Huh?"

"I texted you that you could thank me when I got home, remember?"

"That *was* your thank you and so is this." She kissed him sweetly on the mouth. His tip about Thin Mix and B-Box seeking sponsors had come at the perfect time. Instead of getting the run-around as she had with most other sponsors, Teri Casey and Eddie Phillips had seemed thrilled to have the opportunity to sponsor the new "it" couple. Thin Mix would use them in television ads and the couple would be the face of B-Box's new web ad campaign.

"You're welcome." He pulled her body closer to his.

"You always seem to have the right connections," Zana said. She hadn't bothered to ask him how he'd gotten the tip. He was always running into former classmates, business associates, and family friends. Ever since Zana had been in Hawaii, she'd been surprised and delighted with the interconnectedness of the island people—it was almost as if there were only one or two degrees separation between everyone.

"The right connection is with you."

"Hmmm…" She smiled and closed her eyes, enjoying the sensation of his warm body against hers. It was a rare Saturday afternoon treat. "I hate to be the one to say it, but we've got to get ready for dinner."

"Already?"

"It's a quarter after five. We've got to be there at six-thirty." She pealed herself away and gave him a quick kiss on the nose before heading for the shower.

"It'll be quicker if we wash each other," he said as he climbed in with her.

"I doubt it—too distracting," she said as she soaped up his body.

By the time Jerry pulled his Ferrari into the valet driveway of Hal's Steakhouse, they were twenty minutes late for their dinner with Haley and Sean, who had insisted on taking them out to thank Zana for helping them land more than a million dollars in sponsorship deals in the past month. Once they were inside the restaurant, the maitre d' led them to a large booth where Haley and Sean were seated close together, sipping champagne.

"It looks like you're already celebrating," Jerry said, reaching out to shake Sean's hand.

"You're just in time for a toast," Haley said.

"There's a lot to celebrate," Zana said as she slipped into the half circle booth.

The large room was decorated as the interior of an aged mansion would be, with shelves of century old books and exquisite oil paintings that looked like they belonged in a museum. The waiters wore tuxes and several of them stood in front of guest tables, flambéing cherries jubilee or assembling Caesar salads from scratch.

"Here's to Zana—without her, we would still be living in a two-bedroom condo," Sean said, lifting his glass.

"And here's to Jerry who gave me the leads," Zana clinked her champagne-filled glass with Sean's. "Are you telling us that you're already selling your condo after only a few weeks?"

"We made an offer on a house." Haley smiled, but Zana saw a look of fear in her eyes.

Sean put his arm around her. "We met the seller's asking price so it looks like it's a done deal."

"Are you sure you want to get into something so expensive so quickly?" Zana asked. "The ink is barely dry on the sponsorship contracts and the second Pro Classic is next weekend. You never know what's going to happen."

"That's what I've been telling Sean." Haley took a long sip of water. "I also reminded him that Dieter would have a cow if he saw us drinking champagne."

"You worry too much. Everything's going to be fine," Sean said. "We're going to win the race next weekend and the cash will continue to flow."

They sat in silence and looked at their menus. Zana couldn't concentrate on the offerings after hearing the news about her clients' new house. *Hadn't*

171

they consulted with the financial planner in her office? She'd have a chat with him on Monday.

"What looks good?" Jerry broke the silence.

"They recommend the Caesar salad. I don't usually eat meat, but the steak looks yummy," Haley said.

"Do you think Dieter would have a problem if we indulge just this once?" Zana put a slice of piping hot cheese bread on her plate.

"Dieter can blow it up his ass. I'm eating and drinking whatever I want," Sean said with his mouth full of cheese bread.

Zana made a mental note to call their coach and suggest extra counseling sessions with Sean. Clearly, he was out of control. Donald had warned her about the challenges of pro athletes going from rags to riches overnight. Their comfort zone was being broke, and money would go through their fingers like water until they were broke again, which felt more comfortable. She didn't want to see Sean and Haley lose everything again, and she certainly didn't want to chase sponsors for more money after they spent it all.

"Where's your next race?" Jerry asked.

"San Diego," Haley smiled. "I've never been there before. I hear it's nice."

"If you have time, check out the zoo and Coronado," Jerry suggested.

"We're flying there on Monday so we can get used to the course. We might have some extra time for sightseeing," Sean said.

"Are you going, Zana?" Haley asked.

"I'm planning to arrive there on Thursday. Does that work for you?" Zana took another sip of champagne.

"If you could be there earlier for some of the photo shoots, it would really help." Haley closed her menu.

"Let me take a look at my schedule." Zana pulled her phone out of her purse and examined it. "I can fly in on Tuesday. I also need to be there for Ryan. He's racing and filming a commercial."

"Do you think Ryan will win again?" Haley asked.

"I'll kick dope boy's ass." Sean flexed his bicep.

"We'll see. You're both looking fit," Zana said diplomatically. Any of the top guys could win, but she didn't think Sean stood a chance of placing in the top three. She was pleased that he was confident, but he might do better if he put his energy into his mental game rather than spewing it through his mouth. It had gotten tiresome. Yet another concern she planned to address with Dieter.

They watched as the waiter mixed the fresh ingredients of Caesar salad on a cart next to their table. He then carefully dished it up on their salad plates. The sommelier appeared to open the bottle of wine Sean had ordered, pouring a portion for his approval.

"Excellent," Sean said.

As the waiter was filling their wine glasses, Zana noticed Bud Schubert and his wife being seated at a table on the other side of the room. Bud must have sensed her gaze because he looked up, catching her eye and then gave a nod. Once Sandy was settled in her chair, Bud walked over to their table.

"It looks like you're celebrating," Bud said.

"Yes, thanks to you there's a lot to celebrate." Sean held out his hand to shake Bud's.

"That's just what I was hoping to hear," Bud said, patting Haley on the shoulder. "Have you been able to cash in on your celebrity like I'd hoped?"

"We just landed some impressive sponsorship deals. They're bringing a lot of attention to the sport of triathlon," Zana offered.

Sean interjected, "We're buying a house."

"That's fantastic," Bud said. "I'm sure that if Terry were here, he would be so happy. He'd be thrilled that the guy who lent him his goggles at the Wildflower Triathlon was doing well."

Zana noticed Sean and Haley exchange glances.

"We've got a long way to go, but thanks to you two, the television viewing audience is growing."

"Is next week's race in San Diego going to be televised?" Jerry asked.

"You bet it is," Bud said. "We're going to be advertising heavily and another 'Racing in Paradise' episode will be aired mid-week."

"That's great," Sean said.

"I just have one favor to ask." Bud paused and scratched behind his ear.

"What's that?" Haley looked up at him.

"Try to keep your noses clean. I know you don't have control over the paparazzi, but please don't give them anything to write about. Is that fair enough?" Bud asked.

"Will do," Haley said.

Zana saw Sean nod without meeting Bud's eyes.

Chapter Twenty-five

@FreewheelMV Back to stalking. It can be an invigorating workout. #alternativeworkouts #cross-training

Ryan carefully packed his Kestrel 4000 LTD in its case and placed his helmet, bike, and running shoes, a few pairs of swim goggles, caps, running hats, a bike pump, empty water bottles, and his clothes in a duffle bag, which would be picked up by the airline in a few minutes. It would be easier to have some of his gear delivered directly to his hotel in San Diego so he'd only have to bring his backpack on the plane. The extra cost was inconsequential now that he had some lucrative sponsorship deals—thanks to Zana.

The last few weeks had been torturous after his falling out with Alexia. Ryan had made efforts to apologize, but she'd only started accepting his phone calls a few days ago. It wasn't clear why she began answering after she had ignored as many as thirty attempts in one day. He suspected that when he'd stopped calling all together for three days, she missed hearing his desperate efforts. *Did his calling provide her some comfort?* Alexia didn't say what her motive was for finally answering, but he didn't care. He was relieved to hear her voice. He had been so worried about her that he had started driving by her house at night just to make sure her lights were on and her car was in its parking space.

"Hello," Alexia said after answering on the second ring.

"Hi." Ryan smiled. "Are you okay?"

"Yeah."

"I'm leaving for San Diego tomorrow. Is there anything I can do for you before I leave?"

"No. I'll be alright."

"I'm worried about you." Ryan paced the room.

"Thanks."

"If you need anything—anything at all, I want you to call me."

"Okay," Alexia whispered.

"It doesn't matter what time of day or night. I'm here for you."

"I appreciate that."

"Maybe, we can see each other when I get back?" He silently prayed for a yes.

"Maybe."

"Would you like to see me before I leave?"

There was no answer, but Ryan could hear her light breathing so he knew she hadn't hung up.

"I'll call you when I'm in San Diego. Is that okay?"

"Sure."

After Ryan got off the phone, he moved his bike case and duffle bag to the porch. That task finished, he poured himself a glass of iced tea. He felt his body relax as he sank into the sofa and clicked on the TV. He'd been feeling so tense lately that he had been getting daily massages in order to keep his muscles loose enough to work out. Dieter had insisted that he meet with him, or at least call him every day, to discuss his feelings when he'd learned that Ryan had refused to leave his house for a week. Dieter said that if Ryan wasn't a professional athlete he would have prescribed anti-depressant medication.

The beep of a text elicited a Pavlovian response in Ryan. He grabbed his phone, disappointed that the message was from Zana and not Alexia. I **hope you're doing better. Call me.**

"Hey, Zana," Ryan said after she answered. "What's up?"

"How are you?"

"Better. At least Alexia is answering my calls."

"Are you seeing her before you leave?"

"No. She doesn't want to see me." He gulped. "Maybe when I get back."

"Do you think she might be up for a group outing?" Zana asked. "We could get some people together and hike up Diamond Head?"

"That would be great. I'm not sure if Alexia would go for it, though—when I asked her a few months ago, she said it was for tourists and she preferred to work out in the gym."

"We'll give it a try. I'll give her a call."

He sighed. "Thanks, Zana."

Fueled by the hope of seeing Alexia in a few weeks, Ryan knocked out 50 push-ups and 100 crunches on his carpeted living room floor. He suddenly felt the urge to go for a long run, but then heard Dieter's cautioning voice in his head and so consulted his training schedule, limiting his run to 5 miles. It said nothing of the terrain, so he decided to drive to Makiki, run some hills and pass Alexia's tiny house.

As he ran up and down hills, starting from where he pulled his car over to the side of the road near Punchbowl crater, he thought of surprising her with a knock on the door, imagining it leading to passionate love making. After a few minutes of visualizing their naked bodies intertwined, he realized that his endorphins were messing with his grasp on reality. Alexia was so jumpy there was no way she'd answer the door. It was one thing to call her incessantly on the telephone, but his drive-bys had been under cover of darkness. A daytime run by her house could spook her if he was caught, wrecking everything.

Ryan changed directions and headed towards Pacific Heights.

***

Haley was starting to feel tired, slowing her pace so she trailed Sean, who was carrying Nordstrom, Abercrombie & Fitch, Apple, Hugo Boss, Armani Exchange, and J. Crew bags filled with his purchases. She had bought some clothes at Nordstrom, Anthropologie and H&M, but not nearly as much as Sean. She had never seen his energy level as high as when he was browsing racks of shirts, pants, and jackets and trying on shoes—he seemed almost manic.

"Too bad you're not this driven during races," Haley said when Sean turned to see what was holding her up.

"Very funny. Let's put these bags in the car and head over to Neiman Marcus."

"Haven't we done enough damage for the day?"

"Hell, no. I'm just getting started."

Haley's eyes widened. "You're kidding me, right?"

"You can go back to the hotel if you want. I can meet you there for dinner."

"What about our workout?"

"Fuck that. Shopping is my workout today."

"I'll get an Uber." She left Sean to his frenetic shopping spree and headed out of the mall. In some ways, she understood what was going on with him. He had been switching between his two pairs of pants and three shirts for months. Now that they had money, he was determined to build up the wardrobe he'd always dreamed of having. What she couldn't understand was why he had to accumulate *everything* in one afternoon. Since the race was only four days away, this was a critical workout day— their last six-mile run before the race. Dieter had also instructed them to get in a 1,500-meter swim at the YMCA, which was close to their hotel.

The Palm West Coast Hotel, where they were staying, was only a short Uber ride from the mall. Sean had complained loudly when he saw that the accommodations weren't as fancy as he had anticipated, but Haley loved the well-appointed hotel with its small indoor and outdoor swimming pools, a workout facility, and rooms that were far more luxurious than the low-end flea bags where they'd stayed when traveling to attend university swim or track meets.

After Haley dropped her packages off in their room and changed into her running gear, she took the elevator down to the lobby where the concierge showed her an area map and suggested a running route, which he insisted would be the safest and most scenic.

As she waited at each intersection until the walk signal gave her the go ahead, she lamented that the concierge could not possibly be a runner. The route had her spending more time waiting at lights than she was actually running. Her run ended up being a series of sprints from one busy intersection to the next, and so what normally would have taken her 45 minutes took more than an hour.

When Haley returned to their hotel room, she expected that Sean would be impatiently waiting for her, ready to model his purchases. Instead, the room was empty. She had left her phone in the safe, not wanting its weight and distraction during her run. Expecting that there would be messages and texts from Sean, she felt a rush of panic when she saw that he had made no attempt to contact her even once—and it was close to dinnertime.

"Hello," Sean answered on the first ring.

"Where are you?"

"What time is it?"

She looked at the clock next to the bed. "It's after six—aren't we having dinner?"

"I'm at the Cheesecake Factory with some pro cyclists who I met at Starbucks. There's a thirty-minute wait for a table. By the time you get here, we'll be seated."

"Why didn't you call me earlier and let me know?"

"I tried, but no answer."

"I checked my messages. My phone has no record that you tried to call."

"Well, I did."

Haley rolled her eyes. "Who are those guys you're with?"

"Ben and Trent—I'm not sure of their last names. They know Ryan Peterson from cycling in France."

"Enjoy your dinner. I'll stay here and eat. I'll probably swim at the hotel pool."

"If you change your mind and want to join us, we'll be at the Cheesecake

Factory."

"Okay. Watch what you drink and eat—the race is only four days away."

"I will, Haleyville. Love you."

"I love you, too."

After Haley hung up, she called room service to order a chicken salad to avoid eating alone in public—something she had never done before and didn't want to start tonight. She clicked through every channel on TV, finding nothing to keep her mind off of Sean's deserting her for the evening. Ever since they'd moved to Honolulu, neither of them had made their own friends. For the past four months, they had spent every moment together when they weren't working. While they were in college, they shared a group of friends, but also had their own friends—male and female. It was comfortable and fun. As Haley sat at the desk facing the wall next to the TV, eating her first ever room service meal, she decided that it was time for Sean and her to spend some time apart—he needed some buddies and she would have to develop some female friendships.

After dinner, she went for a swim in the outdoor pool, which was heated and lit up so that it made for a pleasant evening workout, despite its small size and the handful of kids squealing and splashing about. She swam laps, dodging the kids like she was negotiating an obstacle course. Strangely, there was a video monitor set up on one end of the pool showing a movie to some guests who apparently were having an event in the outdoor dining area. Haley noticed that some of the men were more focused on her than on the video screen.

After swimming back and forth in the child-filled pool for almost an hour, Haley pulled her swim cap and goggles off and wrapped herself in a large striped hotel towel. She had to walk through the gathering of people milling by the pool. They were drinking wine and mostly ignoring the video screen.

"Hey sexy," a thirty-something man with a neatly trimmed goatee, wearing an expensive-looking suit said as she walked by his table.

"Can I buy you a drink?" another man who had a receding hairline and wore tortoise shell glasses asked.

"No, thank you." She smiled shyly and kept her eyes down. She walked quickly towards the elevator, glancing back at the men who both smiled and waved. The men looked to be well groomed and nice looking—the kind of men she would be attracted to if she wasn't already in a relationship.

When she got back to the room, it was pitch black. She fumbled with the light switch, hoping Sean would be in bed, asleep after a long day of shopping and socializing.

The bed was empty.

Haley sighed, dropped her towel, tugged off her wet swimsuit, and stepped into a hot shower.

She took her time, enjoying the hot water flowing against her body. After being homeless in Honolulu and living at parks for more than a month, she appreciated the luxuries she used to take for granted. Taking a hot shower in private was probably the one thing she had missed the most.

After washing the chlorine off her body, she shrugged on a white terry cloth hotel bathrobe and climbed into the crisp white sheets feeling their coolness. Most people got into their beds at night thinking nothing of their good fortune to have a mattress, sheets, blankets, and a roof over their heads. Haley looked around the hotel room that Sean had scoffed at. It was beautiful and had everything she needed or wanted. It felt luxurious and would've meant everything to her had someone offered the room for even one night when she had only a damp towel to sleep on in the park.

Haley noticed the shopping bags filled with tissue-wrapped clothing piled up in the corner of the room. It was nice to buy new things—especially new underwear that wasn't someone else's cast-offs. She had bought shorts, skirts, and tops that actually fit, and luxurious crèmes for her face and lotion for her hands. She had gotten a mini-makeover at Nordstrom and purchased everything she needed to make her face soft and pretty again. Her makeup bag had been taken with all of their other possessions and so she had gone sans makeup for the first time since she was fifteen years old. It was an eye-opening experience and she understood how homeless women felt. They were exposed in so many ways—showering and sleeping in public, and revealing to the world their bare faces, disheveled hair, and unadorned earlobes, fingers, necks, and wrists.

As Haley lay in bed waiting for Sean to return, she imagined their lives as their fortunes increased. They would be like any other young couple suddenly bringing in more money than ever before—shopping and accumulating stuff would become a pastime. What hadn't been important when they were barely scraping by would fill most of their waking moments. *Who would they become?*

Haley picked up her phone and texted Ryan: I want to help homeless people through the Freewheel Movement. Let's talk soon. —Haley

Chapter Twenty-six

@FreewheelMV I didn't win today, but I aced my drug test. #racingclean

Ryan stepped off the second tier of the podium, followed by third place winner Sam Donahue. Reporters swarmed around Jeff Paris, photographing him holding up his cardboard check for $100,000 and the stuffed unicorn with its rainbow scarf given to the winners of each Terry Schubert Pro Classic Triathlon. Bud had selected the unicorn because his son had always loved them and the rainbow scarf was symbolic of Terry's involvement in the Gay Pride movement the year before his death.

"Jeff deserves it," Ryan said.

"I know." Sam nodded. "He worked harder than anyone training for this race."

"It just shows you that hard work and concentrated effort pays off." Ryan wiped his brow with a white sponsor towel. "I've been distracted and so I'm very happy to have made it to the podium this week."

"Congratulations, Ryan!" Zana said as she walked up, giving him a kiss on his sweaty cheek.

"Thanks!" Ryan beamed. "How does it feel to be the agent to the women's first place winner?"

"I'm so proud of Haley." Zana clapped her hands together. "She barely edged out Megan Alexander on the run. She's trained hard and it shows."

"How did Sean do?" Ryan asked.

"He finished just out of the prize money—eleventh." Zana frowned. "I'm concerned about his focus."

"I'm sure Dieter will whip him back into shape," Sam said.

"You'll have to excuse me." Ryan put his hand on Zana's shoulder. A man with a USADA shirt was walking towards him and gesturing with his hands. It was time for his post-race drug test.

Ryan walked toward the specially designated port-o-potty where a witness would watch him fill a cup with urine. It was probably the least glamorous part of being a pro athlete. Ryan didn't really mind. He was thankful that after his years doping as a pro cyclist that any sport would have him. For several years, he had used EPO, human growth hormones, and testosterone—anything that his shady team doctor recommended to give him the edge to keep his job as a *domestique*. It wasn't like he was a contender for the podium in the three years he ferried food and water bottles to his team leaders during the grueling Tour de France. But he had managed to win one mountain stage—the extent of the glory for which he paid the price of lifetime expulsion and forever having the reputation as a doper.

After his drug test, Ryan made his way back to the awards ceremony just in time to see Haley hold up her $100,000 check and stuffed unicorn for the adoring public and cameras. He and Bud had spent hours strategizing how triathlon could become a big money sport and had hit the jackpot with the golden couple. Despite Sean's poor finish in today's race, the public loved his boy next-door charm. The ratings for Thursday night's show were through the roof and so they had no problem finding big sponsors for the televised race today.

Ryan was hoping to confirm tomorrow's plans to fly to LA with Zana and looked forward to going to his hotel room to crash for a few hours. The media seemed to be far more interested in Jeff Paris and Haley and Sean, giving Ryan the freedom to walk around without having to stop every few steps to pose for a photograph or answer questions into a microphone. It had been almost 30 minutes since the awards ceremony and the media was still swarming around Haley. Zana stood next to Sean, who seemed to be getting more attention than his mediocre finish warranted.

"Zana," Ryan called, hoping she could break free for a few moments.

"Hey," she said, pushing her way through the crowd of reporters towards him.

"What time are we flying out tomorrow?"

"The car will pick us up at eleven-thirty. If you want to ship your bike back, make sure you bring it to the concierge no later than ten," she said.

"Do we have anything besides the Helen Show on Monday?"

"So far that's it. Helen's guests are Haley and you."

"What about Sean and Jeff?"

"Helen wants to talk about Haley's new project."

Ryan raised his eyebrows. "You might want to fill me in on that if it has something to do with the Freewheel Movement."

181

"Sure, I'll e-mail you the details. She wants to donate half of her prize money from this race to provide hot showers, toiletries, and makeup to homeless women through Freewheel."

"That sounds like quite a project. I don't understand why homeless women want makeup, but we can talk about it."

"Good. Are you going to join us for dinner?"

"I don't think so. I'll be ready at eleven-thirty tomorrow. Just text me if there's anything else I need to know." Ryan suddenly felt his muscles relax with the race out of the way. He smiled at the thought of having more than 24 hours until he was obligated to do anything. His first order of business was a nap. His 90-minute massage in his room was scheduled for 2 p.m. If he didn't fall asleep again afterwards, he planned to sit in the hotel Jacuzzi for a while and then eat an early dinner—hopefully by himself. He wasn't in the mood to talk with any of the Hawaii contingent. Maybe, if he called Alexia tonight, she might answer the phone.

Before he could leave the park, Ryan headed to the transition area to collect his bike and racing gear so he could ride the five miles back to the hotel. Just as he was about to show his ID to the security personnel at the transition area entrance, he heard a familiar voice.

"Is that you, Ryan Peterson?" the voice asked.

"Yeah." Ryan turned around and saw two men whom he hadn't seen since they rode on the same pro cycling team in France. Ben and Trent had both testified against him and had been partially responsible for him being expelled from the sport—even though they had been using drugs themselves. As far as he knew, the guys hadn't been caught yet.

"What's going on, Ryan?" Ben asked.

"I have nothing to say to you." Ryan walked into the transition area. He focused on putting his gear in his backpack. He would leave through a different entrance, not wanting to be seen with those dopers who could only sully his reputation further.

***

Zana was excited about flying to LAX. Jerry had arranged to stay at his Marina del Ray condo that weekend instead of flying back to Hawaii so they could spend Sunday night together. She booked the last available first-class seats for her clients, so she had to sit in coach for the short flight.

"You can have my seat," Haley offered, but Zana preferred coach. She needed a break from Sean's excuses for his poor finish and she wasn't in the mood to discuss get-Alexia-back schemes with Ryan. Her middle seat towards the back of the plane was perfect, allowing her clients plenty of time to collect their luggage and be out of her sight until the next morning when they would meet at the studio for The Helen Show. Ryan offered to wait for her, but she insisted he head to his hotel and get some rest.

After she was finally off the plane, Zana ducked into Starbucks to buy a latte and text Jerry that she would be waiting outside of baggage claim in 15 minutes. By the time she made her way slowly to the baggage carousel, only her bag and a few others were making laps around. Just as she was about to reach for her suitcase, she felt familiar arms wrap around her waist.

"Hey babe," Jerry said as he embraced her from behind.

She laughed and turned to kiss him. but caught sight of Neil standing about 10 feet away with a stern look. "I guess we're not alone."

"I'm never alone anymore," Jerry sighed and reached to grab her bag off the carousel. He wheeled it with one hand and held Zana's hand in the other as they walked to the parking garage.

"I'm so happy to see you. It's been a crazy week," Zana complained.

"Me, too. If we didn't have crazy weeks it would be unusual so why don't we just call them normal weeks?"

"Okay, I've had a normal week."

"That's more like it." He squeezed her hand.

"What's our plan this afternoon?"

"Sweetie, remember when we first started dating—we would talk for hours and just enjoy each other's company? It wasn't so much about doing stuff—it was about spending time together."

"I loved that," she said as she climbed into his Mercedes.

"It's a beautiful day. Let's go for a drive. We can walk along the beach—just spend time together—no set plans."

"Perfect."

"Neil will follow us wherever we go. It'll make the day far more interesting for him."

"I'll bet." She chuckled.

Zana fastened her seatbelt and relaxed in the soft leather passenger seat. She wouldn't tell him that this car was more comfortable than his red Ferrari. It was also nice to be in a less conspicuous vehicle in a big city where Jerry wasn't as well-known as in Hawaii. They sat in comfortable silence listening to soft jazz on the stereo as Jerry pulled onto the freeway and headed south. It was sunny, but the sky was hazy.

"I just realized that the haze is smog." Zana looked up at the sky.

"Yeah, it's not like the fresh humid air of Hawaii."

"Would you ever want to live here full-time?"

"No. Oahu is home. I can't imagine living anywhere else," Jerry said as he exited the freeway. "There's a beach where we can walk. We did some filming here a few weeks ago."

183

After they found a parking place, they made their way down a path to the beach where sunbathers lay on colorful beach towels. A few surfers were in the water.

"How do you like living in Marina del Ray during the week?" she asked.

"I don't feel like I really live there, I'm working so much." They walked hand-in-hand down the beach.

"Is that the first place you ever lived, besides the cottage on your parent's property?" Zana couldn't believe she was finally asking him the question that she had in the back of her mind ever since she found out he owned the Diamond Head Tower condo.

"After I graduated from UH, I lived in a condo in Hawaii Kai for a few years."

"Oh?" Her eyebrows shot up.

"My parents convinced me to move back into the cottage."

"After living away from them for a few years, how were they able to talk you into moving back?"

"It's a long story." Jerry had a pained look on his face.

"We've got all day," Zana said gently. It wasn't often that he opened up, and she wasn't about to let him change the subject.

"I was living with my girlfriend at the time."

Zana swallowed hard. *He had lived with another woman? And, he refuses to live with me?* "What was her name?" she stammered.

"Vienna. At that time, living with a woman without being married was still frowned upon. I was twenty-two years old."

"Why did you move in with her?"

"She was older and she said that it didn't make sense for me to live at my parents' cottage when we were spending so much time with each other. I guess I saw it as a way to have my independence. Since I was a law student, I didn't have much money and couldn't afford my own place."

"What did your parents think about the arrangement?"

"They didn't like Vienna. After we broke up, they admitted they didn't trust her." Jerry glanced at Zana through his sunglasses as they continued their walk on the sandy beach. "They told me they were against me living with a woman—*in sin*—they called it. They didn't want me to wreck my life and marry her, so they tolerated our living situation."

"Your mom and dad seem pretty cool. I had no idea that they would be unhappy with you living with a woman."

"They're old-fashioned. They refused to visit me there and so I didn't see much of them during those few years."

"What happened to your relationship?"

Jerry paused, and with his gaze forward said, "I caught her in bed with another guy."

"Oh, Jer. How horrible."

"Yeah, I left one of my law books at home and in between classes, I drove there to get it. I walked in on them."

"What did you do?"

"I freaked out. I yelled profanities and actually threw one of my law books at them while they were in bed." Zana could hear the hurt in his voice.

"Oh, my gosh!" She didn't know what else to say.

"It hit the guy on the shoulder. He jumped out of bed and we shouted at each other until he left. I immediately packed up my clothes and moved back to my parents' cottage."

"Did you ever find out who the guy was?"

"He was our next-door neighbor. Vienna admitted that the affair had been going on for months. The weird thing is, the guy is a camera man and works on the set for 'Fighting in Paradise'."

"Are you kidding?" Zana stopped in her tracks.

"No. I see him quite a bit. We're actually cordial."

She wasn't sure she wanted to know the answer to her next question. "Do you ever run into Vienna?"

"Rarely. She's an interior designer and last I heard she moved to the mainland—that was years ago."

"Did you live with any other women after that?"

He shook his head.

They continued to walk hand-in-hand, but Zana could feel the tension between them. *Had she blown their fun day by asking too much?*

"That was many years ago," he said, breaking the silence.

"Does that situation have anything to do with why you haven't moved in with me at Diamond Head Tower?" Zana gritted her teeth. She was afraid to hear his answer, but she needed to know.

"No." He stopped and pulled her close to him, and looked deep in her eyes. "I don't want to live with you until we're married."

Chapter Twenty-seven

@FreewheelMV So proud of #ProTriathlete @Haleyville for her contributions to homeless women. Way to pay it forward!

Alexia rubbed her temples, feeling a headache coming on after spending an entire afternoon clicking through more than 1,000 pages of medical records on her computer. The case didn't involve anything gory—just the run-of-the-mill neck and back soft tissue injury—except that the plaintiff had quite a few concurrent medical conditions which made her question whether there might be some other reason for his persistent complaints.

She found a bottle of Aleve in her desk and took two pills with a swig from her water bottle before shutting down her computer. She was looking forward to a relaxing evening at home. Zana texted her last night that Haley was going to be on The Helen Show and she remembered to record it on her DVR. Her evening plan was to eat dinner while watching the show.

Alexia was hooked on the new reality show, "Racing in Paradise", featuring Zana's new clients. Haley was adorable, and her smile lit up the television screen. She was nothing like so many other smug athletes and spoiled young celebrities. She seemed so vulnerable, capturing her heart with the intensity of her brown eyes, her sweet voice, and her love for Sean—the sexy boy next door. Alexia had tuned into the first show with little interest, but quickly became fascinated by the drama of the young couple's homelessness and anxiously awaited the first Terry Schubert Pro Classic Triathlon to see if they would win enough money to put a roof over their heads. After the first race, it seemed like everyone was talking about "the Golden Couple". They suddenly appeared on Youtube videos and commercials promoting everything from cereal to cars.

When Alexia got home, she heated a small bowl of vegetable soup in the microwave—leftovers from the night before—and made herself comfortable in front of the TV to watch Haley's interview with Helen. Alexia nearly dropped her soupspoon when she saw Ryan sitting next to Haley instead of Sean. She turned up the volume and listed to the interview.

Helen: "Haley, how does it feel to have won the Terry Schubert Pro Classic Triathlon on Saturday?"

Haley: "I'm so happy."

Helen: "And, you won a few dollars, right?"

Haley giggled: "Yes, you're right."

Helen: "And, Ryan—you were the big loser. You placed second."

Ryan: Helen, I'm very happy to have placed. My competition was stiff."

Helen: I'll bet they were. Haley, I understand that you have some plans for your $100,000 prize money."

Haley: "I do. When I was homeless, it was so rough living on the beach. I could only take cold showers while wearing my bathing suit and I didn't have any shampoo or conditioner. I just had a bar of soap. My self-esteem suffered so much, because I always felt grubby. When I looked in the mirror, I hardly recognized myself. I looked hideous."

Helen: That's hard to believe."

Haley: "It's true, Helen. I'm finally able to afford makeup and face cream—the kind of things most women who have a roof over their heads take for granted. Just being able to look my best and feel clean has made all the difference in the world."

Helen leaned towards her guest and sniffed: "You do smell nice."

Haley laughed: "I decided to donate $50,000 to be used to buy makeup, lotion, shampoo, conditioner, soap and hot showers for homeless women. It will help them feel clean and better about themselves. I'll be doing this with Ryan's help through the Freewheel Movement."

Alexia watched Ryan as he described the concept of the Freewheel Movement, explaining that it was being used to help homeless, isolated, and many other people in need. He added that it was assisting women who are victims of domestic violence, which struck a chord with her. Watching Ryan's enthusiasm for his charity reminded her that despite his recent unwelcomed interference in her life, he was actually a good guy with a big heart. She had become accustomed to distrusting men, and when he'd gotten too nosey, she instinctively cut him out of her life.

As she watched him, she couldn't help but admire the intensity of his brown eyes when he told Helen about his work. His smile was slightly crooked, but he had a boyish dimple in his left cheek. Even though he was wearing a navy sport jacket with a blue-and-white striped shirt and grey slacks, his six foot body had the fluidity and grace of a well-toned athlete.

After the show, Alexia tried to focus on the novel she was reading, but felt a gnawing sensation in her gut. Her mind kept thinking of Ryan.

She checked her phone, but the last time he called was Saturday night and she hadn't felt like answering. She was somehow frozen in place and couldn't reach the phone in front of her on the coffee table. She watched as Ryan's picture appeared and the "Eye of the Tiger" ringtone played. If she answered the call, she might have to acknowledge that she still had feelings for him, despite every effort she'd made to shut him out of her mind and heart.

A tear slid down her cheek. Since she'd been in Hawaii, Ryan was one of the only people she'd spent any time with outside of work. She'd let him kiss her, make love to her, see her naked and know the truth. *Should she run away again? Or could she trust him?*

Alexia stepped into the bathroom and splashed cold water on her face. Her reflection in the mirror showed a thin blonde woman with bright blue eyes, a straight nose, rosy cheeks and white teeth that few people saw, because she seldom smiled. Her feelings about herself didn't match her outside image. She had heard people compare her to Charlize Theron, Julianne Hough, or Heather Locklear in her youth, but she felt more like one of the popular chubby comedic actresses. Stan had always called her a fat cow and had even made "moo" noises when she entered a room. Now, it was easy to exercise at least two hours a day and restrict calories, but it was impossible to eliminate her insecurities and fear. When she saw Haley on TV, there was something vulnerable about her that reminded Alexia of herself. Haley's eyes had a familiar fearfulness that she could relate to.

Alexia picked up her phone, and after staring at it for at least five minutes, she asked Siri to call Ryan.

The phone rang three times so she wondered if she should leave a message or just hang up. When he answered on the fourth ring, she was almost too surprised to say anything.

"Hi Alexia," Ryan said.

"Hi."

"Are you okay?"

"I'm fine." She was feeling overwhelmed with shyness. She hadn't thought out what she was going to say to the man she was feeling pangs of love for.

"Is there anything I can do for you?"

"Uh, do you still want to walk up Diamond Head?"

"Yeah. Are you up for a hike when I get back?"

"Sure."

"I'm flying back tomorrow morning. We could go as soon as you get off work or another day. Whatever works for you."

"Tomorrow. I'm off at three-thirty. Can Zana come, too?" Zana had texted her about hiking Diamond Head. If his agent went with them, the topic of Stan wouldn't come up.

"Sure, I'll ask her. I'll pick you up at three-forty-five."

"Ryan…"

"Yes."

"You did well on *The Helen Show* today."

"Oh, thanks."

***

Haley had been to Los Angeles for swim meets and a few triathlons, but had never been to Disneyland. As soon as the filming for the show was over, she and Sean climbed into their rental car and headed to Anaheim to visit Mickey and the gang. Even though Sean had finished out of the prize money the day before, she was surprised that he was in an upbeat mood, excited to go on some rides and spend the day relaxing. They had gone for a short run in the morning, but otherwise it was a well-deserved rest day, sanctioned by Dieter himself.

"What did Dieter say about your race?" Haley asked Sean as he was driving towards the next exit.

"I haven't talked to him yet."

"Oh, I thought you were on the phone with him while we were filming this morning."

"No, I was talking to Ben, one of the pro cyclists I met in San Diego."

She placed a strand of hair behind her ear. "Since you were on the phone for so long, I was sure you must be talking with Coach."

"Ben and Trent live in LA and were hoping I could stop in to see them while we're here."

"Too bad that won't work—we're leaving tomorrow."

"Our flight isn't until one. I should be able to meet them in the morning."

"Really?" she said, and then remembered her desire that they each spend time with friends. "Okay, if you want to meet them, I can work out."

"Why don't you get a ride to the airport with Zana and Ryan. I'll meet up with the guys and see you at the airport."

"Sure." At least she'd be able to talk about her victory. With Sean, she didn't feel comfortable saying anything.

"Sounds like a plan." He smiled.

By the time they got to Disneyland, the park was hot and crowded. They waited in line for the rides they had heard about their entire lives—Pirates of the Caribbean, Haunted Mansion, Space Mountain, Jungle Cruise,

Matterhorn Bobsled, and Big Thunder Mountain Railroad. After munching on a dinner of hot dogs and French fries—foods forbidden by Dieter, Haley convinced Sean to go on one more ride—It's A Small World. When he didn't complain and held her hand during the entire ride—seemingly enjoying the dolls coming to life, Haley decided she'd never been happier.

"We should probably get back to our hotel," Sean said after the ride.

"Yeah, it's late. We didn't get to go on the Indiana Jones Adventure."

"No biggy. It'll be here next time we come."

It was past midnight by the time they returned to the hotel and Haley could barely keep her eyes open. Sean offered to carry her to their room, but she said she could manage.

She couldn't remember ever feeling so tired that she didn't have the energy to wash her face. She managed to brush her teeth, but didn't bother to take off her makeup or change into her nightgown before diving into bed next to Sean, who was wide awake and channel surfing.

The next morning, Haley woke to sunshine streaming through the window.

"Sean," she called, assuming he was in the bathroom.

When he didn't answer, she glanced around the room and saw that his suitcase was gone and he'd left a note on her nightstand.

Haleyville,
I'm meeting up with Ben and Trent for breakfast. I'll meet you
at the airport. Please get a ride with Zana and Ryan.
Love, S

Haley smiled at the note. Sean seemed so happy to have new guy friends, which probably took his mind off his poor performance in Saturday's race. Ordinarily, he would lapse into a bad mood when she outperformed him, but he seemed optimistic about his future. It was already 8:45 and so she'd need to give Zana a heads-up that she needed a ride. She texted both Zana and Ryan.

Ryan texted back: **Meet us at the hotel coffee shop at 9:30.**

With only 45 minutes to pack and shower, Haley jumped out of bed. She had to scrape off the make-up she'd been too tired to remove the night before. It was 9:35 by the time she walked out of her room.

"Good morning." Ryan looked up from a menu. "Where's Sean?"

"He's having breakfast with some guys and is going to meet us at the airport," Haley said, taking a seat.

"That's strange."

Haley shrugged. "Not really."

"You're in a city away from home and he ditches you to hang out with some guys. Why didn't he invite you to join them?"

"Sean and I have been spending every minute together for months. This is the first time he's made his own friends. I'm encouraging it."

"How did he make friends in LA in two—"

"Good morning," Zana said, interrupting Ryan as she joined them at the table. The waitress was approaching to take their order. "I'll have an egg white omelet with broccoli and coffee, please."

"That sounds good. I'll have the same." Haley put down her menu.

"Make it three," Ryan said.

"I'm sorry to interrupt," Zana said, holding out her cup as the waitress filled it with coffee.

"I was just asking Haley how Sean had made friends in LA in only a few days," Ryan said.

"He met the guys in San Diego." Haley stirred honey and milk into her coffee. "They're pro cyclists. He said that they knew you, Ryan."

"Come on, seriously? Don't tell me that he met Ben and Trent." Ryan made a face.

"Yeah, that's who he's with."

"What's wrong with them, Ryan?" Zana asked.

"They're bad news." He sighed. "Sean needs to stay away from them."

"Why?" Haley asked.

"You, of course, know why I'm no longer a pro cyclist." Ryan sipped his coffee. "Those guys testified against me at my doping hearings."

"I can see why you don't like them." Haley looked away from the table, worried about Sean.

"We were on the same team and we all used the same doctor. Don't you get it?" Ryan stared in her eyes. "They used as many drugs as I did, and as far as I know, they're still doping."

Zana's eyes widened. "Are you saying that Sean is hanging out with guys who are using performance enhancing drugs?"

"Yeah, I am. Knowing those guys, they're probably selling drugs to Sean as we speak."

Haley clenched her hands under the table.

Chapter Twenty-eight

@FreewheelMV Want to buy a knitted bicycle seat cover? I've got a connection. #CrazyTriathletes

Ryan positioned his lower back close to the Jacuzzi jet so it felt like a massage after the long flight from Los Angeles. The hot water was soothing not only to his body, still a bit sore from Saturday's race, but also to his spinning mind. Zana was sitting across from him in the outdoor Jacuzzi at Diamond Head Tower. She had suggested that before they pick up Alexia for their hike they enjoy a relaxing soak and talk about "a few things"—code for Sean's recent sketchy behavior.

On the flight back to LA, the *turn off electronics and fasten seatbelts* announcement was made seconds before Sean rushed in, sweating and out of breath. "You look like you ran faster to make this flight than you did in the race," Ryan had joked.

Sean wore sunglasses the entire flight and barely said a word. Haley was equally as quiet and asked to switch seats with Zana so she could "cool off" a few rows behind her boyfriend.

Now, back in Waikiki, Zana moved a few inches closer to Ryan so she wouldn't have to shout over the Jacuzzi jets. "Should we tell Dieter?"

"About what?" he asked.

"Sean's meetings with those dopers."

"It doesn't prove anything." Ryan smirked. "Who knows? Maybe the guys are getting together to knit."

"Yeah, I can definitely see them crocheting bike seat covers." Zana laughed. "Maybe Dieter can talk some sense into Sean."

"If Dieter thinks Sean is doping, he'll kick him out of his training program. End of story." Ryan adjusted his position so another portion of his back was pummeled by the Jacuzzi jet. He closed his eyes behind his sunglasses.

"What do you think? Is he doping?"

Ryan lifted a shoulder in a half shrug. "After his poor performance at Saturday's race, if he is, it's not working."

"Haley said that he just met the guys in San Diego. Maybe he was connecting with them this morning to pick up some drugs."

"Hard to tell. We'll have to wait and see. Do you know if Sean is subject to drug testing by Dieter?"

"I don't think so," Zana said. "Sorry to say—I think you're the only athlete he tests."

Ryan winced. "That figures. Maybe we should just keep an eye on him for now."

"Do you mind having a talk with him? Maybe, if he hears your story, he'll think twice about going down the wrong path."

"He knows my story. I had plenty of people have talks with me and I didn't listen to any of them. I was only interested in keeping my job on the team and terrified of the embarrassment if I failed."

"Sean is under so much pressure to succeed." Zana paused. "He went from complete obscurity to world-wide fame in a matter of weeks and now he probably feels desperate to live up to the hype."

"Maybe, but Dieter can counsel him on those issues."

"He already is, Ryan."

"One of my worries is that if Sean is exposed as a doper, all the work that's gone into making triathlon a big money sport will be for naught. The weight of the sport truly is on Sean and Haley's shoulders. I'd hate to see everything crash down on them, impacting all of the pro triathletes." Ryan lifted his torso out of the bubbling water and sat on the side, still soaking his feet and calves. "I hope you don't think I'm being too selfish by saying that."

"Not at all. It's absolutely true."

Ryan thought for a moment. "I think I need to have a talk with Ben and Trent."

"Are you sure that's safe? They sound shady."

"They're as shady as they come. One of the conditions of my being able to compete in triathlon is that I stay away from characters like that."

"That takes that option off the table. As your agent, I don't want you conversing with them."

"Hmm, you're right. Maybe there's someone else who can have a stern word with them." Ryan slipped back into the bubbling water to think about it. "I bet Bud Schubert knows people with the power of persuasion. I'll ask him."

***

"I'm embarrassed to say that I've never hiked up Diamond Head," Alexia said as Ryan helped her into the backseat of Zana's SUV. She gave him an awkward kiss on the mouth after he hugged her, and noticed his face flush.

"You're in for a treat," Ryan said brightly. "It's a decent workout with more than one hundred stairs to climb. The reward is a magnificent view."

"We're going to play a little game today. The one who spots the craziest shoes worn by a tourist wins." Zana looked at Alexia through the rearview mirror as she drove towards Waikiki.

"Do tourists wear Jimmy Choos?" Alexia asked, not sure what she was getting into.

"Close. I don't think they realize that Diamond Head's hundreds of stairs will give their feet blisters unless they're wearing athletic shoes."

From his spot in the front passenger seat, Ryan turned to look at her. "You'll see. It's ridiculous."

Alexia smiled as she gazed out the window. It was always so much fun to get together with Zana. They had started out as work colleagues when she was the adjuster on the Brad Jordan case. Gradually, they became friends after meetings over coffee, lunches, and a few gym workouts. Zana had encouraged her romance with Ryan, which seemed to cement their friendship. Alexia was so determined to protect her secrets that she made every effort to keep people out of her life. But Zana had become a close friend—not close enough to disclose her true identity and abusive past, but close enough to share the details of her life as Alexia Moore.

"You're awfully quiet back there, Alexia," Ryan said.

His comment jolted her out of her thoughts. "I'm enjoying the scenery. I've never driven in Waikiki as a passenger before."

"Have you seen anything new and interesting?" Zana glanced at her.

"Yeah. I didn't realize the sidewalks were so crowded. Look at the long line in front of The Cheesecake Factory," Alexia said. "Oh, there are old men playing chess in that covered picnic area by the beach."

Ryan pointed out the open window. "And look—there's a beach volleyball competition on your right. See the boys jumping off that jetty into the water?"

When they stopped at a red light, Alexia took a picture of the scene with her phone. "I feel like a tourist. When I moved here, I immediately started working and never got a chance to wander around Waikiki or visit any tourist attractions."

"We've both missed out," Zana said. "I'm embarrassed to say that I've never been to Pearl Harbor. Does that make me a bad person?"

"I've never been there, either," Alexia said.

"You're both bad people," Ryan glared at them and then grinned. "That was the first place I went when I moved here. I'm shocked. If you had mentioned that earlier, there's no way I would have gotten in the car with either of you. You call yourself Americans?"

Alexia laughed. It was probably the first time she found something laugh-out loud funny for months. It felt good to be out with her friends, doing something other than working out in a gym, eating rabbit food as Ryan called it, reading magazines or watching TV. Maybe it was time to enjoy life a little. Hiding for almost eight years felt claustrophobic.

"Why are you parking here?" Alexia asked when Zana pulled into a parking lot next to the white church adjacent to Kapiolani Community College. "This isn't Diamond Head."

"We're going to hike from here. It makes it more challenging." Ryan helped Alexia out from the backseat.

"You triathletes—you're such overachievers. You train in three sports and still make your tourist hikes extra hard."

"You should talk." Ryan grinned, showing off the dimple in his cheek. "The woman who works out every day without ever taking a break."

"Are we going to hike or run?" Zana asked. "What do you feel like today?"

"I think we should hike and let Alexia soak in the whole experience." Ryan draped his arm lightly around Alexia's shoulder.

"I'm up for anything." Alexia smiled at Ryan. His touch felt electric. She wanted so much for him to pull her into his arms and kiss her, but knew that before this could happen they would have to finish the hike and talk about continuing their relationship. He was obviously uncomfortable with her marital history and identity. She wondered whether it was time to let go of some of her fears and embrace who she'd become.

"Let's get going," Zana said, grabbing her water bottle from the backseat.

Alexia followed Zana with Ryan behind her as they walked from the parking lot to the street. As they waited for the cars to pass, Ryan grabbed one of Alexia's hands and then grabbed Zana's hand before they ran across.

"You can't be too safe," he said when they made it to the other side. He dropped both of their hands and pulled out his water bottle tucked in the back of his shorts. He then skipped a few steps—*Wizard of Oz* style.

Alexia laughed at Ryan's antics.

They climbed up the steep hill to a tunnel while cars whizzed past them on the road.

"Is there parking up there?" Alexia asked as they walked single file through the dark tunnel.

"Yeah, just beyond the kiosk," Zana shouted to be heard over the cars. "The park closes at six so if you don't have much time, you can park up there and get through the hike in a half hour or at the most forty-five minutes, depending on how fast you are."

"This is a good workout already." Alexia was breathing hard.

"Just wait," Ryan said.

They continued to walk in single file, almost hugging the tunnel wall.

"Be careful," Ryan cautioned.

Alexia followed close behind him, keeping her hand on his back—as if he was guiding a blind person. Once they exited, they walked on the shoulder of the road and could hear each other again.

"How often do you come up here?" Alexia asked.

"About once a week." Zana took a swig of water from the bottle she was carrying.

"I only get up here a few times a month, but it's great fun. A nice change from my ordinary routine."

"There's sure a lot of tourists," Alexia said as they approached the kiosk. Ryan paid for all three of them and then they started on the cement path that would take them to the top.

"It's a must-see for visitors," Zana said as they hiked behind a group of eight tourists from Japan. She silently pointed at one of the women's kitten heels.

"Oh, my gosh," Alexia squealed.

"You ain't seen nothin' yet," Ryan said. "Let's pass them."

He picked up his pace and led Alexia and Zana past the big group. They had open space on the pathway for a couple of minutes before they found themselves behind a family all wearing "Fighting in Paradise" T-shirts.

Ryan tried to pass, but one of the kids stepped in front of him, almost causing him to fall. Looking back at the women, he shrugged his shoulders and waited until the family compressed against the right side of the path before he tried to get by again. When he was able to, he moved quickly so Zana and Alexia could follow close behind.

Alexia was enjoying the rhythm of the hike. They took the steps fast until they got stuck behind a group, and then once they passed the people, they would pick up the pace until they reached another bottleneck. Either Ryan or Zana usually led. Alexia was content to follow close behind.

As they turned a corner, Alexia became separated from her friends, who had passed a couple trying to encourage their young son up the mountain. The three were taking the entire path and Alexia didn't want to be rude and push past them.

She noticed the little boy had dark, wavy hair and a kid-sized Seattle Seahawks jersey. She smiled at the reminder of the city where she was born and raised. She didn't miss the rain, but she desperately missed her parents and her two brothers.

The little boy glanced back at her and Alexia smiled at him, causing him to laugh and turn away shyly. The mother and father took up the entire width of the path, seemingly oblivious to blocking her.

Alexia noticed that the mother was wearing gold sandals with thin straps and a one-inch heel. She could see that with every step, the straps were digging into the mother's feet and causing red marks. Alexia wondered why the woman kept walking when she was obviously in pain.

"Walk faster," the man said harshly to the woman.

Alexia immediately recognized his voice and her heart hammered in her chest. Her first instinct was to run away. And fast.

She couldn't pass them and when she turned around, the group of Japanese tourists and an even larger group behind them were blocking the entire path back down.

Stan turned his head to look at the woman who Alexia assumed was his wife, and recognized his scowling face, reddening with anger and impatience. His wife cowered, looking miserable and trapped—a feeling Alexia remembered well.

Suddenly, a family walking in the opposite direction pushed past Stan's trio, causing him to turn sideways to let them through. When he turned, his eyes focused squarely on Alexia.

She froze, wondering if he recognized that behind her dark sunglasses was the woman he had threatened and beaten so viciously she'd fled to Hawaii to acquire a new identity.

"Daddy, I want a ride," the boy said, shifting Stan's attention to his son. He scooped the child up in his arms and looked away from her.

"Alexia," a male voice shouted, startling her until she saw that it was Ryan who had ran back down the mountain. Alexia didn't want to say a word for fear Stan would recognize her voice. She grabbed Ryan's hand and pulled him with her, running as fast as she could, past Stan and his family. They wound their way up the dirt path, up a steep spiral staircase and into a small cement room.

"Ryan," Alexia pulled him to a stop. She felt like she was going to pass out, she was so out of breath.

"Are you okay?"

"That guy with the yellow shirt and black hat is Stan Finnegan."

"Oh, shit!" Ryan embraced her and spoke softly, "Did he recognize you?"

"I'm not sure. He looked straight at me."

"What do you want to do?"

"I don't want Zana to know."

"I could text her that we went down the mountain and to meet us at the car."

"That would work, but how are we going to get past Stan again?"

"There are two routes to the top. We could head down the other way, and if we see him going that route, we can turn around and head down the way we just came."

"Whatever we need to do is fine. I have to get away from him *now.*" Tears were running down her face, her heart felt like it was beating out of her chest, and she was having a hard time catching her breath. She felt her body crumple underneath her.

"Alexia, I'm here. Are you okay?" Ryan was kneeling by her side.

She nodded, and he helped her up.

She squeezed Ryan's hand as he led her up a few steep stairs out of the cement room. They sprinted down a dirt path, and there was Zana, waiting for them while texting on her phone.

"It's about time you made it. Come up, I'll show you the view." Zana smiled.

"Alexia wants to run down as fast as possible," Ryan said. "She's not comfortable with heights."

Alexia was still holding Ryan's hand as she broke into a run down the outside staircase. They ran down about 20 steps when she saw Stan's yellow shirt. He and his family were making their way up towards them.

Not wanting him to hear her voice, Alexia tugged Ryan's hand and motioned him to turn around.

"You're going the wrong way," Zana said loudly.

"Alexia wants to get a better workout." Ryan quickly changed directions, running behind Alexia back towards where they'd come from.

The three ran up to the cement room, where they lowered themselves so they could go down the interior spiral staircase and then down another steep staircase and into a dark tunnel. The cave-like tunnel was packed with people walking in both directions. Alexia felt her heart racing and sweat drip down her face. It was like being trapped in an MRI machine.

They were forced to slow to a shuffle with Alexia in front, then Ryan and Zana. Ryan put his hands on Alexia's waist as they moved forward with the tide of people through the tunnel. When they emerged from the darkness, Stan and his family were standing five yards in front of them on the narrow path. He looked directly at them and said, "What the fuck are you doing? Following us?"

Ryan stepped in front of Alexia and said, "No, dude." He then turned to let Alexia move forward and created a barrier between her and her tormentor.

Alexia took off as fast as she could down the mountain. She heard footsteps behind her and ran faster, intermittently feeling her feet slide on the gravel. Even with her increased pace, she couldn't lose the person on her tail until she pushed past a group of Japanese tourists. This gave her time to see the person's face. It was Zana.

Alexia was relieved it wasn't Stan, but slowed her pace only a little.

Soon, she heard Ryan call to them from behind. They continued to run on the lower switchbacks of pathways through the obstacle course of tourists down to the upper parking lot. Zana stopped for a moment to rest, but Alexia ran past her, down the road and didn't stop until she reached the entrance tunnel to the park. She paused, wiped the sweat dripping down her forehead and caught her breath while she waited for her friends to catch up.

As soon as Ryan and Zana reached her, Alexia raced through the tunnel, staying close to the wall to avoid oncoming cars. She ran across the road to begin her descent down to the lower parking lot. She could hear their footsteps behind her as she reached the bottom of the hill.

Ryan grabbed her hand as they crossed the busy trafficked street, before sprinting to Zana's SUV in the church parking lot.

"That was a killer workout," Zana said. "I thought we were going to hike up the mountain and spend some time at the top enjoying the view."

Ryan drank from his water bottle. "That was the plan."

"Anyone up for Jamba Juice?" Zana asked.

Alexia shook her head. She put her hands on her knees and leaned over. She was having a hard time catching her breath.

"Are you alright?" Ryan asked.

Alexia could feel her chest tighten again. If she hadn't had panic attacks before, she would have been sure this was a heart attack.

"Let's get you in the car," Ryan said, opening the backseat door and helping her in. "Do you want to go to the hospital?"

Alexia shook her head vigorously. She leaned against the backseat, tears streaming down her face. Ryan wiped her tears with his fingertips, his body blocking Zana's view.

"Do you want me to take you to Kailua?" Ryan whispered in Alexia's ear.

"Yes," Alexia whispered. She didn't feel comfortable going home while Stan was on the island.

"Everything okay?" Zana asked.

"Yeah. She'll be fine. I think she overdid it today," he said. "You can take us to my car. I can drop her off."

Alexia was relieved they were going to Ryan's house where Stan would never find her. The vision of his new wife walking up the mountain had stayed with her. The poor woman wearing sandals digging into her feet at his cruel insistence reminded her of the time when he'd made her dress in a thin sweater, jeans, and tennis shoes without socks. He had suddenly decided they should drive to the mountains to see the snow. Stan was dressed warmly and had a coat, hat, and gloves in the trunk. He'd made her go for a short hike without a coat in freezing weather and completely ignored that she was shivering uncontrollably. When she complained and insisted on going to the car, he'd slapped her hard on the mouth and threatened to leave her there in the wilderness.

Alexia stared out the window as Zana drove slowly out of the parking lot and onto the road.

She waited at the stoplight for traffic to clear so she could take a right onto the road that would lead them towards Kapiolani Park and Waikiki. After about a block, the roadway expanded so there were two lanes going each way, and a black Ford Taurus passed them on the right. The traffic light at the intersection ahead turned red and they stopped next to the Taurus, which Alexia thought looked like a typical rental car. She then noticed the driver was wearing a yellow shirt. It was Stan.

She inched down lower in her seat as the tears fell silently on her cheeks.

Chapter Twenty-nine

@Haleyville They say "Birds of a feather flock together". Is that true of dopers? #HopeNot

"You're looking strong," Dieter said as he stood between Haley and Sean as they pedaled spinning bikes.

"Thanks, I've been working out hard." Sean kept his head down.

"I can see that. You're getting muscles on your muscles," Dieter commented in his heavy German accent.

Ordinarily, Haley would have found Dieter's words amusing, but she wasn't at all impressed with Sean's newly sprouted muscles, his improved energy, or his faster split times that Coach had praised. They were gearing up for the next Terry Schubert Pro Classic in Salt Lake City next Saturday, and the following weekend they'd race in Colorado Springs. They wouldn't be coming home to Honolulu for another five weeks as they flew from city to city, getting used to courses, posing for photo shoots and filming commercials during the week.

Haley knew the truth. He hadn't been following Dieter's training regime at all, but had been slacking off for the first time since she'd known him. Sean now preferred to watch TV or read a magazine rather than run or bike, yet magically appeared more fit and strong. She had rifled through his bathroom cabinets when he'd stepped out to do an errand, but had come up empty. There were no signs of pills, syringes, or drug bottles.

One morning, she had flat-out asked him if he was doping. He had looked at her with what she thought was a mixture of hurt and surprise and said, "Absolutely not."

He had probed her about why she'd asked. "I was just wondering," she replied. She didn't tell him about her conversation with Ryan and Zana about his new doper friends.

"Will Ben and Trent be in Salt Lake City?" Haley asked Sean as they turned on lights in their new million-dollar home after their evening session with Dieter.

"I have no idea," Sean said. "Why does it matter?"

"Just wondering."

He paused and put his hand on her arm. "You've been acting strange lately. Is there something that you want to tell me?"

"Not at all. I was just making conversation."

"Okay." Sean flopped onto the couch with the remote control in hand. "Did Zana give you our travel itinerary?"

"Not yet. How are you feeling about the race?" Haley asked, assuming he'd be even more cocky than usual if he were using performance-enhancing drugs.

"Not bad. We'll see," he said in the most defeated tone he'd ever used when talking about a competition. "How are you feeling?"

"Good. If I place in the top five, I'll be thrilled."

Haley suggested they watch a movie on Netflix so they could relax and think about something other than the upcoming races. She felt more pressure than usual and wondered if it wasn't better to place second or third. First place was too stressful. Everyone expected her to perform well and that took away some of the joy of the sport.

"Does triathlon feel like a job to you?" Haley paused the movie with the remote control and turned towards Sean lounging next to her on the couch.

"Yeah, a job that I don't get paid much for."

"You get paid a lot by sponsors," she said.

"That's true, but the races have lost something since the stakes got so high."

"I wonder if Roger Federer or Serena Williams ever feel that tennis isn't fun anymore."

"Well, if they do, they can count their money. I'm sure that makes them feel better." Sean put his arm around Haley.

"Is money what we really want from the sport?"

"Sure. We all want big bucks. That's every kid's dream—to become pro ball players and cash in."

"Yeah, I guess you're right."

"I think it was a pro basketball player who said something like, I'm tired of all the talk about money. I just want to play, drink Coke and wear Nike."

Haley giggled and threw a sofa pillow at Sean that he deflected with his arm.

"Don't forget how lucky we are not to work our day jobs anymore. We have this big new house and get to do what we love. Few people can say that," Sean said.

"True. It's all happened so fast, Shay. Sometimes, I wish things would slow down a little so we could enjoy ourselves."

"If we had regular full-time jobs in offices, life would be busy, too."

Haley sighed. "Yeah, but we would be home and have evenings and weekends to ourselves."

"That's not necessarily true. A lot of people have to work at night and on Saturdays. What used to be forty hours of work has now become sixty hours, not to mention always being available by cell phone and e-mail."

"You'd think life would have gotten easier with all of these gadgets. I guess we're lucky to get to swim, bike, run and smile for cameras for a living." She gave him her best imitation of a glamorous movie star smile.

"They say the grass looks greener on the other side. Haleyville, I know we're busy, but please try to appreciate our new life. This is what we've always dreamed about having."

"I will. I wish my mother and brothers and sisters could visit us."

"Send them plane tickets. I'm sure they'd love a Hawaii vacation. We have plenty of room."

"Maybe during the off season—I want to at least be here when they visit."

Haley clicked the movie back on, and as she laid her head on Sean's chest, she tried to forget her worries. He laughed out loud at the silly scenes in the movie that she thought were stupid, but she enjoyed hearing the sound of his laughter. At least he seemed happy.

***

Ryan didn't want to leave Alexia by herself, but he had no choice but to get on a plane headed for Salt Lake City. He gave himself no extra time to become familiar with the course or to adjust to the hot, dry weather and elevation, planning to arrive the day before the event. He had never been so late arriving to a pro race site—especially with big money at stake. After seeing her ex-husband, Alexia had calmed down and had even adjusted her routine of staying with him at his house and commuting from Kailua to downtown for work, but she still seemed fragile.

"Do you want to come to Salt Lake City with me?" Ryan asked a few nights before he was leaving.

"To tell you the truth, I haven't traveled outside of Hawaii since I moved here," she said.

"It's time you got a change of scenery."

"It's not a bad idea, but it's too late for me to ask for time off from work."

"Our next cities are Colorado Springs, Chicago, and Miami. If you want to take a trip, I don't mind flying with you both ways, if it will make you feel more comfortable."

"I'll think about it. I'm feeling much better now that your detective reported that Stan left the state and has returned to Seattle. I'll move back into my apartment while you're away."

"I really enjoyed having you here, sweetie."

"It has been nice." Alexia smiled. "Ry, I know I'm not easy to be around because of— Well, I just want you to know—"

Ryan pulled Alexia into his arms and whispered into her ear, "What do you want me to know?"

"I love you," she whispered into his ear.

"I love you, too," Ryan said in a voice louder than a whisper. She had never said those words to him before, even though he had told her many times how he felt about her. She was finally opening up and becoming more relaxed.

Since she'd been at his place for a few weeks, she had actually skipped a few workout sessions in favor of sleeping in and indulged in a barbeque chicken dinner he had made one night. She even enjoyed a small portion of German chocolate cake—beaming with each bite she ate. When she discovered that she didn't immediately turn back into overweight and frumpy Elaine Finnegan, she relaxed the rules a bit.

"Did your rescuers ever say that after so many years you could live a less rigorous lifestyle?" he asked.

"They never put any limits on the rules and I've never seen or talked to them since."

"In view of the fact that your old identity is technically—uhm—no longer living, can't you become who you want to be? Can Alexia create a life that is her own?"

"Hmmm. I guess so. I hadn't really thought about it that way." She paused. "I think you're right."

"I would love to see you enjoy your life. Wouldn't it be fun to do as you pleased? From what you've told me, while you were growing up, your dad imposed so many rules on you that you felt trapped, which led you to marry Stan at a young age. You went from being controlled by your dad to being controlled by your husband."

"That's true."

"I will never try to control you, Alexia. I want you to find out what you love about life and live exactly how you want to. I want you to feel free, my love. I hope what you want to do is be with me, but if there is something else that would make you happy, I hope you find it."

"I'm happy with you." She smiled broadly and looked into his eyes.

"I hope you didn't stay with me only because you were trying to escape

Stan."

"Partly, but I really missed you," Alexia said softly.

"Can we take up where we left off?"

"What do you mean?"

"Being a couple." He didn't know how to describe what they had never before defined out loud.

"I hope so." She grabbed Ryan's hand and led him to the bedroom.

***

It had been months since Zana had made time to get together with her girlfriends, Moana and Shelby. The three used to train together almost every day before Zana joined Dieter's training program in order to rub elbows with the pros. As she sprinkled some parsley on the baked Ono she was preparing, she heard a knock at the door.

"Nice digs." Moana gave Zana a hug. "Security is really lame. We came right up."

"I e-mailed the night security team your names and pictures of you," Zana said.

"So you mean they were comparing us to the pictures?" Shelby hugged her friend.

"That's right. You were watched on cameras the moment you entered the property until you walked inside this condo."

"Creepy," Moana said. "What's cooking?"

"Your favorite fish recipe." Zana wiped her hands on a dish towel.

"I thought you would order something from a restaurant and tell us you cooked it," Shelby said. "Is that what you did?"

"No. I've actually learned to cook since I've lived here. If you spent more time with me, you'd know that I spend a fair amount of my days reading recipes."

"You do not." Moana giggled. "I need a drink."

Zana had already opened a chilled bottle of 2011 Stadlmann Gruner Veltliner and began filling three wine glasses.

"Zana's telling the truth. Every time I call her, she tells me about a new recipe she's discovered. Next thing you know, she'll be cross-stitching kitschy sayings on pillows and wall hangings or growing Chia pets."

Zana chuckled. "It's amazing how a little free time changes someone's life," Zana said, raising her glass to her friends. "Here's to girl's night."

"Yeah, girl's night." Shelby laughed, clinking her glass in a toast.

"We should really be toasting Zana's phenomenal success as a sports agent," Moana said. "Are you still bringing in the big bucks for your clients?"

"They've been doing well." Zana grinned. "I'm flying to Salt Lake City tomorrow."

"Why would you go there? They don't serve wine," Shelby said.

"It's changed a lot since the 2002 Winter Olympics. You can order wine in restaurants," Zana explained. "I'm going there for the third race in the Terry Schubert Pro Classic series. Three of my clients are racing."

"You mean all three of your clients?" Moana raised her glass.

"Yeah—I've got three. But they keep me busy," Zana said. "I have to fly to the mainland for five races in a row for the next five weeks—the races are on Saturdays."

"What about the sexiest man alive—or, should I say, the Cool Cat?" Shelby asked.

"You mean Jerry?" Zana took a sip of wine.

"Have you not seen the Sexiest Man Alive Issue of *People Magazine*?" Shelby reached in her bag and pulled out the magazine issue with Chris Pine on the cover. "I picked it up at Long's today."

"Chris is a sexy guy. What does he have to do with Jerry?" Zana glanced at the magazine in Shelby's hand.

"Look at page seventy-eight," Shelby said, handing the magazine across the black lacquer dining table to her friend.

Zana opened it and quickly found the photograph of Jerry posing on a beige fur rug with his two Siamese cats, Ming and Miko, lying on his chest. Jerry's gaze into the camera was unmistakably sexy. The feature was entitled, "Cool Cats" and showed other stars—Ian Somerhalder, Gilles Marini, Norman Reedus, Max Thieriot, and Ricky Gervais posing with their beloved pets.

"You didn't know about this?" Moana asked.

"I had no idea," Zana frowned. "My boyfriend is smokin' hot."

"Yeah, that's a sexy picture. I'm sure cat-loving women all over the country will have the magazine turned to this page on their nightstands," Shelby said.

"I hope Annabelle doesn't see it." Moana raised her eyebrows.

"I'm not worried," Zana said. As much as she cherished her close friends, she recognized their tendency to dramatize every little thing about the men they dated. When Jerry and his choreographer were spending so much time with each other in Brazil, Shelby and Moana had fueled Zana's jealousy, causing her many sleepless nights. Ordinarily, Zana would have defended her relationship, citing examples of Jerry's devotion to her—she would tell them about gifts of long-stemmed red roses and romantic love notes. This time, Zana felt power in keeping their intimate bond private.

As Moana and Shelby flipped through the magazine, Zana savored thoughts of Jerry's recent hints about marriage. She was looking forward to her upcoming five weeks on the road with her clients and flying to Los

Angeles to see Jerry for several days each week between races—using his condo as her home base. He had even bought a desk and leather chair for her so she would have her own work space while he was busy with filming at the studio. She was looking forward to running along the beach and exploring Marina del Ray's shops. She could even pop over to Starbucks in the afternoons for a latte.

"You look deep in thought," Shelby observed. "I hope I didn't upset you by showing you this article."

"Not at all. It's a gorgeous picture." Zana grabbed it out of her hand. "I may even frame it."

"You'll have to get your own magazine. You know how I feel about Chris Pine." Shelby took the magazine back and put the cover with her star crush's picture close to her face. "Don't we look like the perfect couple?"

"Yeah, maybe Jerry and I can go on double dates with you and Chris," Zana said, getting up to pull the baked fish out of the oven. "I hope you're hungry."

Zana heard the beep of a text after she dished up the fish, sautéed green beans with almonds, and saffron rice on three plates.

It was from Jerry. Take a look at People. Ming, Miko and I are Sexy Cats! Can't wait to see my favorite Zana-kat. I Love You, J

"Who texted you?" Moana asked.

"Nothing important," Zana told them, but inside she felt butterflies. She spent the rest of dinner thinking about the secret text.

Chapter Thirty

@ZLaw Sometimes I'm sentimental about my days slaving away at my law firm—dodging briefs hurled at me by a senior partner. #Sigh

Zana took a double take. *Was Sean really passing Jeff Paris?* She checked her list of race numbers. Number 22 was assigned to Sean, and he had passed number 1 on the run with 100 yards to go.

The announcer said, "And Ryan Peterson is the winner of the Salt Lake City Terry Schubert Pro Classic Triathlon! Sean Bennett follows in second place!"

Zana checked to see if Dominic and his cameraman were capturing this huge upset. Yup, Dominic hustled to the finish line so he would be in position to interview Sean. Sean had proven himself, and his fans would be atwitter about their favorite triathlete reality star.

Zana edged closer so she could hear the interview.

"How does it feel to win fifty thousand dollars in prize money?" Dominic pushed the microphone to Sean's face before he was able to take a sip of the water bottle he accepted from a volunteer.

"Wonderful. I'm very pleased with this outcome. It was a close race." Sean smiled into the camera, his dimples as explanation points.

"Why do you think you've improved so much?"

"Years of hard work." He shrugged. "It's finally paying off."

"Have you heard how Haley's doing?"

"Not yet. Do you know?" Sean glanced at the finishing line.

Zana expected Haley to be in the top three. She watched as Dominic cut the interview short when he heard the announcer mention the women's race. His cameramen were in place at the finish line and so he jogged the

100 yards down the road for a good vantage point.

The first female runner appeared—Megan Alexander, followed by Brenda Jackson with Trisha Brady on her heels.

Where is she?

Zana searched for Haley, but couldn't see her.

When Haley finally ran through the arch with the race's title sponsor's Buddy's Bike Shop logos plastered all over it, she was in a disappointing 13th place. She shrugged her shoulders for the camera, grabbed a bottle of water from a volunteer and took a long swig.

"What happened out there, Haley?" Dominic asked, putting the microphone near her mouth.

"It wasn't my day." She wiped some sweat from her face with the back of her hand.

"Did you have any problems on the course?"

"A few flat tires—some bad luck." She winced.

"Did you know that Sean came in second place?"

"No. Really?" She raised an eyebrow.

Watching Sean's unexpected podium finish caused Zana's stomach to twist into knots, and she felt the beginning of a headache. *Were their suspicions right and Sean was doping? Did she have an ethical obligation to report on him? If so, to whom?* Donald had assured her that without any solid evidence that Sean was cheating, Zana had no obligations whatsoever. He had suggested she keep a close eye on her client and steer him in the direction of clean and fair play.

"Sean, great job," Zana said with little emotion after Sean's interviews were over. She noticed that her client looked to be in much better shape than he was when he was rushed to the medical tent after the San Diego race.

"Thanks," he beamed.

"What's your secret? » She probed. « You've improved so much."

"I listened to Dieter—I didn't over-train for a change."

"Haley mentioned that you've been relaxing and watching TV instead of training."

"I highly recommend it."

"Did you get drug tested?" she asked.

"What do you mean?"

"They're doing random drug testing here. Didn't you know that?"

"I thought they were only testing Ryan," he said, an edge to his voice.

"In the triathlon federation races, they test all the athletes. Since this race is new, there's only one person doing the testing and so it *is* random." Zana watched for his reaction. "That will probably change very soon."

"Okay, good to know, I guess." He was wearing sunglasses, so she couldn't see his eyes.

"Are you concerned about that?"

"No. Should I be?"

He sounded defensive. Zana backed off. "Just wondering. If you ever need to talk with me about *anything*, I'm here for you."

"Okay, sounds good." He looked at his feet for a moment and then said, "I'm going to find Haley."

She watched him walk away. There was nothing about his appearance that made it obvious he was using PEDs. She wondered if his explanation that he hadn't over-trained plausibly explained his second place finish, or was he using steroids, human growth hormones, EPO, or something else? She'd been so busy negotiating with sponsors and coordinating five weeks of appearances, photo shoots, filming, and racing schedules that she hadn't had a chance to research the drugs she suspected Sean of taking.

Zana noticed the medical tent was virtually empty save for a single IV connected triathlete sprawled out on an army cot.

"I can't see my phone screen in the sun. Do you mind if I stand in the corner of your tent in the shade for about five minutes and take a look at the Internet?" she asked a nurse who was sitting in a camp chair in front of the tent.

The nurse nodded. "It's okay as long as no one else comes in."

Zana stood close to the edge of the tent and focused on her Google search of anabolic steroids, learning that they might cause a man to develop prominent breasts, baldness, shrunken testicles, infertility, and impotence. Other possible symptoms were severe acne, increased risk of tendinitis and tendon rupture, liver abnormalities and tumors, negative impacts on cholesterol, high blood pressure, heart and circulatory problems, prostate gland enlargement, aggressive behaviors—rage and violence, psychiatric disorders and some other problems. It was like a drug commercial on TV. Zana sighed as she studied the list more carefully. Most of the side effects would not be visible and he probably hadn't been using the drugs long enough to cause anything observable.

She typed in a search for human growth hormones. They could cause joint pain, muscle weakness, fluid retention, carpal tunnel syndrome, cardiomyopathy, high cholesterol, diabetes, or high blood pressure. So far, it looked like Sean would need to submit to a medical exam and have diagnostic testing in order to detect any such problems. Even with a thorough medical evaluation, side effects could have other causes and it would be difficult to identify illicit drug use without urine and blood testing. She'd hoped her Internet search would yield information on how to visibly assess whether her client was doping so she could confront him. Even if he complained of joint pain or had a few zits, she wouldn't be able to reasonably connect those to performance enhancing drugs. Knowing Sean, he'd blame other potential causes—his joint pain was from vigorous training; his pimples were from those potato chips he ate the day before.

"You're going to have to leave, Miss," the nurse said, gesturing to a few athletes with road rash who had limped into the tent.

"No problem." Zana slipped her phone in her pocket. "Thanks so much."

She spotted Ryan talking with some other athletes and headed towards him. About 30 yards away, Sean was being interviewed by a reporter with Haley watching.

"What's going on?" Ryan asked, turning away from the athletes who he'd been talking with.

"How long before the awards ceremony?" she asked.

"A few minutes. You look upset."

"We can talk about it later."

"I'm sure I can guess. You're wondering how Sean could have possibly placed in second place. Am I right?" he asked, lowering his voice so no one could overhear.

She nodded.

"There's absolutely nothing you can do, Zana. If he's doping, that's his problem."

"But—I'm his agent."

"So what? Unless you're sticking needles in his butt or force feeding him pills, what Sean does is his business."

"I need to have a talk with him."

"Believe me, Sean won't listen to a word you say. If he's clean, he'll deny any allegations. If he's using, he'll be in denial. You can't win."

She took a deep breath. "Isn't there anything we can do?"

"Wait and see. If he's clean, there's nothing to worry about. If he's not, he'll get caught eventually. He'll be kicked out of triathlon. Maybe he can get his barista job back."

"What about the sport?" Zana asked. "Sean has become the face of triathlon and has attracted so many sponsors. No offense—but if he's exposed as another Ryan Peterson, fans will promptly lose interest and we'll be back where we started."

"True," Ryan said. "Before Sean gets caught red-handed with the EPO jar, we should probably find another sexy, young male triathlete to take his place."

"It was Haley and Sean's rags to riches story that caused loads of people to tune in to triathlon for the first time. All of you guys have six pack abs and sexy smiles. The public wants more. They want the vulnerability the golden couple brings to the screen, which inspires them to buy cereal, toothpaste, and running shoes."

"And condoms."

"You saw Sean's ad for Smooth?"

He chuckled. "How could I not? It's on every bus in Los Angeles."

"Let's just hope he's clean," Zana said softly as she watched Sean talk into a reporter's microphone.

"Yeah, the future of big money professional triathlon depends on it."

***

Haley and Sean were seated near the window enjoying a stunning view of Utah's Wasatch Mountains. They were munching on carrot and celery sticks from a crudité plate instead of the creamy artichoke dip and fried calamari Sean wanted to order. After Haley's poor finish, she'd talked him into adhering to the rules—for her sake. So, instead of enjoying champagne to celebrate Sean's second place victory, they toasted with their iced tea glasses.

"I wish we could celebrate like normal people," Sean complained.

"You mean by drinking champagne and eating rich food?" Haley munched on a celery stick.

"Exactly. We now have all this money and we can't even buy the most expensive bottle of wine on the menu."

"That's probably a good thing," she said, smiling at her boyfriend. His brown hair was disheveled from when he pulled off his sweatshirt and he was staring at her with his hazel eyes that looked brown in the light. She felt fluttering in her stomach for the first time since they'd graduated from college. The feeling reminded her of when they first met and couldn't get enough of each other. They'd become inseparable and called each other their soul mates. Gone were her fears about doping—at least for tonight.

Sean broke the spell when he spoke. "They have the most amazing filet mignon and prime rib here, and we're eating baked halibut with vegetables."

"There was a time not long ago when we were lucky to have peanut butter and jam sandwiches for every meal."

Sean winced, then sipped his iced tea. "Well, if you put it that way, we don't have much to complain about. At least we can have sorbet for dessert."

She shook her head. "Too much sugar. The waiter said he'll bring fresh strawberries and blueberries." Haley didn't like being the dessert police, but with Sean's sweet tooth she usually stepped into the role.

"Only four more races to go and then we can enjoy our new swimming pool and Jacuzzi."

"Assuming we don't blow it like I did today." She cast her eyes downward, not wanting Sean to see her disappointment.

"It was a fluke. You don't get flat tires very often, and rarely more than one." He reached for her hand. "You'll do better next time."

"I hope so. How does it feel to move up the ranks?"

"I'm loving it. I wish I could lie naked in my fifty thousand dollars."

Haley laughed. "Sweet."

"You know what it's like, Hayleyville," Sean said. "It's so weird that the money is just pouring in. It was only a few months ago when we were counting our pennies at the thrift store and debating about how much fifty cent used underwear we could afford."

"I'm wearing a pair tonight."

"No way. That's disgusting."

"Yeah, I'm just kidding." She laughed. "I went to La Perla and bought shopping bags of new thongs and other delightful sexy bits of naughtiness."

"Check please," he raised his hand. "I'm not sure if you should be talking that way *before* our entrées."

"I'll save it for later." She winked.

"Back to the money—we have a ridiculous amount of sponsors. I can't even get my head around how much money is coming in. Can you?"

Haley took a sip of iced tea and wondered what he would say to her next question. She'd been stewing over this so much she was losing sleep. She opened her mouth and then closed it before she could speak.

"Were you going to say something?" Sean said.

She felt her heart racing. "You can say no if you want."

"To what?"

She closed her eyes and said what was on her mind. "I'd like to buy my mother a house."

"Sure—go ahead. That won't even make a dent."

"I can't wait to see her face when I give her the key." Haley looked out the window at a hawk flying in the distance.

Chapter Thirty-one

@Haleyville A beautiful resort, a four-poster-bed and a Jacuzzi with a TV. What more can a formerly homeless girl ask for?

Haley stood in awe at the reservations desk at the Broadmoor, the famous 5-star resort where she'd never dared dream to stay during her four years as a poor student. When she traveled to Colorado Springs for college swim meets, the team stayed at a Holiday Inn close to the airport, spending some of their down time visiting the famous resort frequented by movie stars and athletes since it was built almost a century ago.

While Sean was handling check-in, Haley studied the history of the resort on framed pictures on the walls.

"We *booked* a suite," Sean raised his voice.

"We have you in a very nice corner room with a view of the lake with a king bed," said the young woman whose nametag read "Betsy".

"That's absurd. Put us in a suite."

Haley turned away from the photographs to stare at Sean, who was leaning over the reservation desk, his face red with anger. He had always been so patient with people and never seemed to care what hotel room they booked as long as it had a big bed. Now, Sean was berating this polite young woman with a demand for a suite Zana would never have booked for them. As their agent, she insisted they not be extravagant and had suggested they save money by staying at the Cheyenne Mountain Resort instead of the expensive Broadmoor.

Since both Sean and Haley had always dreamed of staying at this resort, Zana had been easily persuaded, but reminded them that this was a special treat and their accommodations would return to three and four-star hotels for the remainder of the season.

"Honey, let's just take the room we're assigned to," Haley interjected.

"I want a suite." He slammed his fist on the counter, startling Haley and the woman.

"I'm sorry sir, as I said, there are no suites available," the woman said in a slightly louder, but still polite voice.

"Can I assist with anything?" a man with a gold "Manager" badge asked as he approached them.

"Everything's fine. We'll take the room." Haley grabbed the small folder with the plastic key cards, put her hand on Sean's arm, and led him away from the desk.

"I want a suite," Sean said loudly.

"I know, sweetie," she whispered. And then in his ear, she said, "I really want a regular room. It's more cozy to make love in."

Her words seemed to calm him. They followed the bellman, whose expression told her that he had overheard her whispered promises. The bellman's cart was piled high with their bike cases and luggage, which he pushed towards their room located in an adjacent building.

"This is a great location, if you plan on using the spa and gym facilities," the bellman said.

"Perfect." Haley smiled and squeezed Sean's hand. Now that he'd calmed down, she could take in the beautifully landscaped grounds as they followed the bellman.

They rode up the elevator a few flights to their corner room with its four-poster bed and view of the lake. A large Jacuzzi tub separated the bedroom from the vanity and shower, and Haley noticed a second flat screen TV in the bathroom that could be viewed from the large tub.

"This is heaven," Haley said as she gave the bellman a generous tip.

As soon as he left, Sean grabbed her by the waist and pulled her onto the bed, kissing her roughly and yanking down her shorts. He wasn't usually this aggressive, but she appreciated the added excitement and went along with it.

Their clothes were strewn about within seconds. Soon he was inside her, pounding with vigor without any of their usual gentle foreplay. Haley felt squished lying under him. His sweat dripped onto her body and he let out loud, animal-like grunts.

Usually, when they made love, his eyes would lock on hers. As she felt him push firmly inside of her, they would make quiet sounds of pleasure together that would gently escalate for as long as they could hold out. This time, he was closing his eyes tightly and seemed to be in his own world, oblivious of her needs. Within minutes, his animal noises became guttural, his sweaty body stiffened, and he collapsed on the bed away from her.

Haley felt frustrated by his oblivion to her needs and left him sleeping on the bed. She headed to the bathroom, filling the Jacuzzi tub with hot water and the resort's lavender bath salts. She turned on the bathroom flat screen to a cooking reality show, and as soon as the tub was full, stepped in to enjoy the pressure of the jets against her body. She closed her eyes and willed herself to fully relax, but couldn't stop ruminating about Sean's sudden changes in behavior.

He must be doping. He had inexplicably gotten second place in Salt Lake City, beating Jeff Paris and so many other guys who were much faster swimmers and cyclists. He'd blown his top at the front desk of the Broadmoor for no logical reason, and he was so aggressive in bed she'd hardly recognized him. The only way his uncharacteristic behavior made sense is if he was using drugs.

After she soaked in the tub for the remainder of the cooking show, she toweled off and slipped on her running gear. With another race on Saturday there was no way she was going to miss her workout even if Sean was dead asleep.

She texted Zana. **Meet me for a run in 15?**

Her plan was to get in a warm-up and then, hopefully, pick up Zana.

It was late afternoon and still stifling hot, but that didn't matter to Haley. In order to properly prepare for the race, she'd have to run in the worst conditions and get used to this high altitude quickly. As she'd hoped, Zana—in her running bra and shorts—was waiting for her in the front lobby.

"How's Ironman training going?" Haley asked as they fell into step together.

"Not well. With all of this travel, I'm finding it hard to get any long bikes and swims in."

"Yeah, tell me about it."

"Where's Sean?" Zana asked.

"Sleeping."

"I'd think he'd be concerned about getting a run in today."

"Apparently not."

Zana slowed her pace. "What's going on, Haley?"

"I'm sure he's using."

"Did you find something?" Zana's eyes widened.

"No."

"Then, how do you know for sure?"

Haley turned her face towards Zana's and slowed to a jog. "Let's just say that gentle, patient Sean has become a 'roid raged pig."

"Are you sure?"

"I wouldn't say this if I wasn't."

"This really sucks," Zana said as they ran side-by-side along the tree-lined street.

"Is there anything we can do to help him?"

"I don't know. I've been talking to Ryan about our suspicions, but he seems to think that Sean will have to lose everything before he'll stop."

"Can't Ryan convince him to stop? It's not like this has been going on very long."

"No," Zana said. "He refuses to intervene, because he said it doesn't work."

The women ran silently for a few minutes and then Zana said, "He's afraid that if it's publicized that Sean is a doper, sponsors and the public with lose interest in triathlon. Everything Bud Schubert has worked for on behalf of his son will be destroyed."

"That's probably true. I'd rather go back to being broke than have Sean win prize money because of drugs." Haley felt tears well in her eyes.

"I'll talk with Ryan again."

***

"Directions to Colorado Springs Airport," Ryan said loud enough so Siri could hear.

"Finding directions for Colorado Springs Airport," the computer voice from his iPhone said.

Ryan was concerned that he might have gone a little overboard with his cologne in his excitement to pick Alexia up at the airport. When he woke up this morning, her text read: Taking the red eye. Will be in Colorado Springs at 2:27 p.m. tomorrow. Pick me up at airport?

She called him from LAX early in the morning and said, "I miss you. We need to talk". If she hadn't flown all the way to Colorado and hadn't prefaced her words with "I miss you," he would have assumed it was a bad news "we need to talk." He couldn't help but wonder if Stan had found her and she had quickly left the state in order to escape him again. He would have to wait and see.

Ryan looked over his shoulder after he parked his car. He wondered if Stan might be following him. He shook his head at the grim thought. Ryan headed for the baggage claim area where he popped into the bathroom to wash off some of the cologne. He didn't want Alexia to smell him before she descended the escalator into the area beyond security, and he certainly didn't want her to acquire a cologne-induced headache that might interfere with his plans for romance back in his hotel room later.

The baggage claim area was virtually empty, save for a few stragglers picking up identical black 20-inch suitcases that had been circling the carousel over and over again. He watched the owners visibly relax when they spotted their bags. He was so caught up in the reunions between bags and owners, he didn't notice Alexia until he felt her arms wrap around him from behind.

"Sweetheart, you made it!" Ryan gushed.

"Finally." She kissed him with a passion he'd never before felt from her.

"Where did that come from?" he asked softly.

"That's how I greet my boyfriend."

"Your boyfriend, eh?"

"Yeah."

He closed his eyes and breathed in her fresh scent. His knees felt weak. He pulled her in closer.

After holding each other for a few more minutes, they slowly pulled away, but kept their arms around each other—their hips touching.

"Do you have any luggage?" he asked.

"One bag." She took Ryan's hand and they made their way over to the empty carousel assigned to her flight, now surrounded by waiting passengers.

"I thought you didn't want to come to the mainland," Ryan said, watching a line of suitcases spilling down the metal chute.

"I changed my mind."

"How did that happen?"

"There's my bag." She pointed to a generic looking black suitcase.

"Are you sure?"

"Yeah. See the pink agriculture sticker? I don't think there were many people on my LA to Colorado Springs flight from Hawaii," she said.

Ryan snatched the black bag off the moving carousel and placed it on its wheels.

"I'm anxious to hear your story about why you changed your mind," he said, then realized that he'd probably spend the next few days pleading with her to open up. If Stan was the reason, he needed to know now so he could protect her.

They walked hand in hand along the sidewalk leading to the parking area. "I'm no longer Elaine Finnegan," Alexia said in a voice that was louder than he expected. She had guarded her secret for so long, Ryan was surprised at her statement made in public even though there was no one within listening distance.

"That's progress."

"I finally realized that Elaine Finnegan was the old me. She took Stan's abuse and was afraid of a world bigger than her small three-bedroom rambler and the cubicle at the bank where she worked," Alexia said as Ryan opened the rental car's trunk and placed her suitcase carefully inside.

"A few nights ago, after a particularly crazy day at work, I drove home, did my usual workout and then stayed inside with the curtains pulled. I ate the same boring salad."

"Uh huh," he listened as he opened the passenger door for Alexia and helped her in.

"I realized that the only difference between being in the Seattle home and living in Hawaii was that in Seattle, Stan physically hurt me."

"Have you seen him?" Ryan asked after he positioned himself in the driver's seat. He wasn't completely sure he understood what she was explaining, but he did know that if he ever saw Stan go near his girlfriend, he might kill him—or, at least hurt him very badly.

"No, I haven't seen him again. What I mean is, that in Seattle, Stan controlled my every move. I couldn't go to the grocery store without permission. I realized that the habit of having Stan control my life hadn't changed with my new hair color, body, or location. He's been controlling me from the minute I took on a new identity. My name may be different, but my heart is still the same."

"Has your heart changed—" Ryan paused, not sure if he should finish his question.

She gave him a reassuring smile.

"Has you heart changed towards me?" he asked.

"Yesterday, instead of getting up at four a.m. to work out, I decided to sleep in. When I finally woke up, it was almost seven. I didn't have time to flat iron my hair or put on much makeup or I'd be late for work. I actually put my frizzy hair in a ponytail."

"I'm sure you still looked beautiful," Ryan said focusing more on what Alexia was saying than where he was driving. He hadn't wanted to interrupt by asking Siri how to return to The Broadmoor.

"The weird thing was that when I went to Starbucks, I didn't even get hit on. I felt invisible."

"Did anyone say anything to you at work?"

"They asked me if I was sick—almost everyone."

"What did you tell them?"

"I didn't say anything, but Caron told me to take the day off. I think she thought I'd infect the other employees—with my dowdiness."

"I'm sure you didn't look *dowdy*."

"Not as dowdy as Elaine Finnegan. Maybe a little more like a relaxed Alexia."

"Do you mind if I ask why you decided to fly to Colorado?" Ryan glanced at her and then managed to miss the exit he remembered seeing on the list of directions to the resort.

"I went home and realized that all I ever do is work, exercise, and eat rabbit food. I was bored."

"Okay. Well at least you must find me more interesting than sitting around the house."

"I missed you, Ryan."

"You did?"

"Yeah. Caron thinks I'm sick. I was able to get a decent airfare online and so here I am. Are you okay with that?"

"More than okay." Ryan realized that his not paying attention to where he was driving was now directing them to Denver. "I'm going to have to pull over and figure out where we are. I don't think this is the right direction."

He took the next exit, taking a right into a strip mall parking lot with a Panera Bread restaurant, a Supercuts, and a Burger King.

"There's a Panera. Shall we get salads?" Ryan asked, parking the car.

"I'm in the mood for a Whopper."

Ryan laughed and pulled her close.

Chapter Thirty-two

@ZLaw Triathletes don't have one-track-minds. They have three-track-minds: #Swim, #Bike, #Run.

Zana would ordinarily feel like the fifth wheel, tagging along to dinner with two cozy couples, but she hardly gave it a thought tonight as she pulled on a jersey knit black dress she had rolled up in her suitcase just in case there was occasion to wear something more elegant than a track suit or jeans. When they traveled for races, they seldom went out for a nice meal, preferring to dine on steamed fish or broiled chicken and vegetables delivered by room service or prepared in the most casual restaurant on the hotel premises. Tonight was special. She had managed to peel Ryan off of Alexia long enough to discuss her concerns about Sean, and together they'd hatched a plan with the assistance of a scientist at the United States Olympic Training Center nearby. The dinner was part of their scheme.

"I'll scooch over." Haley moved to the middle of the backseat, so she was sitting between Sean and Zana. They were on their way to the restaurant with plenty of time to make their 7 p.m. reservation. Alexia sat up front with Ryan, who was driving.

"Where are we going?" Sean asked.

"The Blue Moon Restaurant." Ryan maneuvered the car past a limo parked in front of the Broadmoor. It looked like a bridal party was pouring out of the back. Three young women wearing identical burgundy silk chiffon dresses with matching burgundy pumps, and several men wearing black tuxes and burgundy cumberbunds were whooping and hollering, apparently on their way to the reception.

"Why aren't we eating in the hotel?" Sean asked.

"Change of pace." Zana glanced over at him. "Aren't you bored of hotel

221

food?"

"Yeah, but isn't a nice restaurant kind of a waste?" Sean's voice sounded whiney.

"Their chicken breasts might taste better." Haley put her hand on her boyfriend's knee.

Ryan glanced in the rearview mirror at Sean. "We can watch Alexia eat."

"Yeah, right. A salad with dressing on the side." Zana laughed.

"You never know—Alexia might surprise you." Ryan winked at his girlfriend.

The restaurant was close by and, after making a few wrong turns, Ryan pulled into the cramped parking lot. Zana noticed that Alexia and Ryan seemed to be in their own little world, holding hands, stealing kisses and staring into each other's eyes. She felt like she was intruding on their time together, but their plan to confirm that Sean was doping took precedence.

A hostess immediately escorted them to a table close to the open kitchen in full view of the chefs at work. Zana and Alexia waved off the waiter's invitation to order drinks in deference of the pro athletes who Dieter prohibited from ordering anything stronger than water with lemon so close to the race. Their coach even instructed them to ask for lemons on a side plate for fear of illness-causing bacteria from the rinds. Even small errors in judgment could mean the difference between winning $100,000 and nothing at all.

After they selected their bland dishes, the five chattered on for a few minutes about the upcoming race, discussing unique elements of the course and the anticipated weather on Saturday morning. The men debated whether to wear wetsuits, and in the end, decided it would be a good idea even though the race rules made it optional.

"You're making triathlon seem like a lot of fun." Alexia smiled at Ryan, and he moved his chair closer to hers.

"Have you ever considered doing one?" Haley asked.

"You're so fit." Zana poured balsamic vinaigrette on her small dinner salad. "I'm sure you'd have no problem competing."

"I'll think about it," Alexia said. "I'm not much of a swimmer, but I rode my bike everywhere when I was a kid, and of course, anyone can run."

"There are some decent beginner triathlon training groups in Honolulu." Ryan took a bite from his cup of minestrone soup. "There's a Women's only group and several others that would be perfect. It depends on your preference."

"Let me think about it. I'm getting a little bored with my gym workouts." She winked at her boyfriend. "It would be nice to get outside and train with other newbies."

"If you start competing in triathlons, you can become obsessed like all of us." Haley smiled.

Alexia rolled her eyes. "That is the one thing holding me back. From my observation, triathletes have one-track minds and never feel like they've trained enough."

"You've obviously been hanging around with this guy too much," Sean punched Ryan lightly on his upper arm.

"Oh, come on." Ryan put his other arm around Alexia. "I do have a one-track mind, but it's focused on my beautiful girlfriend."

Zana nodded. "See, triathletes can think about other things besides training."

"Not me. Hey, wouldn't it be fun to run up Pike's Peak tomorrow?" Sean asked.

"That's far too strenuous so close to the race." Zana's eyes widened. She tapped Ryan's shin with her foot under the table.

"Okay, coach," Sean said sarcastically.

Ryan exchanged looks with Zana, turned to Sean and said, "We're going to the Olympic Training Center tomorrow morning."

"What for?" Sean raised his eyebrows.

"Some testing." Zana looked down at her almost empty salad plate.

"What kind of testing?" Sean began bouncing the table with his shaking knee.

"VO2 Max." Ryan steadied the table with his hands.

"I've done that before." The intensity of Sean's knee bouncing increased. "There's no reason to do it again."

"Dieter's orders," Zana lied. She didn't want their coach to know the test results for fear he'd kick Sean out of the program. Ryan had talked a friend who was conducting a VO2 max study with Olympic athletes into testing them and keeping the results confidential. Since he was testing athletes all day, it wasn't any problem for him to add Sean, Haley, and Ryan to his schedule.

"We're testing at altitude," Ryan explained.

"Can we ride our bikes to the training center so we can get a workout?" Haley asked.

"I don't see why not." Zana relinquished her empty salad plate to the waiter. "I'll ride with you. I really need to get a long ride in." She'd brought her bike with her, hoping to get some training rides in. She'd gotten behind on her Ironman training with so much travel.

The waiter placed the fresh Alaskan salmon special with a baked potato in front of Zana. He delivered sauce-less versions of the salmon special to Ryan, Haley, and Sean, who were also eating baked potatoes with a sparse amount of butter and extra vegetables. Alexia had ordered a filet mignon,

223

but she seemed to be monopolizing the breadbasket.

Zana noticed that Sean was quiet throughout dinner. He occasionally jumped into the conversation and laughed at one of their jokes, but seemed a bit moodier than usual. She also noticed that Haley and Sean's body language didn't even suggest they were a couple. Their chairs were far apart and they seemed to be avoiding eye contact. She hoped the 'roid rage Haley mentioned earlier hadn't turned into abuse.

***

The next morning, Ryan, Zana, and Haley straddled their bikes wearing bright colored bike jerseys as they waited for Sean to run back into the hotel to use the restroom before they rode to the United States Olympic Training Center. It was a clear, sunny morning and already warm enough for short sleeves.

"I'm surprised he's going through with it," Ryan said quietly, not wanting Sean to overhear should he return.

"He was really quiet after dinner." Haley fiddled with her bike computer. "He went to sleep immediately after we got back to our room."

Zana turned to Ryan. "Are you sure your friend is trustworthy?"

"Absolutely. He knows what's at stake." Ryan didn't feel the need to tell Zana about Jake's doping history. Jake had been a *domestique* on his cycling team in France when Ryan was singled out for using drugs. If Ryan hadn't been caught, Jake would have continued on the same path. Instead, Jake cleaned up his act and won a few stages of the Tour de France. He'd accumulated enough money to go back to school and earn his PhD. His research on VO2 max and Olympic athletes had landed him a job at the training center.

"Who knows what's at stake?" Sean asked approaching the group.

"Dr. Feldman. He'll be doing the testing," Ryan said quickly, hoping Sean wouldn't guess they'd been talking about him. "I told him about the prize money."

"Let's get going." Sean mounted his bike.

Ryan clipped into his pedals and sprinted ahead. He had studied a map of the area and had planned their bike route. He glanced over his shoulder to make sure the others were following. Haley was directly behind him, then Zana, and Sean was taking up the rear.

Ryan rode slowly through the tree-lined streets, stopping at every stop sign until they made their way down the base of the mountain and were able to pick up speed by riding on the side of a highway. The traffic wasn't too bad and so Ryan sunk down onto his aero bars and picked up speed. He sensed that Haley was on his back wheel and focused on his cadence and body position all the way to the training center. As he turned into the parking lot, he stopped at the security kiosk with Haley and Zana behind him.

"We're here to see Dr. Jake Feldman," Ryan said to the security guard, who picked up his phone to make a call.

"Where's Sean?" Haley asked. They'd stopped their bikes in the parking lot near the entrance.

"I don't know." Zana turned to look down the road. "I was trying to keep up with you guys. Remember, I'm not as fast."

Ryan looked down the street in the direction they'd come but didn't see him.

"We probably dropped him. Maybe he got lost." Haley took a swig from her water bottle.

"Everyone around here knows where the US Olympic Training Center is. He can ask for directions." Ryan didn't think Sean had gotten lost, but didn't want to tell the others that if he was doping, he probably never intended to go through with the testing.

"He can use his navigation on his phone." Haley thought for a moment. "I think he has it with him."

"I'll text him." Zana pulled her phone out and tapped on the keys.

"Tell him to let the security guard know that he's with us and he'll direct him to where he needs to go. We're already about five minutes late and Jake has limited time," Ryan explained.

After the security guard checked them in, they headed to a main building where they would sign some papers and obtain visitor's passes. They passed large photographs of athletes representing Olympic sports and colorful silhouettes of athletes and a huge Olympic rings display—so large that some tourists were posing in the colorful rings as their friends took their picture.

Haley stopped and looked around. "This place is amazing."

"After we're done with the testing, we should explore. We can take pictures of each other in the rings," Zana suggested.

"Did you train here when you were on the US Olympic team, Ryan?" Haley asked.

"Yeah. It was an awesome experience. You should see the cafeteria." Ryan smiled. "There are so many choices of quality food."

Zana took her phone out to take a quick selfie with the Olympic rings in the background. "I'll bet it's healthy."

Ryan nodded.

"Dieter would love it." Haley laughed.

"Has Sean texted back?" Ryan led the girls towards the building where the testing would be conducted.

Zana checked her phone. "Not yet."

Haley put her hand briefly on Ryan's shoulder. "If Sean isn't here, why are we doing this?"

"If he doesn't show up, that speaks volumes." Ryan hoped his sunglasses prevented the women from seeing his resigned expression. Sean wouldn't show up.

"He's going to have some whopping excuse about why he didn't make it," Haley said with an edge to her voice. "He'll say that we dropped him and he got lost, and decided to go back to the hotel."

Zana looked towards the entryway. "Should I ride back the way we came and look for him?"

"No." Ryan led them into the building. "If only one of us finds him, he's not going to agree to come here. He'll conjure up some excuse. Let's just do this testing. Zana, you can take Sean's place if he doesn't show up."

After they entered the Testing Center, a man who looked to be in his early thirties with a shaved head, wearing a white coat approached them. "Good morning Ryan, my friend," Jake said, walking over to shake hands.

"Jake, thanks so much for helping us today." Ryan hugged his friend and made introductions. "This is Haley O'Neill and Zana West. Unfortunately, the gentleman I told you about seems to have disappeared on our ride over."

"From what you told me of the situation, I'm not surprised," Jake said, shaking hands with Haley and then Zana. "If he were clean, he'd be standing here with you."

Haley turned away and wiped her eyes. Ryan put his hand on her shoulder, hoping she'd be able to cope. The best he could do was offer his support and direct her to a support group when she was ready.

He turned back to Jake. "I'm curious about my VO2 max at altitude." Ryan looked around at the equipment. He wished Dieter could see this.

"Sure," Jake said. "If Sean shows up, I'll connect him—even if I have to adjust some of my scheduling today."

"Thanks, buddy. I really appreciate it," Ryan said, patting Jake's upper arm affectionately.

"We don't have much time, let's start with you first, Ryan." Jake motioned for him to step onto a treadmill. "Why don't you take off your shirt and I'll attach the leads.

"I'm sure you're all familiar with VO2 max," Jake said, "but as a reminder, it's the maximum rate of oxygen consumption as measured during exercise and reflects the aerobic fitness of an individual. It's a determinant of your endurance capacity during prolonged, sub-maximal exercise." Jake adjusted the leads on Ryan's chest.

"Will the test show whether someone is using performance enhancing drugs?" Zana asked.

"It depends on what drugs they're using. If I have a person's past testing and compare, that might help, and of course your VO2 max will be reduced at altitude—the conditions we have here. If someone is blood doping, there should be an increase, but if someone is using steroids, there may not be." Jake put an oxygen mask on Ryan and positioned him on the treadmill.

"I doubt that Sean is using EPO." Haley sniffed.

"My suspicion is steroids," Zana offered.

"Sean may not know exactly what testing we're doing today," Jake said. "By failing to show up, he's provided you with further evidence that he's using performance-enhancing drugs. In my experience, drug users find excuses to avoid voluntary testing." Jake adjusted the speed of the treadmill while Ryan began to run—connected to electronic leads and wearing an oxygen mask. "We have to look at the whole picture."

After Ryan was tested, Haley and Zana took their turns. Jake went over their results with them, explaining how they compared with Olympians. Ryan was pleased with his results, but wasn't surprised that his VO2 max wasn't as good as it had been when he was last in Colorado Springs—training before the 2012 Olympics. He was still in excellent shape, but had been distracted by Alexia and now Sean.

After they were done and held their results in hand, Ryan thanked Jake. "Let's ride back to the hotel."

"Wait, I got a text from Sean." Haley brightened.

"What does it say?" Zana asked.

"He's been arrested!"

Jake shot Ryan a knowing look, and Ryan cringed.

Chapter Thirty-three

@ZLaw TV Star #JerryHirano suggested we fly to Paris. I said "No". What is wrong with me? #SeriouslyMessedUp

Zana turned the TV on out of habit, flipping through the channels, hoping to find a favorite movie or sitcom to keep her company—like an old friend. She wasn't interested in a depressing drama or the news. *Chelsea Lately* or *The Big Bang Theory*—or, even a *Two and a Half Men* re-run would be perfect for another night in a hotel room alone. She settled on the latter and kept the volume low. Even though The Broadmoor room was exquisite, it was still a hotel room—and so by her definition—a lonely place.

She busied herself with putting her sweaty workout clothes into the hotel laundry bag and then filled out the form so she could spend outrageous sums to have her clothes laundered by the hotel. At least she wouldn't have to hang out in some random Laundromat, counting the minutes between spin cycles.

Just as she was trying to decide whether to spend $4.00 to launder each pair of panties, the theme song to "Fighting in Paradise" played on her phone.

"Hi Jer-bear." Zana smiled into her iPhone.

"Hi babe. Watcha doin'?"

"You called at just the right time." She dropped the laundry bag to the floor, muted the television, and plopped onto the king size bed.

"Why's that?" His tone was soft and loving.

She sighed loudly. "I'm lonely—" her voice cracked "—and stressed out."

"I wish I were there to take your loneliness away. What's so stressful?"

"Sean got arrested today."

"Are you kidding me?" The rise in Jerry's tone startled her.

"No. He blew off our diabolical plot to have his VO2 max tested and went to some gym for a workout without telling us."

"Last I heard, that's not illegal," Jerry said. "But what do I know? I'm just a lawyer."

She giggled at his attempt at a joke. "He got into a fight."

"How did that happen?"

"He's been a jerk lately." She twirled a long strand of her straight hair in her fingers. "We think he's using steroids."

"What did he do?"

Zana rolled her eyes and made an effort to be diplomatic. "I'm sure there are two sides to the story, but he claimed that some guys picked a fight and he was defending himself."

"Did you hear what the other side of the story was?"

"I went with Ryan and Haley to the police station. As his agent, I talked with the arresting officer. He told me that the owner of the gym called 9-1-1 after Sean began throwing free weights around. Apparently, he went into a rage when he had to wait too long to use a machine."

"Did anyone get hurt?"

"Some big guys at the gym grabbed him and held him down. Sean claims he has a sprained wrist, but I don't think it's anything serious." Zana stood up from the bed and began pacing.

"Is he still in jail?"

"No, Haley bailed him out. She's absolutely furious."

"I'll bet."

"She moved out of their hotel room and got her own room." Zana continued pacing.

"It sounds like lots of drama."

"It sucks." She paused and sat on the edge of the bed. "What are you up to?"

"We just finished shooting." He sounded relieved.

"What now?"

"Paris?"

"I wish." Zana sprawled out on the bed and closed her eyes.

"Come on, Zana. Can't your clients fend for themselves for a few weeks?"

"If they didn't use drugs and get arrested. I need to be here for Sean and Haley until things get sorted out."

"Should I come to Colorado Springs? I can hop on a plane."

"That would be fantastic." She came to life and jumped up off the bed, stood before the window and looked at the expansive view of the lake in the foreground with cloud-capped mountains in the background. "The Broadmoor is so romantic. When we're not enjoying the in-room Jacuzzi and king-sized bed, you could golf."

"My kind of place." Jerry paused. "Since we can't seem to make time for our Paris trip, I guess I'll follow you across the country and help babysit Sean."

"That will solve my loneliness problem. *Two and A Half Men* are not doing enough to entertain me." She glanced at the show still playing on TV.

"How 'bout I solve that with one whole man?"

"I can't wait." She grinned.

***

Haley clicked on the television shortly after she woke up alone on the far-right side of her hotel bed. It would keep her company until breakfast. Against her better judgment, she had said "yes" to Sean's texted invitation. *At least they could talk about how he was blowing his chance for an amazing life.* She clicked through the TV channels and settled on CNN. She watched the story of a plane crash in North Carolina and then Sean's picture flashed on the screen.

Sean had helmet hair and dirt smeared on his cheek. The news anchor reported "pro triathlete and reality star, Sean Bennett, was arrested in Colorado Springs for allegedly starting a fight in Pump It Up Gym."

Haley sighed and clicked the TV off. She took a quick shower, brushed her teeth, and washed her face in silence. She didn't dare turn on the bathroom television she'd been delighted with only a few days earlier. Her stomach felt queasy at the thought of talking to the man she lived with, but hardly recognized anymore. She dressed in running shorts and a workout top for a quick transition from breakfast to a gym workout before a planned bike ride with Zana in the afternoon.

On her way to the hotel coffee shop, she dawdled in a few shops along the way and finally arrived about 15 minutes late.

"Good morning, sweetheart," Sean said as she joined him at a table. A coffee, a package of Greek yogurt, and a banana were waiting for her.

"Hey." She sat down hard in the chair, avoiding eye contact.

"I'm really sorry," he pleaded.

"I know. You said that already," she said flatly. She sipped her coffee and then began unpeeling the banana.

"How can I make it up to you?"

She shrugged. "The damage is already done."

"It wasn't my fault. I told you already." He leaned forward.

She finally glanced up and saw the look of hurt and confusion in his eyes. The last time she'd seen that expression on his face was after she told him the city had taken their tent and all of their possessions at the park.

"What if our sponsors drop us?" She could feel her hands shake as she attempted to open the yogurt.

He took the yogurt and opened it for her. "They won't drop *you*."

"Sean, you've got to stop this. If you had come to the training center with us, none of this would have happened."

"I told you, I couldn't keep up with your pace. When I saw the gym, I figured I could at least get in a solid workout."

She shook her head. "I'm tired of your excuses." She focused on eating the yogurt, shoveling it into her mouth in time with the beat of an 80s disco song playing in the background.

"You've got something there." Sean wiped off some yogurt that had collected on the corner of her mouth.

She looked up at him. "Are they going to let you race on Saturday?"

"Why wouldn't they?"

"I don't know—because you're a felon?"

"I'm not a felon." Sean laughed. "I'll appear in court on Monday and maybe pay a small fine. It's not like we can't afford it."

"You don't get it. We *can't* afford it. The cost of this behavior is your— *our*—reputation. That's all we have to sell." She slammed down her spoon and looked at him intently. "How we finish in races and the prize money we earn is nothing compared to the value of our images to sponsors. Unless we're squeaky clean, we'll end up back on the streets."

"Everything's going to work out, Haleyville," Sean said in a tone that ordinarily made her smile. This time, it sounded disingenuous, sarcastic.

"I've got to go work out." She stood up and walked out without looking back. Yoga, lifting weights, and a treadmill run while listening to her play list would hopefully distract her. Just as she was about to open the gym door, she ran into someone she'd hoped to avoid.

"We need to get some footage of you," Dominic said. "I also need an up close and personal interview."

Haley resisted flipping him the bird. Instead, she turned around and ran as fast as she could through the hotel grounds, around the lake and up a hiking trail.

***

Ryan couldn't remember a pro race at which he felt so distracted. He woke up feeling Alexia snug in his arms and breathed in the lilac scent of her hair. Her bare skin felt warm against his and it took every bit of energy to pull away from her at 3:30 a.m. He had laid his clothes and gear out the night before so he could quickly and efficiently be ready in time for the van ride to Prospect Lake.

In the old days, before so much money was at stake, he would've rode his bike the 6 miles to the race site. Now, with Dieter and Zana at the helm, he was not permitted to ride, save for a warm-up on the roads near the lake before the start time of 6 o'clock. He needed to get some food down immediately so it would digest and provide him fuel for the race. He chewed a banana and plain bagel without noticing their taste or texture. Food used to fuel his performance gave him no pleasure at all. He ate as prescribed by his coach, hoping for an edge over his competition.

He arrived at the entryway to the hotel before any of the others and had time to give his bike another thorough check, making sure the tires had sufficient pressure and there was nothing loose or broken. He'd ridden it yesterday, performing the same checks and pumped his tires before going to bed. He re-checked the chinstrap on his helmet to make sure it buckled properly. He wouldn't take the risk of having the helmet fall off his head if he crashed as happened to Terry Schubert—the namesake of the race.

"You're here early," Haley said, wheeling her bike up to where Ryan was standing.

"It's a big day." He noticed that Sean wasn't with her. "Where's your other half?"

"He's on his own this morning."

"That's understandable. Any chance he won't race?"

She reached into her backpack for a water bottle. "I have no idea."

"Does Dieter know what happened?"

"Of course. It's all over the news." Haley's hands were shaking, causing her to fumble the water bottle. It dropped onto the sidewalk spilling half of its contents. "Shit!"

Ryan reached down and picked the bottle up for her.

"Has Dieter said anything?" Ryan asked quietly, handing it over.

"Not a word. He gave me my coaching instructions by e-mail and invited me to call him if I wanted to discuss anything. He didn't mention Sean."

Ryan nodded and straightened his backpack.

"Good morning." Sean rolled his bike up next to Haley.

"Hey," Haley said, and Sean kissed her on the lips.

Ryan didn't want to look at Sean, who reminded him too much of who he used to be. When he had first met Sean, he was so energetic and happy, despite his Muhammad Ali-like cockiness. If he hadn't been connected to the hip with Haley, Sean would have been everyone's best buddy. It wasn't surprising that the media labeled him "the boy next door with the chiseled abs."

Now, he looked bloated. He had traded his cocky attitude for a negative, brooding demeanor. Ryan had read tweets and Facebook posts commenting that fame had changed Sean, but knowing his association with Ben and Trent, his behavior was more likely drug-induced.

Zana drove up with the van she'd rented, large enough to transport the athletes, their bikes, and gear.

"Is Alexia coming with us?" Zana asked.

"I let her sleep. She set her alarm for five so she can catch the race start."

"Okay, I'll look for her."

After they all piled in, they rode to the race site in silence. It was time for Ryan to visualize his performance and put his game face on. During the 13-minute drive, he mentally rehearsed the entire race from the start of the swim to the end of the run. He planned to do a few more visualization exercises before the race start, rather than talking to anyone. This was his job and he was here to work.

As soon as he opened the door to the van, bright lights shone and a half dozen reporters stuck their microphones in their faces. Before Colorado Springs, the questions had been about the race. Now, all questions were focused on Sean's violent behavior at the gym and his subsequent arrest.

"Sean, how much time did you spend in jail?"

"Did you throw weights in the gym as alleged?"

"Ryan, what do you think of Sean's arrest?"

Ryan grabbed his backpack and bike, ignored the reporters, and headed straight to the transition area to set up. He used his mental discipline to focus on what he was doing, his breathing, how his body felt, and how he was going to use his muscles to carry him through the course in a relaxed, efficient, and powerful way. He never once looked back at the media circus. It was none of his business and irrelevant to his racing strategy.

Ryan noticed Sean in the water when they were seconds away from the swim start. Sean positioned himself a few swimmers away, which made sense since they were similar in ability. After the gun went off and Ryan went to work focusing on his most fluid swim stroke, he didn't see Sean again until after the race.

This time, Jeff Paris edged him out for the win by less than a second. It was a closely contested race with Ryan pulling ahead of Jeff on the bike, only to have Jeff catch up with him on the run. They were neck and neck for the last four miles. Jeff had more energy reserves and was able to sprint faster into the finish line. Ryan was happy for Jeff, but a bit disappointed that he wasn't able to keep up his winning streak. He certainly couldn't complain about the $50,000 prize money, and saw that Zana seemed pleased with his second place finish, putting cash in her pocket. Not bad for a morning's work.

He was standing near the finish line when Sean came in eighth—earning very little prize money, but still attracting the attention of the media who swarmed him the moment he stepped across the line. The reporters and cameramen were so pre-occupied with Sean they didn't notice when Haley crossed the finish line for the women.

It wasn't until an announcement was made that she won $100,000 that Ryan realized she was the women's winner.

"Congratulations, Haley!" Ryan said as he gave her a sweaty hug.

Chapter Thirty-four

@ZLaw The best package arrived today. If it weren't a slow news day, it would have been heaven.

Zana was leaning against the reception desk after receiving a call that there was a package waiting for her. She felt his familiar hands wrap around her, and then turned to see Jerry's grinning face.

"You're here!" Zana embraced him, inhaling a faint scent of Polo cologne.

"After we talked, I hopped on the next plane available," Jerry said softly into her ear. "You'll laugh when I open my luggage. I just threw everything in—not bothering to fold it. I guess I can buy whatever I forgot to bring."

"We can fold your clothes together—at least that will give us something to do."

"I have other things in mind." He winked.

"Oh, yeah?"

"Where's that beautiful room of yours."

"But, I have a package."

"*I'm* your package!" He laughed and grabbed her hand.

She led him from the hallway by the hotel coffee shop to her room in the adjacent building. "Let's test the bed and make sure it's up to five-star resort standards."

"Yeah, we can report our findings on Travelocity.com."

It was the afternoon post-race, and Zana had already spent time with her clients, rehashing their performances. Her work with Sean took much longer than usual, since she had to coach him on how to respond to the media—using phrases Donald e-mailed her the day before in response to her questions about how to best spin Sean's arrest. Jerry's arrival was perfectly timed. She was heading to the coffee shop for a latte when he'd shown up. Her afternoon caffeine infusion was forgotten in favor of passionate lovemaking in her hotel room's big comfy bed, followed by a soak for two in the Jacuzzi tub.

"Shall we turn on the TV?" Jerry asked as they soaked.

"Ordinarily, that would completely destroy the mood, but how often do we have a flat screen TV a few feet away from the tub?"

"My thoughts exactly." Jerry clicked it on using the remote control within reaching distance of the Jacuzzi.

"Maybe there's a good movie on."

He laughed. "We'll turn into prunes." He clicked through the channels, dismissing cooking, sports, cartoons, talk shows, news, crime dramas, and animal shows.

"What was that? Turn back a few channels." She sat up higher in the tub, splashing water onto the floor.

"That's Sean," Jerry said as images of the triathlete and two men arguing in loud voices in a restaurant appeared on the screen.

"Turn up the volume."

The men were yelling at each other. Then, Sean punched the guy with stringy, long hair in the face, causing him to slump to the ground. The other guy, who was tall and lanky, swung at Sean, barely missing when Sean ducked out of the way. Sean shoved the tall guy against a wall of framed photographs. A restaurant employee appeared on camera and Sean quickly made his escape out the front door.

The news reporter explained that the brawl was caught on the restaurant security camera and that all three men left the establishment before police arrived. Pro triathlete and television personality Sean Bennett was identified as one of the men in the scuffle. The reporter reminded the viewing audience about Sean's arrest a few days ago for a "fighting incident" that allegedly occurred in a gym. He was scheduled to appear in court on Monday.

"Damn!" Zana jumped out of the tub on the bedroom side, dripping water all over the carpet.

"Here, babe." Jerry stepped out of the bath, grabbed some towels, and wrapped one around Zana. He gestured to the trail of water she'd left on the carpet.

She flung her hands up. "I've got to talk to Ryan."

"I'll straighten up in here. Why don't you text him to come over."

She grabbed her phone, surprised there was already a text from Ryan. OMG! We need to talk.

After a few texts back and forth, she put down her phone.

"He's coming over in ten minutes." Zana pulled on her jeans that lay crumpled on the floor and quickly threw on a bra and a Terry Schubert Pro Classic Triathlon T-shirt.

As Jerry was tidying up in preparation for Ryan, Zana sat on the edge of the now made bed watching more news coverage about Sean.

"It must be a slow news day," Jerry said as he pulled out crumpled shorts and a T-shirt from his suitcase. "How is Sean's little scuffle such a big deal?"

"I don't get it, either. Anything having to do with Sean or Haley is always blown out of proportion." When she heard Ryan's knock, Zana stood up to answer the door.

"WTF," Ryan said, walking into the room.

"I know, right?" She shook her head and raised her eyebrows.

Ryan sat in an upholstered chair in the corner and Jerry pulled out the chair from the desk while Zana positioned herself on the edge of the bed as they stared silently at the television screen showing commentary of Sean's fall from grace.

"He's screwed." Ryan stared at the TV.

"Is there *anything* we can do?" Zana asked.

Ryan thought for a moment. "If it weren't for the news stories, we could do something."

Jerry looked at his watch. "It's only two p.m.—most people are still out and about on a Saturday afternoon."

"In an hour, it will be five o'clock on the east coast and millions will be tuning into the news." Ryan grimaced.

Zana consulted her phone. "I'm surprised that I don't have any e-mails from Sean's sponsors."

"Just wait until Monday morning. Believe me, they'll all be cutting him off." Ryan shook his head. "I should know."

"I wonder if Haley has seen this." Zana looked at her texts and emails to see if there was anything from her client.

"I don't know." Ryan shrugged. "As soon as Alexia and I saw it, I texted you and asked Alexia to go find Haley and keep her busy. I think they went to the pool."

"Should we try to reach Sean?" Jerry asked.

"I already texted him, but haven't heard back." Zana looked at her phone again.

For the next 40 minutes they sat watching the news loop, showing the story over and over with news anchors providing little varied commentary. Sean was portrayed as a psychologically unstable, troubled young man. There were some speculations about possible drug or alcohol use, but mostly the focus was on his trajectory from rags to riches. Perhaps he was having a hard time adjusting to fame and fortune, one commentator speculated.

"Alexia texted me, wondering what we're up to." Ryan looked up from his phone. "She's not sure how to keep Haley away from the media much longer."

"If Haley wasn't in training, I'd suggest that they have some stiff drinks," Jerry said.

"I'll tell her to take Haley for coffee." Ryan typed into his phone.

Zana stood up and looked out the window. "She'll find out eventually."

"If we can buy some time before she knows, at least we can figure out a game plan," Ryan scratched his head. "Sean's actions could bring Haley down with him."

"It's two forty-five." Zana looked at the time on her phone. "In fifteen minutes, the east coast will hear all about Sean—it'll be headline news."

"There's nothing we can do." Jerry stood up and began pacing.

They stared at the TV in silence, listening to the story about Sean over and over again. Every few minutes, an image of his mug shot flashed on the screen, followed by video of him racing in triathlons and the most recent fight scene footage. An expert psychologist was now being questioned about whether Sean might be suffering from some sort of diagnosable condition.

"Breaking News: We have just learned that Callie Walsh, Grammy-nominated pop star, has been shot. We don't have much information yet. It appears that she was the victim of a home invasion," the commentator said. "She was taken away by ambulance and we don't know whether she's alive or dead. We'll be giving you up-to-date coverage of this breaking story throughout the evening. For those who just joined us, pop star, Callie Walsh has just been shot at her home in Malibu, California."

"OMG! It's two fifty-five. There's no way that Sean's story of punching someone will be shown now." Zana flipped to other news channels, now reporting the story of the tragic shooting.

"Sean dodged a bullet." Ryan wiped his forehead with the back of his hand. "No pun intended."

Tears welled in Zana's eyes as she realized how close Sean had come to being the biggest news story of the weekend.

Ryan tapped out a text.

"What are you doing?" Zana asked.

"I just texted Sean. He said he's in his room." Ryan stood. "I'm going over there to have a talk with him."

"I thought you said it wouldn't do any good." Zana's eyebrows shot up.

"We're out of options. This is our last shot before he loses everything," Ryan said before walking through the doorway.

***

Sean's room was in the same building, so Ryan didn't have much time to collect his thoughts as he rode the elevator up to the 5th floor. He remembered what it was like when he was using performance-enhancing drugs out of desperation to be who he thought everyone wanted, or at least, expected him to be. He had felt so trapped, not able to escape the choices he made until his life was destroyed.

Maybe Sean didn't have to endure the consequences that he had faced—losing his pro cycling career and the woman he loved. When Ryan was doping, he was engaged to Lucie, a stunning young French woman he had met at a coffee shop in Andorra. After being fired from his team, Lucie and her family didn't want anything to do with him and he had flown back to the US with his tail between his legs.

His parents were upset, but embraced his return, helping him through his recovery from dependence to drugs. His father had seen the Ironman Triathlon on television and had suggested to Ryan that he take up the sport, since pro cycling wouldn't take him back. It turned out that even though his swimming skills were not at the level of the other pros, his cycling speed and years on his high school track team put him in the upper echelon of triathlon after a year of serious training. He started winning local races, became a pro, and ultimately won a gold medal in the Olympics, which in retrospect made his many struggles worth it. And now he was dating Alexia, and making a very good living as a professional triathlete and owner of the Freewheel Movement. He was finally living his dream.

Ryan was surprised when Sean opened the door immediately after his first knock.

"What took you so long?" Sean asked.

"What do you mean? It took me about three minutes to get here from Zana's room."

"You've wanted to talk with me for weeks." Sean motioned for Ryan to come in.

"Not really." Ryan stepped into the room. It was so messy it didn't look like a hotel maid had cleaned for days. The bed was unmade and clothes were strewn all over the floor.

"Trent told me that you would want to have a talk with me."

"That guy's a sleaze ball. I'm not sure you realize that, Sean." Ryan approached the upholstered chair in the corner—the same style and color as the one in Zana's room, but was piled high with empty pizza boxes. He moved them and sat down, motioning for Sean to sit in the desk chair.

"Why are you here?" Sean asked.

"You're about ready to lose your sponsors."

"So?" Sean ran his fingers through his thick, brown hair.

"If you think your life sucked when you were homeless, it's going to be fucking shitty on Monday when you're dropped by all of your sponsors."

"They're not going to drop me."

"Now that your face appeared on the early news punching and pushing guys in a bar, yes, you *will* be dropped. Believe me—I know."

"That's not true." Sean shook his head.

"Haley's going to dump your ass."

"No way." He knocked over the pizza boxes piled high on the desk with his elbow and they crashed to the floor.

Ryan ignored the mess and looked Sean squarely in the eyes. "You placed eighth—what did you make—around a thousand dollars?"

"It was a bad day." Sean broke eye contact.

"I don't know what you're taking—testosterone, HGH, EPO—whatever it is, it's not doing you any good."

"How can you say that?" Sean jumped up and punched a lampshade, causing the lamp and shade to tumble to the floor. The light flickered out so they were in the dark, except for the sliver of light coming from the door to the hallway.

"You came in fucking eighth place, Sean. I came in second with disciplined training."

"You're an Olympian."

"Damn right, and I did that clean."

Sean put his head in his hands and sank back into the chair.

"Admit to me right now that you've been using drugs." Ryan stood up and placed a hand on his shoulder. "I can help you."

"How can you possibly help me?" Sean looked at Ryan with pleading eyes.

"It can stay between you and me. No one needs to know."

"Dieter will kick my ass out of the program."

"I won't tell him. You and I will fly to California and get you into a rehab program for thirty days." Ryan kneeled in front of Sean.

"Rehab? That's so lame."

"No, it isn't. If you can get through that program, you'll keep Haley and your sponsors."

"There's no guarantee."

"What do you think will happen if you don't go?" Ryan asked.

Sean was quiet for a few minutes as he stared at the ceiling. He put his face in his hands and began crying.

Ryan stood and put his arm around him.

"I've been there, buddy," Ryan said quietly. His eyes filled with tears.

After a few minutes, Ryan pulled the upholstered chair next to Sean's and sat close to him in the dark room. It smelled of sweaty clothes and stale food. His mind drifted to a time long ago when the team owner, the coaches, and the other cyclists used him as a scapegoat to fend off public criticism about doping in cycling. He was singled out, and not one person reached out to help him. He would do anything he could to help Sean avoid the pain, devastation, and loneliness he'd endured. Up until now, he felt a hands-off approach was best, but with Sean's recent behavior, he was obviously spiraling out of control. It was time to step in.

Sean sobbed for a while, but now was quiet. His knee was shaking, and he was rocking slightly in the chair.

"Okay," Sean said quietly.

"Okay, what?"

"I'll go…I'll get treatment."

Epilogue

@ZLaw They say in order to beat #jetlag, it's best to stay up. I agree. #VivalaFrance

Zana showed her passport to the customs agent at the Charles de Gaulle Airport in Paris, trying not to smile for fear she might look like she was trying to get away with something.

"How long will you be in France?" the agent asked in a thick accent.

"A few weeks." She grinned without realizing it.

"Have a nice time." The agent stamped her passport. "Next."

"We're here!" Zana joined her boyfriend who was waiting for her beyond the customs officers.

"It's about time." Jerry grabbed her hand. "Let's get our luggage. We have a fun day ahead of us."

She had never been out of the United States before, except for brief trips to Canada and Mexico, so even though they were in an airport baggage claim area, it seemed exotic. She listened to the alien-sounding French announcements and wished she'd paid more attention in high school French.

"Do you understand what they're saying?" Zana asked.

"I haven't a clue," Jerry said. "I took Japanese in high school. I don't know any French, except *bon jour*, *je t'aime* and *c'est la vie*."

"I suppose that could come in handy. We should probably start saying *oui* and *merci*. That's easy enough."

"*Oui*," he said, taking her hand and kissing it.

"*Merci*." Zana giggled.

Jerry grabbed their rolling suitcases off the luggage carousel. They wheeled them out the door into an area where a dozen or so people were holding signs with passengers' names on them.

Zana saw a man dressed in a suit holding a sign with "Jerry Hirano" on it. She pointed to the sign.

"That's our driver," Jerry said. "He's taking us to the Hyatt Regency near the airport."

"We're staying at an airport hotel?" she asked, feeling her heart sink. She had always dreamt of staying in more quaint accommodations in the heart of Paris, rather than an American airport hotel.

"Only for tonight. It's a stunning, modern hotel and will allow us to get some much needed sleep before we wander around and enjoy the city."

Zana smiled and felt her shoulders relax. "Sounds terrific."

They followed the driver to a black Mercedes. After a five-minute drive, they pulled up to a large, modern hotel.

"What should we do? It's only two p.m.," Zana said after they'd reached their spacious room.

"It's two a.m. back home." Jerry yawned.

"I feel great. I caught up on sleep almost the entire plane flight."

"I should know, I have drool stains on my shirt."

Zana laughed. "Sure you do. Those beds that lay down flat in first-class are so amazing. I feel totally rested."

"Well, if we're going to adjust to Paris time, we'll have to stay up."

"That's fine with me. I can't wait to explore the City of Lights."

"I could use a shower." Jerry kissed her, then pulled his toiletry kit out of his suitcase. "I'm still in shock that I was able to drag you away from your clients in the middle of the race series."

"It feels wonderful to get away." Zana walked over to the window and flung open the blackout curtains. "I'm worried about Sean, but Ryan insisted he'll be alright."

"The Betty Ford Clinic is the best place for him now." Zana burst into laughter.

"What's so funny?"

"Can you imagine Donald in his plaid pants at races with Ryan and Haley? It was nice of him to take my place, but off of a golf course, he's completely lost."

"You're right, that's hilarious."

Zana stood by the window and looked out at their street view. "Dieter seemed to take the news well."

"How could he not? Sean's one of his most famous athletes."

Jerry stepped into the shower while Zana pulled an outfit out of her suitcase. When it was her turn, she showered quickly, anxious to explore Paris.

"Can we see the Eiffel Tower?" Zana asked as she dried herself with a thick, white towel. Jerry was already dressed, wearing dark jeans, a crisp white shirt with a skinny black tie and a black sport jacket. "You're so dressed up."

"It's Paris, baby."

Zana giggled. She decided against wearing jeans and a T-shirt and pulled a red, no-iron wrap dress out of her suitcase. She quickly applied make up and blow-dried her hair.

"I arranged for a car," Jerry said as they walked out of their room hand in hand. The romance and excitement of finally being in Paris with the man of her dreams made Zana feel giddy and not one bit jetlagged.

She beamed as the limousine pulled up and the driver opened the door for her. A dozen long-stemmed red roses adorned the seat. Jerry presented them to her, and helped her into the back where a bottle of champagne was on ice. After they toasted to their Parisian adventure, the driver headed to the heart of the city.

She sipped champagne and stared out the window, taking in the large, old buildings, the ornate churches and the sparkling Seine.

"What do you think?" Jerry squeezed her hand.

"It's stunning." Zana admired the Eiffel Tower as it came into view. She pressed her face against the window. There was a long line of tourists waiting to buy tickets to go to the top of the structure. "The queue is so long."

"Don't worry. I have VIP tickets and dinner reservations." He helped her out of the limo. "Let's explore the gardens first."

They strolled hand in hand along the walkway. The sun was shining and the temperature was so pleasant, the park was filled with Parisians and tourists, picnicking, reading, socializing, or playing Frisbee with their dogs. Zana looked up at the Eiffel Tower as they walked toward it.

"I've been waiting for this moment for so long," she said.

"So have I," Jerry said, leading her into the garden next to beautiful pink and blue flowers she couldn't identify.

He then dropped onto one knee, took her hand in his and presented her with a diamond ring. He looked into her eyes that were now welling with tears and said, "Zana, will you marry me?"

Her legs felt weak and her throat was dry, but she managed to whisper "*Oui.*" His face brightened, and then in a louder voice she said, "Absolutely."

He placed the ring on her finger, and picked her up and twirled her around in the shadow of the Eiffel Tower. Jerry then pulled her close and she felt breathless as she looked into her future husband's eyes.

If you enjoyed *VO2 Max* by Katherine M. Nohr, you may enjoy these other titles from Written Dreams Publishing.

Death by G-String

A Coyote Canyon Ladies Ukulele Club Mystery

C.C. Harrison

Can Viva Winter find the truth before it's too late?

The Coyote Canyon Ladies Ukulele Club is gearing up for a ukulele competition when their flamboyant star player, Kiki Jacquenette, is found strangled to death with a G-string. Not only is a first place win in jeopardy, the entire folk music festival is put on the verge of collapse. A murderer on the loose is sure to keep tourists away.

Chronicle editor Viva Winter had hoped to make Coyote Canyon the folk music capitol of the Colorado mountains, and was also trying to raise money to help repay the townspeople bilked by her father's phony investment scheme. With much to gain by Kiki's death, Viva soon comes under suspicion, so she must uncover the truth before her whole life turns into one sour note, and a tourist trade boom falls flat.

Easy Kill

An EZ Kelly Novel

Charles DuPuy

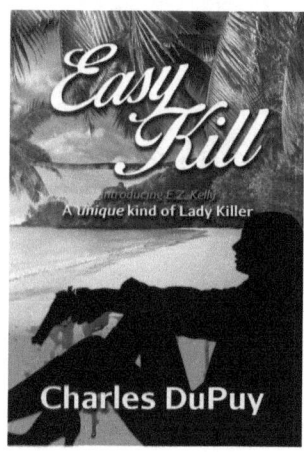

Will dangerous lady EZ Kelly succeed in finding the real culprit?

EZ Kelly is intent on becoming a travel agent, but trouble finds her wherever she goes. It's good that self-defense was a high priority among the lessons taught to her by her Special Forces father.

Expecting a boring night shift at the hotel where she works, EZ is surprised when night after night the place is targeted by thieves. Taking the thieves down one by one is a simple task for her.

Unafraid of the threats, she continues to work at the hotel and cooperates with the Miami Police's investigation to discover the reason why the hotel is being hit.

As they dig further into the case, she discovers that terrorists have a plan to detonate nuclear devices in three large US cities simultaneously. Will EZ be able to take the terror cell down before she gets herself killed?

Assume Guilt

A Matt Barlow Novel

Paul M. Lisnek

With loyalty, family secrets, and death involved, Matt Barlow must discover the real facts.

Attorney Matt Barlow vowed he'd never be part of a criminal case again, not after failing to save an innocent man from the death penalty. A jury consultant on civil cases, Matt doesn't waver until...

When Chicago's top real estate developer and aspiring politician Charles Marchand is charged with the death of his wife, Sandra, loyalty to an old friend pushes Matt into signing on as the jury consultant for the defense. But the case is about much more than guilt or innocence.

As Matt—and his staff—delve deeper into the evidence, they uncover information Marchand himself would just as soon stay buried, including the death of a college classmate that links him to the corrupt Leo Toland, Governor of Illinois. Before the truth and lies are untangled, Matt even finds himself secretly working with his half-brother, who just happens be on the governor's payroll.

Acknowledgements

A big mahalo to my editor Brittiany Koren for her skill and patience in making this 3rd novel in my Tri-Angles series a reality.

None of this series would have been written if it hadn't been for my writers group and so I offer my sincere thank you to Steve Novak, Brian Malanaphy and Karin O'Mahony. It's not easy to write book after book, and so I thank those friends who have played an important and supportive role during this year of editing VO2 Max: Mark Coberly, Cindi John, Lisa and Jim Ghahramani, Mary Alexander, Kristie Byrum, Dianne Johannson, Brian Rosa, Donna Good, Angela Hayslett, Nathalie Pettit, Cheri Moore, Cheri Huber, Melissa Deats, Winston Dang, and Dr. David and Elizabeth Samsami.

Mahalo to my forever besties: Kristina Selset, Ramona Emerson, Lesia Schafer, Tamara Gerrard, Prebah Covetz, Deborah Blackman, Jennifer Papastephanou, Karin Polivy, and Heather McVay.

A special thanks to my friends and employees: Lenore Ogawa, Emmy Nation and Celeste Moore, because what would I do without you?

And, all my love to my family: Kim and Hannah Nohr, Ed Haney, Shane and Joyce Sullivan, Gerrie Nohr, Jill, Gordy and Drew Gradwohl, Jay Iversen, Jeff Iversen, Rick and Kelly Shewey, Sandy Crouse, Wendy Monette, Lois and Paul Wilson, Chris and Patricia Wilson, Kiana and Kalin Uluave, Lucie Poehere Wilson, Marsha and Shan Fu and family, Kelly and Mary Graves and family, Kathleen and Brian Sheffield and family, Ed, Krystle and Rachel Kendrick and the Christensen family.

A special thanks to the Honolulu Association of Insurance Professional board and members and to IAIP friends and members.

And, most important of all, thank you to my boyfriend, Bill Touth, and purrs to my Siamese kitty children, Ninja and Tashi.

About the Author

Katharine M. Nohr is the author of *Managing Risk in Sport and Recreation: The Essential Guide for Loss Prevention* and the mysteries *Land Sharks, Freewheel,* and *VO2 Max* of the Tri-Angles Series. She speaks internationally on Olympic Games and professional athlete risk management. Ms. Nohr served as Regional Coordinator of Officials, appellate hearings officer and member of the Pacific Northwest Council for USA Triathlon. Ms. Nohr served as a Judge (per diem) of the Honolulu District Court and continues to practice insurance defense litigation in Hawaii. Ms. Nohr is a past Regional Vice President for International Association of Insurance Professionals and was awarded Insurance Professional of the Year in 2012. She is a principal of Nohr Sports Risk Management, LLC and Claim Crazy, Inc. and the owner of the Law Offices of Katharine M. Nohr, LLC.

Currently, she is working on several projects. Visit her websites at KatharineNohr.com, nohrsports.com; or claimcrazy.com. Find her on social media: Twitter: @TriathlonNovels, Instagram: @TriathlonNovels; Linkedin: Katharine Nohr, and on Facebook: Katharine M. Nohr or Tri-Angles Series.